PENGUIN BOOKS

LEAVEN OF MALICE

Robertson Davies has had three successive careers: first
as an actor with the Old Vic Company in England; then
as publisher of the Peterborough Ontario Examiner;
and most recently as a university professor and first
Master of Massey College at the University of Toronto,
from which he retired in 1981. He has over thirty books
to his credit, among them several volumes of plays, as
well as collections of essays, speeches, and *belles lettres*.
As a novelist he has gained fame, especially for his
Salterton trilogy, *Tempest-Tost, Leaven of Malice,* and *A
Mixture of Frailties*—and his Cornish trilogy—*The Rebel
Angels, What's Bred in the Bone,* and *The Lyre of
Orpheus*. His most recent novel, *Murther & Walking
Spirits,* is also available in Penguin. He was the first
Canadian to become an honorary member of the Ameri-
can Academy and Institute of Arts and Letters. He is a
companion of the order of Canada, and honorary fellow
of Balliol, and has received an honorary degree from
Oxford. He and his wife now divide their time between
homes in Toronto and in Caledon, Ontario.

Grant us to to put away the
leaven of malice and wickedness
that we may alway serve Thee
in pureness of living and truth
THE PRAYER BOOK

ROBERTSON DAVIES

LEAVEN · OF · MALICE

Penguin Books

PENGUIN BOOKS
Published by the Penguin Group
Penguin Books USA Inc., 375 Hudson Street, New York, New York 10014, U.S.A.
Penguin Books Ltd, 27 Wrights Lane, London W8 5TZ, England
Penguin Books Australia Ltd, Ringwood, Victoria, Australia
Penguin Books Canada Ltd, 10 Alcorn Avenue, Toronto, Ontario, Canada M4V 3B2
Penguin Books (N.Z.) Ltd, 182–190 Wairau Road, Auckland 10, New Zealand

Penguin Books Ltd, Registered Offices: Harmondsworth, Middlesex, England

First published in Canada by Clarke, Irwin & Company Limited 1954
First published in the United States of America by Charles Scribner's Sons 1955
Reprinted by arrangement with Clarke, Irwin & Company Limited
Published in Penguin Books 1980
This edition published in Penguin Books 1994

1   3   5   7   9   10   8   6   4   2

PUBLISHER'S NOTE
This is a work of fiction. Names, characters, places, and incidents either are the product of the
author's imagination or are used fictitiously, and any resemblance to actual persons, living or
dead, events, or locales is entirely concidental.

ISBN 0 14 01.6789 7
(CIP data available)

Printed in the United States of America

PART ONE

IT was on the 31st of October that the following announcement appeared under 'Engagements', in the Salterton *Evening Bellman*:

> Professor and Mrs Walter Vambrace are pleased to announce the engagement of their daughter, Pearl Veronica, to Solomon Bridgetower, Esq., son of Mrs Bridgetower and the late Professor Solomon Bridgetower of this city. Marriage to take place in St Nicholas' Cathedral at eleven o'clock a.m., November 31st.

Few of the newspaper's readers found anything extraordinary about this intimation, or attached any significance to the fact that it was made on Hallowe'en.

WHEN FORTUNE decides to afflict a good man and rob him of his peace, she often chooses a fine day to begin.

The 1st of November was a beautiful day, and the sun shone with a noble autumn glory as Gloster Ridley, editor of *The Bellman*, walked through the park to his morning's work. The leaves rustled about his feet and he kicked them with pleasure. It was like tramping through some flaky breakfast food, he thought, and smiled at the unromantic fancy. That was not in the least what his colleague Mr Shillito would think about autumn leaves. He recalled what Mr Shillito had written yesterday on the subject of Hallowe'en—which Mr Shillito had managed five times to call All Hallows' Eve and twice 'this unhallowed Eve'—and his face darkened; the Old Mess had been at his most flowery

1

and most drivelling. But Ridley quickly banished Mr
Shillito from his mind; that was a problem to be dealt with
later in the day. Meanwhile, his walk to his office was his
own, for his own agreeable musings. His day had begun
well; Constant Reader had prepared an excellent breakfast
for him, and the hateful Blubadub, though faintly audible
in the kitchen, had kept out his sight. He sniffed the de-
lightfully cool and smoky autumn air. The day stretched
before him, full of promise.

In less than a week he would be fifty. Middle-aged, unquestionably, but how much better he felt than ever in his
youth! From his seventeenth year until quite recently,
Anxiety had ridden him with whip and spur, and only when
well past forty had he gained any hope of unseating her. But
today . . . ! His bosom's lord, he told himself, sat lightly
in his throne. Who said that? Romeo. Pooh, Romeo knew
nothing about the quiet, well-controlled self-satisfaction of
a man who might well, before he was fifty-one, be a Doctor
of Civil Law.

To be Doctor Ridley! He would not, of course, insist upon
the title, but it would be his, and if he should ever chance
to be introduced to a new acquaintance as Mister, there
would almost certainly be someone at hand to say, probably
with a pleasant laugh, 'I think it should be Doctor Ridley,
shouldn't it?' Not that he attached undue importance to
such distinctions; he knew precisely how matters stood.
After what he had done for Waverley University they must
reward him with a substantial fee or give him an honorary
doctorate. Waverley, like all Canadian universities, was per-
petually short of money, whereas its store of doctorates was
inexhaustible. They would not even have to give him a
gown, for that glorious adornment would be returnable
immediately after the degree ceremony. It would be a
doctorate, certainly, and he would value it. It was a symbol
of security and success, and it would be another weapon
with which to set his old enemy, Anxiety, at bay. He would
feel himself well rewarded when he was Doctor Ridley.

He had fairly earned it. When it had occurred to some of
the Governors of the University two years ago that Waver-

ley ought to establish a course in journalism, it had been to
him that they turned for advice. When the decision was
taken to make plans for such a course, he had been the only
person not directly associated with the University to sit upon
the committee; tactfully and unobtrusively, he had guided
it. He had listened, without visible emotion, to the opinions
of professors upon the Press and upon the duty which some
of them believed they owed to society to reform the Press.
He had discussed without mirth or irony their notions of
the training which would produce a good newspaperman.
He had counselled against foolish spending, and he had
fought tirelessly for spending which he believed to be necessary. Little by little his academic colleagues on the committee had recognized that he knew what he was talking
about. He had triumphed in persuading them that their
course should occupy three years instead of two. His had
been the principal voice in planning the course, and his
would certainly be the principal voice in hiring the staff.
Next autumn the course would be included in the Waverley
syllabus, and now his work was almost done.

One task still lay before him, and it was a pleasant one.
He was to deliver the first of the Wadsworth Lectures for
the current academic year. These public lectures, founded
twenty years before to inform the university opinion on
matters of public importance, were to be devoted this year
to 'The Press and The People'. A Cabinet Minister would
speak, and the United Kingdom High Commissioner; a
celebrated philosopher and an almost equally celebrated
psychologist were also to give their views. But the first of
the five lectures would be given by himself, Gloster Ridley,
editor of the Salterton *Evening Bellman*, and he was determined that it should be the best of the lot. For, after all, he
knew at first hand what a newspaper was, and the other
lecturers did not. And it was widely admitted that under his
guidance *The Bellman* was a very good paper.

Yes, he thought, he had a shrewd idea what the Press was.
Not a cheap Press, nor yet the pipedream Press that the
university reformers had talked about at those early meetings. And he knew about the People, too, for he was one of

3

them. He had had no university education. That was one of the reasons why it would fall so sweetly upon his ear to be spoken of as Doctor Ridley.

Oh, yes, he would tell them about the Press and the People. The Press, he would explain, belonged to the People—to all of the People, whether their tastes and needs were common or uncommon. He would speak amusingly, but there would be plenty in his lecture for them to chew on. He would begin with a quotation from Shakespeare, from *All's Well that Ends Well;* a majority of his listeners, even in a university audience, would not have read the play, but he would remind them that people outside university halls could be well-read. Of a newspaper he would quote, 'It is like a barber's chair that fits all buttocks; the pin-buttock, the quatch-buttock, the brawn buttock, or any buttock'. And then he would develop his theme, which was that in any issue of a good daily paper every reader, gentle or simple, liberally educated or barely able to read, should find not only the news of the day but something which was, in a broad sense, of special concern to himself.

It would be a good lecture. Possibly his publisher would have it reprinted in pamphlet form, and distribute it widely to other papers. Without vulgar hinting, he thought he could insinuate that idea into his publisher's mind.

Musing pleasantly on these things, he reached the newspaper building.

HE CLIMBED the stairs to his second-floor office somewhat furtively, for he did not want to meet Mr Shillito and exchange greetings with him. He was determined to do nothing which might appear two-faced, and Mr Shillito's greetings were of so courtly and old-world a nature that he was often enticed into a geniality of which he was afterward ashamed. He must not feed the Old Mess sugar from his hand, while concealing the sword behind his back. But his path was clear, and he slipped into his office unseen by anyone but Miss Green, his secretary. She followed him through the door.

'No personal mail this morning, Mr Ridley. Just the

usual. And the switchboard says somebody called you before nine, but wouldn't leave their name.'

The usual was neatly marshalled on his desk. Miss Green had been solicitous about the morning's letters since the day, more than three days ago, when somebody had sent him a dead rat, wrapped as a gift, with a card explaining that this was a comment upon *The Bellman's* stand on a matter of public controversy. She had failed, since then, to intercept an envelope filled with used toilet paper (a political innuendo) but in general her monitorship was good. There were ten Letters to the Editor, and he took them up without curiosity, and with a thick black pencil ready in his hand.

Two, from 'Fair Play' and 'Indignant', took the Salterton City Council to task, the former for failing to re-surface the street on which he lived, and the latter for proposing to pave a street on which he owned property, thereby raising the rates. Both writers had allowed anonymity to go to their heads, and both had added personal notes requesting that their true names be withheld, as they feared reprisals of an unspecified nature. From 'Fair Play's' letter Ridley deleted several sentences, and changed the word 'shabby' to 'ill-advised'. 'Indignant' required more time, as the writer had not used enough verbs to make his meaning clear, and had apparently punctuated his letter after writing it, on some generous but poorly conceived principle of his own.

The third letter was so badly written that even his accustomed eye could make very little of it, but it appeared to be from an aggrieved citizen whose neighbour spitefully threw garbage into his back yard. Other iniquities of the neighbour were rehearsed, but Ridley marked the letter for Miss Green's attention; she would return it with the usual note declining to publish libellous material.

The next three letters were legible, grammatical and reasonable, and dealt with a scheme to create a traffic circle at a principal intersection of the city. They were quickly given headings and marked for the printer.

The seventh letter urged that a hockey coach who had trained some little boys the winter before be prevented, by force if necessary, from training them in the winter to come.

He was, it appeared, a monster and a heretic whose influence would prove the ruin of hockey tactics and the downfall of that sport in Canada. It was signed with a bold signature and a street address, but the editor's eye was not deceived. He consulted the Salterton *City Directory* and found, as he had suspected, that there was no such number as 183 Maple Street, and no such person as Arthur C. Brown. With a sigh for the duplicity of mankind, he threw the letter into the wastepaper basket. He was a little pleased, also, that the intuition which suggested to him that a signature was a fake was in good working order.

The eighth letter was from a farmer who charged the Salterton Exhibition Committee with great unfairness and some measure of dishonesty in the matter of awarding prizes in the Pullet sub-section of the Poultry Division of the Livestock Competition at the fall fair. He was aware, he said, that the fair had taken place seven weeks ago, but it had taken him a little time to get around to writing his letter. It went into the waste basket.

The ninth letter caused Ridley both surprise and annoyance. It read:

Sir:

Warm congratulations on the editorial headed 'Whither The Toothpick' which appeared in your edition of 28/x. It is such delightful bits of whimsy as this which raise the tone of *The Bellman* above that of any other paper which comes to my notice and give it a literary grace which is doubly distinguished in a world where style is rapidly becoming a thing of the past. This little gem joins many another in my scrapbook. Happy the city which can boast a *Bellman!* Happy the *Bellman* which boasts a writer who can produce the felicitous 'Toothpick'.

Yours, etc.
ELDON BUMFORD

No error about that signature; old Bumford, at eighty-four, was reversing the usual tendency of old men to damn everything, and was loud in his praise of virtually everything. No reason not to publish it. Dead certainty that if it did not appear within a day or two old Bumford would be on the telephone, or worse still, in the chair opposite his desk, asking why. And yet it was out of the question that the thing should be published. Ridley laid it aside for later consideration.

The tenth letter was in a well-known hand, in green ink. Letters in that hand, and in that ink, appeared on Ridley's desk every two weeks, and their message was always the same: the world had forgotten God. Sometimes it showed this forgetfulness by permitting children to read the comic strips; sometimes drink—invariably referred to as 'beverage alcohol'—was the villain; sometimes it was the decline in church attendance which especially afflicted the writer; in winter the iniquity of ski-trains, which travelled during church hours and bore young people beyond the sound of church bells, was complained of; in summer it was the whoredom of two-piece bathing suits, and shorts which revealed girls' legs, which was consuming society. The writer was able to support all her arguments by copious quotations from Holy Writ, and she did so; now and then she related a modern enormity to one of the monsters in Revelation. The letter at hand urged that the Prime Minister be advised to declare November 11th a National Day of Prayer, in which, by an act of mass repentance, Canada might be cleansed of her wrong-doings, and at the end of which her iniquity might be pardoned. The letter was marked 'Urgent—Print this At Once'. Wearily, Ridley laid it aside. This was, perhaps, the voice of the people, and the voice of the people, no editor is ever permitted to forget, is the voice of God. It was a pity, he reflected, that God's utterances needed such a lot of editorial revision.

Disposing of the remainder of the morning's mail was easy. Ridley ran his fingers quickly through it: propaganda, some of it expert and much of it amateurish, from a dozen bureaux maintained by a dozen foreign Governments. *The Bellman* was invited to espouse two opposed causes in India; it was offered a ringing denunciation of the partition of Ireland; it was urged to celebrate the 250th anniversary of a French poet whom Ridley could not recall having heard of; it was reminded of seven quaint celebrations which would take place in Britain during November.

There were four long mimeographed statements from four trades unions, setting forth extremely complex grievances which the Government was admonished to settle at once. There was a pamphlet from a society which wanted to reform the calendar and had received the permission of Ecuador, Liberia, Iceland and the Latvian Government-in-exile to go ahead and do it. There was a mass of material from United Nations. There were five printed communications of varying length from religious and charitable societies. There was something stamped 'Newsflash' in red ink, advertising a new oil well in terms which were not intended to sound like advertisement. A bluebook, to which was attached the visiting card of a Cabinet Minister, presented a mass of valuable statistics, eighteen months out of date. Four packages offered *The Bellman* new comic strips of unparalleled funniness, which Ridley read through with undisturbed gravity.

He threw the whole lot into the waste basket, filling it almost to the brim.

THERE WAS a rich, rumbling sound outside his door, a voice which said, 'Ah, Miss Green, as charming as ever, I see. Nobody with the Chief, I presume?' and the door opened, admitting Mr Swithin Shillito.

Mr Shillito was seventy-eight years old, and frequently put people into a position where they had to tell him that he did not look it. His white hair, parted in the middle, swept back in two thick waves. His white moustache was enormous, and was shaped like the horns of a ram. Lesser moustaches, equally white, thick and sweeping, served him for eyebrows. His very large, handsome head appeared to be attached to his small, meagre body by a high stiff collar and a carefully knotted tie, in which a nugget of gold served as a pin. On his waistcoat hung a watch-chain with huge links, from one of which depended an elk's tooth, mounted in gold. Other interesting elements in his dress were brightly shined high boots, an alpaca working coat, and wicker cuff-guards on his sleeves. Gold pince-nez hung from a little reel on his waistcoat, ready to be hauled out and nipped on his large nose when needed. He carried some papers in his hand.

'Nothing strange or startling this morning, Chief,' said he, advancing with a jaunty step. 'I thought I'd do my stint a little early. Nothing heavy: just one or two odds and ends that may prove amusing, and fill up a corner here and there. I wanted to get my day clear, in order to do some digging. I tell these young chaps in the news room, "Dig, dig, it's the secret of the Newspaper Game. I'm seventy-eight and still digging," I say. Some of them won't believe it. You'll do the leader yourself, I suppose?'

'Yes Mr Shillito,' said Ridley. 'I have two or three things I want to write about today.'

'And I dare swear you have them written in your head at this moment,' said Mr Shillito, wagging his own head in histrionic admiration. 'Plan, plan; it's the only way to get anything done on a newspaper. They won't believe it, the young chaps won't, but it's the gospel truth.'

'I have been reading one or two reports on the seaway scheme which suggested some ideas to me.'

'Ah, that's it! Read, read. Dig, dig. Plan, plan. That's what takes a journalist to the top. But the young chaps won't listen. Time will weed 'em out. The readers, the diggers, the planners will shoot to the top and the rest—well, we know what happens to them. Do you want to cast your eye over those things while I wait?'

I'm damned if I do, thought Ridley. Mr Shillito loved to watch people reading what he had written, and as he did so he would smile, grunt appreciatively, nod and in other ways indicate enjoyment and admiration until all but the strongest were forced by a kind of spiritual pressure to follow his lead. In his way, the old fellow was a bully; he was so keen in his appreciation of himself and his work that not to join him became a form of discourtesy.

'I am rather busy, at present,' said Ridley. 'I'll read them later.'

'Ah, you don't have to tell me how busy you are,' said Mr

9

Shillito; 'I know, perhaps better than anyone, what the pressure is in your job. But if I may I'll drop in again later in the morning, when you've had time to read those. I've noticed that a few of my things haven't appeared in print yet, though you've had them in hand for a fortnight or more. Now, Chief, you know me. I'm the oldest man on the staff, perhaps the oldest working journalist in the country. If there's any falling-off, any hint of weariness in my stuff, you've only to tell me. I know I'm not immortal. The old clock must run down some day, though I must say I feel in wonderful form at present. But be frank. Am I getting too old for my job?'

Oh God, thought Ridley, he's beating me to it! He's making me say it the meanest, dirtiest way. He's putting me in the position of the Cruel Boss who throws the Faithful Old Employee into the street! I must seize the helm of this conversation from Mr Shillito's skilled hand or all will be lost.

'You mustn't think in those terms, Mr Shillito,' he said. 'Your work seems to me to be on the same level as always. But it is not my wish or that of the publisher to rob you of the ease to which your seniority entitles you, and in the course of a few days I want to have a talk with you about the future. Meanwhile, I have some pressing matters to attend to, and if you will excuse me—'

'Of course, of course,' said Mr Shillito, in a voice which suggested movement, though he remained firmly in his chair. 'But you understand how matters are with me. I don't wish to be sentimental. Indeed, you know that any display of feeling is repugnant to me. An Englishman, and what I suppose must now be called an Englishman of the Old School, I will submit to anything rather than make a display of my feelings. But you know, Chief, that the News-paper Game is all in all to me. When the Game becomes too rough for me, I don't want to watch it from the sidelines. If I have a wish, it's that I may drop in harness. I'm not a conventionally religious man; my creed, so far as I've had one, has been simple Decency. But I've prayed to whatever gods there be, many and many a time, "Let me drop in harness; let the old blade wear out, but not rust out!" '

Mr Shillito delivered this prayer in a voice which must have been audible in the news room, even though the presses had begun the morning's run, and Ridley was sweating with embarrassment. This was becoming worse and worse. To his immense relief, Miss Green came in.

'An important long-distance call, if you can take it, Mr Ridley,' said she.

'Aha!' he cried. 'You'll excuse me, Mr Shillito? Confidential.' He hissed the last word, as though matters on the highest government level were involved. The lover of the Newspaper Game raised his great eyebrows conspiratorially, and tip-toed from the room.

'What is it, Miss Green?' asked Ridley, mopping his bald brow.

'Nothing, really, Mr Ridley,' said Miss Green. 'I just thought you might like a change of atmosphere. There was a call a few minutes ago. Professor Vambrace wants to see you at eleven.'

'What about?'

'Wouldn't say, but he was rather abrupt on the line. He said he had called earlier.'

'Professor Vambrace is always abrupt,' said Ridley. 'Thank you, Miss Green. And I am always busy if Mr Shillito wants to see me, for the next few days.'

Miss Green nodded. She was too good a secretary to do more, but there was that in her nod which promised that even the gate-crashing talents of Mr Shillito would be unavailing against her in future.

SIGHING, RIDLEY turned to his next task, which was a consideration of the editorial pages of thirty-eight contemporaries of *The Bellman*, which had been cut out and stacked ready to hand. He would have liked to take ten minutes to think about Mr Swithin Shillito and the problem which he presented, but he had not ten minutes to spare. People who form their opinions of what goes on in a daily newspaper office upon what they see at the movies imagine that the life of a journalist is one of exciting and unforseen events; but as Ridley intended to say in his Wadsworth lecture, it was rooted deep in a stern routine; let the heavens fall and the earth consume in flames, the presses must not be late; if the reading public was to enjoy the riotous excess of the world's news, the newspaperman must bend that excess to the demands of a mechanical routine and a staff of union workers. Before one o'clock he must read all that lay on his desk, talk to the news editor, plan and write at least one leading article, and see any visitors who could win past Miss Green. He could spare no ten minutes for pondering about Mr Shillito. He must read, read, dig, dig, and plan, plan as the Old Mess himself advised.

Upon the right-hand drawboard of his desk was his typewriter; he slipped a piece of paper under the roller and typed a heading: *Notes and Comment*. It was an ancient custom of the paper to end the editorial columns with a few paragraphs of brief observation, pithy and, if possible, amusing, and Ridley wrote most of them. It was not that he fancied himself as a wit, but the job must be done by somebody, and better his wit than Shillito's; the Old Mess had a turn for puns and what he called 'witty *aperçus*'. He picked up the first of the editorial pages, and ran his eye quickly over it: a leader complaining of high taxation, and two subsidiary editorials, one sharply rebuking a South American republic for some wickedness connected with coffee and another explaining that the great cause of traffic accidents was not drunkenness or mechanical defects in cars, but elementary bad manners on the part of drivers. There were no paragraphs which he might steal, or use as priming for the pump of his own wit, and only one joke. It read:

WAS LIKE HIM

Office boy: Man waiting to see you, sir.
Boss: I'm too busy for time-wasters. Does he look important?
Office Boy: Well, not too much so, sir. About like yourself.

Ridley sighed, and put the sheet in the waste basket. The next three yielded nothing that he could use. The fourth contained a note which looked promising. It was:

An American doctor says that hairs in the ears help hearing. Barber, hold those shears!

Surely a witty *aperçu* could be wrought from that? He pondered for a moment, and then typed:

A Montreal physician asserts that hairs in the ears are aids to hearing. In future, it appears, we must choose between hearing and shearing.

When it was on paper he eyed it glumly, changed 'asserts' to 'says' and picked up the next sheet. It was from a prairie paper, whose editor was of the opinion that the chief cause of motor accidents was faulty brakes. None of its notes were worth stealing, but tucked in a corner was:

ONE FOR THE BOSS

Boss: You say there is a man at the door wishes to see me. Does he look like a gentleman?
Office Boy: Well, not exactly like a gentleman, sir. Just something like yourself!

The next three papers brought him no inspiration, but among the *Notes* in the fourth appeared the following:

A local merchant is still reeling from the answer he received when he asked his secretary to describe a visitor. 'Nobody important,' replied the fair one, 'pretty much like yourself.'

Ridley hurried on. The next page which came to hand carried a sharp warning to the Government that continued high taxation would beget a dreadful vengeance at the next general election, and a lesser piece which said that modern children would be less prone to delinquency if they read fewer comic books devoted to the doings of criminals and fixed their admiration upon some notable hero of the past, such as Robin Hood. This paper also carried an editorial which took issue with some opinions *The Bellman* had expressed a few days before, on prison reform; the editor of *The Bellman*, it was implied, lacked a kind and understanding heart. Ridley made a note to write a counterblast, pointing out that Robin Hood was a criminal and a practical communist, and that no one but a numbskull would hold him up as a hero to children.

Thus he worked through the pile of contemporary opinion. He paused to read what a medical columnist in one paper had to say about gallstones. They could, it appeared, 'sleep' for years, causing little or no distress beyond an occasional sense of uneasiness. Ridley wondered if he had sleeping gallstones; he certainly had a sense of uneasiness, though it was nothing to what it had been a few years ago. To sit in an editor's chair, even reading epidemic jokes and groping for witty *aperçus*, was a good life; better, certainly, than his days as a reporter and, later, as a news editor. He read on, plunging deep into the pool of Canadian editorial opinion: the wickedness of the Government, the wickedness of the nation in spending several times as much on liquor as it gave to charity, the wickedness of the U.S.A. in not sufficiently recognizing Canada's greatness, the wickedness of Britain in not spending more money in Canada: he scanned these familiar topics without emotion, thinking only that the newspapers, like the churches, would be in a poor way if there were no wickedness in the world. Indeed, a good many editors seemed to think of themselves, primarily, as preachers, crying aloud to a godless world to repent of its manifold sins. Some, who did not regard themselves as preachers, appeared to think of themselves as simple, shrewd old farmers; they wrote nostalgically of a bygone, Arcadian era, when everybody was near enough to the farm to have a little manure on his boots, and they appeared to think that farmers were, as a class, more honest and less given to gaudy vice than city folk. Ridley, who had lived in a rural community for a few years when a child, had never been able to find out where this opinion had its root. Other editors, who were disguised neither as preachers nor farmers, donned newsprint togas and appeared as modern Catos, ready to shed the last drop of their ink in defence of those virtues which they believed to be the exclusive property of the party not in power; these were also exceedingly hard upon the rising generation, whom they lumped together under the name of 'teen-agers'. To be an editor was to be a geyser of opinion; every day, without fail, Old Faithful must shoot up his jet of comment, neither so provocative as to drive subscribers from his paper, nor yet so inane as to be utterly contemptible. The editor must not affront the intelligence of the better sort among his readers, and yet he must try to say something acceptable to those who really took the paper for the comics and the daily astrology feature. Truly, a barber's chair, that fits all buttocks.

While musing, Ridley had drawn moustaches and spectacles on pictures of four statesmen which appeared in a paper under his hand. He sketched a wig of curly hair on a bald man. With two deft dots of his pencil, he crossed the eyes of a huge-breasted girl under whose picture appeared the caption: 'Miss Sweater Girl for this month is lovely Dinah Ball, acclaimed by outstanding artists for her outstanding physique'. If a new Sweater Girl every month, why not an Udders Day, for the suitable honouring of all mammals? Could a witty *aperçu* be made of that? Probably not for a family journal.

But this was idleness. He must work. The editor of an evening daily has no time for profitless musing until after three o'clock. He tore up the defaced pictures, so that Miss Green should not find them, and turned once again to his task.

When another twenty minutes had passed he had perused the editorial outpourings of his thirty-eight contemporaries and had produced four more paragraphs of *Notes and Com-*

ment. It was possible, he knew, to buy syndicated material of this sort, but he rather liked writing his own; the technique had its special fascination. It was possible, when desperate for material, to make an editorial note about virtually anything, or out of nothing at all. Consider, for instance, his startling success of the previous June: a mosquito in his office had annoyed him, and when he mentioned it to Miss Green she borrowed an atomizer filled with some sort of spray from the janitor, sought out the monster, and stifled it. 'There's a spray for every kind of bug now, Mr Ridley,' she had said. 'Except the humbug, Miss Green,' he had replied, thinking of Mr Shillito. And there had been a Note, ready to hand. He had typed it at once:

> An eminent scientist asserts that there is now a spray for the control of every form of bug. Excluding, of course, the humbug.

One always attributed any foolish remark upon which one intended to pun either to an eminent scientist, a prominent physician, or a political commentator; it gave authenticity and flourish to the witty *aperçu* which followed. This gem, so quickly conceived and executed, had been copied by eighteen other newspapers, with appropriate credit to *The Bellman,* stolen by several more, and had appeared a month afterward in the magazine section of the New York *Times,* attributed to the late Will Rogers.

It was now time for him to settle down to work on the leader for the day, his editorial on the St Lawrence seaway. This was a nervous moment, for he hated to make a beginning at any piece of writing. As the Old Mess had told him, it was already written in his head, but what is written in the head is always so much more cogent and firmly expressed than what at last appears upon the page. He longed for a discretion, something that would postpone beginning for a few more minutes. His wish was gratified; Miss Green came in, carrying three books.

'Shall I put these with the other review books, Mr. Ridley?'

'No, let's have a look at them, Miss Green.'

Books for review always gave him a moment of excitement. There was the chance, faint, but still possible, that among them there would be something which he himself would like to read. But not this time. The first was a volume of pious reflections by a well-known Canadian divine; just the thing for Shillito. Next was a slim volume of verse by a Canadian poetess. Why are such volumes always 'slim', he wondered; why not 'scrawny', which would be so much nearer the truth? Miss Green could polish off the poetess. Next—ah, yes, the choice of an American book club, a volume somewhat larger and heavier than a brick, with a startling jacket printed upon paper so slick as to be somewhat sticky to the touch. *Plonk* was its title, and the inside flap of the jacket declared that 'it lays bare the soul of a man and woman caught up in the maelstrom of modern metropolitan life. Rusty Maloney fights his way from Boston's Irishtown to success as an advertising executive, only to fall under the spell of Siva McNulty, lovely, alluring but already addicted to Plonk, the insidious mixture of stout, brandy and coarse-ground poppyheads which brings surcease to screaming nerves and abraded passions. An Odyssey of the spirit on a scale rarely attempted, this novel is redolent of . . . .' No use giving that to Shillito; his usual reviewer of novels which were redolent of something was in hospital, having a baby, and he did not want the Old Mess being offensively moral through four inches in the review column. Who, then? Ah, Rumball!

He rang the bell and asked Miss Green to find Mr Rumball and send him in. Meanwhile he made a bet with himself that the first sex scene in *Plonk* would be found between pages 15 and 30. He won his bet. It was by no means a certainty. Sometimes this important scene came between pages 1 and 15.

Henry Rumball was a tall, untidy young man on the reportorial staff; his daily round included visits to the docks, the university and the undertakers. He presented himself wordlessly before the editor's desk.

'I thought you might like to review *Plonk*,' said Ridley. 'I know you take an interest in the modern novel. This is rather special, I believe. Stark stuff. Say what you think, but don't frighten any old ladies.'

'Thanks, Mr Ridley. Gosh, *Plonk*,' said Rumball, seizing the volume and seeming to caress it.

'You know something about it?'

'I've seen the American reviews. They say it moves the novel on to an entirely different plateau of achievement. The *Saturday Review* man said when he'd finished it he felt exactly as if he had been drinking plonk all night himself. It's kind of tactile, I guess.'

'Well, say so in your piece. Tactile is a handy word; tends to make a sentence quotable.'

Rumball rocked his weight from foot to foot, breathed heavily, and then said, 'I don't know that I really ought to do it.'

'Why not? I thought you liked that kind of thing?'

'Yes, Mr Ridley, but I'm trying to keep my head clear, you see. I'm avoiding outside influences, to keep my stream unpolluted, if you know what I mean.'

'I don't know in the least what you mean. What stream are you talking about?'

'My stream of inspiration. For *The Plain*. My book, you know.'

'Are you writing a book?'

'Yes. Don't you remember? I told you all about it nearly a year ago.'

'I can't recall anything about it. When did you tell me?'

'Well, I came in to ask you about a raise——'

'Oh yes, I remember that. I told you to talk to Mr Weir. I never interfere with his staff.'

'Yes, well, I told you then I was writing a novel. And now I'm working on my first draft. And I'm not reading anything, for fear it may influence me. That's the big danger, you know. Influences. Above all, you have to be yourself.'

'Aha, well if you don't want *Plonk* I'll find someone else.

Will you ask Mr Weir to see me when he has a free moment?'

'Could I just talk to you for a minute, about the novel? I'd appreciate your help, Mr Ridley.'

'This is rather a busy time.'

But Rumball had already seated himself, and his shyness had fallen from him. His eyes gleamed.

'It's going to be a big thing. I know that. It's not conceit; I feel it just as if the book was somebody else's. It's something nobody has ever tried to do in Canada before. It's about the West——'

'I recall quite a few novels about the West.'

'Yes, but they were all about man's conquest of the prairie. This is just the opposite. It's the prairie's conquest of man. See? A big concept. A huge panorama. I only hope I can handle it. You remember that film *The Plough that Broke the Plain?* I'm calling my book *The Plain that Broke the Plough*. I open with a tremendous description of the Prairie; vast, elemental, brooding, slumbrous; I reckon on at least fifteen thousand words of that. Then Man comes. Not the Red Man; he understands the prairie; he croons to it. No, this is the White Man; he doesn't understand the prairie; he rips up its belly with a blade; he ravishes it. "Take it easy," says the Red Man. "Aw, drop dead," says the White Man. You see? There's your conflict. But the real conflict is between the White Man and the prairie. The struggle goes on for three generations, and at last the prairie breaks the White Man. Just throws him off.'

'Very interesting,' said Ridley, picking up some papers from his desk. 'We must have a talk about it some time. Perhaps when you have finished it.'

'Oh, but that may not be for another five years,' said Rumball. 'I'm giving myself to this, utterly.'

'Not to the neglect of your daily work, I hope?'

'I do that almost mechanically, Mr Ridley. But my creative depths are busy all the time with my book.'

'Aha; will you ask Mr Weir if I may see him?'

'Certainly, sir. But there's just one thing I'd like your

advice about. Names. Names are so important in a book. Now the big force in my book is the prairie itself, and I just call it the Prairie. But my people who are struggling against it are two families; one is English, from the North, and I thought of calling them the Chimneyholes, only they pronounce it Chumnel. The other is Scandinavian and I want to call them the Ruokatavarakauppas. I'm worried that the vowel sounds in the two names may not be sufficiently differentiated. Because, you see, I want to get a big poetic sweep into the writing, and if the main words in the novel aren't right, the whole thing may bog down, do you see?'

'I want to see Mr Weir at once,' said Ridley, in a loud, compelling voice.

'I'll tell him right away,' said Rumball, moving toward the door, 'but if you should happen to think of a name that has the same rhythm as Ruokatavarakauppas but has a slightly darker vowel shading I'd be grateful if you would tell me. It's really going to be a kind of big saga, and I want people to read it aloud as much as possible, and the names are terribly important.'

Reluctantly, he left the office, and shortly afterward Edward Weir, the managing editor, came in and sat in the chair from which Rumball had been driven with such difficulty.

'Anything out of the ordinary last night?' asked Ridley.

'Just the usual Hallowe'en stuff, except for one story we can't track down. Some sort of trouble at the Cathedral. The Dean won't say anything, but he didn't deny that something had happened. Archie was going home a little after midnight and he met Miss Pottinger coming from the West Door of the Cathedral. He asked her if anything was wrong and she said, "You'll get nothing out of me," and hurried off across the street. But she had no stockings on, and bedroom slippers; he spotted them under her coat. Now what was she doing in the Cathedral at midnight on Hallowe'en with no stockings on?'

'At her age lack of stockings suggests great perturbation

of mind, but nothing really interesting. Did Archie try to get into the church?'

'Yes, but the door was locked. He could see light through the keyhole, but there was nothing to be heard.'

'Probably nothing at all happening, really.'

'I don't know. When I called Knapp this morning he was very short, and when I asked him if it was true that someone had tried to rob the Cathedral last night he said, "Where did you hear about that?" and then tried to tell me he meant nothing by it.'

'Why don't you try the organist? You know, that fellow— what's his name?—Cobbler. He never stops talking.'

'Called him. He said, "My lips are sealed." You know what a jackass he is.'

'We'd better keep after it. Tell me, is that fellow Rumball any good?'

'Fair. He was better when he first came on the staff. He moons a good deal now. Maybe he's in love.'

'Perhaps Mr Shillito could give him one of his talks on the virtue of digging in the Newspaper Game.'

'God forbid. Are you going to do anything about that matter?'

'I'm moving as fast as I can. It's very difficult. You have no heart, Ned. How would you like to be thrown out of your job at seventy-eight?'

'If I had a pension, and a house all paid for, and a nice little private income, and probably a good chunk of savings, like Old Shillito, I would like nothing better.'

'Has he all that?'

'You know it as well as I do. He just likes to prowl around this office and waste everybody's time.'

'He says he prays to whatever gods there be that he may drop in harness. He's not a conventionally religious man, but that is his prayer.'

'The old faker! When he caught on to this Cathedral story this morning he was in my office like a shot out of a gun. "Ned, my boy," he said, "take an old newspaperman's advice and let this thing drop; I've been a staunch churchman all my life, and there's nothing I would not do to shield the church against a breath of slander." Of course I tried to find out if he knew anything, but he shut up like a clam. Gloster, why don't you give him the axe? He's just a pest.'

'I inherited him. And he was editor himself for a few months before I was appointed. I don't want anybody to be able to say that I was unfair to him.'

'It's your funeral. But he's a devil of a nuisance. Always in the news room, keeping somebody from work. The boys are sick of him. They aren't even civil to him any more, but he doesn't notice.'

'I'm going to do something very soon. I just want to be able to do it the right way. If we could ease him out gloriously, somehow it would be best. I had a notion involving an illuminated address which might work. But leave it with me for a few days more. Nothing else out of the way?'

But the day's news was barren of anything else which the managing editor thought Mr Ridley should know, and he went back to his own office leaving the editor once more with the task of writing his leader. To postpone the dread moment a little longer he picked up the few typewritten sheets which Mr Shillito called 'his stint', and read that which was uppermost.

A VANISHING AMENITY

That the walking-stick is disappearing from our streets —nay even from our hall-stands—is a fact not to be gainsaid by the boldest. Where once:

> Sir Plume, of amber snuffbox justly vain
> And the nice conduct of a clouded cane,

took pride in possessing half-a-score different sticks for every occasion—for dress, for church, for the town stroll and the rural ramble—your modern man, hastening from business to home and from home to club in his comfortable car, needs none and, be it said, desires none. Macaulay's schoolboy, young model of erudition, might be excused today for failing to distinguish between rattan and ebony, between cherished blackthorn and familiar ashplant. Beyond question the walking-stick has—*hinc illae lacrimae*—gone where the woodbine twineth.

Ridley sighed and then, slowly and painfully, was possessed by rage. His weakness in failing to get rid of the Old Mess condemned him to publish this sort of hogwash in the paper of which he was known to be the editor. The mantle of the eighteenth century essayist—old, frowsy, tattered, greasy and patched with Addison's gout-rags and the seat of the gentle Elia's pants—had fallen upon Swithin Shillito, and he strutted and postured in it, every day, in the columns of *The Bellman*. And why? Because he, Gloster Ridley, lacked the guts to tell the Old Mess that he was fired. He hated himself. He despised his weakness. And yet—a pious regard for old age and a sincere desire to be just and to use his power wisely restrained him from acting as he would have done if the offender had been, for instance, Henry Rumball. And, who could say, might not many readers of *The Bellman*—even a majority of them—share the opinion of Eldon Bumford, who revelled in Mr Shillito's essay on the fate of the toothpick and exulted in his discussions of the importation of snuff and birdseed? To what extent was he, Gloster Ridley, justified in imposing his taste upon the newspaper's subscribers? Still, was it not for doing so that he drew his excellent salary and his annual bonus reckoned upon the profits? What about the barber's chair; might there not be a few buttocks for Shillito? But he could go on in this Hamlet-like strain all day. There was only one thing for it. He rang for Miss Green.

'Please call Mr Warboys and ask if I may see him for half an hour this afternoon,' said he.

'Yes, Mr. Ridley. And Professor Vambrace called again and said he couldn't come at eleven and insists on seeing you at two.'

'Very well, Miss Green. But what is all this about Professor Vambrace? What does he want to see me about?'

23

'I don't know sir, because he wouldn't give me any hint on the phone. But he was very crusty. He kept repeating "Two, sharp," in a way I didn't like.'

'He did, did he? Well, whenever he comes, keep him waiting five minutes. And I don't want to be disturbed until lunch.'

'Yes, sir. Here are a few letters which came with the second mail.'

These were quickly dealt with. A temperance league called for 'renewed efforts', and Moral Re-Armament asserted in three paragraphs that if everybody would try to be decent to everybody else, all problems between management and labour would disappear. A young Nigerian wrote, 'I am African boy but always wear American shoes,' and wanted a Canadian pen-friend, preferably a girl between 14 and 16. Another, deeply critical of *The Bellman*, was so eccentric in grammar and spelling that it took five minutes of Ridley's time to prepare it for the printer; there is nothing that makes an editor feel more like St Francis—a loving brother to the ass—than this sort of remedial work on a letter which accuses him of unfairness or stupidity. At last Ridley was ready to write his leader.

After all his fussing it came out quite smoothly, and by mid-day he had everything prepared for the printers and was ready to think about his luncheon.

CONSIDERING THAT he prepared and ate it in strict privacy, Gloster Ridley's lunch was a matter of extraordinary interest to a great many people in Salterton. There are some ways in which a man may be eccentric, and nobody will think anything of it; there are others in which eccentricity becomes almost a moral issue. Having no wife to return to at the middle of the day, the obvious thing was for him to eat at an hotel or a restaurant. But instead he preferred to prepare his own luncheon and eat it in his office. This oddity might have been overlooked if he had uncomfortably devoured a sandwich at his desk, and washed it down with milk; such a course might have won him a reputation as a keen news-

paperman, unwilling to relax for an instant in his con-
templation of the day's horrors; it might have brought him
those stigmata of the conscientious and ambitious executive,
a couple of ulcers. But he was known to prepare and eat a
hot dish, and follow it with some cheese or a bit of fruit,
and make himself black coffee in a special percolator. It was
even suspected that he sometimes took a glass of sherry
with his meal.

These enormities might have been forgiven if he had
made a joke of them, or had asked other men of business
to come and share his repast. But he obstinately considered
his lunch to be nobody's business but his own. Consequently spiteful things were said of him, and it was hinted
that he wore a blue apron with white frills while preparing
his meal, and more than one Letter to the Editor had suggested that if he knew as much about politics, or economics,
or world affairs or whatever it might be, as he did about
cooking, *The Bellman* would be a better paper.

Cooking, however, was his hobby, and he saw no reason
why he should not do as he pleased. He would probably
have admitted—indeed, often did admit to his particular
friend Mrs Fielding—that he was a bit of an old woman,
and fussed about his food. He hated to eat in public, and
he hated the kind of food which the restaurants of Salterton
offered. In a modest way he was a gourmet. He cooked his
own dinners in his apartment, and often asked his friends to
dine with him. They agreed that his cooking was excellent.
He permitted his housekeeper (whom he always thought of
as Constant Reader because she devoured *The Bellman*
nightly and gave him unsought advice about it daily) to
cook his breakfast, but otherwise he took care of himself
in this respect. He did not realize that his daily luncheon
was taken almost as a personal affront by several ladies in
Salterton who regarded all unattached men with suspicion,
and if he knew that other men laughed at him he did not
care.

Perhaps the most irritating part of the whole business to
those who disapproved of his custom was his extreme thin-

ness. A man who makes so much fuss about his food ought, by all laws of morality and justice, to be fat. He should bear about with him burdensome evidence of his shameful and unmanly preoccupation. But Ridley was tall and thin and bald, and was referred to by the staff of *The Bellman,* when he was out of earshot, as Bony.

He liked his lunch-time, because it gave him an opportunity to think. On this first of November he moved the little hot-plate out of his cupboard as usual, took two eggs and other necessaries from his brief case, and made himself an excellent omelette. He sat down at a small table near his window and ate it, looking down at the Salterton market, which was one of the last of the open-air markets in that part of Canada, and a very pretty sight.

He was thinking, of course, about Mr Shillito. When he saw his publisher that afternoon, he would explain that Mr Shillito must go, and he would ask Mr Warboys to help him to ease the blow. Execrable as Mr Shillito might be as a writer, and detestable as he might be about the office, he was an old man with somewhat more than his fair share of self-esteem, and Ridley could not bring himself to wound him. But there must be no half-measures. Shillito must have an illuminated address, presented if possible by Mr Warboys himself. The whole staff must be assembled, and Mr Shillito must be allowed to make a speech. Perhaps the Mayor could be bamboozled into coming. And a picture of the affair must appear in *The Bellman,* with a caption which would make it clear that Mr Shillito was retiring of his own volition. It would all be done in the finest style. Why, if Mr Warboys were in a good mood, he might even suggest a little dinner for Mr Shillito, instead of a staff meeting. Ridley found that his eyes had moistened as he contemplated the golden light in which Mr Shillito would depart from *The Bellman.*

But why do I worry about him? he asked himself. Does he ever give a thought to my convenience? Doesn't he use me shamelessly whenever he can? What was that incident only a week ago? Shillito had burst into his office with some dreadful freak in tow, a grinning little fellow called Bevill Higgin—how tiresome he had been about the lack of a final 's' on his name—who wanted Ridley to publish half-a-dozen articles by himself on some method of singing that he taught. Print them and pay for them, if you please! Ridley had been furious, but when really angry he did not show it. Instead he gave them both what he thought of as the Silent Treatment. He had allowed little Higgin to chatter on and on, making silly jokes and paying him monstrous compliments, while he sat in his chair, saying nothing and only now and then gnashing the scissors which he held in his hand. The Silent Treatment never failed, and at last Shillito had said, 'But we mustn't detain you, Chief; shall I make arrangements with Mr Higgin for the articles?' And he had replied, 'No, Mr Shillito, I don't think we need trouble you to do that.' Higgin had blushed and grinned, and even the Old Mess knew that he had been snubbed. But if people invaded his office unasked and tried to force upon him things which he did not want, did they deserve any better treatment? One of Shillito's worst characteristics was that he looked upon *The Bellman* as a sort of relief centre and soup kitchen for all the lame ducks he picked up in a social life which yielded an unusual number of lame ducks. A lunatic, lean-witted fool, presuming on an ague's privilege, he quoted to himself, and at once felt sorry for the Old Mess. But he really must stop thinking of him as the Old Mess. It was one of his worst mental faults, that trick of having private and usually inadmissible names for people. Some day a few of them were sure to pop out. When he was on the operating-table, under anaesthetic, for instance.

Thus, rocking between anger against Mr Shillito and pity for him, Ridley ate his biscuits and cheese, drank his excellent coffee, put his dishes on Miss Green's desk to be washed, and composed himself for his invariable twenty-minute after-lunch sleep in his armchair.

MISS GREEN coughed discreetly. 'Professor Vambrace is waiting,' she said.

Ridley leaped from his chair. He hated being caught thus; he had an uneasy conviction that he was unsightly when asleep. And he had overslept by ten minutes. 'Keep him till I ring,' he said.

When Miss Green had gone he combed his hair and rinsed his removable bridge in his tiny washroom. Sitting at his desk, he fussed with some papers, but he could not calm himself. He was disproportionately ashamed of having been found asleep. His nap, like his lunch, was no guilty secret, but he hated to be caught unprepared. How long had Miss Green watched him, perhaps listened to his snores, considered the dry and iridescent matter, like the sheen on a butterfly's wing, which formed on his lower lip when he slept? To escape this uncomfortable train of thought he rang his bell, and Professor Vambrace stalked from the door to the space before his desk, and glared down upon him.

'Well,' he said, and his deep voice vibrated with anger, 'have you decided what you are going to do?'

'As I have no idea what you are talking about, Professor,' said Ridley, 'I can't say that I have. Won't you sit down?'

The Professor sat, majestically. 'I do not believe you, but I'll soon tell you what I'm talking about,' said he, 'and I'll tell you what you're going to do, as well.'

Walter Vambrace was a tall, gaunt man who looked like a tragedian of the old school; his large, dark eyes glowed balefully under his demonic eyebrows. From an inner pocket he produced a wallet, and drew a clipping from it with great care. Ridley, to whom the faces of newspapers were as familiar as the faces of his friends, saw at once that the clipping was from *The Bellman*, and prepared himself for trouble.

'In the next three issues of your paper you will publish this, and the retraction and apology which I shall also give you, in large type at the top of your front page,' said Professor Vambrace.

'Aha,' said Ridley, in a noncommittal tone. 'May I see the clipping, please?'

'Do you mean to tell me that you are not aware of its contents?' said the Professor, working his eyebrows menacingly.

'I have no idea what you are talking about.'

'Good God, don't you read your own newspaper?'

'Of course I do, but I still don't know what has offended you.'

'Refresh your recollection, then,' said the Professor, with a rich assumption of irony, and handed Ridley the scrap of newsprint upon which was printed the engagement notice with which the reader has already been made familiar.

The editor read it carefully. 'This seems quite in order,' said he.

'In order! There is not one word of truth in it from beginning to end. It is a vile calumny!'

'You mean that your daughter is not engaged to Mr Bridgetower?'

'Is not, and never will be, and this damnable libel exposes me and my wife and my daughter to the ridicule of the entire community.'

Ridley's heart sank within him. Physicians say that this cannot happen, but editors know a sensation which may not be described in any other phrase.

'That is most regrettable. I shall do everything possible to find out how this notice came to appear in print. But I can assure you now that we have a system which provides every possible safeguard against this sort of thing, and I cannot understand how it could have failed.'

Professor Vambrace's expression, which had been one of anger, now deepened to a horrible grimace in which rage and scorn were mingled. 'You have a system!' he roared. 'Read it again, you fool, and then tell me, if you dare, that you have a system, or anything except the mischievous incompetence of your disgusting trade to explain the insult!'

Ridley was thoroughly angry himself, now, but caution was ingrained in his nature, and he turned his eyes once again to the clipping.

'To take place November 31st,' hissed the Professor. 'And when, you jackanapes, is November 31st? Is that date provided for in your system? Hey?' he was shouting, now.

All Ridley's anger was drained out of him, and a great but not unfamiliar weariness took its place. He was a good editor, and when praise came to *The Bellman* he took it on behalf of the staff; when blame came to it, he took that alone. He was, in law and in his own philosophy of journalism, personally responsible for every word which appeared in every issue of his paper. He looked into the eyes of his visitor and spoke the speech which was obligatory on him on such occasions.

'I cannot tell you how much I regret this,' he said; 'however, it has happened, and although this is my first knowledge of it, I accept the full blame. Someone has played a tasteless joke on the paper, and, of course, upon you and your family as well. I am deeply sorry that it has happened, and I will join you in doing everything that can be done to find the joker.'

'Pah!' said Professor Vambrace, with such violence that quite a lot of spittle shot across Ridley's desk and settled upon the papers there. 'What kind of newspaper do you call this, where nobody knows how many days there are in November? That alone should have been enough to warn any intelligent person, even a newspaper editor, that the thing was a vile hoax. Quite apart from the ludicrous implication in the notice itself; whatever made you think that my daughter would marry that nincompoop?'

'As I have explained, I have not seen this notice until this moment. And how should I know whom your daughter might or might not marry?'

'Don't you see what goes in your own paper?'

'I see very little of it, and certainly not the engagement notices. These matters are left in the hands of our staff.'

'A fine staff it must be! The thing is preposterous on the face of it. Do you know this Bridgetower?'

'I have met him two or three times.'

'Well? An idiot, nothing better. What would my daughter be doing with such a fellow?'

'I do not know your daughter.'

'Do you imply that she would take up with any simpleton who came along?'

'Professor Vambrace, this is beside the point.'

'It is not beside the point. It is the whole point. You have linked my daughter with this fellow Bridgetower. You have coupled them in the public mouth.'

'I have done nothing of the sort. *The Bellman* has been the victim of a practical joke; so have you. We must do what we can to set matters right.'

'Exactly. Therefore you will publish this notice on your front page, along with the apology which I have here, for the next three days, beginning today.'

'We shall publish a correction . . . .'

'Not a correction, an apology.'

'A correction, but not on the front page, and not for three days.'

'For three days, beginning today.'

'Impossible. The paper has gone to press.'

'The front page.'

'The page on which these announcements appear. For you must understand that our correction will appear for one day only, in the same place that the erroneous notice appeared.'

'That is what you will publish.' The Professor pushed a piece of paper at Ridley. It began rather in the rhythm of a Papal Encyclical: *With the uttermost apology and regret we make unqualified retraction;* Ridley read no more.

'Look here, Professor,' said he, 'we've both been made to look like fools, and we don't want to make matters worse. Leave this matter in my hands, and I'll deal with it in a way that will make an adequate correction and attract no unnecessary attention.'

'This will be settled in my way, or I'll take it to court,' said Professor Vambrace.

'All right, then, take it to court and be damned,' said Ridley.

The Professor glared horribly, but it was the glare of a man who was wondering what to say next. Ridley saw that he had the advantage for the moment and followed up his lead.

'And spare me your histrionics,' said he; 'I am not intimidated by them.'

This was a shrewd thrust, but tactically it was a mistake. The Professor was a keen amateur actor, and fancied himself as the 'heavy' of the Salterton Little Theatre; Ridley's remark disconcerted him, but deepened his anger. However, the editor had at last secured the upper hand, and he continued.

'You must understand that I have had more experience in these matters than you have.'

'That is a confession of incompetence rather than a reassurance,' said Vambrace.

'Kindly allow me to say what I have to say. *The Bellman* will not apologize, because it has acted in good faith, and is just as much a victim of this hoax as yourself. But we will correct the notice, printing the correction in the same place and in the same size of type as the original; we shall do this once only, for the notice appeared only once. If you will think about the matter calmly, you will see that this is best; you do not want an undignified fuss, and you do not want people to hear about this false engagement notice who have not heard of it already. Comparatively few people will have seen it——'

'My family is not utterly obscure,' said the Professor dryly, 'and the Personal Notices are one of the few parts of your paper which are widely read. Scores of people have been asking me about this already——'

'Scores, Professor Vambrace? Did I understand you to say scores?"

'Yes, sir, scores was the word I used.'

'Now, now, precisely how many people have spoken to you about it?'

'Don't take that tone with me, if you please.'

'My experience has been that when angry men talk about scores of people they mean perhaps half-a-dozen.'

'Do you doubt my word?'

'I think that your annoyance has led you to exaggerate.'

'A man in your trade is hardly in a position to accuse anyone of exaggeration.'

'Now let us be reasonable. Of course we shall do everything in our power to find out who perpetrated this joke—'

'I don't call it a joke.'

'Nor do I. This outrage, then.'

'That is a better word. And what do you propose to do?'

It was here that Mr Ridley lost the advantage he had gained. He had no idea what he proposed to do. Therefore he looked as wise as he could, and said, 'That will take careful consideration. I shall have to have a talk with some of the other men on the paper.'

'Let us do so at once, then.'

'I shall talk to them later this afternoon.'

'Let me make is plain to you that at this moment my daughter and my whole family rest under a vile imputation of which this newspaper is the source. Anything that is to be done must be done at once. So get your men in here now, and I will talk to them just long enough to find out whether you really mean to do anything or whether you are stalling me off. And unless you have an immediate plan of action I shall go straight from this office to my lawyer.'

The Professor had the upper hand again, and this time he did not mean to lose it. Ridley rang for Miss Green. 'Will you find Mr Marryat and ask him if he will join us here,' said he; 'it is urgent.' When the secretary had gone he and the Professor sat in painful silence for perhaps three minutes until the door opened again, and the general manager of *The Bellman* appeared.

Mr A. J. Marryat's principal interest was in advertising, and he had the advertising man's optimism and self-assurance. He came in smiling and greeted the Professor warmly. He told him that he was looking well. 'And how is Mrs Vambrace?' said he.

'My wife is in bed, under strong sedatives, because of what you have done here,' replied Vambrace, and breathed noticeably and audibly through his nostrils.

Ridley took the general manager by the arm, guided him to a chair, and explained the trouble as briefly as he could.

Mr Marryat's rule was never to display perturbation. He continued to smile. 'That's bad,' he said, 'but we'll find out who did it, and then we'll show him a joke or two. He laughed comfortably at the prospect; but under cover of his bonhomie he was taking stock of the situation. Ridley, obviously, was in a tight spot or he would not be discussing a matter of this kind with himself in front of the injured party. Well, A. J. Marryat knew all there was to know about tight spots, and one of his most valuable pieces of knowledge was that the sharpest anger can be blunted by good humour, courtesy and a relaxed manner, all of which could be combined with a refusal to do anything you did not want to do. He turned to Ridley, 'Let's hear the details,' said he.

When he heard the details concerning November 31st, Mr. Marryat was disturbed, but his outer appearance of calm was maintained without a ruffle.

'That was inexcusable stupidity,' he said, 'but I'm sure you know, Professor, how hard it is to get people to pay attention to things of that kind.'

'It is your work to do so, not mine,' said the Professor. 'I am only concerned with the fact that your paper has involved my family in a scandal. My professional dignity and my family honour make it imperative that this announcement be denied, and a full apology made, with the least possible waste of time. I want that done in today's paper.'

'That's a mechanical impossibility,' said Mr Marryat. 'The presses will begin rolling in about fifteen minutes.'

'Presses can be stopped, can they not?'

'They can be stopped at very great expense.'

'Probably less than it will cost you if I take this matter to court.'

'Now just a minute, Professor. Let's not be fantastic. Who's talking about court?'

'Your associate, Mr Ridley, told me to take my case to court and be damned.'

'I apologize,' said Ridley, 'but you were very provocative. You called me a fool and a jackanapes, you know.'

'I did, and I see no reason to retract either term.'

'Oh, come now, Professor,' said Mr Marryat, with his genial and ready laugh; 'let's not lose our perspective on this thing.'

'Mr Marryat,' said the Professor, rising, 'I have not come here to be cajoled or lectured. I came to tell you what you must do, and it is plain to me that you will twist and squirm all day to avoid doing it. I have no time to waste and this atmosphere is repugnant to me. You will shortly hear from my lawyers.' The Professor walked rapidly out of the room.

'WELL, HOW do you like that?' said Mr Marryat.

Mr Ridley moaned, and wiped his brow.

'The gall of that guy,' said Mr Marryat. 'Professional dignity! Family honour! You'd think we did it on purpose. And what's all this scandal he talks about? Do you know this fellow Bridgetower?"

'Yes. He's a junior professor.'

'Well? Has he got two heads, or a common-law wife, or something?'

'So far as I know there's nothing against him except that he is the son of old Mrs Bridgetower.'

'That's plenty, mind you. And Vambrace's daughter, what about her?'

'I haven't seen her for two or three years. I think she's in the Waverley Library, somewhere, but I never meet her there. So far as I know she's just a girl.'

'Probably she's engaged to somebody else. That notice was somebody's half-baked joke. Well, I'll trace it. I'll get busy on it right now, and if we hear anything from Vambrace's lawyers, we can explain to them. They'll soon put a stop to that talk about scandal.'

'I'd be grateful if you'd let me know anything you find out as soon as possible, A.J.,' said Ridley.

'At once,' said Marryat, smiling the smile of a man who knows that he has an office system which cannot go wrong.

IT WAS an hour and a half later when Mr Marryat returned. 'Well,' he said, sitting down opposite Ridley's desk, 'this isn't going to be as easy as I thought.'

'What's wrong?' said Ridley.

'If I've told them once, I've told them a million times that we have to have a record of every personal notice and classified ad that goes in the paper,' said Mr Marryat. 'When the yellow form is written out for the composing room a carbon copy is made on the blue form that goes into the files; the customer gets a pink form with all this on it, as a receipt. All three forms have to be initialled by the girl who takes the order, and the advertiser. You'd think it was fool-proof. But look at this.' He handed Ridley a blue form.

It bore the text of the offending engagement notice and some marks which meant nothing to the editor, but Mr Marryat was already explaining them.

'Number of insertions: one. Payment: cash with order, $3.25. Date received: October 30th. Date of insertion: October 31st. Order received by: L.E. Advertiser: blank. Now what do you think of that?'

'It doesn't give the name of the advertiser,' said Ridley, who knew that this was a foolish answer, but obviously the one expected of him. When playing straight-man to Mr Marryat or anyone else with a load of grief, these steps must not be omitted.

'Exactly. And do you know why?'

'No. Why?'

'It's the kind of thing that sickens you; you think you've got a staff trained so that this kind of thing won't happen; you think you can trust everybody; then it happens.'

'Yes. But how?'

'Lucy takes all these classified ads. A dandy girl. Comes

from a fine family. But she's young, and by God, sometimes I swear I won't have another woman in the office that isn't over fifty. Whenever she leaves the desk she's supposed to tell Miss Ellis; she's allowed fifteen minutes every morning and afternoon for coffee and a rest, and for ordinary purposes besides. But if Miss Ellis is out of the office, Lucy likes to slip off to the girl's room for a smoke. This ad was taken at 11.42 on October 30th. Miss Ellis was in my office, going over some figures for the monthly statement. Lucy was downstairs for a cigarette and Miss Porter took the ad, and Lucy initialled the form when she came back.'

'I see.'

'It took me over an hour to get that story out of them. Tears! The more these damned girls are in the wrong, the more they cry.'

'Hadn't Miss Porter enough sense to make whoever-it-was sign in the space for the advertiser's name?'

'She swears she did. And she swears he signed. My guess is that he signed the customer's own pink receipt slip and put it is his pocket and she didn't notice.'

'Aha, then she knows it was a man?'

'Yes, at least she remembers that. And he gave her the copy, typewritten, and she clipped it to the order for the composing room. Here it is. But it doesn't tell us anything.'

'Except that the writer was not used to a typewriter; and it is done on a piece of cheap linen correspondence paper; and the ribbon was in poor condition. What does she remember about the man's appearance?'

'She thinks he wore a blue suit. It might have been a dark grey.'

'Useless. What else?'

'Not a thing. Believe it or not, she can't remember whether he was young or old, dark or fair, wore glasses or not. She does remember that he had what she calls a funny voice.'

'What kind of funny voice?'

'Just funny. I asked her to imitate it, and she opened her mouth and let it hang open; then she cried again. Would

37

you believe anybody could be so dumb and not be in an institution?'

'Most people are very unobservant.'

'You can say that again. Well, you can see what this does to us.'

'We haven't a leg to stand on.'

'Not a leg.'

'Still,' said Ridley, 'the advertisement isn't libel, and Vambrace's lawyers won't advise him to go ahead on that line.'

'Of course not,' said Mr Marryat, 'but if they ever find out that there was any carelessness here they'll make our lives miserable. So I'm taking these papers out of the files and putting them in the safe till we know what's going to happen.'

'I've got to see Mr Warboys this afternoon about another matter. Should I mention this to him, do you think?'

'What for? It won't come to anything. I wouldn't bother him.' And after a few more reflections upon the untrustworthiness and tearfulness of girls Mr Marryat withdrew.

It was half-past three, and Mr Ridley was to see his publisher at half-past four. At four o'clock he received a call from the legal firm of Snelgrove, Martin and Fitzalan, asking that he see Mr Snelgrove at ten o'clock the following morning on a matter of urgent importance.

CLEREBOLD WARBOYS was not primarily interested in the publication of the Salterton *Evening Bellman*; he had been born wealthy, and in the process of becoming much wealthier he had acquired several properties, of which *The Bellman* was one. It had come upon the market as an ancient and almost bankrupt newspaper, and he had bought it because he did not want to see an institution which was so much a part of his native city disappear from that city's life; he also thought that the application of business acumen to the newspaper might improve its fortunes. He was right, as he usually was about such matters, and Mr Marryat and Mr

Ridley had made *The Bellman* not only a very much better paper than it had been before, but a profitable business, as well.

Mr Warboys never interfered with the paper, and this was a source of disagreement between himself and his daughter-in-law, Mrs Roger Warboys, who lived with him and was his housekeeper and hostess. Mrs Roger Warboys, who had been widowed before she was forty, had a great store of energy which was not fully absorbed by her steward-ship for Mr Warboys and the many women's causes into which she threw herself. Her dearest dream was to 'take over' *The Bellman* and to give it a policy more in line with her own opinions. She had a passion for crusading, and she felt that with a newspaper at her command she could do tremendous things to defeat juvenile delinquency, the drug traffic, comic books, immodest bathing suits and other evils which were gnawing at the foundations of society; she would also be able to do much to improve the status of women which, in her view, was unsatisfactory. But her father-in-law, who had passed the greater part of his life in public affairs and had acquired a considerable store of worldly wisdom, refused to pay any attention to her wishes. He was wont to say; 'Nesta, you have what most of the world wants: leisure and the money to enjoy it; why don't you relax?' But for Mrs Roger Warboys there could be no happi-ness which was not also turmoil and the imposition of her will upon other people. Perhaps twice a year she renewed her attack upon her obdurate father-in-law, and the rest of the time she seized what opportunities she could to call his attention to what she believed were fatal weaknesses in the editorship of Gloster Ridley.

It was with no quickening of the spirit, therefore, that Ridley found Mrs Roger Warboys in the publisher's study, pouring tea.

'Ridley,' said his employer, 'I've got the title for my book, at last.'

'Splendid!' said Ridley, with false enthusiasm.

'Yes. *Politics: The Great Game.* What do you think of
that?'

'Absolutely first-rate!'

'Really? Don't give a snap decision. Do you really think
it's what I want?'

'It's very original,' said Ridley.

'It sounds well. But of course most people won't hear it.
They'll read it. How do you think it would look? Nesta, give
me that dummy.'

His daughter-in-law handed him a book from the desk.
Upon it Mr Warboys had put a piece of white paper, to
resemble a dust jacket, and had crudely lettered *Politics:
The Great Game,* by CLEREBOLD WARBOYS, across it.

'Very fine,' said Ridley: 'it has a kind of ring about it,
even in print.'

Conversation as they drank their tea was all about Mr
Warboy's book. This work had been *in utero,* so to speak,
for eight years, but even at the age of seventy he could not
find time to write it. Instead, he made copious notes for it,
which he revised whenever a political contemporary died;
when they were all dead, and the decks cleared, he might
actually write it. Meanwhile he sustained the enthusiasm of
an author at a remarkably high level, year in and year out,
and Ridley rarely visited him without being asked for advice
on some point relative to the great work. But at last the
moment came when Ridley was able to raise the question
of Mr Shillito.

'It is by no means easy,' he explained, 'because Mr
Shillito is in a sense a legacy from the former management.
He is a link with the past of the paper. But the sort of thing
he writes no longer has a place in *The Bellman,* and I feel
that it is not in the best interest of the paper to postpone his
retirement.'

'There's no doubt about it that he's a bloody old nuisance
and not worth his keep,' said Mr Warboys, who was only
eight years younger than Mr Shillito and felt no need to
beat about the bush. 'Well; we've got a pension scheme.

What's it for? We'll bounce him with all honours, as you suggest.'

'Mr Shillito never subscribed to the pension scheme,' said Mrs Roger Warboys, unexpectedly.

'How do you know?' asked her father-in-law.

'He asked me to tea on Sunday last. The poor old man is getting very frail, Father, and he has some nice things he wants to see in good hands before he dies. He was really very touching about it. He gave me the loveliest little bronze bowl—Chinese, and very good; I have it in my sitting-room. He hasn't much in the way of money, he says, but he has a few treasures, and he doesn't want them to go to just anybody when he dies. He told me that he had never felt able to contribute to the pension scheme.'

'I don't know how that could be,' said Ridley. 'Miss Ellis has always been very good about arranging payment plans for anybody who needed special help.'

'Perhaps you don't understand Mr Shillito's way of looking at things, Mr Ridley,' said Mrs Roger Warboys, quietly censorious. 'He's one of those proud old Englishmen who would rather die than ask anybody for help.'

'Then why didn't he take advantage of the pension scheme?' asked Mr Warboys.

'Because he didn't think he would ever live to enjoy it,' said his daughter-in-law. 'He told me that he worked himself so hard in the last few years before you took over *The Bellman* that he never expected to reach his present age. He has always expected that he would drop in harness.'

'Well, let him have the good sense to get out of harness,' said Mr Warboys, 'and he needn't drop so soon.'

'I know I have no right to interfere,' said Mrs Roger Warboys, in the tone she always used when she meant to do so. 'I think Mr Shillito should have every consideration. His judgment alone should be worth something. Even if he simply stays at *The Bellman* to keep an eye on things in general, he would be valuable. His knowledge of the city and its people is surely the most extensive of anyone now on the staff. For instance, I'm sure he would never have passed that ridiculous engagement notice about Pearl Vambrace and young Bridgetower.'

'That matter is in hand,' said Ridley, turning white.

'That's just as well,' said Mrs Roger Warboys, smiling unpleasantly. 'For Professor Vambrace phoned me about it this afternoon, just to make it clear that if he has to take it to law, there is nothing personal intended toward myself. I have worked very closely with him for years,' she explained, 'on the Board of the University Alumni.'

It was then necessary for Mr Ridley to explain to Mr Warboys what the dispute was between *The Bellman* and Professor Vambrace. Mr Warboys was not inclined to pay too much attention to it. 'These things soon blow over,' said he.

'Nevertheless, I think my point about Mr Shillito is well taken,' said Mrs Roger Warboys. 'The Professor was hardly off the phone before Mr Shillito called about it. He said that the minute he saw it he knew there had been some dreadful blunder, for the feud between the Vambraces and the Bridgetowers dates from when Professor Bridgetower was alive. He just wanted me to know that he would never have permitted such a thing to appear in print, but of course his power on the paper is very limited—at present.' These last words were directed with a special smile to Ridley.

'The damned old double-crosser,' said Mr Warboys, who understood these matters very well.

Ridley could think of no comment save lewd and blasphemous variations on that of his publisher, so he held his peace, and soon returned to his office.

IT WAS after six o'clock when he reached it. He stopped in Miss Green's office, and after some rummaging, he drew a sheet of paper from a file and took it to his desk. It was an obituary, prepared some years before and kept up to date, for use when it should be needed. It read:

VAMBRACE, WALTER BENEDICT, b. Cork, Eire, March 5, 1899 only son Rev. Benedict V. and Cynthia Grattan V., a second cousin to the Marquis of Mourne and Derry; Educ. at home and Trinity Coll. Dublin. (M.A.) Emigrated to Canada 1922 joined classics dept. Waverley as junior professor. Married Elizabeth Anne Fitzalan dr. Wolfe Tone Fitzalan, June 18, 1925, one daughter Pearl Veronica b. 1933. Full professor 1935; head classics dept. 1938. Supported for Dean of Arts 1939 but defeated by one vote by the late Dean Solomon Bridgetower. Did not stand again after Dean Btwr's death in 1940. Author: *Contra Celsum with Notes and Commentary* 1924; *Enneads of Plotinus Newly Considered* 1929 (*Times Litt. Supp.* says 'valuable though controversial' in review which might have been by Dean Inge) *Student's Book of Latin Verse* 1938 (sold 150,000).

Professor Vambrace was no austere scholar, but a man who gave richly of himself to a variety of worthy causes. Always accessible to his students, he opened to them the stores of scholarship which he brought from famed Trinity College, Dublin. Graduates of Waverley will long remember the rich and thrilling voice in which he read Latin poetry aloud, seeming to—as one graduate put it—'call Horace smiling from his tomb and Vergil from the realm of the shades.' This same noble organ was for years to be heard in performances given by the Salterton Little Theatre, of which Professor Vambrace was at one time Vice-President. His most notable performance by far was as Prospero in *The Tempest,* of which *The Bellman* critic of that time, Mr Swithin Shillito, wrote: 'It was said of Kean's Shylock, "This was the Jew, That Shakespeare drew"; still borne aloft upon the wave of poetry evoked by Walter Vambrace (away with all Misters and Professors in the presence of Genius) your annalist can but murmur, "This is the Mage, From Shakespeare's page." '

After fifteen minutes' careful work Ridley had revised this paragraph to read thus:

Professor Vambrace, an austere scholar, was associated

43

with many causes. To his students he brought a store of scholarship from famed Trinity College, Dublin. Graduates of Waverley will long remember the voice in which he read Latin poetry aloud, seeming, as one graduate has put it, to call Horace from his tomb and Vergil from Hades. The late Professor Vambrace had a strong histrionic bent and was for some years an amateur performer with the Salterton Little Theatre.

It was not much, and it might be years before it bore fruit, but it made him feel a little better.

PART TWO

IT was not for Gloster Ridley only that November 1st was embittered by the incident of the fraudulent engagement notice. The first person, who was in any way concerned with that notice, to read it in *The Bellman* was Dean Jevon Knapp, of St Nicholas' Cathedral. Returning to the Deanery at half-past five on October 31st he picked up his copy of the evening paper, and having prudently brought his handsome wrought-iron footscraper indoors so that naughty boys would not run off with it in celebration of Hallowe'en, he went into his study to read the news. It was his professional habit to turn first to the column of Births, Marriages and Deaths—Hatch, Match and Dispatch as he called it when he was being funny—to see if there was anything there which called for his attention. He read of the engagement of Pearl Vambrace and Solomon Bridgetower with annoyance; if people proposed to be married in his church it was the least they could do to tell him before announcing it to the world. He spoke to his wife about it during dinner.

'I resent the casual assumption that I shall be on call, and the Cathedral ready, whenever anyone chooses to be married,' said he. 'And how stupid to announce a marriage for November 31st; everybody knows that there is no such day.'

'The Vambraces are very odd people,' said Mrs Knapp. 'Mrs Vambrace is a Catholic, I believe; I never knew that he was anything. Of course it is Mrs Bridgetower who wants the marriage to be in the Cathedral.'

45

'Then why has not Mrs Bridgetower said so to me?' asked the Dean. 'I called on her only last week, and she did nothing but moan about Russia and her heart. She gave me to understand that unless the Russians change their tune at UN she will have a heart attack, presumably to spite them. She never breathed a word about her son's marriage. And nobody has booked the Cathedral for the last day of November, which is presumably the day they mean. I will not be taken for granted in this irritating way.'

'Well, Jevon,' said his wife, 'why don't you call up Professor Vambrace and say so?'

'I shall call him after dinner,' said the Dean, though he did not relish the idea. He hated wrangles. But at eight o'clock precisely he was on the telephone.

'Good evening, Professor Vambrace, this is Dean Knapp of St Nicholas' speaking. I hope you are well?'

'Good evening, Mr. Knapp.'

'I saw the notice of your daughter's engagement in *The Bellman* this evening, and I wished to speak to you about it.'

'You are under some misapprehension, Mr Knapp; my daughter is not engaged.'

'But her engagement is announced in this evening's paper, and her wedding is said to be at St Nicholas'.'

At this point the Dean's telephone clicked, and a steady buzzing told him that his communication with the Professor had been cut. So he patiently dialled the number again, and heard Vambrace's voice.

'Who is it?'

'This is Dean Knapp of St Nicholas' speaking. We were cut off.'

'Listen to me, whoever you are, I consider your joke to be in the worst of taste.'

'This is not a joke, Professor Vambrace. I am Dean Knapp——'

'Dean Humbug!' roared the Professor's voice. 'Do you suppose I am not aware, whoever you are, that this is Hallowe'en?' And the line began to buzz again.

The Dean was angry, but he was not one of those lucky

men who are refreshed and stimulated by anger; it shook
his self-confidence and upset his digestion and put him at a
disadvantage with the world. He was ill-prepared, therefore,
when the telephone rang a few minutes later and Professor
Vambrace's angry voice roared at him.

'So there was a notice of my daughter's engagement in the
paper!'

'Yes, of course, Professor Vambrace, that was what I
called you about.'

'And what do you know about this outrage, eh?'

'I know nothing about it. I wished to know more.'

'What? Explain yourself.'

'That is what I intended to do, but you rudely rang off.'

'Never mind that. What do you know of this?'

'I saw the notice. I had heard nothing of any such wedding, and I called to make inquiries.'

'What about?'

'Well, I am Dean of St Nicholas' and when a wedding is
announced there I feel that I should be informed first.'

'The whole thing is an outrage!'

'To what do you refer, Professor Vambrace?'

'My daughter is not engaged to anyone. Least of all is she
engaged to that yahoo of a Bridgetower.'

'Indeed. Then how do you explain the notice?'

'I don't explain it! How do you explain it?'

'What have I to do with it?'

'Isn't your church mentioned?'

'Yes, and that is what I called you about in the first
place.'

'I have nothing to do with it, I tell you!'

'You need not shout, Professor.'

'I do well to shout. What do you know about this? Answer
me! What do you know?'

'I only know that if you did not authorize the announcement, and it is dated for an impossible date, it looks as
though the whole thing were a practical joke.'

'Joke? Joke! You dare to call this dastardly action a
joke?'

'Professor, I must ask you to moderate your tone in speaking to me.'

There was an angry howl from the other end of the line, and the communication was cut for the third time, presumably because the Professor had slammed his telephone down in its cradle. Dean Knapp's evening was ruined; for an hour he expostulated with his wife, whom he tried to cast in the role of Professor Vambrace, but she sustained it so poorly that he sank into silence and pretended to read a book. But all the while he was thinking up crushing retorts which he should have made when the opportunity served. There is nothing worse for the digestion than this, and before he went to bed the Dean took a glass of hot milk and two bismuth tablets.

HE WAS in his first sleep when the telephone bell rang, and after a little prodding from his wife the Dean trudged downstairs to answer it, sleepily counting over in his mind those among his parishioners who were so near death that they might need him at this hour. But the voice on the telephone was tremulous with life and excitement.

'Mr Dean! Mr Dean!'

'Dean Knapp speaking. Who is it?'

'It is I, Mr Dean. Laura Pottinger.'

'What is the matter, Miss Pottinger?'

'Something terribly wrong is going on at the Cathedral, I know it. Lights are flashing on and off. And I am sure that I can hear the organ.'

'The organ, Miss Pottinger? Surely not.'

'Yes, the organ; I went out on my steps, and I am sure I heard it. And shouting. A dreadful, unholy sound.'

'Not from the Cathedral, Miss Pottinger. You must have been mistaken.'

'Indeed I am not mistaken. And I have called you so that you may take proper action at once.'

'What do you expect me to do, Miss Pottinger?'

'Do, Mr Dean? It is not for me to tell you what you

should do. But if something is wrong at the Cathedral, do you not know what you should do?'

'But I am sure that you must have been deluded in some way, Miss Pottinger.'

'Deluded, Mr Dean? Do you suppose that because I am no longer young I do not know what I hear with my own ears? Do you mean to disregard this matter? Who knows what it may be—sacrilege of some sort, or robbery. There is a lot of fine plate in the Cathedral, Mr Dean, and it is not in the safe, as you know.'

This was a telling thrust. The Dean liked to have the Communion plate laid out at night, ready for the morning, and many of his parishioners, of whom Miss Pottinger was one, felt that it should be kept in the safe until it was needed. If anything were stolen, this quirk of the Dean's would not be forgotten, so he said, 'Very well, Miss Pottinger. I shall go over and see that everything is all right.'

'I shall meet you at the West Door.'

'No, no; you must not think of venturing out.'

'Yes, I shall. I want to know what is happening.'

'If there is anything amiss there might be trouble, and you must not be in any danger.'

'I am a soldier's daughter, Mr Dean.'

'Miss Pottinger, as your priest, I forbid you to come to the Cathedral. Now please go back to bed and do not worry any more.' And with that the Dean hung up his telephone, hoping that he had quelled her. Miss Pottinger, who was over eighty, and very High in her religious opinions, rather liked to be ordered about by clergymen, and was always impressed by the word 'priest'.

By this time the Dean was thoroughly awake, and cold and miserable. His stomach was churning within him and he wanted to go back to bed. But unless he went to the Cathedral he would never hear the end of it. The chances were that Miss Pottinger was mistaken, and his journey would be for nothing: but on the other hand there might be something wrong, and he would face—what? The Dean had been through the 1914-18 war and he felt that his brave days were over. All he wanted now was a quiet life. But the service of the Church was terribly unquiet, sometimes. So he went back to his bedroom, and put on a pullover, and his socks and shoes, and drew on his cassock over his pyjamas. His wife, who was accustomed to night calls, did not stir. He found the large cloak which he wore for winter funerals in the coat-cupboard in the hall, and set forth.

It was only a block from the Deanery to the Cathedral, and the night was bright with moonlight, and mysterious with a film of mist. As the Dean drew near to the Cathedral his heart sank, for unmistakably there was music on the air, a loud and merry tune played upon the organ, mingled with singing voices and an occasional shout of laughter. And unquestionably there was light in the large church, not much, but some. As he approached the West Door the Dean thought that he saw a lurking figure, but when he drew near it had vanished. St Nicholas' Cathedral in Salterton is not one of your common Canadian cathedrals, in sham Gothic; it is a reproduction, on a much smaller scale, of St Paul's, and it has a periwigged dignity of its own. The West Door was under a columned portico, darkly shadowed at this time of night.

The Dean took out his key, and listened. The music and the laughter were not so plainly to be heard here as in the street, but they were plain enough, and eerie. The Dean admitted to himself that he was frightened. He was a devout man, and while devotion undoubtedly brings its spiritual rewards it brings its spiritual terrors too. This was All Hallow's Eve, and if he truly believed in All Saints on the morrow, why should he not believe in the Powers of Darkness tonight? He had never been the sort of Christian who wants to have things all his own way—to preach the love of God and to deny the existence of the Devil. Well, if he had to meet the Devil in the line of duty, he would do so like a man. He muttered a prayer, unlocked the door and tiptoed into the vast shadows of the church.

At first it seemed to him that the chancel was filled with people, but when his astonishment subsided he judged the number to be six or seven. In his own stall—the Dean's stall!—a man was standing on his cushion, waving his arms in time to the music of the organ and the voice of the organist. It was a good tenor voice, and it was singing:

> *Man, Man, Man,*
> *Is for the woman made,*
> *And the woman for the man!*

On the chancel steps a group of people, hand in hand, were circling in a dance, a sort of reel, and now and then one of them would cry 'Heigh!' in the high voice used by Highland dancers.

> *As the spur is for the jade*
> *As the scabbard for the blade,*
> *As for digging is the spade*
> *As for liquor is the can,*
> *So Man, Man, Man,*
> *Is for the woman made.*

The voice was full and joyous and the accompaniment skirled and whistled from the reed pipes of the organ. The Dean stood amazed for a time—it could not have been long, but he was so astonished that he was unable to make any estimate of it—and then wondered what he should do. These were no devils, and as people they did not look very frightening. Indeed, he realized with astonishment at himself that he had been looking at their antics with admiration, thinking what a pretty sight they made, dancing there, and how beautiful his Cathedral looked in this light, with this music and with these inhabitants. Such thoughts would never do. He strode forward and shouted in a loud voice: 'What is the meaning of this?'

The effect was everything that he could have desired, except that the music did not stop. The men roared, and scurried for cover behind the choir stalls; the women—or

51

girls, he judged them to be—shrieked and hid themselves; one leapt into the Bishop's throne and slammed the little door behind her, and another dived into a pew where, on the principle supposed to be favoured by ostriches, she hid her head, but left a great deal of silk-stockinged leg and some inches of thigh in clear view.

> *Be she widow, wife or maid,*
> *Be she wanton, be she staid*
> *Be she well or ill array'd*
> *Whore, bawd or harridan,*
> *So Man, Man, Man,*
> *Is for the woman made,*
> *And the woman for the man!*

The voice concluded triumphantly. Then as the notes of the organ seemed to fly away into the shadows at the roof of the chancel it cried again: 'How was that?'

'Mr Cobbler, what is the meaning of this?' called the Dean sternly.

'Oh, my God!' said the voice, dismayed, and from the organ console emerged the figure of Humphrey Cobbler, the Cathedral organist, dishevelled and ill-dressed, badly in want of a haircut, plainly drunk, but with an air of invincible cheerfulness which shone through even his present discomfiture.

'Mr Dean,' he said, fatuously, 'this is an unexpected pleasure.'

'Mr Cobbler,' said the Dean, now fully in command of the situation, 'answer my question: What is going on here?'

'Well, Mr Dean, it isn't altogether easy to explain. Very odd, on the face of it. As I shall be the first to admit. But when taken in the light of everything that has gone before, and viewed historically, if I may so express myself, quite inevitable and defensible and not in the least reprehensible, if I make myself clear.'

Cobbler delivered this speech with a fine rhetorical air, and there was an appreciative snigger from one of the hidden figures.

'Who are these people?' said the Dean, gesturing broadly. When he had entered the Cathedral he had suffered from the sense of insufficiency which afflicts a man who is wearing no trousers under his cassock: now he was free of that disability, and had indeed acquired the spacious and authoritative manner of a man who is wearing, and has a right to wear, a handsome cloak. 'Come out, all of you, at once,' he cried.

'If you please, Mr Dean,' said Cobbler, 'don't ask that. This is entirely my fault, and I accept the full responsibility. Don't ask them to come out. Not fair to them. My fault.'

'Be silent, Mr Cobbler,' said the Dean sternly. 'Come out, all of you, and be quick.'

Shuffling and scraping, they came out. And the Dean was amazed to see, not a pack of middle-aged roisterers, but four boys and three girls of university age, plainly students at Waverley, and all looking shame-faced enough to melt a harder heart than his.

'Students, I see,' said the Dean, because he could think of nothing better to say.

'My students, Mr Dean, and here entirely because of me,' said Cobbler. 'I hope that you will allow me to send them away, now, for they are really not to blame for what has happened.'

'You must all go away, at once,' said the Dean. 'And I shall see you, Mr Cobbler, at the Deanery at half-past ten tomorrow morning. Now go.' And he herded them toward the West Door.

But as they drew near to it, he had a sudden thought, and pushing past the boys and girls he opened the door a crack and peeped out. Yes, there was a figure, lurking, which could only be Miss Pottinger. The Dean was annoyed. He wanted time to make up his mind about this matter, and he did not want any interference. He was angry with Miss Pottinger for snooping around the Cathedral when he had told her to stay at home. Perhaps unreasonably, he was angrier with her than with the sheepish students who had been making merry in his Cathedral. So he turned, and without explanation, drove them before him to a door which communicated with the Church House and Sunday School annex of the Cathedral, and from there he dismissed them into a street far from where Miss Pottinger kept her vigil. When they had been gone a few minutes he followed them, and went back to the Deanery wrapped in thought.

Miss Pottinger, shivering with cold and disappointed curiosity, hung about the West Door until Archie Blaine, *The Bellman* reporter, returning late from the office, approached her and asked if anything was wrong. And, as often happens when something is wrong, Miss Pottinger denied it vehemently and scampered across the street to her own house.

IT WOULD probably be unjust to Miss Laura Pottinger to describe her as a busybody; she preferred to think of herself as one who possessed a strong sense of her responsibility toward others. She was a soldier's daughter, as she had told the Dean; her father had for many years been a colonel of militia, and if he had not been somewhat too busy for service when the first Boer War broke out, and somewhat too old for it when the second Boer War came along, he would undoubtedly have distinguished himself in the field. He was a very successful wholesale grocer, and his business yielded the means to support his military dignity on the highest level; indeed, in his household it was possible to maintain the most idealistic concepts of military honour, of good breeding and of Victorian Anglicanism, without ever being troubled about such base considerations as money. Miss Pottinger, in her advanced years, had yielded nothing to the spirit of the times; two world wars had beaten vainly against her sense of propriety, and the reduction of her means (though she was very comfortably off) had only served to increase her devotion to what she believed to be the public good.

She was aggrieved, but not surprised, that Dean Knapp had behaved so oddly in the matter of the midnight disturbance in the Cathedral. She had long ago decided that

the Dean lacked those qualities ot decision, censoriousness
and command which she included under the general heading of 'gimp'. But she was devoted to the Cathedral, and
was ready to put all her own boundless stock of gimp at its
service. Therefore she made her way to early Communion
on All Saints' Day in a martial spirit, and as soon as the
service was over she buttonholed Mr Matthew Snelgrove,
the lawyer, as he made his way toward the door.

'You are not locking up the Communion plate, Mr Snelgrove?'

'Surely that is not necessary, Miss Pottinger? There will
be another service at eleven.' Mr Snelgrove was chancellor
of the diocese, and although it was not strictly his duty to
do so, he usually locked the church valuables in the vault,
and made himself responsible for their safe keeping.

'I hope that there was nothing missing this morning?'

'Not that I know of. Why would there be?'

'There was something very odd going on in the Cathedral
last night, at midnight and after. A dreadful clamour, as
though the place were full of rowdy people. I called the
Dean, and I believe he took some action, though of course
I don't know. Naturally I was anxious. After all, there were
many fine pieces on the altar all night, including the chalice
which father gave to St Nicholas' on the successful conclusion of the South African War. I was concerned. And of
course I concluded that you, as chancellor, would have news
which would be some time in getting down to those of us
who are merely parishioners.'

Simple though this speech appears, it contained many of
those qualities of hidden meaning and implication which
made Miss Pottinger a remarkable, if unrecognized, rhe-
torician. It aroused suspicion in the mind of Mr Snelgrove,
and warmed up his well-developed animosity against the
Dean; it suggested sacrilege, which to his lawyer-like mind
was deeply repugnant; it brought into the open the old
quarrel about whether the altar should be decked with
Communion plate at night (which was convenient) or in
the morning (which was safe); it reminded Mr Snelgrove

that the Pottingers had been an influential and generous family in Cathedral life for almost a century, and that when Miss Pottinger died her small fortune might come to the Cathedral if she got her way in some Cathedral affairs; its mock humility flattered the chancellor, while goading him, and gave him an excuse to harry the Dean. Mr Snelgrove's keen legal mind grasped all these points at once, and after a few more words with Miss Pottinger he hurried off to the vestry, like a ruffled old stork, to tackle the Dean about it.

IT MUST not be supposed, because Dean Knapp was not in every respect satisfactory to Miss Pottinger, Mr Snelgrove and some others among his parishioners, that he was less than capable as a clergyman. He was, on the contrary, a man of more than ordinary ability in his profession. But in every church there are people who, for reasons which seem sufficient to them, do not approve of their pastor and who seek to harry him and bully him into some condition more pleasing to themselves. The democracy which the Reformation brought into the Christian Church rages in their bosoms like a fire; they would deny that they regard their clergyman as their spiritual hired hand, whom they boss and oversee for his own good, but that is certainly the impression they give to observers. Dean Knapp attracted this sort of bullying, for he had his share of personal vanity, and it was his desire to be considered urbane. Although he lived in Canada, in the middle of the twentieth century, his clerical ideals were those nineteenth-century clergymen in England who were witty men of the world, as well as men of God. His aptitude for this sort of masquerading was not great, but he tried hard, and often committed innocent follies in pursuit of his urbane goal. He made little literary jokes which people did not understand; he sometimes suggested that certain minor sins were unimportant and rather funny, instead of ignoring them completely as a really tactful Canadian clergyman should; he lacked zeal for the more

uproarious sorts of boys' work, and when it was necessary
to raise money for good causes he did not show that whole-
hearted reverence for money which is so reassuring to a
flock composed predominantly of business people. And,
worst of all, he sometimes refused to be serious when dealing with people who were angry. It was this characteristic of
the Dean's which especially annoyed Mr Matthew Snelgrove, who was often angry and who liked people to share
his anger or tremble at it. A surprising amount of Mr Snelgrove's time was spent in trying to make the Dean be serious
when the Dean wanted to be urbane.

Mr Snelgrove entered the vestry, with the most cursory
of knocks, just as the Dean had removed his cassock and
was about to put on his waistcoat and coat. It is not as easy
to be urbane in shirtsleeves as when fully dressed.

'What's this I hear about trouble in the church last night?'
asked Mr Snelgrove.

But Dean Knapp was not to be caught that way, and he
replied: 'Well, what do you hear about it, Mr Snelgrove?'
He then smiled, as though to say that Mr Snelgrove was
making a fuss about nothing.

'Miss Pottinger thought that there might be some danger
to the plate which was on the altar. It is of considerable
value, you know.'

'It is certainly more valuable that one might think, without being as valuable as the donors suppose,' said the Dean,
and laughed urbanely. Not bad, thought he, for a man who
has not yet had his breakfast. But Mr Snelgrove was not
pleased.

'We should have our work cut out to replace it, if any of
it were stolen,' said he.

'Then perhaps we should increase the insurance,' said
the Dean.

'The insurance is all right as it is,' said Mr Snelgrove.
'But associations, and sentiment, and the devotion to the
Cathedral which those pieces represent can't be replaced
with insurance.'

'No, of course not,' said the Dean, pulling in his horns. He rarely had the temerity to be urbane straight through even the shortest conversation.

'What was happening here last night?'

'What was not happening last night? Hallowe'en, you know. The first thing to happen was that someone made an impudent use of the Cathedral's name in connection with a practical joke.' And then the Dean told Mr Snelgrove about the false engagement notice, and the unreasonable treatment to which he had been subjected by Professor Vambrace. But that was not enough to assuage the curiosity of the lawyer.

'And what was happening at the Cathedral? Miss Pottinger spoke of some rowdiness here.'

'Some people got in and were skylarking, but they meant no harm. I quickly cleared them out.'

'If they got in someone must have let them in. There are not so many keys. Who admitted them?'

'I did not ask.'

'Didn't ask, Mr Dean! And why didn't you ask? Is it nothing that people should break in here and skylark, as you call it? Did Smart let them in?'

'Smart is the most discreet of caretakers, Mr Snelgrove.'

'Who, then? Was it Cobbler?'

'I assure you, Mr Snelgrove, I have the matter in hand and will take steps to prevent it happening again.'

'Then it was Cobbler. I have said many times, Mr Dean, that we ought to get rid of that man.'

'Mr Cobbler has his faults, but he is an excellent musician. It would be easier to get rid of him than it would be to replace him.'

'I know little about music, Mr Dean, and frankly I care little. But Cobbler's character is such that it will one day bring disgrace upon this church, and if you insist upon defending him you may be seriously implicated.'

'That is not a risk which worries me, Mr Snelgrove. And as Mr Cobbler comes directly under my authority I think that the matter of disciplining him may safely be left to me,

And I must remind you, by the way, that it is you, and not
I, who associate him with the trifling disturbance here last
night.'

'And you have not denied that he was responsible. I must
remind you, Mr Dean, that as a lawyer I am not unaccustomed to evasiveness.'

'That is very frankly stated, Mr Snelgrove,' said the Dean,
and the two men parted, each feeling that he had been
called evasive by the other, and resenting it.

ALTHOUGH IT seemed to Mr Snelgrove that he had made no
impression upon the Dean and had been rebuffed by him
with something approaching impertinence, he had in fact
worried the Dean considerably. In a life spent in church
work, the Dean had never become accustomed to the vigi-
lance of parishioners in observing his every movement, or
to the rapidity with which rumour and surmise circulated
among them. If their zeal for their salvation, he thought,
began to equal their zeal for minding his business, the New
Jerusalem would quickly be at hand. He wanted to pass
off the affair of the students in the Cathedral as quietly as
possible; he hated rebuking people, partly from timidity
and partly from genuine kindness, and he valued the Cathedral organist highly. Working with Cobbler he had been
able to raise the aesthetic standard of the Cathedral services
to a level in which he took pride; he was continually astonished by the slight effect which this work of his appeared
to have upon his congregation. Indeed, the better Cobbler's
music was, the more the organist's personality seemed to
grate upon a number of influential Cathedral parishioners.
As the Dean looked at Cobbler when the latter appeared
in his study at half-past ten on All Saints' Day, he wondered
if these disapproving parishioners were not, perhaps, in the
right.

The organist had assumed what was, for him, ceremonial
garb for this solemn occasion. That is to say, he wore an
ill-fitting and rather dirty blue serge suit, the trousers of
which were so short that no one could miss seeing that

he wore no socks, and that of the laces in his scuffed black shoes, one was black and one was brown. His shirt was clean but ragged, and his tie had ridden toward his left ear. His hair, which was black, thick and very curly, stood out from his head like a Hottentot's; he had cut himself several times while shaving, and had staunched the blood with tufts of cotton wool. But it was not the man's poverty or untidiness which made him a disturbing object; it was the smiling concentration of his lean, swarthy face, and the nervous rolling of his large, black, bird-like eyes. He looked like a gypsy. His appearance was of the sort which causes housewives to lock up their spoons and their daughters.

'This is a serious matter, Mr Cobbler,' said the Dean, who found it hard to begin.

'Serious, indeed,' said Cobbler agreeably.

'I had hoped that your escapade of last night would not become widely known, but already the Press has been plaguing me with questions about what has been happening in the Cathedral.'

'Tck, tck.' Cobbler clucked his tongue sympathetically.

'The Press,' said the Dean, finding himself suddenly incensed against *The Bellman,* 'is a powerful and often a mischievous agency.'

'Dreadful,' said Cobbler, with feeling.

'I cannot guarantee that the story of your escapade may not become known,' said the Dean. And indeed he could not tell whether Miss Pottinger or Mr Snelgrove might not babble something which a reporter might pick up. 'You realize what a juicy morsel it would make?'

Cobbler closed his eyes, giving an unconvincing imitation of a man whose thoughts lie too deep for utterance. The Dean knew that he was not achieving the effect he sought. He decided to try another line.

'Mr Cobbler, have I not always tried to be fair with you in all matters relating to your duties at the Cathedral?'

'Mr Dean, your sympathetic co-operation makes my work a pleasure, as the gynaecologist said to the lady contortionist,' said Cobbler, earnestly. The Dean blinked, but decided to ignore the similitude.

'Then why are you not fair to me?' he asked. 'You must know that it is not always easy for me to defend you against people in the Cathedral who disapprove of you. Why do you provoke trouble in this wanton fashion?'

'The move into the Cathedral was unpremeditated,' said Cobbler. 'I never expected that there would be any trouble.'

'Rowdy singing! And dancing! And you say you did not expect any trouble!'

'It happened very simply. I had been talking to a group of students about music. Walking home, I had another idea, and as I happened to have my key with me, we popped into the Cathedral for a brief illustration.'

'You were singing what sounded to me like a bawdy song.'

'The words are misleading. The tune is a roundelay, and true roundelays are not easy to find. Poets use the word, but you know what loose thinkers poets are. The words are insignificant.'

'Those young people were dancing. And three of them were girls. Young, attractive girls,' added the Dean, severely, for as every moralist knows, youth and charm in a woman makes any deviation from ordinary conduct doubly reprehensible.

'Stirring about rhythmically, perhaps. You know how musical people are.'

'Dancing. Unquestionably they were dancing. I saw a lot of leg.'

Cobbler said nothing, but his eyes rolled in a way the Dean did not like.

'If it was all so innocent, why did they hide when I came upon them?'

'Frightened, I suppose. After all, it was Hallowe'en.'

'What is that, Mr Cobbler?'

'I only meant that you are an awe-inspiring figure in your cloak, Mr Dean.'

'You had been drinking, Mr Cobbler.'

'Not really. I mean, I've usually been drinking. But only

a sip here and a sup there. Nothing, really. I might have
had a beer, early in the evening.'

'Mr Cobbler, let us be plain. You had been drinking,
and you brought a rowdy group into the Cathedral. You
played secular music, very loudly, and you sang a song of
obscene implication. Because of the excellence of your
work in general, I might overlook such conduct once, but
how am I to defend you against parishioners who feel
themselves affronted by your conduct?'

'You mean Auntie Puss?'

'You should not speak so disrespectfully of Miss Pottinger.'

'No disrespect whatever, Mr Dean. All her dearest friends
call her that.'

'You are not one of her dearest friends.'

'Through no fault of mine, I assure you.'

'You annoy her, and others.'

'In what way, Mr Dean? Apart from last night, I mean.'

'It's something about you. You don't look like a Cathedral
organist.'

'That's lucky for me. Funny chaps, a lot of them. Seem
to have no faces. But what can I do about it?'

'You might dress more neatly. You look too Bohemian
for your position.'

'Oh, not that, surely. Bohemian is a word we use of the
bad habits of our friends. I'm sure Auntie Puss doesn't say
I look Bohemian.'

'If you wish to know, she says you look like a gypsy
golliwog.'

Cobbler opened his mouth very wide, and laughed a
loud, long laugh, which made several ornaments on the
mantelpiece ring sympathetically. 'I wouldn't have thought
the old faggot could think up anything so lively,' he said
when he had done.

'You must not call Miss Pottinger an old faggot.'

'Why not, if she can call me a gypsy golliwog?'

The Dean was greatly troubled now. 'You will not be
serious,' he said.

62

'Oh come, Mr Dean. That's what Auntie Puss says about *you*. We mustn't get our characters mixed.'

'I mean that you will not look at your situation in a proper way.'

'I know. That's what one of my teachers used to say. "Er ist nicht ernst," he would mumble, because I wouldn't get all sweaty about Brahms.'

'You must be serious. You have a wife and children to support. That is serious, I suppose?'

'Not really.'

'What is serious then?'

'Music, I suppose, in a hilarious sort of way,' said Cobbler, ruffling his hair and grinning.

'The Cathedral is not serious?'

'Perhaps the Cathedral is too serious,' said Cobbler. 'It is the House of God, isn't it? How do we know that God likes His house to be damned dull? Nobody seems to think that God might like a good time, now and then.'

'We are achieving nothing by this conversation,' said the Dean wearily. He felt the old weakness coming over him. He agreed with half of what Cobbler said, and in order to keep from being completely won over he was driven into a puritanical position which he did not enjoy, and in which he had little belief. Before they parted, he had won something resembling an apology from the organist, and a promise that the outrage of the previous night would never be repeated. When they parted, Cobbler's step was light, and the Dean was sitting hunched up in his chair, greatly troubled. Anyone coming upon them suddenly would not have known that the Dean had been rebuking and disciplining his organist; it looked as though the reverse had been the case.

PROFESSOR VAMBRANCE was not a man to utter an empty threat. When he left the office of *The Bellman* after his unsatisfactory talk with Mr Ridley and Mr Marryat, he went at once to the chambers of his lawyers, Snelgrove, Martin and Fitzalan.

Chambers is the only possible word to describe the place in which this old-established firm discharged their affairs. Offices they were not, for an office suggests a place touched by modern order and efficiency. Nor were they simply rooms, for they had lofty architectural pretensions, and enclosed a dim light and a nineteenth century frowst which distinguished them from common apartments. They partook largely of that special architectural picturesqueness which is only to be found in Canada, and which is more easily found in Salterton than in newer Canadian cities. Now the peculiar quality of this picturesqueness does not lie in a superficial resemblance to the old world; it is, rather, a compound of colonialism, romanticism and sturdy defiance of taste; it is a fascinating and distinguished ugliness which is best observed in the light of Canadian November and December afternoons. This picturesqueness is not widely admired, and examples of it are continually being destroyed, without one voice being raised in their defence. But where they exist, and are appreciated, they suggest a quality which is rather that of Northern Europe—of Scandinavia and pre-revolutionary Russia—than of England or the U.S.A. It is in such houses as these that the characters in the plays of Ibsen had their being; it was in this light, and against these backgrounds of stained wood and etched glass that the people of Tchekov talked away their lives. And, if the Canadian building be old enough, the perceptive eye may see faint ghosts from Pushkin and Lermontov moving through the halls. This is the architecture of a Northern people, upon which the comfort of England and the luxury of the United States have fallen short of their full effect.

To reach the offices of Snelgrove, Martin and Fitzalan the Professor had to climb a long flight of stairs, which had a marked list to the right, and an elaborate balustrade which seemed to have no purpose but to keep the climber from pitching into the wall which rose directly beside it. The central room of the law chambers was lofty, and suggested a Victorian railway station and a vestry, without precisely resembling either. In it, at a number of tables and desks, sat several stenographers working at typewriters, and as these instruments tapped, the milky opaque glass which composed the partitions which shut off the private rooms of the partners rang and jingled protestingly. Mr Fitzalan was not engaged, and the Professor was shown at once to his private room.

This was a small apartment, much too tall for its floor area, and consequently rather like a well. Its single window looked out on the street, but as the exposure was a north-easterly one it was dark in November. The partition which separated it from the main office was composed of Gothic groining in wood, and the varnish on this wood had, through the years, acquired the rough and scaly surface of an old lizard. In the arches of the partition was a frosted glass, in which an elaborate floral scrollwork had been cut. In such a setting, Ronnie Fitzalan looked oddly frivolous and out of place. He was in his early forties, and on close inspection he looked it, but a first glance did not take in his bald spot, the mottled red of his cheeks, and his dull and drooping eye; it was the jaunty twist of his moustache and the elegance of his tie which held the gaze. He was a cousin of Vambrace's wife, and he greeted the Professor with cordiality.

Vambrace told his story, displayed the offending clipping from *The Bellman,* and demanded to know how quickly he could bring an action for libel. But Fitzalan gave him little comfort.

'You'd better forget all about it, Wally,' said he. 'Libel's the very devil even when you've got a good case, and you've got no case at all. Who put the thing in the paper? You don't know. You want to sue *The Bellman*. Right? Well, they'll fight just as hard as you will. You'll get all kinds of publicity you don't want. That'll do you no good and *The Bellman* no harm. Suppose you win; what've you got? Suppose you lose—and you could lose, you know, just as easy as dammit—you've got a big bill for costs and you've been made to look a fool. You'd better take *The Bellman's* offer of an apology.'

'But they will not apologize,' said Vambrace.

'Not the way you want them to,' said Fitzalan. 'How can you expect anybody to eat dirt like that? But they've made you an offer, and it's the best one for you. It'll save face for you, and save face for them, and it won't attract a hell of a lot of attention, which is what you seem to want. Damn it all, Wally, do you want to make little Pearlie look like a fool? Do you want to spoil her chances of ever nabbing a husband, poor kid? If you do, just go ahead and shout her name around the court for a few days, or get it on the front page of *The Bellman*, suggesting that some poor chap has had his head knocked off for pretending he was engaged to her.'

'You are far away from the facts,' said Vambrace.

'I know that, Wally, but not half as far as the general public will be after you've had your fun. They'll get all the details jumbled up, and rumours will be everywhere that Pearl threw down some chap in a nasty way, or that you are such a jealous father that nobody dares come near your girl. You've got to give some thought to Pearlie, Wally. And this fellow Bridgetower; you've got to give him some consideration.'

'Why?' said the Professor.

'Why? Well, for decency's sake, that's why. He's at the University, isn't he? So are you. Do you want to kick a colleague around? Maybe you do, but it wouldn't look well.'

'Decency has never troubled the Bridgetower family in their relations with me,' said Vambrace.

'Oh, I know all about that old quarrel with this fellow's father. But it was never as bad as you pretended.'

'I think I am the best judge of that. And this young man has offered me insults which I cannot brook.'

'Listen, Wally, stop talking like a novel by Sir Walter Scott. You should have some thought for Liz and Pearlie.'

'I have. That is why I intend to see this thing through to a finish. It shall not be said that I allowed any reflection to be cast upon them.'

'Wally, you're crackers. Libel is the slipperiest charge you can take into court. Most libel cases are not worth a damn to anybody but the lawyers. And before you've finished with this one, some smart cross-examiner will make you look like a monkey, and then you'll be worse off than ever.'

Although he despised his cousin-in-law's vocabulary, and detested being called Wally, and hearing his wife and daughter called Liz and Pearlie, the Professor respected Fitzalan's ability as a lawyer, and in spite of his protests he was beginning to think that he might forgo the excitements of a law case, and accept *The Bellman's* limited apology. But it was at this moment that the senior partner of the firm, Mr Matthew Snelgrove, put his head in at the door.

'I'm very sorry,' said he, 'I didn't realize there was anyone with you, Fitzalan. I was looking for a book.' He made as though to withdraw, but did not do so, for the fact was that he had learned from the office girls that Professor Vambrace was with his junior partner, and after his chat with the Dean that morning, he thought that he could guess why. So after some symbolic shuffling, intended to signify polite withdrawal, he said to the Professor, 'I hope that it is nothing unpleasant that brings you to us, Professor Vambrace.'

'Something most unpleasant,' said the Professor, falling into the trap.

'Really?' said Snelgrove, feigning surprise and concern. 'If I had suspected that anything was really wrong I would not have inquired. Please overlook my poor attempt at jocularity. Of course any advice that we can give you is at your disposal.'

'My cousin has been giving me what I presume is good advice; he urges me not to go to law.'

'A libel action, Mr Snelgrove,' said Fitzalan. 'I've been

telling Wally how tricky they can be. Never like to advise anyone to start a libel case—unless it's something really rough, and when you have a chance of winning.'

'Now what do you think of that?' said Mr Snelgrove, smiling at the Professor with an urbanity which Dean Knapp might have envied. 'Imagine a lawyer advising a client not to go to law! Still, Fitzalan has a very level head about these things. Libel is very strange; very strange indeed. But if you think two heads are better than one, I'd be happy to hear the facts—at no extra charge, of course.' And again he laughed in a manner which was supposed to convey his knowledge that Fitzalan would not charge a relative for advice, and that he concurred in such generosity. And in another minute Mr Snelgrove was sitting down, the door was closed and the Professor was rehearsing his grievance against *The Bellman* once more, just as Mr Snelgrove intended.

MATTHEW SNELGROVE presented, in himself, one of those interesting and not infrequent cases in which Nature imitates Art. In the nineteenth century it appears that many lawyers were dry and fusty men, of formal manner and formal dress, who carried much of the deportment of the courtroom into private life. Novelists and playwrights, observing this fact, put many such lawyers into their books and upon the stage. Actors deficient in observation and resource adopted this stock character of the Lawyer, and he was to be seen in hundreds of plays. And Matthew Snelgrove, whose professional and personal character was being formed about the turn of the century, seized upon this lawyer-like shell eagerly, and made it his own. Through the years he perfected his impersonation until, as he confronted Professor Vambrace, he was not only a lawyer in reality, but also a lawyer in a score of stagey mannerisms; a lawyer who joined the tips of his fingers while listening to a client; a lawyer who closed his eyes and smacked his lips disconcertingly while others talked; a lawyer who tugged and polished at his long nose with a very large handkerchief; a lawyer who coughed dryly before speaking; a lawyer who used his eyeglasses not so much as aids to vision as for peeping over, snatching from the nose, rubbing on the lapel, and wagging in his listener's face. He was a master of legal grimace—the smile of disbelief, the smile of I-pity-your-ignorance, the smile of that-may-safely-be-left-in-my-hands, as well as a number of effective frowns, signifying disapproval, impatience and disgust. Like many another professional man, Mr Snelgrove had become the prisoner of a professional manner, and as his legal skill was by no means extraordinary it was often impossible to tell whether he was really a lawyer or an indifferent character actor playing the part of a lawyer. Whatever the truth of the matter, his life-long performance had brought him great respect and no small measure of wealth.

For the practice of the law he had no particular intellectual endowment except an enthusiasm for the *status quo* and a regret that most of the democratic legislation of the last century could not be removed from the statute books. If Dean Knapp's ideal was the urbane cleric of the nineteenth century, Mr Snelgrove's was the lawyer-squire of the eighteenth; he was a snob, ready to play the dignified toady to anyone whom he considered his superior, and heavily patronizing to those beneath him; it was with people who might be considered his equals that he was uneasy and contentious. But as no client can be considered the full equal of his lawyer during a professional consultation he was quite at ease with Professor Vambrace.

As he listened to Vambrace's story he realized that this was a case peculiarly fitted to his own talents and temperament. Fitzalan could not be expected to understand it. The law firm of Snelgrove, Martin and Fitzalan was composed on a familiar principle; Mr Martin was particularly adept at corporation law and did all the firm's business in that line; Fitzalan was a Catholic and a Liberal in politics, and brought a good deal of business into the office from those quarters; Mr Snelgrove was a Conservative who liked to be called a Tory, and he attracted Tory business

69

in wills and estates. But he also considered himself the firm's expert on what he called 'the niceties' — meaning matters of offended honour, as opposed to vulgar rape and breach of promise. Obviously the matter of the false engagement notice was a 'nicety', and he would pronounce upon it himself. When the Professor had finished, Mr Snelgrove fitted the tips of his fingers together, smacked his lips, raised his eyebrows and peeped over his pince-nez, and feeling that this was enough of what actors call 'business' for the moment, gave utterance.

'I see what Fitzalan means, of course. It would not be easy to determine whether the publication of this distasteful notice constitutes libel. Libel, as you are probably not aware, is that which brings a man into hatred, contempt or ridicule, or which lowers a man in the estimation of his fellows; where there is a defamatory imputation which can be plainly shown to the court, it is not necessary to prove special damage—loss of money, or some actual loss of that sort. If this is a case at all, it is a border-line case. Judges as a rule do not like border-line cases, and if you were to go to court on this matter you might be badly disappointed.'

'Just what I mean,' said Mr Fitzalan, who had not been with Mr Snelgrove long enough to know when to keep his mouth shut. When Mr Snelgrove was rolling the sweet morsels of the law under his tongue, he did not care to be interrupted, and he put on the face of one who thinks he detects an escape of sewer gas, but is not quite sure. But Fitzalan went on: 'You see, Wally, you've got to decide who would be the plaintiff in a case you brought. How old is Pearlie?'

'My daughter Pearl is twenty-two,' said the Professor.

'Well, you see, she's not a minor. Is she to be the plaintiff? Who has suffered the libel, you or her? Does she want to bring a case?'

'I have naturally not discussed such a painful and distasteful matter with her.'

'Well, you'd better do it before you go any farther. If Pearlie doesn't put a good face on it in court, and act like a girl who is wronged the judge will think you've forced her into the action, and the defence lawyers will get it out of her, and you'll look like a tyrant and a fool as well. You'd better watch your step, Wally.'

'My wife and daughter and I have all suffered more than you can suppose, Ronald, from this iniquitous thing,' said the Professor. 'It is not inconceivable that we might appear as joint plaintiffs.'

'Oh, now, hold on, Wally,' said Fitzalan. 'You know what a mess Liz would make of it in the box; anybody could make her swear that black was white. You're making a mountain out of a molehill. Anyhow, what have you to gain by an action?'

'I have this to gain: I should make those idiots on *The Bellman* feel something of the pain that I have felt. I should make them smart.'

'Oh, Wally, never go to law for simple vengeance; that's not what law is for. Redress, yes; vengeance, no. You talk as if *The Bellman* did it to spite you. Of course it was damn silly of them to take an ad with a date like November 31st in it, but wrong dates are common enough. You'd be surprised how many law cases hang on a wrong date. But they were just as much the victims of this practical joker as you.'

'Precisely,' said Mr Snelgrove, snatching the conversation to himself. 'Now my advice, Professor Vambrace, is this: to threaten an action for libel is not necessarily to go to court and fight it. You think *The Bellman* has been negligent, and I agree with you. A sharp lesson will do them no harm. I have no special affection for the Press; indeed, in a long career in the courts, I have despaired of teaching the Press manners. Rather than face an action, *The Bellman* would probably consider some reparation out of court. But it would not be good strategy to let them think that we would do so. If you care to leave the matter in our hands, I should like to think it over, and advise you.'

Thus Professor Vambrace experienced that sensation of bereavement which so often comes to a man who seeks professional assistance with a grievance, and shortly finds that his grievance is no longer his own personal property, and that much of the flavour has gone out of it.

WHEN THE Professor had left the office, Mr Snelgrove sat silent, his finger-tips together, peering over his spectacles, until Fitzalan spoke.

'Do you want to see the people at *The Bellman* or shall I?' said he.

'Perhaps I had better attend to it,' said Mr Snelgrove. 'You are a relative of Professor Vambrace, are you not?'

'I'm his wife's cousin. I thought you knew that.'

'I wasn't sure just where the kinship lay. I think there might be some indelicacy about your appearing too openly in such a matter. I'll be glad to deal with it.'

'As a mater of fact, Mr Snelgrove, I'm not at all sure that anything should be done. I told Wally to forget about it, or take *The Bellman's* apology.'

'I don't agree with you. The Vambrace family has undoubtedly sustained some injury of reputation. They have a right to expect some reparation.'

'I always think it's better to swallow a little hurt to a family reputation than to get tangled in a lawsuit, or a law wrangle in private. It always comes out, and sounds worse. Wally's cracked on his family reputation. Doesn't amount to a damn. Who cares, anyhow?'

'Isn't Vambrace related to a noble family in Ireland?'

'Second cousin to the Marquis of Mourne and Derry. He brings it up fairly often, in order to say that such things mean nothing to him.'

'Aha; and isn't his wife's family, and yours, rather a distinguished one, among the Irish families in this part of Canada?'

'Well, we didn't emigrate during either of the Potato Famines. I suppose that's something. Liz's father, old Wolfe Tone Fitzalan, drank a bottle of whisky a day for thirty years and was never drunk. That's distinction, of course.'

'You make light of it, but these things have their significance. Fine old families should not suffer affront in silence.'

'Don't you worry that Wally will be silent. He'll belly-ache about this till the day he dies. I just hope he doesn't scare all the boys away from Pearlie because of it. Her chances aren't first rate, anyhow, working in Waverley Library; there's a graveyard of matrimonial hopes, let me tell you!'

'I'll undertake it, and let you know what happens.'

'If you insist, sir, there's nothing I can say. But I'm against it. You're fighting *The Bellman,* but they're as much a victim of this joke as Wally and his family, and they may dig in their heels and refuse to pay up.'

'Ah, yes, the anonymous practical joker should come in for his share of the punishment, of course, or the matter cannot be considered closed.'

'Exactly. And how do you think you'll find him?'

'As a matter of fact,' said Mr Snelgrove, pausing at the door before making a well-timed exit, 'I have a shrewd idea that I know who he is.'

And with this remark he went, leaving his junior impressed against his will.

WHO READS a newspaper? In a very large city, where news-papers are many, the question is of real concern to pub-lishers, to editors, to circulation managers. But in such a city as Salterton, though it is no mean city, there is little question as to who reads *The Bellman;* it is no great exag-geration to say that everybody reads it. But with what a range of individual differences they read it!

Even in our time, when there is supposed to be so much rush and bustle, there are people who read a newspaper solemnly through, taking all evening to do so, missing nothing; international news, district correspondence, local affairs, editorials, special articles and advertisements even down to the humblest adjuration to 'End Pile Torture Quickly', all are grist to their mill. What it means to them is never easy to discover; they are usually aged and uncommunicative people, and they rarely make themselves known to the staff of the paper which affords them so much entertainment, unless it is to confess to a reporter on a ninetieth birthday that they are still able to read *The Bellman* without glasses. How different are they from those others, usually women, who confess under questioning that they have 'skimmed through' the paper, but who appear to have missed the chief news of the day. It was to this class of skimmers, perhaps, that the lady belonged who was discovered in London in 1944, and who admitted that she had never heard of Hitler. The vagaries of female readers, however, are beyond all reason; the simplest group for study is that which reads the paper from back to front, dropping its central portions to the floor early in the proceedings, and reassembling the whole on a principle which makes it intolerable to those who attempt to read it later.

Inevitably the literacy and comprehension of a newspaper's readers ranges over the widest scope. *The Bellman* had readers who read the column headed 'City and Vicinity' every night of their lives, and never failed to speak of it as 'City and Vinicity'. At the opposite pole to these were some members of the Waverley faculty who affected a fine superiority to the paper, spoke of it as 'the local rag' and were alternately amused by it or angry with it; indeed, they were almost ashamed to be seen ordering half a dozen extra copies when some references to themselves or their work appeared in it. But there were others at Waverley who thought differently, and who knew something of the part which the old paper had played in the history of its country. Of course there were readers who asserted that *The Bellman* was not nearly so good as it had been when they were younger; they found that this stricture applied to much else in life as well.

Gloster Ridley's editorials were read by people who were interested to know what *The Bellman* thought about current affairs, as well as by people who wanted to know what the paper thought in order that they might, as a matter of principle, disagree with it. Of these readers, only a very few bore in mind that each editorial was simply an expression of opinion by one man, who had made up his mind after some consultation with perhaps two or three other men; the majority thought of newspaper editorials as the opinions of a group of remote beings, like the Cabinet, or the justices of the Supreme Court, but with this difference: it was a mark of grace to dissent from them, if only in some slight particular. Thus it was that many people who met Ridley for the first time said, 'I always read your editorials; of course I don't agree with all of them'—as though this revealed a special independence of spirit in them, and put the editor in his place. Many people feel it necessary to be especially belligerent when talking to an editor, to show that they are not afraid of him; for however foolish an editor may be in private life, when he puts on his editorial 'We' he is like a judge who has put on his wig, and has added a cubit to his stature. And the readers who least resembled these editor-quellers were those who read the paper chiefly for its comic strips. Not that these were frivolous; the solemn devotion with which they followed the snail-like progress of those serial adventures was as great as that of the devout who read the syndicated Bible comment which was published every Saturday.

Devout also, but rarely edified, were the readers of the sports pages. It is a tested axiom of newspaper work that the sporting fraternity are never content. Although the proportion of most newspapers which is devoted to sport is far greater than the proportion of the population which is seriously interested in sport, sports lovers usually feel that a niggardly allowance of space has been given to their hobby. They tend to be zealots, and they believe their kind to be more numerous than is really the case; and because they are frequently superstitious, and possess a strong mythopoeic faculty, they attribute to newspaper sports reporters grudges and malign intentions toward their favourites of which those hard-working men are innocent. It sometimes seems to harassed sports editors that sports enthusiasts read the papers only to find food for their vast disgruntlement.

The Bellman was closely perused by countless specialists,

and by none more keenly than the specialists in morality; the reports from the police court were their special meat, and they acquired and retained a wide knowledge of who had been before the magistrate, and upon what charge; reckless driving, drunkenness, non-support of wives, all the common offences were docketed in their minds, enlivened now and again by a lively fist-fight or tasty bit of indecent exposure. Everybody looks at a police court report now and then, but the specialists never missed one; wherever a report might be printed, separated by some mechanical necessity from others of its kind, they would sniff it out, make it part of their mental fabric, never forget it, and recall it when the offender died, or when his daughter married, or when some distinction or piece of good fortune brought him once again into the news. They were good people, these moralists, who rarely offended against the law themselves; but if by chance one of their kind were found, say, drunk and in charge of a car, they knew at once all the details—that his wife was pregnant, or his aged mother trembling upon the threshold of death (for these are the two commonest afflictions of wrongdoers, as every newspaperman knows) and bemoaned his fall with an intensity which might almost have been mistaken for relish.

To set down all the special interests to which a paper like *The Bellman* ministers every night would be a gigantic task and weary reading. For who, in his heart, really wants to give much of his time to another man's concerns? Most people will sympathize with the schoolchildren who search the columns of the paper for items about 'Current Events' to take to school to appease a teacher who approaches history by that path. But who except a physician searches the columns of accident news, to see what other physicians may be mentioned; and who but a lawyer gives special attention to the lawyers who are named in the reports of court cases? Professional etiquette forbids the gentlemen of the short and the long robes to advertise their skill, but they do not like to be overlooked in the news columns; as Mr. Marryat sometimes bitterly remarked, they were fond enough of advertising when they did not have to pay for it.

Even the clergy are not above this human weakness; they may personally choose to do good by stealth, but their congregations like themselves and their pastors to be frequently and favourably mentioned. The page of social news was read with eagerness by those who hoped to be included, or who admired or envied those who were named, for even in democratic Canada the fire of social ambition burns with a hard, gem-like flame in many bosoms. There were thousands among *The Bellman's* readers who apparently never wearied of reading that 'lovely flower arrangements and tapers in dainty silver holders graced the table'; they always wanted to know who had 'poured', at afternoon teas, for to 'pour' is for many ladies the pinnacle of social achievement. And the wedding photographs were keenly scanned by all the photographers, of course, to see whose work had been printed and what could be found wrong with it.

Specialists of all sorts find the daily newspaper a mine of treasures for their delight. Sometimes this delight lies in indignation, and here both labour and management can be accommodated by a single item of news, for both are convinced that newspapers never use them with complete fairness. Indignation, also, was sought by the old lady who nightly scanned *The Bellman* for pictures of girls in bathing-suits; upon finding such a picture, she never failed to write to Gloster Ridley, threatening to cancel her subscription if the offence were repeated. The advent of the two-piece suit, with its inevitable concomitant of a few exposed navels, was an unlooked-for source of delicious indignation to her. There were the people who read everything about royalty, and pasted it in a scrap-book, and the people who did the same with all news about movie stars. There were the people who always worked the simple crossword puzzle, or who read the article on bridge. There were the people who read the advice to the lovelorn, sometimes for laughter but usually in deep earnest. There were the people who read the nightly article of the medical columnist, seeking always a new name to apply to the sense of insufficiency, of dissatisfaction, of heart-hunger which gnawed at them. And of course everyone who had written a letter to the editor sought early for it until it was printed, or until hope died and resentment came to fill its place.

As well as these specialists there were of course the professional newspapermen who read the paper closely for their own reasons. Mr Rumball read all that he himself had written to see whether the city editor (who was, of course, jealous) had cut that splendid paragraph of 'colour' in his report of a street accident. Archie Blaine looked to see whether, as he suspected, he had not written considerably more news reporting than anyone else; he was not jealous, but he sometimes wondered whether the fellows who had taken journalist courses at universities would ever write as much, as fast, as well, as he did. Mr Swithin Shillito invariably read all that he had written aloud to Mrs Shillito, and then pondered aloud on possible reasons why some of his witty *aperçus* ('Quite good enough for *Punch,* though I say it myself, my dear') had not been printed. Jealousy, he feared; yes, it was a pity that poor Ridley could not rise above jealousy. Nevertheless, his brilliant couple of paragraphs about the decline in the quality of shoelaces had been used, and certainly Mr Eldon Bumford would comment on it when next they met.

Matthew Snelgrove read his evening copy of *The Bellman* with a special gloomy relish, for it never failed to yield several instances in which rampant democracy had been guilty of some foolishness which could never, he was convinced, have happened under the old squirearchy—particularly if a sufficient number of squires happened also to be lawyers. Life, as he conceived of it, was a long decline from a glorious past, and if a reader approaches a newspaper in that spirit, he can find much to confirm him in his belief, particularly if he has never examined any short period of the past in day-to-day detail. Bleak also in her approach to *The Bellman* was Mrs Solomon Bridgetower, the mother of that Solomon Bridgetower whose name had been unwarrantably linked with that of Pearl Vambrace. She was a lady whose life had been devoted in great part to the study of world politics; when she was a young and keen-witted undergraduate of Waverley she had explored and dreaded the Yellow Peril with an intensity which was beyond her years, and won the admiration of her professors. As a young wife during the First World War she had been a great expert on German atrocities; she had successively foreseen and dreaded the Jazz Age, the Depression, the Rise of Fascism and the Second World War, but she had always had a soft spot for her first dread, the Yellow Peril, and insisted on regarding the rise of Russia to world power as an aspect of it. Higher education and a naturally acute mind had enabled her to dread all these things much more comprehensively and learnedly than most ladies of her acquaintance, and had won her a local reputation as a woman of capacious intellect. She read her *Bellman* with a special pair of scissors at her side, so that she might cut out and keep any particularly significant and doom-filled piece of news.

The only other reader of the Salterton paper who used scissors was the secretary to the archbishop of the Roman Catholic diocese which had its cathedral there. Unknown to each other as they were, Monsignor Caffrey and Mrs Bridgetower had both read and been impressed by a book written in the 'twenties by a French abbé, who recommended the clipping of newspapers as a method of clarifying and understanding what appeared in them. But while he did not use scissors, Gloster Ridley made it his nightly duty to read *The Bellman,* using a blue pencil to mark every error of spelling, punctuation, proof-reading and grammar; from time to time he confronted his staff with these marked papers, as a means of urging them toward the perfection which danced before him, an ever-fleeting goal.

There was one other paper-marker in Salterton, and that was Mrs Edith Little, Ridley's housekeeper, and it was this habit of hers which made him think of her as Constant Reader.

'COME ON there, Ede, come on! Let some of the rest of us have a look at the paper!' It was Mrs Little's brother-in-

law, George Morphew, who spoke, and he playfully
punched the November 1st issue of *The Bellman* from
behind, as he did so, startling her from her absorption.

'You can have it in a few minutes,' she said, with dignity.
'Just be patient.'

'Patient, hell! I got to check up on my investments.'
George laughed loudly.

'Oh, your investments! You're more of a baby than Earl.
And speaking of Earl, just mind your language, George.'

'He's in bed.'

'But not asleep. He can hear everything. And he just
picks up everything he hears. So just let's have a little less
of H and D, please.'

George's reply was to belch, long and pleasurably. His
sister-in-law gave him a sharp glance, and although his
face was solemn, she knew that he was kidding her. George
thought of himself as a great kidder. Pity there was such a
coarse streak in George. Still, that was how it was with most
men; swear or burp or even worse, and think themselves
funny. She went on with her painstaking reading of the
paper; from time to time she wetted her pencil and marked
a typographical error. It was not long until her sister came
in. George caught his wife by the wrist and drew her down
into his lap. He kissed her with relish, while she struggled
and giggled in his arms.

'Cut it out, Georgie,' she cried.

'A fine thing!' said George, feigning dismay. 'A fellow
comes home after five days on the road, and he can't even
get a little smooch!'

'Not in front of Ede,' said his wife.

'Cripes! Can't swear because of Earl; can't give you a
smooching because of Ede! What the heck kind of house is
this anyway?'

'Don't mind me,' said Edith, but she was blushing.

'Lookit, Ede's blushing!' cried George, delighted. 'Come
on, Kitten, let's show her a real burner, and she'll go up in
smoke!' He seized his wife again, and kissed her in what he
believed to be a Hollywood manner.

'George, that's enough!' said Kitten. 'You got to remember that Ede's living a single life, and that kind of thing
isn't fair to her. She's got her feelings, you know.'

'O.K., O.K.,' said George, with assumed docility, and as
his wife sat on his lap rearranging her hair, he whistled
When I Get You Alone Tonight, rolling his eyes in rapture.
This caused Kitten to give him a playful punch in the chest,
to which he responded by slipping his hand under her skirt
and snapping her garter against her thigh. Edith sniffed
and glowered at the paper. These nights when George came
home from 'the road' were always difficult. She wondered
how Kitten could stand for it. Funny how some people
seemed to lose all the refinement they'd been brought up
with, after marriage. These thoughts of hers were well
understood by her sister, who thought that what Ede needed,
maybe, was a little cheering up. Nothing raw, like George
wanted to pull, but some fun.

'Ede's marking up the paper for her fella,' said she, winking at her husband.

'Oh, that's it, eh?' said George. 'Say, how's the big
romance coming along, Ede?'

'I haven't the slightest idea what you're talking about,'
said Mrs Little, blushing again.

'Go on! Sure you have. You and Mr Shakespeare Ridley.
Have you named the day?'

'Things between Mr Ridley and I are just exactly what
they've always been, to wit, strictly formal as between employer and daily homemaker.'

'Strictly formal, eh? Like the time he was sick and asked
you to give him a bed-bath?' said George.

'George Morphew, you made that up out of whole
cloth, and I'd just like you to understand I don't like it!'

'Well, cripes, Ede, keep your shirt on! Cripes, it's nothing
to me if you give him a bath. For all of me you can get into
the tub together,' said George, who delighted in this subtle
baiting of his sister-in-law and was prepared to continue on
these lines for an hour. But Mrs Little's cheeks were very
red, and there were tears in her eyes.

'I'd just like you to know, George, that I'm a part owner in this house and I don't have to put up with that kind of talk,' said she. 'And if there's any more of it, I'll march right out of here with Earl, and you can carry the whole thing, mortgage and all.'

'Now you've made her sore, George,' said Kitten. 'Why do you always have to go so far? Can't you ever kid without getting raw? Lookit, now you've got her bawling.' She went to her sister and set about those shoulder squeezings, proffering of bits of partly-used Kleenex, and murmurings, with which women comfort one another.

'O.K., O.K., you don't have to take that line with me,' said George who, like many great kidders, quickly became aggrieved. 'I know we've got a mortgage just as well as anybody else in this house, and if you don't want Earl to know it too, you better not shout so loud. You don't have to throw the mortgage up in my face, just when I get home from five days on the road.'

'When you get back from the road, all you want to think about is One Thing,' said Mrs Little, with an air of injured virtue.

'Yeah? Well, just because you're not getting any of it yourself you don't have to pick on me,' said her brother-in-law, who now firmly believed himself to be the injured party.

'Georgie! You just take that right back!' It was his wife who spoke. 'Just because Ede's had hard luck and is left to fend for herself and her kiddie you got no right to taunt her because she's living the life of a single girl and it gets her all nervous and stewed up—'

'I'm not stewed up,' shrieked Mrs Little, and hid her face in the sofa cushions, sobbing.

'Now look what you done!' roared George, happy to blame his wife for something.

'Mo-o-ommie!' The child's voice floated down the stairs.

'Oh, God, you've wakened up Earl,' said Mrs Little, hastily mopping her eyes. 'Coming, Lover! Mommie's coming to you right away!' She hurried from the room.

'Well, now you've made a fine mess of it,' said Kitten.

'Aw, hell, Kitten, she's not the only one that's nervous. I've been five days on the road and I'm nervous as a cat. You know how I get.'

'I certainly do,' said Kitten, in what she meant to be a disapproving voice, but there was a strong hint of self-satisfaction in her tone.

'Well, all right; you wouldn't like it if I didn't come home that way, would you? Best compliment a wife can have. You don't have to jump on me, just because I kid Ede a little bit. I tell you how Ede is: you got to kid her to keep yourself from taking a punch at her.'

'Now, Georgie, that's my sister you're talking about.'

'Sure, sure, I know. But she gives me a heartburn the wrong end of my digestive track, like the fella says. We ought to have a place of our own, Kitten.'

'We've been over all that lots of times, Georgie. We can share this big house with Ede a lot cheaper than we can live separate. We share the mortgage, and there's what we get from the boarder, don't forget.'

'I don't like having a boarder.'

'It's all money, and Mr Higgin is no trouble. With you on the road most of every week, it doesn't bother you much. You wouldn't want a room to stand empty, would you?'

'I guess not. But in this house everything's for the boarder, or for Ede, or for that kid.'

'Aw now, honey-bunch, don't be sore. There's one thing in this house that's all for Georgie.'

'Yeah? What?'

'Me,' said Kitten, and gave her husband a long and passionate kiss. She was a pretty little woman, and because she loved and was loved in return, she was rounded and attractive. Edith, though she had a child, looked sharp and unfruitful compared with her childless sister.

George was an unromantic figure, a travelling salesman for a food company, whose hair was thinning in front, and whose slack paunch slid down into the front of his trousers when he stood up. But so far as his nature allowed, he loved

Kitten, and would have fought tigers for her. He kissed her
now, greedily, and slipped his hand expertly into the bosom
of her dress. And thus they remained, for perhaps a minute,
until a key turned in the front door and the boarder came
in.

'I hope I don't intrude,' said he, popping his head around
the corner from the hallway.

'Oh, not a bit. Come in, Mr Higgin,' said Kitten, jump-
ing up and tidying her hair and frock.

'Jeez, Kitten, you don't have to jump like that. I guess
it's legal, after six years married,' said George. 'Take a chair,
Mr Higgin.'

BEVILL HIGGIN was a small, very neat man, so small and
neat that the shininess of his suit and the oldness of his
shoes did not at once attract attention. Although he was not
eccentrically dressed, there was something old-fashioned
in his appearance. His face was of a fresh, salmon pink, and
his eyes were of a light and shiny blue. Although the top of
his head was shiny and bald, the rusty hair which fringed it
was long, and was brushed upward in an attempt to min-
imize his baldness, and this gave him a look of surprise.
He had a long, inquisitive nose, and his little mouth was
usually drawn into a bow, but from time to time it expanded
in a smile which showed very white, very shiny false teeth.
He was a teacher of elocution by profession, and, unlike
many of his kind, he spoke in a pleasant voice with no
particular accent, though an expert in such matters would
have detected him as an Irishman. He perched himself
neatly on a chair, and twinkled his eyes and his teeth at
George and Kitten.

'I shan't stay long,' said he. 'I see that you are—busy,
shall I say?' And he laughed; his laugh was of a kind in-
frequently heard, which can only be suggested by the syl-
lables tee-hee, tee-hee. 'I wanted to ask a favour. I am
acquiring a few pupils now, quite a number, really, and it
is not always convenient for me to teach them in their
homes. Many of them are business young men and women,

who live in lodgings. I hoped that I might beg the use of this room for a couple of nights a week—when you are from home, naturally, Mr Morphew—for two or three hours' teaching?'

'Well, I'd have to give that some thought, Mr Higgin,' said Kitten.

'Naturally, I should wish to pay extra for the extra accommodation. But perhaps we could leave the matter of fixing a sum until I found out just how many hours I would need the room,' said Mr Higgin.

'Well —' Kitten was always open to suggestions which would bring more money into the house. There was that mortgage.

'Perhaps we might make some reciprocal arrangement,' said Mr Higgin. 'I would be very happy to make the extra payment in lessons. You yourself, Mrs Morphew, have a delightful voice; a little training, and who can say what might not come of it? Or the little boy—a charming child, but think how his opportunities in life would be increased if, from infancy, he learned to speak with—shall I say?— an accent which would at once make him *persona grata* among persons of cultivation?'

'Yeah, that'd be great,' said George, the kidder rising triumphant above the frustrated lover in him. He put one hand on his hip, and patted at his back hair with the other, speaking in what he believed to be the accent of a person of cultivation: 'Good mawning, mothaw deah. Did I heah Uncle Georgie come in pie-eyed lawst night? Disgusting, yaws? Haw!' After this flight of fancy he could contain himself no longer, and burst into a guffaw.

'Georgie, that's not funny,' said Kitten. Like many women, she had a superstitious reverence for teachers of all sorts, and she did not like to see Mr Higgin affronted. But Mr Higgin was tee-heeing happily.

'Oh, it's easy to see where the talent lies in this house,' said he. 'You have a real gift for comedy, Mr Morphew. I'd give a great deal to do some work with you, but I know you men of affairs. You'd be too busy.'

'Eh?' said George. 'Well, some of the boys think I'm pretty good. Stunt night at the club, and that kind of thing.'

'Indeed, I know it,' said Mr Higgin. 'I've had a wide experience of club smokers myself. Not for ladies, of course,' he cried, tee-heeing at Kitten, 'but very good, oh, very good. It's a pity so much talent is lost to business, but I don't suppose anything can be done about it. Still, it would be a pleasure to help you.'

'You mean, give me a few lessons?' said George. 'Well, I don't see why not. Maybe I could work up a little new material, eh. For club night?'

'Do you know a song called *The Stub of Me Old Cigar?*' Mr. Higgin's eyes twinkled wickedly. 'Or, *If You Don't Want The Goods, Don't Maul 'Em?*' His eyes fleetingly sought Kitten. 'Both delightful songs. I know *all* the verses.'

'It's a deal,' said George, excitedly, and he would have closed with Mr Higgin then and there, but his sister-in-law came downstairs at that moment, greeted Mr Higgin formally, and sat down again to her paper, pencil in hand.

'What do you think, Ede,' said George. 'Mr Higgin is going to give me a little training in a few little take-offs and sketches. Get a little new material.'

'Your brother-in-law and sister have talent, I feel,' said Mr Higgin. 'One develops an instinct for such things. And you, too, Mrs Little; I feel that you are by no means the least talented of this gifted family. But your flair is for the serious rather than the comic. You and your sister might pose for a study of Comedy and Tragedy. You know the famous portrait of Garrick between Comedy and Tragedy? What a tableau you might make, with you, Mr Morphew, as Garrick, of course.'

'Never heard of Garrick, but I'm strong on garlic,' roared George. He was one of those men to whom onions, in all forms, were exquisitely comic.

'Oh, Mr Morphew, what an impromptu!' cried Mr Higgin, tee-heeing until his face was a deep carrot colour. 'What a radio M.C. you might make! Or television!' Mr Higgin waved a tiny hand, as though indicating boundless

vistas of achievement before George. But George was not
the only one who had fallen under his spell.

'Funny you should compare Kitten and I with Comedy
and Tragedy,' said Edith, 'because that's the way our lives
have always worked out. Hers is a great big joke, all the
time, but I've always seemed to get the dirty end of the
stick.'

'Aw now, Ede, it's not as bad as that,' said Kitten.

'That's how it seems to you,' said Edith, 'but you haven't
gone through what I've gone through.'

'Husband ran out on her,' said George, who had no sense
of artistic form and did not understand that such a revelation as this should have come after much preliminary hinting. 'Left her with the kid.'

'Left her before the baby came,' said Kitten. 'What I
said at the time was, how big of a stinker can a fella get?'

Mr Higgin said nothing, but he looked at Edith very
seriously, his mouth so pursed as to be completely circular.
At last he said, 'Perhaps you were well rid of him.'

'I was,' said Edith, who was enjoying the situation. 'But
if there's one thing means more to me than anything else,
it's duty, and he's got a duty to little Earl, and the dearest
wish of my life is to see that duty done.'

'Yes?' said Mr Higgin, for that seemed to be what was
wanted of him. But once again George clumsily robbed
Edith of her moment.

'Wants to catch up with him,' said he, 'to dig money out
of him for the kid's education. But no luck, so far.'

'Your boy will bless you for it,' said Mr Higgin, turning
his eyes solemnly upon Edith. 'A parent cannot give a
child anything finer than an education to fit it for life. As I
was suggesting a few moments ago to Mrs Morphew, I might
perhaps undertake the little lad's speech-training; a really
well-trained voice, from his earliest years, would put him far
beyond ordinary children, who speak very carelessly in
Canada, I must say. And in such a talented family—'

'No, Ede, don't you do anything that'll make the kid talk
different from other kids,' said George. 'A kid's got to be

regular. Other kids hate a stuck-up kid. If a kid isn't just like other kids it keeps him from getting to be outstanding, and going ahead in the world. Nope, I won't go for any teaching the kid to speak like a sissy.'

'And what's it got to do with you?' said Edith coldly.

'The kid's got no father and I feel a kind of a duty to give the advice a father'd give. You want the kid to grow up regular, don't you?'

'I'm not sure I want him to grow up to travel in canned goods,' said Edith.

'Oh, and what's wrong with travelling in canned goods? Just as good as being a house-painter, I'd say.'

'Earl's father was a sign-painter and letterer,' said Edith haughtily.

'And you have found no trace of him?' said Mr Higgin, who wanted to steer the conversation into calmer waters.

'Not hide nor hair,' said Kitten, and added portentously, 'and from that day to this Ede has lived without men. Bob Little was the first and the last.'

'Oh, not the last, I'm sure,' said Mr Higgin gallantly. 'He will be presumed dead, after a time, and then I am sure that you will have suitors galore. Galore,' he repeated, savouring this fine word.

'A widda with a kid isn't going to draw much of a crowd,' said George, with more gloom than seemed really necessary.

'Oh, I must contradict you,' said Mr Higgin, tee-heeing. 'A widow is a very attractive creature,' and he began to sing softly:

> *Have you heard of the widow Malone?*
> *Ochone!*
> *Who was bred in the town of Athlone?*
> *Alone!*
> *Och, she bothered the hearts*
> *Of the swains in them parts,*
> *So lovely the Widow Malone*
> *Ochone!*
> *So lovely the widow Malone!*

This outburst was so surprising that no one offered to speak immediately after it, and Mr Higgin followed up his advantage.

'Not only a rare melancholy beauty, but also literary taste and intellect, Mrs Little,' and with his hand he indicated the newspaper and the pencil which she was holding.

'Oh, that,' said Edith, blushing for no reason that she could think of. 'Oh, that's just a hobby of mine; every night I go through and mark the mistakes.'

'Ede keeps house for the editor,' said George. 'Fella by the name of Ridley.'

'Mr Gloster Ridley,' said Edith primly. 'I oblige him as a daily homemaker.'

'Washes the dishes after he cooks,' sniggered George. 'Cooks all his own meals. Wears an apron, too, I bet. That's what happens to kids that aren't regular.'

'Mr Gloster Ridley?' said Mr Higgin. 'And you mark errors in the paper for him. Do you find many?'

'Not really for him,' said Edith. 'But I feel I ought to help all I can. I can't say he's very grateful. In fact, I don't mention it very often; I just take my marked paper and leave it where he'll see it. Usually he doesn't look.'

'How interesting. What kind of errors do you find?'

'All kinds. Names reversed under pictures, and misprints, and that kind of thing. Like this—' She pointed to a mark she had made on the social page. 'See here, in this report of the Catholic Women's League tea, it says: "The table was centred with a mass of dwarf nuns." Of course, that ought to read "dwarf mums".'

'Mums? Mothers, do you mean?'

'No. Chrysanthemums. He'll be sore when he sees that. But I won't be the one to point it out. Sometimes he's as good as hinted that he'd as soon I didn't mark the paper.'

'Ah, touchy?'

'Very touchy. Yesterday there was a wrong date in an engagement notice. Said a marriage would take place on November 31st. What do you think of that?'

'I think some poor guy is probably making the mistake of his life,' said George, winking at Kitten, who punched him affectionately.

'I wouldn't mention it to him. He marks a paper himself, and I just happened to see it this morning, before he went to work, and he hadn't caught it. There'll be trouble about that.'

'I should think so,' said Mr Higgin, his eyes wide. 'Was it the engagement of anyone you knew?'

'Not to say I actually know them,' said Edith. 'One was the daughter of a professor at the University and the other was Solly Bridgetower. I guess everybody knows about him; a while ago he was chasing after that Griselda Webster, but you wouldn't catch a rich girl like that marrying a poor wet like him. They said his mother broke it up.'

'Well, wouldn't it be interesting to know what happened about that,' said Mr Higgin, laughing his little laugh. 'If you know this young Bridgetower, you will probably hear all about it.'

'Oh, it isn't as if we actually *know* him,' said Kitten. 'But you know how it is; we've lived in Salterton all our lives, and we get to know about a lot of people we don't actually know to *speak* to, if you understand me.'

'I must speak to my friend Mr Shillito about it,' said Mr Higgin. 'He is very highly placed on *The Bellman,* and he has been most kind to me since I came to town. Indeed, it was he who sent me to see Mr Bridgetower at the University.'

THE CONVERSATION moved to more immediately interesting matters, such as the latent talent of the Morphews and Mrs Little, the striking cleverness of little Earl, the nobility and fortitude of a grass-widow of thirty-two who brought up her fatherless child single-handed, the desirability of daily home-making as a career over factory work (in that it allowed a refined person to keep herself to herself), the vagaries of life on the road, the art of salesmanship and the toll it took of the salesman, and kindred topics. So congenial did Mr

Higgin prove that they sat until twelve o'clock, drinking some beer and eating cheese and crackers. They were greatly surprised to find how late it was, and when Mr Higgin sang as much as one man could of the Midnight Quartet from Flotow's *Martha* (an opera in which, he said, he had once toured in Southern Ireland) the Morphews were lifted to such a romantic pitch that they did not observe that Mr Higgin had taken Edith's hand and was pressing it tenderly to the breast pocket of his shiny blue suit. As Edith undressed in her own room—dark, so that Earl might not wake—she could hear his light tenor voice singing in the boarder's room, and she reflected that however distant Mr Ridley might be, not all men of cultivation were unmoved by her presence.

PART THREE

IN the music room of Waverley University Library, Pearl
Vambrace had abandoned herself to a deplorable form
of self-indulgence. If Mr Kelso, the lecturer on music,
were to find her he would certainly be angry. If Dr Forgie,
the Librarian, were to find her he would be angry too, for
although he had no ear for music he knew an idle assistant
when he saw one. But the chances were good that nobody
would find her, for Mr Kelso had cancelled his Music
Appreciation Hour for that afternoon, and everybody knew
it but Dr. Forgie. So Pearl had seized her chance. It had been
a hateful day, and it would undoubtedly go on being hateful. She sprawled in a large armchair, her head resting on
one arm and her legs dangling over the other, and gave
herself up to illicit, healing pleasure.

The phonograph in the Music Room was of the largest
and most expensive kind; it would play a great many
records without being touched. But it was temperamental,
like so many great artists, and only Mr Kelso and Pearl,
who acted as his helper during music lectures, were permitted to go near it. Under Mr Kelso's extremely critical
eye Pearl had learned to pick up recordings by their edges
only, to wipe them with a chamois, and to place them on
the spindle of the costly, fretful machine. She was permitted to act as Mr Kelso's handmaiden, and as nursemaid
to the phonograph, because she had, in her own undergraduate years, been a particularly apt pupil in Music
Appreciation; she could appreciate anything, and satisfy
Mr Kelso that her appreciation was akin to, though natur-

ally of a lesser intensity than, his own. Play her a Gregorian
chant, and she would appreciate it; play her a Bartok
quartet and she would appreciate that. And what brought
a frosty and unwilling smile to Mr Kelso's lips was that her
appreciation, like his own, was untainted by sentimentalism;
she did not rhapsodize foolishly about music, as so many of
his students did; she really seemed to understand what
music was, and to understand what he said about it in his
singularly unmusical voice. When Pearl, the autumn after
her graduation, was taken on the Library staff, Mr Kelso
had asked that she be allowed to help him in the Music
Room, when he lectured there.

It would never occur to Mr Kelso that Pearl was a hypo-
crite, or that Music Appreciation, as taught by him, was
something which a stone-deaf student could learn and pass
examinations in. But such was the case, and her post as
bottle-washer to Mr Kelso and the machine gave Pearl
occasional chances for indulging what she fully knew to be
a base side of her nature.

Among the very large collection of phonograph records
which the Library maintained were perhaps a hundred
which Mr Kelso called his Horrible Examples. These were
pieces of music which he despised, sung or played by people
whose manner of interpretation he despised. Now and then
Mr Kelso would play one of these, in order to warn his
students against some damnable musical heresy. It had
taken Pearl a long time to recognize and admit to herself
that just as there were times when she had to buy and eat
a dozen doughnuts in one great sensual burst, there were
also times when the Horrible Examples, and nothing else,
were the music she wanted to hear.

As she lay in the chair on the afternoon of November 1st,
a bag in which there were still ten delicious greasy doughnuts was on the floor at her side, and on the turntable of the
phonograph was what she called, to herself, a Vambrace
Mixed Concert. At present, in the concert hall of her mind,
the world-renowed pianist, Pearl Vambrace, was playing
Sinding's *Rustle of Spring*; as the cascades of sound gushed

and burbled from the instrument the audience asked itself
how it was that this frail girl could produce a body of tone
which might have been (and in plain fact *was*) that of two
players with a piano each: and the only reply that the
audience could give itself was that this was the mastery
vouchsafed to an artist who lived wholly for her art. . . .
Spring ceased to rustle, the gramophone gave a discreet,
expensive cough, and at once broke into the rather thin
strains of *I'll Sing Thee Songs of Araby*. Pearl Vambrace,
the contralto marvel of the age, stood by the piano, singing
the sweet ballad with a melancholy beauty which suggested
very strongly the voice of a once-great Welsh tenor. . . . To
cheat thee of a sigh, or charm thee to a tear. . . . With heart-
breaking loveliness, with ineffable, romantic silliness, the
exquisite voice mounted to the last note, and Pearl's eyes
were wet as her hand stole down into the bag for another
doughnut. . . . This lot of records was nearly done. Only
one more to be played. It was Sibelius' *Valse Triste,* which
Mr Kelso was accustomed to call an aberration of genius,
but which Pearl thought of in quite different terms. This
time she appeared upon the stage of her imagination as
Pearl Vambrace, the great ballerina, floating with pathetic
grace through a dance of love and death. It was unbearably
beautiful, and yet, somehow, it made life much more bear-
able. It made it possible, for instance, to think with some
composure about Father.

Sherlock Holmes was accustomed to think of a difficult
case as a three-pipe problem. In Pearl's life, Father was
becoming more and more a dozen-doughnut problem.
Without the greasy, bulky comfort of a dozen doughnuts
distributed at various points through her digestive tract the
Professor's daughter found it hard to think about him at all.
His behaviour last night, for instance; his terrible rage, his
rhetorical ravings after he had finished talking on the telephone with Dean Knapp; it was all that she could do to
bring herself to think of them. He had not been so much
angry as amazed, to begin with, but gradually, over an
hour's time, he had worked himself up to a pitch of shouting

fury. And what a personal fury! Great as his rage was, it was only big enough for himself. She and Mummy might have been the culprits, rather than the sharers in any disgrace or scandal that there was.

Mummy had taken it, as always when there was trouble, incoherently and in tears, and finally in agonized prayer. That Mummy loved Father there was no shadow of doubt, and that Mummy loved God was equally apparent. But she seemed always to be so frightened and guilty before them both. Perhaps if Father had not forbidden Mummy to bring Pearl up a Catholic things would have been easier at home. Pearl knew, of course, that when they had married, Father had promised (but 'as good as promised' was the exact phrase that Mummy used on the rare occasions when she spoke of it to Pearl) to join his wife in her faith, but he had refused to do so (or as Mummy always said, 'had been unable to do so'). He had insisted that Pearl be brought up an agnostic, like himself. Nor was this done by neglect of religion, or silence about it; long before she could understand what he was talking about Father had lectured her on the nature of faith, of which he had a poor opinion. And as Mummy became more and more devout, and gave more and more of her time to meditation and spiritual exercises, Father's unbelief grew rawer and more aggressive. Home was not easy. But Pearl was a loyal daughter and it never occurred to her that home was, in many ways, a hell.

Last night Mummy had spent at least two hours at the *prie-dieu* in her bedroom, weeping softly and praying. Pearl had no such refuge. Father had paced the floor, his eyes glaring, and at one time foam, unmistakable foam, had appeared at the corners of his mouth. He had talked of a plot, on the part of a considerable number of unknown persons, to bring him into disrepute and mockery. He had been darkly conscious of this plot for some time; indeed, it had begun before he had been done out of his rightful dignity as Dean of Arts. That was when the late Professor Bridgetower had been voted into the dean's chair. Bridgetower! A scientist, a geologist if you please, who would not even have been in the Arts faculty if the composition of the Waverley syllabus had not been ridiculously out of date! What if the man was called Professor of Natural Philosophy; in the present day such terminology was as ludicrous as calling a man Professor of Phrenology. They had been out to defeat him and they had done so. But, not content with that shabby triumph, they now sought to disgrace him through his family. Through his only child—a daughter! What would they have contrived, the Professor demanded of the world at large, if he had had a son?

The first part of the Vambrace Mixed Concert had come to an end, and Pearl rose to put a new pile of records on the turntable. But that which was uppermost in the group she had chosen was a violin rendition of *The Londonderry Air,* and she felt suddenly that she could not bear anything Irish, however good it might be. So she put on Tchaikovsky's Symphony Number Six, and in no time, in that vast imaginary concert hall, the great woman conductor, Pearl Vambrace, was letting an enchanted audience hear how unbearably pathetic the *Pathétique* could be.

No, decidedly nothing Irish. Pearl was pleased, in a vague way, to be of Irish blood on both sides of her family, but she had had enough of Ireland last night. Professor Vambrace was strongly conscious of his own Irish heritage, and in periods of stress it provided him with two character roles which appealed deeply to his histrionic temperament. The first of these was the Well-Born Celt, proud, ironical and aristocratic of manner; was he not a cousin of the Marquis of Mourne and Derry? The other was the Wild and Romantic Celt, untrammelled by pretty Saxon considerations of reason, expediency, or indeed of fact. When this intellectual disguise was on him he assumed a manner of talking which was not quite a brogue, but which was racy, extravagant and punctuated by angry snorts and hollow laughter. His mode of expression owed a good deal to the plays of Dion Boucicault, which the Professor had seen in his boyhood.

It was a hammy performance, but Pearl and her mother were too near to it to be critical; they feared the Professor in this mood, for he could say very bitter things.

Last night the Professor had given one of his most prolonged and elaborate impersonations in this vein. He was, he said, being persecuted, hounded, mocked by those who were jealous of his intellectual attainments, of his integrity, of his personal dignity. People who hated him because he was different from themselves had found a new means by which they hoped to bring him low. Ha, ha! How little they knew their man! He was unpopular. He needed no one to tell him that. His letters to the City Council about garbage disposal had won him no friends; he knew it. His wrangle with the Board of Education, when he had refused to have Pearl vaccinated at their request, still rankled; no one needed to tell him that. He had spoken out at meetings of the faculty of the University; no man who attacked incompetent colleagues—in public, mind you, and not like a sneaking, night-walking jackeen—need hope for popularity, let alone preferment. His success as an amateur actor was bound to create jealousy; his performance as Prospero had been something of a triumph, in its small way, and every triumph created detractors. He had fought in the open, like a man, against stupidity, and Bumbledom, and mediocrity, and he knew the world well enough to expect a bitter return.

But that he should be attacked through his daughter! Even his realism had not forseen that! A false announcement of an engagement when they all knew that no suitor had ever so much as darkened the door of his house! That was cruelty. That was catching a man in a place where he could hardly be expected to defend himself. He was, ha ha, surprised that they could rise to cruelty, for cruelty on that level demanded a touch of imagination, and that was the last thing he had expected. If they could accuse his daughter of being engaged, they would next be spreading a report that his wife was a witch.

Tchaikovsky, filtered through the splendid machine, was dying by inches; his groans, his self-reproaches filled the room with Slavic misery. Pearl's eyes were full of tears, and she reached for the second-to-last doughnut.

It had been Mummy who broke first, and went weeping to her room. Pearl knew that Mummy's unhappiness was for her, as well as for her husband. Of course Daddy didn't realize that it was painful to have it said so many times, and in so many different ways, that no young man had ever been interested in her. She didn't care for herself, but she supposed a girl had a duty to her family in such a matter; nobody likes it to be thought that their daughter lacks charm.

Once, by an odd chance, this same Solomon Bridgetower had taken her to the Military Ball, the great event of Salterton's social year. But that was when they were both in a play, and he hadn't meant anything by it. Anyway, it was four years ago and she had not spoken a dozen words to him since. And he was the recognized property, though low on her list, of the local heiress and beauty, Griselda Webster. It was queer that anyone should think of playing a trick in which her name was linked with his. Anyway, no young man had asked her to go anywhere with him since then.

No; that was not quite true. No young man with whom she could be bothered had approached her. She had been conscious, recently, that Henry Rumball, a reporter on *The Bellman* who came every day to the University, seeking news, was persistently attentive to her. But he was a joke among all the girls in the Library.

Solomon Bridgetower, however, was not. That morning she had been aware as soon as she put her coat in her locker in the staff-room that something was in the air, and that it concerned her. The first to congratulate her had been her great enemy, Miss Ritson in Cataloguing.

'Well,' said she, 'aren't you the sly one? Carrying him off right from under Tessie's nose! No ring yet, I see. Or don't you choose to wear it at the daily toil? Congratulations, dear.'

Miss Ritson moved away, humming. It was an ironical hum, but it was lost on Pearl, whose father had been so determined that she must be an agnostic. For Miss Ritson was humming *God moves in a mysterious way, His wonders to perform.*

Tessie was Miss Teresa Forgie, daughter and principal secretary to the Librarian. She was of classic features (that is to say, horse-faced) and formidable learning. It was obvious that she would make a wonderful wife for any ambitious young professor, and it was well known among her associates in the Library that she had chosen Solly Bridgetower as the recipient of this rich dower. But Miss Forgie was as high-minded as she was learned, and when she greeted Pearl no one would have guessed that she had cried herself to sleep the night before.

'I am so deeply happy for you, Pearl,' she said. 'There is so much that a man in academic life needs—so much of simple femininity, as well as understanding of his work.' She glanced around, and continued in a lower tone. 'So many needs of Body, as well as of Mind. I hope that I may continue to be a dear, dear friend to you both.'

Pearl understood the import of this very well. She was in charge of Reference, and that included a locked section of the book-stacks called Permanently Reserved, where books were kept which could only be read on the spot, upon presentation of a permit signed by the Librarian. Tessie plainly thought that Pearl had won Solly by subtle arts learned from the Hindu Books of Love, and from Havelock Ellis' *Studies in the Psychology of Sex.*

All of the girls had congratulated her, in one way or another, within an hour of opening time. Some of them seemed genuinely glad that she was to make her escape from the Library. And Pearl had said nothing to arouse further curiosity. Was this wise? But with Daddy talking about lawyers and suits she did not know what else to do; there would be trouble enough in time. She had trembled, when she overheard some of the girls talking in whispers about arranging a shower for her.

A shower! She had intimate knowledge of these affairs, at

which the friends of an engaged girl lavished everything from handkerchiefs to kitchenware upon her. What would she do if she suddenly found herself the recipient of twenty handkerchiefs, or a collection of candy-thermometers, lemon-squeezers and carrot-dicers? As Tchaikovsky moaned his last, Pearl cowered in the armchair, licking the sugar from the last doughnut off her fingers, and sweated with fright.

Suddenly the light flashed on in the dark room. It was old Mr Garnett, the Library janitor, with his trolley of cleaning materials.

'Sorry. Didn't know anybody was here.'

'It's all right, Mr Garnett. I'll just put away these records, and then I'll be through. Please go ahead with your work.'

'O.K., Miss Vambrace. Looks pretty clean in here anyways.'

'There wasn't any class this afternoon. I was listening to some music alone. You won't tell anybody, will you?'

'I never tell what ain't my business. You got a right to be alone, I guess. Won't be alone much longer, I hear.'

'I'll put these records away at once.'

'That's what they say about marriage. Never alone again. Well, that can be good, and it can be pure hell, too. Ever think of it that way?'

'I'll just throw this bag right into your wastepaper box, shall I?'

'What's the fella's name?'

'I beg your pardon?'

'The fella. The fella you're engaged to? Somebody mentioned it, but I forget, now. One of our fellas, isn't it?'

'Oh, you know how people talk, Mr Garnett.'

'It was in the paper. That's not talk. When it's in the paper, you mean business. What's the fella's name?'

'Oh. I forget.'

'What? How can you forget?'

'Oh—well—the name in the paper was Mr Solomon Bridgetower.'

'Yeah. Yeah. Young Bridgetower. Well, I knew his father. I've seen worse.'

Pearl had replaced the records, and she fled. Oh, what despicable weakness! She had named him, as her fiancé, to someone outside the family! What would father say? How would she ever get out of this hateful, hateful mess?

IN TWENTY-FIVE years of marriage Professor Vambrace and his wife had never reached any satisfactory arrangement about food; she was preoccupied, and thought food a fleshly indulgence; he liked food, but disliked paying for it. In consequence they lived mainly on scraps and bits. Now and then Mrs Vambrace would parch, or burn, or underdo a large piece of meat, and the recollection of it would last them for two or three weeks. They never had sweets, because the Professor did not like them, but they ate a good deal of indifferent cheese. They never had fruit, because the Professor considered it a dangerous loosener of the bowels, though he made an exception in favour of stewed prunes which he thought of as regulators, or gastric policemen. Their refrigerator, which seemed to be in permanent need of de-frosting, and smelled, was always full of little saucers of things which had not been quite finished at previous meals, and they always seemed to be catching up with small arrears of past dishes. They were great keepers of bowls of grease in which, now and again, things were fried. They tended also to fall behind with their dish-washing.

Nevertheless the Professor, as became a cousin of Mourne and Derry, firmly believed that there was a formal programme which governed their eating, but which they had temporarily agreed to set aside. The most substantial meal of their day was always eaten at one o'clock, give an hour or so either way, but he would not permit it to be called dinner, for only common people ate dinner then. It was luncheon. Not lunch; luncheon. If he chanced to be at home during the afternoon he always suggested that they skip tea. They had never actually had tea in years. Supper, he maintained, was a meal which one ate before going to bed, and as the food they ate between six and eight could not possibly be called dinner, it was usually referred to as 'the evening meal.'

When Pearl came home after her music-and-doughnut orgy at the Library it was well after six o'clock, but nothing had yet been done about the evening meal, so she prepared it. As she had acquired her notions of housekeeping from her mother, and as the cloth and such things as salt and pepper and sugar were never removed from the dining-table, this did not take long. She called her mother, who had been having a nap on her bed, and tapped at the door of her father's study, and the evening meal began.

For a time no one spoke. Pearl, glutted with doughnuts, worried a plate of stewed prunes and some bread. Mrs Vambrace ate a kind of cardboard which her doctor had recommended to her years before, as a bread substitute during a brief illness, and took a little jelly which had been left from luncheon two days ago, and which had withered and taken on a taste of onion in the refrigerator. The Professor, as became a man, was a heavier eater, and he had a saucer of cold macaroni and cheese, upon which he poured a little milk, to liven it; he followed this with the remains of a custard, the component parts of which had never really assembled, but which had a splendidly firm skin. Hunger partly satisfied, he was ready to talk.

'I have struck the first blow in my campaign, today,' he announced.

'Yes, dear?' Mrs Vambrace had a calm and sorrowful face, which belied her character, for she was inclined toward hysteria. She had also a low and pretty voice.

'It is a good policy to carry the war into the enemy's camp. I have instigated a suit against *The Bellman*.'

'Oh, Walter! A lawsuit?'

'Of course a lawsuit. What other kind of suit could I possibly mean?'

'But Walter! A lawsuit can be such a dreadful thing.'

'You should know, Elizabeth. Your family have been lawyers for long enough.'

102

'Did you talk to Ronny?'

'Yes, and little good it did me. Ronny shares your opinion, Elizabeth. He too thinks that a lawsuit is a dreadful thing. I would think that with his objection to suits he would get out of the law and find some other profession.'

'But Walter, I am sure that if Ronny advised against a suit he meant to spare you pain. Father always said that Ronny was a very good lawyer, for all his flippant way.'

'Your father himself enjoyed a great reputation as a lawyer, Elizabeth, and much of it was founded on his habit of persuading people not to go to law. He was a sentimentalist, I fear. It is the curse of a certain type of Irishman. Ronny would naturally appeal to him.'

'If you don't consider Ronny competent, Walter, why did you go to him?'

'That is a ridiculous question, Elizabeth. He is one of the family. Of your family, that is to say. Family means something. Not much, but something. My own family is not entirely inconsiderable, though I do not attribute a pennyworth of my own success in my chosen career to that. Still, there is the connection with Mourne and Derry. There is what I suppose may be called the aristocratic tradition, which is chiefly a tradition of not allowing oneself to be trampled over by a pack of louts and cheapjacks. So far as family gives one courage to resist what is vulgar and intrusive and impertinent, family is a very good thing. Ronny may not understand that, but his senior partner certainly does so.'

'Mr. Snelgrove?'

'Yes.'

'Oh dear, Walter.'

'What about him?'

'Father always disliked him so.'

'Very possibly. Your father disliked many people.'

'Only superficially, Walter. But he really disliked Mr Snelgrove. He said he was one of those men who gravitate to the law because they delight in mischief.'

'Your father was quick to find some fanciful reason for discrediting a man who had defeated him in court.'

'That is unkind, Walter. And Mr Snelgrove never defeated Father anywhere. Father was a great advocate.'

'Everyone says so, Elizabeth. It is generally admitted that if it had not been for his weakness he could have done anything he chose.'

'He had a very large heart, Walter. We had such a happy home.'

'I dare say.'

The thought of that home made Mrs Vambrace weep a few tears, perhaps because of the contrast between those laden tables and her loving, witty, drunk-every-night father, and the stewed prunes which she shared with the invincibly sober Vambrace. Pearl, who had not wanted to speak until she had heard more of her father's campaign, cleared away the dishes and set in place the inevitable *pièce de résistance* of a Vambrace evening meal, a large plate of soda crackers and a pot of very strong tea.

'I also visited the editor of *The Bellman*,' said the Professor, when he had buttered a biscuit very thickly and sprinkled it generously with salt.

'Yes?' said his wife. Her resistance, such as it was, had been broken for the evening.

'There's a fool, if you happen to be in search of a fool,' said the Professor, while crumbs flew out of his mouth. 'Family is little enough, as I said. But there's a fellow with no family. A self-made fellow. And what a thing he has made of himself! He crumpled up at once, when I told him what I intended to do. I despised him. First of all, he has no character. That's where family comes in. Then he has no real education. That's where the university comes in. To think that a mind of that quality should be in charge of a newspaper! Is it any wonder that the Press is the engine of mischief that it is! When I told him I meant to sue he went as white as a sheet.'

'Did you go to him first?' said Mrs. Vambrace.

'Of course.'

'You threatened a suit before you had seen your lawyers? Oh Walter!'

'Elizabeth, you really have the most curious notion of the place of a lawyer in a man's life. I decide to sue, and I tell my lawyer to go ahead with it. I do not ask his advice; I give him my instructions.'

'Father.' Pearl spoke now for the first time. 'What will the suit mean?'

'It will mean justice, I trust. Retribution. An absolute retraction of this foul attack, and substantial damages. The private citizen has some redress in cases of this sort, I hope. The Press is powerful, but it has not quite got us all under its thumb.'

'Will I have to appear in court?'

'I don't suppose so. Why should you?'

'If I don't, who will?'

'Don't be absurd, Pearl. I shall appear, of course.'

'Are you bringing the suit?'

'And who else would bring it?'

'But in my name?'

'Not at all. Why in your name, of all things?'

'Because if anyone has been wronged, it's me.'

'It's I. How often have I ——'

'Listen, Father. I won't go.'

'What do you mean? Won't go where?'

'To court. I couldn't bear it.'

'What makes you think you would appear in court? I am defending you. You are my daughter. Why should you appear anywhere?'

'Father, I'm over twenty-one. You can't defend me that way. If I have been offended, I must at least appear and say so.'

'Nonsense. You don't know anything about law.'

'I know that much. Father, please don't go on with it.'

'Of course I shall go on with it. How can you speak so ungratefully, Pearl? I know what must be done. You are still very much a child.'

105

'In law I'm not a child. I'm a grown woman. And I won't go to court and be made a fool of. I'll talk to Cousin Ronny.'

The Professor pushed his teacup aside and brushed some crumbs into a heap on the cloth.

'I refuse to continue any such discussion as this at the table,' said he. As a cousin of Mourne and Derry he kept up a strong pretence that there are certain things which cannot be discussed while eating. As he was an inveterate quarreller-at-the-table himself it was never easy for his family to know what these things were.

The Professor and his wife went into the living-room and sat in their accustomed chairs on either side of the fireplace. Pearl gathered up the dirty dishes, took them to the kitchen, held them briefly under the cold water tap and stacked them up, to be washed at some indefinite future time. It was a received belief of Vambrace housewifery that dishes might be left thus if they had been rinsed. She then went and stood between her parents, waiting to be recognized, but as neither of them would look at her she screwed up her courage and spoke.

'Father, please don't have a lawsuit.'

'I beg your pardon?'

'Please don't have a lawsuit.'

'I shall do what I think best.'

'Yes, but think what it will mean for me.'

'And what, precisely, will it mean for you?'

'I'll have to go into court and say it was all a mistake, or a joke, or whatever it was. They'll ask me questions. I'll be a laughing stock.'

'Your honour will be vindicated.'

'It'll make me look silly.'

'And how, pray, do you suppose you will look if this foul lie is not exposed for what it is?'

'But what's foul about it?'

'What? How can you ask such a question? Haven't you realized that this is a blow at me? A public statement that my daughter is to marry the son of a family which has always sought to push me aside and belittle me—is that nothing at all?'

'I thought you had given up all that about the Bridge-towers?'

'And what made you think that, may I ask?'

'You've been in the Little Theatre with Solly for quite a while.'

'Solly? I had not known that you were on terms of familiarity with him.'

'Everybody calls him Solly.'

'Do you do so to his face?'

'No. Not exactly. But I don't see him often.'

'That is as well.'

'But Father——'

'Yes?'

'Well——'

'Yes, yes, yes. If you have something to say, say it.'

'I—well, I——'

'Come along, Pearl. What is it?'

'It's hard to put it in words.'

'Then you are not ready to speak. What is clearly apprehended is capable of being clearly expressed. Think again. And I venture to say that when you have thought this matter over you will be in agreement with me.'

Pearl went to her bedroom, changed into a better frock, and made herself tidy. She was not skilled in presenting herself, and when she had made her best efforts she still looked somewhat tousled and distracted in her dress. As she dabbed at her face in front of her small mirror (which had a whorl in it) she worried about her failure to impress her father. How could she possibly tell him what she really felt? How could she tell him that such a lawsuit as he contemplated would harm, and perhaps ruin, her chances of ever marrying?

Because she had never been able to look at her parents from any distance, Pearl was unable to guess why they were as they were, but she knew that they would take in very bad part any suggestion from her that she was interested in marriage, or regarded her chances of marriage as an important factor in her life. She was certainly not clear on the subject herself. She had done nothing to attract any man, and men had shown little enough interest in her. She had no clear notion of what marriage would be like, or the kind of husband she wanted. But she had, deeply rooted in her nature, a feeling that she wanted a husband, and that if she did not get one, of some kind, at some time, her life would be incomplete. She was humble. She did not expect a Prince Charming, and she did not think that it would be easy to marry anybody. But she did not see any reason why, when girls no more attractive than herself were able to marry, she should not manage to do so.

She also knew that if there were a lawsuit, and her father said that she must appear in court, and look like a fool, that she would do so. She would protest, of course, but it was unthinkable that he should be disobeyed.

She would dearly have liked to go out without saying anything to her parents, but she knew that such a course was quite impossible. So when she had put on her coat she went to them.

'I don't expect to be very late.'

'You are not going out?' The Professor looked at her with histrionic amazement.

'The Yarrows are having a party. They've asked me.'

'When did they ask you?'

'At least a week ago.'

'And, in the light of what has happened, you are going?'

'Well—why not, Father?'

'Why not? Pearl, are you utterly out of your mind? Here we are, facing a law action because your name has been publicly linked with that of the one man in Salterton, above all others, whom you should avoid, and you ask me why you should not appear in society! Have you no sense of fitness?'

'But Father, are we to keep ourselves locked up until the case is over? It will be months, probably.'

'Surely, the very night after this false notice appeared, you wish to keep out of sight?'

'Well, it isn't my fault, really.'

'Has anyone questioned you about this matter?'

'Some of the girls at the Library congratulated me today.'

'And you told them the truth?'

'I didn't say anything. I didn't know what to do. I thought I should wait until you had thought it over. Father——'

'Well?'

'Couldn't the newspaper just publish a retraction, or an apology, or something?'

'They utterly refuse to do so.'

'You asked them?'

'I gave them a written form of apology. They refused it. With insolence.'

'I think I'll have to go. It will look awfully funny if I don't.'

'You are determined?'

'Well—you see how it is, Father.'

'I see that you are determined not to be guided by me in this matter. You are your own mistress, I suppose.'

'Please don't feel badly.'

'You are over twenty-one.'

'I really think I ought to go. I promised.'

'This is the spirit of the age, and of the New World, I suppose. I had hoped that as a family we would see one another through this.'

'Well, of course I'll stay at home if you feel like that, Father.'

'No, no. Go. You want to go. Don't stay at home and look at me reproachfully all night.'

And so, after a few more interchanges, Pearl went, feeling thoroughly ashamed of herself.

WAVERLEY WAS a staid university. The establishment of a School of Journalism was being undertaken only after long debate and a considerable measure of opposition; as Professor Vambrace complained, there was still a Professor of Natural Philosophy attached to the Faculty of Arts who was also, in effect, the Dean of Science. But the University had a very active Chaplain, and as his work had become so heavy that he needed an assistant, his department had been enlarged in September by the inclusion of Norman Yarrow, Ph.D., whose first academic appointment it was.

Norman Yarrow was in his early thirties, and for two years after receiving his doctorate he had worked in the social service department of a large Canadian city. When he was invited to join the staff at Waverley he had been able to marry Yolande Spreewald, a young woman who was also in social service, as an assistant director of recreation.

It was agreed in the circle in which they moved that Norm Yarrow and Dutchy Spreewald were made for each other, and that they would be an invincible team. Norm was not, the social workers agreed, one of those nut psychologists. He did not appear to belong to any special school of psychology. He frankly admitted that he relied upon his own commonsense, rather than theory, to guide him in dealing with people who seemed to need psychological assistance. Confronted with somebody whose mental hygiene appeared to be defective, he first asked himself, 'How does this guy deviate from what's normal?' Having found that out, he knew how to proceed. He just had to jolly the fellow into a normal attitude, and that was that.

If anyone asked him how he knew what was normal, he would smile his slow, boyish smile, and explain that he was pretty normal himself—just an ordinary guy, really—and he took that as his guide. He was tall and well-built, and if his eyes were small, they were kindly and bright. If his hair had not become thin in his twenties, he might have been considered handsome. Worried women, and boys in their 'teens, were attracted by him and found him reassuring. He put great faith in what he called The Personal Influence in Guidance. He was very popular with his colleagues on his own level, and it was unfortunate that he had attracted the jealousy of his immediate superior. It must have been jealousy, for why else would his superior have suggested that he seek another position? Jealousy of that kind is not normal, and Norm had lost no time in handing in his resignation and seeking an academic post at Waverley. After some sifting of applicants, and some disappointments, the Chaplain had given Norm a contract for a probationary year. Whereupon Norm had married Dutchy.

Dutchy was every bit as normal as he. She was a girl of abounding and restless energy, physically attractive in a muscular way, of whom it was said that 'she made things go'. She was well suited to her work as a recreation director, for she was convinced that any sort of inactivity was evil, and that people who had worked all day needed to be guided into some sort of activity at night. She was immensely popular with people who agreed with this belief, and who acknowledged her superiority as a leader. She worked wonders with most children, and with amiable and submissive adults. Like everyone in her line of work she met with the occasional screwball who refused to be assimilated into the group; she directed such screwballs at once to Norm, who did what he could to jolly them into a more normal attitude. But her failures were few. Her work lay chiefly among people who were poor, without being in poverty, and among such people resistance to recreational programming and creative activities can usually be overcome.

She loved Norm in a normal, healthy way. That is to say, she was determined to do everything that lay in her power to advance him in the world, without herself being swallowed up in marriage. For marriage, as she told a great many people, was an equal partnership, with nobody on top.

Norm loved her, as was to be expected, normally. Which meant, as he explained to Dutchy while their romance was ripening, that as long as their marriage proceeded in a perfectly normal way, he was for her one hundred per cent.

Their many friends said, many times, that they made a swell couple. They received many wedding presents, including a set of twelve table mats, of spongeable glacé leather, made and given by the Sixth Ward Women's Leather-working Class, which was Dutchy's first achievement in organized recreation. And after their wedding they had a wonderful party, which Dutchy had organized, at which, for once, everybody knew all the figures of every square-dance that was performed.

THE PARTY for which Pearl was bound was the first that Norm and Dutchy had given in Salterton; indeed, their wedding party was the only one that they had given before it. But they had made friends quickly. Norm was a success with the students, with some of the younger faculty members, with the administrative and Library staff, and he was already on terms of apparent intimacy with a great many people. There was something about him which attracted confidence. Perhaps it was the frankness and ease of his manner; perhaps it was his title of Doctor, which is enough in itself to break down the reserve of many people; perhaps it was the widespread notion that a psychologist is a fountain of good counsel. Whatever it was, Norm had managed in six weeks to become the confessor of a surprising number of people who had never felt moved to confide in any of the members of the official staff of the Psychology Department. He wanted to entertain these trusting souls, and some others who, for one reason or another, might repay cultivation. And Dutchy was only too happy to organize a party; after all, that was her business. Though she told Norm several times that she was scared to death to make her first appearance at a party as a prof's wife.

'I mean,' she said, as they were cleaning their teeth together in the small bathroom of their apartment one night, 'in the ordinary way in a new town you'd get things rolling even before they came in the door by hanging up a sign "Please Remove Your Shoes Before Entering". Get people with their shoes off right away, and the ice is broken. But at a university—Gee, I don't know how far this dignity stuff has to go.'

'Just carry on as you would anywhere, Dutchy,' advised her husband. 'These people are all regular. All nice and normal, really. Some of them have talked to me pretty freely, and I think they could do with some shaking up. They need what you've got to give.'

'O.K.,' said Dutchy, and later, as they lay together in bed, she told Norm that the wonderful thing about him was his insight, and the way he sensed that practically everybody is really a great big kid at heart.

PEARL WAS one of those who had succumbed to Norman Yarrow's charm. She had first met him in the stacks at the Library, when she was checking a reference for Dr Forgie in Locke's *Essay on Human Understanding*. 'Can I help you?' the strange man had said. 'I doubt it; I'm looking for *Understanding*,' she had replied. Norman Yarrow was not a man to miss such an opening; 'Aren't we all?' he said, and when Pearl blushed he did not laugh or pursue the conversation. But two days later he had appeared in Dr Forgie's outer office with some questions about books for his students, and since then they had had two or three conversations in which Pearl, who was not used to a sympathetic male listener, had said a good deal more than she meant to say about her life. And thus the invitation for this evening came about.

When Pearl heard the rumble of a party through the apartment door she realized that she had not expected a big gathering, and had been secretly hoping for a very small one, perhaps a simple evening with understanding Dr Yarrow and his wife, who was certain to be equally understanding. But she had already rung the bell, and when the door opened the noise of the party seemed to jump out at her, like a big dog. And there was a young woman who must be Mrs Yarrow, radiating vitality like an electric heater, who seized her hand in a painfully muscular grasp.

'You're Pearl,' she shouted, in a voice pitched for the noise within; 'I'm Dutchy. Come on in, we're just warming up and you're a couple of drinks behind. Here's the bed-room, throw your coat on the bed. Yeah, it's a double bed and its legal; ain't that wonderful!' Dutchy laughed the loud and shameless laugh of the enthusiastic bride. 'The john's in there; if you don't want it now, you sure will later. Now don't waste time primping, kid; they're waiting for you inside.'

Dutchy had lost any misgivings she might have had about being a prof's wife. Gin had banished it. Neither she nor Norman had been what they called 'drinkers' when in social service work. But as people rise in the world their social habits change. Dutchy knew that as a prof's wife she ought to make some advances in what she was unselfconscious enough to call 'gracious living' and Alcohol, though bad for the poor, was probably expected in academic life. Norm was, after all, a Ph.D. and she herself was a trained social worker, and had written an unusually good thesis, at the age of nineteen, on *Preparing the Parent for the Profession of Parenthood*; they were not the kind of people who were brought to ruin by drink, and so they had made a few experiments.

Gin had come to Dutchy like fire from heaven. At the first swallow she was conscious of that shock of recognition with which psychologists and literary critics are so familiar. It was as though, all her life, she had been dimly aware of the existence of some miraculous essence, some powerful liberating force, some enlightening catalyst, and here it was! It was gin! Why be nervous about being a prof's wife, why worry about a party going well, when gin could make the crooked straight and the rough places plain? Dutchy, as Norm laughingly said, had taken to gin as a duck takes to water.

Pearl was hauled into the combined living and dining-room of the apartment by the hand, while Dutchy cried, 'Gangway! Here's a poor erring sister who's a couple of drinks behind!' She was conscious of some familiar faces, but she saw no people whom she knew well. On the dining-table was a large glass jug, containing a purple liquid, and from this Dutchy poured a tumblerful, slopping a good deal on the table, and forced it upon her. 'Drink up!' she ordered.

Pearl sipped suspiciously. It was gin; unquestionably it was a great deal of gin, to which some grape juice and ice water had been added.

Dutchy subdued the conversation by shouting 'Hold it! Hold it!' and when she had comparative silence she harangued her guests thus: 'Now, gals and guys, we've come to the second part of the party. Maybe you didn't know a party had a second part? Sure it has. There's the Hello; that's the beginning, when you meet everybody. You've had that. The second part's the What Now? That's where we've got to. This is the crossroads of a party. You can either go on to the Ho Hum, when everybody wishes it was time to go home, or you can go on to the Whee! What's it to be? The Ho Hum, or the Whee?'

The guests, who were unfamiliar with up-to-date techniques of recreational programming, looked somewhat astonished, and made no reply. But Dutchy was used to carrying crowds on her own enthusiasm, and she immediately made enough noise for all.

'The Whee! The Whee! Come on, let's hear it! Whee!'

A few guests politely said Whee, in rather low voices.

'OKAY!' shouted Dutchy, in a clarion voice, and in no time at all the Whee was in progress.

Pearl was not quite able to see how the Whee worked, it was so rapid and so noisy. A bowl containing scraps of paper was shaken under her nose, and she chose one. All the people in the room seemed to be engaged in some very rough game. In her surprise and dismay she hastily gulped some of the sickly gin drink, and as someone jostled her she spilled it on her front. She was dabbing at herself with her handkerchief when a man seized her slip of paper, gave a yell, and darted away, to return at once dragging a protesting young man who had been lurking at the far end of the room. Before Pearl knew what was happening another man pressed a large piece of adhesive plaster over her lips, she was forced back to back with the protesting young man, who was similarly gagged, and they were tied, by the wrists and ankles with grocer's string. This had been happening all

115

over the room, and only Dutchy and two or three of her muscular lieutenants were free. Dutchy addressed her trussed-up guests.

'Now folksies, this is just the start of the Whee! You chose your partners by lot, and now you've got 'em. I'm going to time you, and the first couple to get untied without breaking the string, and to pull off the adhesve tape without using your hands, gets the Grand Prize. Ready? Go! She discharged a cap pistol which she held in her hand.

Pearl had heard of people wishing to die, in books, but she had never experienced that feeling herself until now. For the young man with whom she was bound and gagged was Solomon Bridgetower.

PROFESSOR VAMBRACE did not sit long in his chair after Pearl had gone. A plan was working in his mind, like yeast. That is to say, part of a plan was there, and he was sure that the remainder of it would follow soon. But he did not want to wait until the plan had completed itself. He wanted to be up and doing. He was still smarting from the feeling that his grievance and his lawsuit had been taken from him and had become the property of Mr Snelgrove. Pearl's unwillingness to play the role of a submissive, wronged daughter with perfect trust in his power to win justice for her had nettled him. Nobody, it appeared, saw this matter in the proper light. But he was not a man without resource, and he would uncover the whole plot—for a plot it surely was.

'I shall be out for a time,' he said to his wife, and added mysteriously, 'on this business. If anyone should call, say that I'm in but cannot be disturbed. You understand?'

'Oh Walter!' said she; 'you are not going to do anything rash, are you?'

The Professor laughed, for it pleased him to be accused of rashness.

'You need not worry about me, Elizabeth,' he said, almost kindly. 'I know what I am doing.'

This latter claim was perhaps an exaggeration.

The Professor went to the coat cupboard, and put on,

first, a thick cardigan under his jacket, and then a heavy, long scarf which was a relic of his university days. Next he brought out, from the back of the cupboard, a very long, very heavy tweed overcoat, belted across the back, which he had not worn for years. He put this on, and a pair of heavy gloves, and from the depths of the hall-seat he recovered a tweed cap, which he had not worn since the days when they were fashionable wear for golfers. He took a blackthorn walking-stick from the umbrella vase, and surveyed himself in the small, dim mirror in the back of the hall-seat. No question about it, he was effectively disguised, ready for rough weather and rough exploits, a man not to be trifled with. In fact—he finally admitted the word into his conscious thoughts—he looked like a detective. He left the house and strode briskly up the street.

Disguised the Professor was, in the sense that he was unusually dressed. He was not, however, unobtrusive, looking as he did like a fugitive from some Irish racecourse. A tall, gaunt man, nothing could disguise his characteristic long, swift stride, nor the thin, whistling sound which he made with his nostrils as he walked. But faith is a great gift and, atheist as the Professor was in matters of religion, he was not troubled by even the slightest agnosticism concerning himself and his abilities. In his own opinion, he was wrapped in a cloak of invisibility.

He was not sure where he was going, nor what he meant to do when he arrived, but he thought that a general reconnaissance would be a good beginning to his detective work. Therefore he made his way to the house in which Gloster Ridley's apartment was. This was a Victorian mansion toward the middle of the city, and when the Professor reached it, there were lights on all three floors.

It is well known to readers of detective stories—and Professor Vambrace liked to relax his mind in that way—that detection must be conducted according to the School of Force, or the School of Intellect; the detective can either burst into rooms and fight whomever he may find there, or he can collect infinitely tiny pieces of information, fit them together into a mosaic, and astonish the simple by his deductions. The Professor was unhesitating in his adherence to the latter school. Looking carefully in all directions to make sure that no one was watching, he hastened to the back of the Victorian mansion and literally stumbled upon valuable evidence in the form of a collection of garbage cans. They made a clatter, and almost at once the back door on the ground floor opened and a female voice said, fiercely, 'Get out of that, you filthy brute!'

The Professor, in detective parlance, 'froze'. That is to say, he crushed himself flat against the wall, ducked his head, and stopped breathing. Unfortunately, in this manoeuvre, he dropped his heavy stick among the garbage cans and made another clatter.

The unseen woman came further out of the house, and said, 'Scat!'

There was an inaudible question from within.

'It's those damned dogs again,' said the woman. She heaved half a brick among the garbage cans, frightening the Professor, and hurting him when the brick bounced and hit him on the shin. But she then went inside, and after a few rigid moments he carefully extricated himself from the cans, and observed them closely. Upon one was roughly lettered RIDLEY. Aha! Well, he had known that Ridley lived in this house, but there was satisfaction in proving it in this thoroughly detective-like way. Here was another can with the same mark. Tut! He had heard that Ridley was unnaturally interested in food; a glutton, it was said, for all his thinness. Still—two garbage cans for a single man! It was effete.

As this part of the house yielded no further evidence the Professor crept around to the front, and went into the main entrance, which was in a square Victorian tower which ran up the façade of the house. Three cards were enclosed in three brass frames. George Shakerly Marmion; yes, it had been Mrs Shakerly Marmion who had mistaken him for a dog. Gloster Ridley; the second floor apartment. Mrs. Phillip West; top floor. Well, he now knew *precisely* where Ridley lived; he had seen lights on the second floor; Ridley was within. No car was parked near the house; Ridley was probably alone. Deduction was going smoothly, and bit by bit was being added to the mosaic. True, there was nothing absolutely new in any of this, but Rome was not built in a day.

Then, all of a sudden, there was a sound on the stairs within the door which was marked with Ridley's card! The detective was nonplussed, and in his confusion he did what he knew at once was a silly thing. He tried the door of the Shakerly Marmion's apartment, and when it would not yield, he rang the bell. The footsteps in Ridley's entrance grew louder, and the Professor was conscious that the hair on his head was stirring. He pressed his face against the Marmion's door, to conceal it, and thus he could not tell who it was that came out of Ridley's door and stood so near to him. Why didn't the man go outside, and let him make his escape before the Marmion's door was opened! But no; there were mail boxes in the hall, and whoever it was put a key in one of them, and stood by it, presumably examining some letters. The door of the Marmion's apartment opened, and there was Mrs Shakerly Marmion, whom he knew slightly, and who might be expected to recognize him, looking him in the face. It was a moment of ingenuity, and the Professor rose to it.

'Would yez like to subscribe to *The War Cry*?' he asked, disguising his voice as completely as he could, and assuming what he later realized was the broadest possible Cork accent, recollected from childhood. To give colour to his performance, he winked confidentially at Mrs Shakerly Marmion, who immediately slammed the door in his face.

The man in the hall had gone. The Professor hurried into the street, and—yes, there he was, just turning the corner. After him!

It was Ridley, and Vambrace set out to—detective parlance—tail him. After a block or so, however, he became conscious that his quarry was hurrying in a nervous fashion. Aha, Ridley knew that he was being tailed! But the Professor was equal to that; he halted for a moment, and then changed his step to a limp—a good, audible limp, such as a man with a club foot might own. That was disguise! In his exertion to maintain his limp and a high rate of speed, the Professor's nasal whistling became positively uproarious, and cut through the November night air with astonishing clarity.

Ridley, almost on the run, turned into a house, rushed up the steps and entered without knocking. Vambrace knew it. It was the home of the Fieldings. Well, it had been an exciting chase. Now he would, in the best detective fashion, lounge unobtrusively at some little distance, ready to follow his man when he came out again.

PEARL'S FIRST coherent thought after her chaotic dismay at finding herself bound and gagged with Solly Bridgetower, was that this was what came of disobliging her father. He had not wanted her to come to this party; she had insisted on coming; this was the shameful result. It was so often like this! Whenever she tried to assert herself, and to prove to Father that she was an adult, she got into some dreadful scrape. It was as though Father were in league with God. In spite of her atheistic upbringing Pearl still had, at the back of her mind, a notion of God as a vindictive old party who was determined to keep her humble and uncertain. God and Father were not mocked. Mock them, and what happened? Some kind of unpredictable, farcical hell, like the Whee.

There was little time for painful reflection. Having briefly enjoyed the spectacle of her guests in bonds, Dutchy was moving around the room, giving advice.

'It's a technique,' she said; 'best thing is to get the plaster off your mouths first. Then you can work out of the string. Come on, folksies, don't be shy!'

Norm, who had been tied to a lady in middle life who was secretary to the University registrar, showed the way. It involved rubbing the face against the face of the partner, until the sticking-plaster could be rolled off. The middle-aged lady, who had a bad breath and a short temper, was not fully co-operative, but this only added to the fun of the thing, for Dutchy. Couple by couple the guests, realizing that this was the price of freedom, set about a sheepish rubbing of face upon face. For men who had not shaved since morning, for women who wore heavy makeup, it was a painful and messy business. Their necks were twisted; the string bit into their wrists and ankles; some stockings were torn and a good deal of dust was picked up from the floor. Most of the guests weakly pretended to think their predicament funny; a few were inwardly raging but still, borne down by Dutchy's overwhelming gaiety and a weight of painfully acquired politeness, they did not break into open rebellion.

Pearl knew Solly Bridgetower well enough by sight. She had once acted in a play—that same performance of *The Tempest* in which Mr Swithin Shillito had so admired her father—of which he was assistant director. She had met him a few times at social gatherings; she had seen him from time to time in the Library. But these were scarcely preparations for rubbing her face repeatedly against his, while their eyes watered, and they breathed stertorously. Her hair fell forward, and when she tried to throw it back with a jerk of her head she bumped Solly sharply on the nose with her chin. His nose was long and apparently very sensitive, for from beneath his sticking-plaster came a sound which might have been a cry of pain, or an oath.

Dutchy, who was running about the room, encouraging and exhorting, stopped beside them.

'Say, I only just heard about you two,' said she, excitedly. 'Congratulations, kids! But this ought to be duck soup for you two. Come on! Do it like you meant it! Say, I'll bet this was a plant. I bet you fixed it so's you'd get his name, Pearl!'

'No, I arranged that,' said one of her assistants, a large, dark, genial dentist. 'I didn't even look at her piece of paper; just grabbed Solly and tied them up.' He laughed the self-approving laugh of one who knows that he has done a good deed.

Pearl's mouth was free at last. 'I want to get out of this,' she said.

'Sure you do,' said Dutchy. 'And seeing it's you, I'll give you a hint; the way the string's tied, you can get loose at once if he lies down flat and you crawl right up over his head; then the string drops off without untying the knots. 'Bye now.' And she was off to encourage other strugglers, who lay in Laocoön groups about the floor.

Solly made a noise which sounded like entreaty. Pearl, maddened by the arch looks of the dark dentist, leaned forward, seized a loose corner of his sticking-plaster in her mouth, and jerked her head backward savagely. Solly howled.

'I think you've killed me,' he said when he could speak.

'I wish I had,' said Pearl, venomously.

'It's not my fault. I didn't ask to be tied to you.'

'Oh, shut up!'

'No use shutting up, when we're tied together like this. Let's get out. What's the trick? I lie down and you crawl over me, or something.'

'I won't.'

'You must.'

'Don't you dare tell me I must.'

'You're being a fool. If we don't get out of this mess we'll be the last, and you'll have to do it with everybody looking. Come on; I'm lying down.' And he did lie down, and Pearl had no choice but to lie down also. Solly was on his face on the floor, and she lay flat on his back.

Inch by inch she hitched herself upward along his spine and at every move Solly groaned. But as she moved the strings became looser, and at last, as she hunched her bottom over his head, they were free enough to permit her to shake them off, and stand up. In a moment Solly, much ruffled, stood beside her.

They were one of the last couples to escape, but they were not observed by the others, who were too much occupied in trying to straighten and dust their clothes to pay close attention to anything else. Nor did Dutchy leave them time for embarrassment; swift passage from one delightful experience to another was part of the technique of partygiving, as she professed it. Very rapidly she herded her guests into a circle of alternate men and women.

'Now this one's easy, kids,' she said. 'Here's an orange, see? You stick it under your chin, Jimmy, see?' Jimmy, the dark, zealous dentist, did so. 'Now you just pass it to the lady on your right, not either of you using his hands, see, and she gets it under her chin, and so you pass it all around the circle back to me. Anybody drops it, they have to fall out of the game.'

This last remark, as Dutchy quickly realized, was an error. The more reticent and more selfish people made haste to drop the orange as soon as it reached them, sometimes without any pretence at gripping it. There were, however, eight or nine people who either feared Dutchy's disapproval, or felt some necessity to do as their hostess wished, or who positively liked passing oranges from neck to neck, and they remained in the middle of the room, while Dutchy spurred them on the finer flights. After the orange they passed a grapefruit in the same way; after the grapefruit came a melon. And after the melon appeared a watermelon, which Dutchy and Jimmy the dentist passed merrily between them a few times, just to show that it could be done. The watermelon had been borrowed from the freezing locker of a neighbour in the apartment building, and its coldness was the matter for much mirth. But the secretary to the registrar was not amused.

'When I was a girl I always hated the kissing games at parties,' said she, 'and until tonight I thought that they had gone out of fashion.' Her tone was low, but a surprising number of the guests heard her, and the dissatisfied faction gained heart. So much so, indeed, that Dutchy sensed a change of atmosphere, and decided that she would not continue with her programme as she had planned it. Dutchy was not stupid, but she had not had much previous experience with people whom she could not dominate—

who did not, indeed, welcome domination. She passed the purple drink, and became conciliatory. She asked her guests what game they would like to play next.

It is as dangerous, in its way, to ask a group of people associated with a university to choose their own games as it is to leave the choice in the hands of a trained director of recreation, like Dutchy. The secretary to the registrar immediately set out to explain a kind of charades which she called The Braingame; it was, she declared, a barrel of fun.

'It's just like the old kind of charades we played as children,' said she, 'except that a letter must be dropped from each syllable as it is guessed, in order to get the right answer, and when the group acts out the full word, it must express both the full word, and the word which is left when the superfluous letters are dropped. Is that clear?'

It was not clear.

'Let me give you an example. Suppose, for instance, that your real word—the word the others must guess—is "landscape". Well, the word which the group acts is "blandscrape". They pretend to be eating a pudding, and putting more salt in it; that gives the word, "bland". Then "scrape" is easy; you simply act somebody in a scrape.'

'As it were, crawling backward over a complete stranger?' asked a masculine young woman from the Dean's office, who had had to do this not long before with a young man from the classics department, who had playfully pinched her bottom. The registrar's secretary laughed lightly, and went on.

'Now, recall that your word was "landscape"; you must now act the whole word, or rather, both words. So you act "blandscrape". One of the group is being given a smooth shave, while the others peer admiringly at an imaginary view. You see? Blandscrape and landscape at once. Of course after a round or two we can have some really hard ones.'

The party seemed depressed by this notion. The masculine young woman seized her chance to make the cunning suggestion that they play a game in which they could all sit down. This was greeted with such eagerness that she launched at once into an explanation.

'Simple as ABC. Just Twenty Questions, really, but with knobs on. Somebody's It. They go outside and make up their minds that they are somebody—movie star, games champ, person in history—anybody at all. Then they sit in the middle of the room and we ask them questions to find out who they are. But—this is what makes it fun—if we ask them who they are we do it indirectly or by definition only, and they must show they know what we're talking about, or they're out of the game. I mean, I'm It. You question me. You find out I'm a famous literary woman who lived long ago. So you say, "Did you live on the Isle of Lesbos?" And I say, "No, I'm not Sappho"——'

'And we all laugh,' said the registrar's secretary in a voice which was not quite low enough.

Dutchy had not met with tensions of quite this kind in her career of recreation planning. But she was learning rapidly the arts of a faculty wife, and she intervened at this juncture in time to prevent a lively exchange between the two ladies, who were enemies of several years' standing. Such games, she said, would be wonderful for the clever university people, but there were a few dopes like herself and Jimmy present, whose minds did not work that way. Therefore they would play The Game.

As always, there were a few people present who did not know what The Game was, but they were told that it was a form of accelerated charades, and after sides had been chosen they played it quite peaceably and even with enjoyment.

Pearl and Solly were on the same side, and although she could act quite well, and make her ideas clear to the others, he was without skill in this direction. He became confused when it was his turn to act; he scowled and beat his brow; he pawed the air meaninglessly with his hands. He could not remember the rule that everything must be done in silence, and made despairing and inarticulate sounds. Pearl

watched him with contempt; it was to this idiot that an
unknown practical joker had linked her. She understood
better what her father meant when he raved about the
insult of it.

If there is anyone who has not played The Game, it may
be explained that two teams are chosen, and that each team
gets its chance to present the other team with a number of
pieces of paper, upon which proverbs, quotations, catch-
words and the like are written; each player is given one of
these, and his task is to convey its meaning to his team by
means of pantomime. If they guess what he is trying to tell
them, they score a point. The other team, knowing the
secret, watch the struggle with enjoyment.

In the fifth round of The Game, Solly was handed his
paper by Norm, as captain of the opposing team, and when
he read it he moaned, and muttered 'O God!' and gave
every sign of despair. Norm and his team were delighted.
Solly turned toward his own team in misery, and stood with
his mouth hanging open, sweating visibly.

'How many words?' asked the Registrar's secretary, who
had a very businesslike approach to The Game.

With his fingers Solly indicated that there were thirty-five
words.

There was a roar of dismay from his team. Protests were
made that this was impossible. Norm's team merely
laughed in mockery.

'Is it a verse?' demanded the Registrar's secretary.

Solly shook his head.

'A saying?'

Solly looked confused, nodded, shook his head, and
nodded again. Then he contorted himself violently to
signify his despair.

'A quotation?' went on the Registrar's secretary, who had
the phlegm of a Scotland Yard detective.

Solly nodded violently.

'Quotation from a writer?'

Solly thought for a moment, made a few meaningless
gestures, then took up a rhetorical stance, and pointed

toward the wall. Becoming frantic, he walked toward the Registrar's secretary and waved his hands before her face; he repeated this manoeuvre with a man, then seemed to lose heart, and stood once more at a loss, shaking his head.

Pearl's voice was heard, low and calm: 'You can fool some of the people all of the time, and you can fool all of the people some of the time, but you can't fool all of the people all of the time.'

There was an instant of silence, and then a roar from the opposing team. Solly gaped, and, forgetting that he was now privileged to speak, pantomimed extravagant delight.

'Is that right?' demanded the Registrar's secretary.

'Sure it's right,' said Norm; 'how did you guess it, Pearlie?'

Pearl was abashed. 'I don't know,' said she; 'but he somehow looked a little bit like Lincoln, and then he pointed south, toward the States, and I just said it.'

This brilliant stroke won the game, and it was time for refreshments. Consequently the company had plenty of time to talk about what Pearl had done. Although such uncanny guesses are by no means uncommon in The Game they always arouse excitement when they happen. Solly, upon being questioned, said that he did not know that the saying was attributed to Lincoln, nor had he been aware that he was pointing south; he had merely tried to behave like a man who was fooling some of the people some of the time—obviously a politician. This made Pearl's feat even more remarkable. It was Norm who, as a psychologist, offered the explanation which the company liked best.

'When people are very close, they often have the power of communicating without words,' said he. 'For instance, sometimes in the morning when I don't want an egg for breakfast, it will occur to me while I'm shaving, and then, when I get to the table, I'll find that Dutchy hasn't cooked me an egg; maybe it will turn out that there isn't even an egg in the house. It doesn't always work, of course. But obviously there's a Thing between Pearlie and Solly right now

—at this stage of their relationship, I mean. It certainly looks as if they were made for each other.'

This remark naturally brought inquiry, for only Norm and Dutchy, and their friend Jimmy, appeared to have read of their engagement. Professor Vambrace would undoubtedly have been astonished that ten of the people present were utterly ignorant of the shame and insult which had been forced upon him. But when Norm had finished his explanation they knew all about it, and offered their congratulations in the shy and affectedly casual manner in which people felicitate acquaintances. Dutchy, however, insisted that a toast be drunk in the purple fluid, and hurried about, filling glasses.

'Oh no, please don't!' cried Pearl.

'Oh, don't be so modest,' shouted Dutchy.

'I'd really much rather you didn't!'

'Now Pearlie, you've got to conquer that shyness,' said Norm, in a fatherly manner.

Pearl turned a look of desperate appeal upon Solly, but he was sitting with his head down, in a condition of abjection. She was furious with him. What a fool! Oh, Daddy was so right! What a nincompoop!

Norm rose to his feet, his glass held at eye-level in that curious gesture which people never use except when they are about to propose toasts.

'Friends,' said he, making his voice full and thrilling, 'let's drink to Pearlie and Solly. Dutchy and I can't claim to be old friends of either of them, but we know what married happiness is, and I think that gives us a kind of claim to speak now. Pearlie we know a good deal better than Solly. I do, that is to say, because we've had some talks. I guess you all know that Pearlie is one hell of a swell kid, but life hasn't been much fun for her. A shy kid, brainy, not the aggressive type, she's had the idea that she's a failure in life—that she isn't attractive. A religious problem, too, which I won't touch on now, but I guess all of us who have a sincere but modern and scientific Faith know that it's pretty lonely if you haven't got that and are wandering around in the dark, so to speak. I don't want to introduce a solemn note now but as a psychologist and as a professional in guidance I know what can happen in a life which lacks what I call the Faith Focus, and there's nobody more pleased than I—and I know here that I speak for Dutchy too—that Pearlie has found herself, and that all those doubts and fears and misgivings are sublimated in that vast Power the happiness of which is something upon which Dutchy and I feel ourselves peculiarly qualified to speak. I mean getting engaged, of course. So I ask you to drink to Pearlie and Solly, and if I can remember it I'll just recite a little verse that seems to fit the occasion. Now let's see—ah. "Hurrah for the little god with wings"—no, that's not it. Oh, yes——

> *Hurrah for the little god of Love,*
> *May he never moult a feather,*
> *When his big boots and her little shoes*
> *Are under the bed together.'*

This speech was granted a mixed reception. Some of the guests appeared to be stunned. Others took it in the spirit in which it was offered, and, led by Jimmy, broke feebly into 'For they are jolly good fellows'. Pearl was miserable, but angry enough to keep back her tears; Solly looked very weary. When the song died down, he said 'Thanks', and his tone was such that even Norm and Dutchy did not press him for more.

THE FIELDINGS' comfortable drawing-room rang with the brilliant arpeggio passages of the *Mink Schottische*, which Humphrey Cobbler was playing on the piano. As far as possible from the instrument, Gloster Ridley sat with Mrs Fielding on a sofa. He disliked music, and wished that the noise would stop. In a nearby chair sat Miss Vyner, Mrs Fielding's sister; she was a soldierly lady, at the last of youth but not yet begun upon middle age, and she was working her way through a box of fifty cigarettes, helped by occasional swigs at a whisky-and-soda. She too disliked music, and thought Cobbler a bore and a fool; these were the only two opinions she shared with Ridley, and as neither had given voice to them, this agreement could do nothing to lessen the hatred which had sprung up between them on sight. Mr Fielding, however, was enjoying himself greatly, and as he sat in his deep chair he wagged one finger, bobbed one foot, and occasionally made little noises in his throat, appreciative of the music. His wife, also, appeared to be perfectly content, which maddened Ridley, for he wanted to talk to her.

It could not be said of Ridley that he coveted his neighbour's wife. He was more than happy that Richard Fielding should live with Elspeth Fielding, sleep with her, be the father of her children and be first in her heart so long as he, Gloster Ridley, was free to call on her whenever he pleased, talk to her, confide in her, and enjoy the solace of her presence. He kissed her on her birthday, on Christmas, and on New Year's Eve, and was never ambitious to do more. Yet he loved her more truly than many men love their wives, and she and her husband both knew it. He loved her because she was beautiful, wise and kind; he also loved her because she was married, safe and would never want him to do anything about it. Such affairs are by no means uncommon nor, whatever the young may think, are they despicable.

'Wonderful stuff, Humphrey, wonderful!' said Mr Fielding, as the schottische came to a rousing finish. 'You ought to make a collection of things like that.'

'Nobody wants them,' said Cobbler. 'Music is a serious business. You may publish collections of literary oddities, but nobody wants musical oddities.'

'Then why not a concert? That's the idea! You could tour, playing a programme of forgotten Victorian music.'

'Not enough people want to hear it. And rightly so, I suppose. It's trash, though fascinating trash. It's the trashy art of an age which gives us its real flavour, far more than its handful of masterpieces. Don't you agree?' He turned his black eyes suddenly on Miss Vyner.

'Haven't a clue,' said that lady, morosely.

'But this is authentic Canadiana,' said Cobbler, 'A suite of dances, composed in this very city in 1879 and dedicated to the Marchioness of Lorne. Title: *The Fur Suite*. I've played the *Mink Schottische*. I can give you the *Beaver Mazurka*, the *Lynx Lancers*, the *Chinchilla Polka* or the *Ermine Redowa*. Every one of them re-creates the loyal gaiety of Victorian Canada. You name it; I've got it. What'll it be?'

Miss Vyner said nothing, but gave him the look of bleak, uncomprehending boredom which the unmusical wear when they are trapped among musicians. Mr Fielding elected for the *Ermine Redowa*, and quickly its solemn but scarely sensuous strains filled the room. Ridley sighed audibly.

'Why don't you talk, if you want to?' said Mrs Fielding.

Ridley muttered and made a gesture toward the piano.

'Oh, that's not the kind of music you have to be quiet for. Dick and Humphrey will be at it all night. What's bothering you?'

'I was followed here tonight by Professor Vambrace. I really think he's off his head. He was lurking near my door, pretending to be a solicitor for the Salvation Army,' said Ridley. And at some length, and with the sort of anguished exaggeration which he could use when talking to Mrs Fielding, but which was denied him otherwise, he told the story of his afternoon. Mrs Fielding was sympathetic, asked a great many questions, and they became so absorbed in their talk that they did not notice that the *Ermine Redowa* had finished, and that they had the full attention of the others until Miss Vyner spoke.

'Well, I suppose you have to expect that kind of thing with newspapers,' said she. 'I'm not a socialist, thank God, but I'd like to see the newspapers taken over by the Government. Or a strong control put on them, anyhow. They need some responsibility knocked into them.'

Miss Vyner was looking for a fight. She was a lady with a

large stock of discontent and disapproval always on hand, which she could apply to any question which presented itself. She had been a guest in the Fieldings' house for three days, and its atmosphere of easy-going happiness grated on her. She knew that Ridley was a special friend of her sister and brother-in-law and she felt that for the good of everyone she should insult him. But Ridley was not in a mood for further insult that day.

'Quite possibly you are right,' said he. 'But what you would get then would not be newspapers free of error, or newspapers edited according to some splendid principle, but gazettes of fact, probably no better authenticated than the facts in newspapers at present. You see, newspapers are written and edited by journalists, and journalists are rather special people. Drive them out of the newspaper offices, and send in civil servants to replace them, and I do not think you would like the result.'

'I haven't noticed anything very special about the journalists I've met,' said Miss Vyner.

'Perhaps not, but why should you? Nevertheless, a journalist is not something which just happens. Like poets, they are born. They are marked by a kind of altruistic nosiness.'

'That's what I don't like about them,' said Miss Vyner. 'They're always poking their noses into what doesn't concern them.'

'Certainly. But they also poke their noses into what concerns everybody. This nose-poking isn't something you can turn on and off like electricity. If you want the benefit of what journalists do, you must put up with some of the annoyance of what they do, as well.'

'Of course you have to stick up for them, I suppose. That's how you get your bread-and-butter.'

'Yes, and I like getting my bread-and-butter that way. I like being a journalist and a nose-poker. I like it not only because I am made that way, but because journalism is one of the few jobs which has been able to retain most of its original honesty about itself.'

'Don't let Pat bother you,' said Mrs Fielding, who

thought that her sister was being surly. 'We all know that journalism is a very honourable profession.'

'Excuse me, Elspeth,' said Ridley, 'but I don't like to hear it called a profession. That word has been worked to death. There are people in the newspaper business who like to call it a profession, but in general we try not to cant about ourselves. We try not to join the modern rush to ennoble our ordinary, necessary work. We see too much of that in our job. Banking and insurance have managed to raise themselves almost to the level of religions; medicine and the law are priesthoods, against which no whisper must be heard; teachers insist that they do their jobs for the good of mankind, without any thought of getting a living. And all this self-praise, all this dense fog of respectability which has been created around ordinary, necessary work, is choking our honesty about ourselves. It is the dash of old-time roguery which is still found in journalism—the slightly raffish, *déclassé* air of it—which is its fascination. We still live by our wits. We haven't bullied and public-relations-agented the public to the point where they think that we are gods walking the earth, and beyond all criticism. We are among the last people who are not completely, utterly and damnably respectable. There is a little of the Old Adam even in the dullest of us, and it keeps us young.'

'That's what I like to hear,' said Cobbler, and played an Amen on the piano. 'That's what's wrong with my job, too, you know. Too much talk about the nobility of it, and how the public ought to get down on its knees before the artist simply because he has the infernal gall to say that he *is* an artist, and not enough honest admission that he does what he does because that is the way he is made. My life,' he declared, rolling his eyes at Miss Vyner, 'is a headlong flight from respectability. If I tarted up in a nice new suit and a clean collar, I could spend hours and hours every week jawing to Rotary Clubs about what a fine thing music is and how I am just as good as they are. I'm *not* as good as they are, praise be to God! As a good citizen, I am not fit to black their boots. As a child of God, I sometimes think I have a considerable bulge on them, but I'm probably wrong. Sometimes I have a nightmare in which I dream that I have gone to heaven, and as I creep toward the Awful Throne I am blinded by the array of service-club buttons shining on the robe of the Ancient of Days. And then I know that my life has been wasted, and that I am in for an eternity of Social Disapproval. Wouldn't it be an awful sell for a lot of us—all the artists, and jokers, and strivers-after-better-things—if God turned out to be the Prime Mover of capitalist respectability?'

His eye was still upon Miss Vyner, who was uncomfortable. She never thought about God, herself, but she had a sleeping regard for Him, as a Being who thought very much as she herself did, though more potently. Dragging God into a conversation embarrassed her deeply. The organist continued.

'Your story fascinates me. Particularly the part about Vambrace playing sleuth. That explains what he was doing out in the street when I came here, dolled up like a race-track tout. It never struck me that he was avoiding notice. Quite the most eye-taking figure in town tonight, I would have said.'

'It's the engagement that interests me,' said Mrs Fielding. 'Of course I saw the piece in the paper; I never miss them. I thought it a splendid match. Solly needs a wife dreadfully, if only to get away from his mother, and Pearl is a dear child, and a great beauty as well.'

This comment made Ridley and Fielding start.

'A great what?' said her husband. 'Why, the girl looks as if she had been dragged backward through a hedge.'

'I haven't seen her in some time,' said Ridley, 'but it certainly never occurred to me that she had any looks.'

'That's because you are both getting a little old,' said Mrs Fielding. 'When a man doesn't notice that a girl under thirty has any looks, just because she is a little rumpled and doesn't know how to present herself, he is far gone in middle age. That's why men like you take up with obvious, brassy little blondes, when you take up with anything at all. You can't see real beauty any more. Give me Pearl Vambrace and five hundred dollars, for a week, and I will show you a beauty that will make even your eyes pop. She's quite lovely.'

'Elspeth and I never agree about looks,' said Mr Fielding. 'She's always pretending to see beauty that I can't see. Now my idea of a real beauty is Griselda Webster.'

'Very nice, I grant you,' said Cobbler, 'but I agree with your wife. The Vambrace girl has something very special. Mind you, I don't mind 'em a bit tousled,' said he, and grinned raffishly at Miss Vyner, who was, above all things, clean and neat, though she tended to smell rather like a neglected ash-tray, because of smoking so much. 'This business of good grooming can be carried too far. For real attraction, a girl's clothes should have that lived-in look.'

'I suppose you really like them dirty,' said Miss Vyner.

'That's it. Dirty and full of divine mystery,' said Cobbler, rolling his eyes and kissing his fingers. 'Sheer connoisseurship, I confess, but I've always preferred a bit of ripened cheese to a scientifically packaged breakfast food.'

Miss Vyner found herself without a reply. She felt, though no socialist, that a man who talked like Cobbler ought to be taken over by the Government, and taught responsibility.

'Unfortunately, there appears to be no question of this suitable match coming off, Elspeth,' said Ridley; 'and meanwhile I am in very hot water, and I am not even sure that I can leave this house without having trouble with Vambrace. I had to run the last few yards in order to get here at all.'

'I thought that was what you liked,' said Miss Vyner. 'From what you said just now I thought you wanted to go back to the days when editors were horsewhipped by people they had injured.'

'But as you doubtless overheard me saying to Elspeth, I have not injured the Professor. Somebody else has injured him, using my paper. If I am to be horsewhipped, I at least want to have my fun first.'

'I have to go now,' said Cobbler. 'I'll lure the Professor away.'

Ridley protested, for he did not like Cobbler, and certainly did not want to be under an obligation to him. The editor was ready to play the raffish journalist in order to annoy Miss Vyner, but the genuine raffishness of Humphrey Cobbler disturbed him. But it was impossible to shake the organist's determination, and when at last he left the house even Miss Vyner joined the other three in peeping through the window curtains, to see what he would do.

PROFESSOR VAMBRACE, cold and cross, was leaning against a tree in the park which was on the other side of the street from the Fieldings' house. To be fair to him, he would not have been noticed by anyone who was not on the lookout for him. He saw Cobbler hurry down the walk, cross the street until he was standing at the edge of the park directly in line with himself. And then Cobbler began to dance, and to sing in a very loud voice:

> *This is the way to the Zoo, the Zoo,*
> *The Zoo, the Zoo, the Zoo;*
> *The monkey cage is nearly full*
> *But I think there's room for you;*
> *And I'll be there on Saturday night*
> *With a bloody big bag o' nuts—*
> *NUTS you bastard!*
> *NUTS you bastard!*
> *Bloody big bag o' nuts!*

The Professor attempted to creep away unseen among the trees, but even he could not deceive himself that the song was not an aggressive act of derision, aimed at himself. And all his detective enthusiasm melted from him, leaving him naked to his own scorn. For the Professor, who was immoderate in self-esteem, was similarly immoderate in his condemnation of himself, and as he strode swiftly toward his home he hated himself as a buffoon who had spent an evening, ridiculously dressed, stumbling among garbage cans,

skulking among trees, and spying on people who had, unquestionably, spent the whole evening comfortably indoors,
laughing at him. Not only was it bitter to be mocked; it was
worse still to feel that he was worthy of mockery.

DUTCHY AND Norm were a little surprised that their party
ended so soon. But immediately after refreshments had been
served the guests showed a restless eagerness to leave, ex-
cepting Jimmy the dentist and one or two others whose
thirst for organized Whee was not fully slaked. Solly and
Pearl spoke in undertones over their coffee.

'Come on. I'll take you home.'

'You will not.'

'Don't argue. Get your things.'

'Don't speak to me like that. I'll go by myself.'

'And chance what Dutchy will have to say about it? You
come with me. I've got to talk to you.'

'I don't want to talk to you.'

'Yes you do. Don't be a fool. We've got to get together
about this thing or we'll never hear the end of it.'

'I can't go with you. I don't want to see you, ever again.'

'I know all that. But we've got to leave this place together. Please.'

And so they left the party as quickly and unobtrusively
as they could, and Solly helped Pearl into his tiny Morris
quite as though they wanted to be together.

'Now,' said Solly, when they had gone a short distance,
'I suppose you don't know anything about all this?'

'Of course I don't,' said Pearl. 'How would I?'

'I didn't suppose you did. But before I can do anything
about it myself I have to be quite sure.'

'Before you do anything about it?'

'Yes. Didn't it occur to you that I might want to contradict that notice?'

'Surely I am the one to do any contradicting that is done.'

'Why, precisely?'

'Well—because I'm the one that's been dragged into this
mess.'

'Why you more than me?'

'Because——' Pearl was about to say 'because I'm a girl,' but she felt that such a reason would not do for the twentieth century. There was a short silence.

'I think that you had better get things straight,' said Solly. 'You haven't been dragged into the mess any more than I have. And I am every bit as anxious to contradict this story as you are.'

Pearl was surprised to feel herself becoming angry. It is one thing not to want to marry a young man; it is quite another thing to find that the young man is offended that people should think he wants to marry you. She sat up very straight and breathed deeply through her nose.

'There's no sense snorting about it,' said Solly. 'And you needn't expect me to be gallant about it, either. This damned thing has put me in a very queer position, and God only knows what will be the upshot of it. It could very easily ruin everything for me.' He frowned over the wheel at the dark street.

'You mean when Griselda Webster hears about it?' said Pearl, in a well-simulated tone of polite interest.

'Yes. That's what I mean,' said Solly. 'Though what you know about it, or how it concerns you, I don't understand.'

'I only know what everybody knows. Which is that you have been hounding Griselda for the past three years; and that on her long list of suitors you rank about fifteenth; and that now she is in England you write to her all the time, and even take her little sister Freddy for drives to get the news of Griselda that she doesn't trouble to write to you. And as for how it concerns me, well—I am sure Griselda will hear it from somebody, by air-mail, probably the day after tomorrow, and she will be glad because it will relieve her of the nuisance of thinking she has blighted your life. However, if it will relieve your mind, I will write to her myself, and tell her that you are still her faithful slave, and that contrary to public report, I haven't stolen you away from her.'

'You!' said Solly, with so much scorn and horror and—

worst of all—amazement, that Pearl was goaded beyond bearing.

'Yes—me!' she shouted.

By this time they had reached the Vambrace home, and by unlucky chance Solly stopped his car just as the Professor was about to open his front gate. Her father heard Pearl's indignant shout, and in an instant he had pulled open the door of the Morris and, bending more than double from his great height, thrust his head into it.

'What does this mean?' he demanded.

Solly was weary of feminine illogicality, and was delighted to see a fellow man, with whom he could argue in a reasonable manner.

'Professor Vambrace,' said he, 'I've been wanting to see you. Pearl seems to have some very queer ideas about this mix-up—you know, this newspaper nonsense—and I think we ought to get together and straighten matters out.'

'Do you so!' roared the Professor, in such a voice that the whole body of the tiny car hummed with the sound. 'Is it get together with you, you sneaking little cur? There's been too much getting together with you, I see! Get out o' that contraption!'

This last remark was addressed to his daughter.

'Daddy,' said she, 'there's been a mistake——'

'Get out of it!' roared the Professor. 'Get out of it or I'll pick you out of it like a maggot out of a nut!' And with these words he brought his stick down on the roof of the Morris with such force that he dented it badly and smashed his treasured blackthorn to splinters.

'Daddy,' said Pearl, 'please try to understand and be a little bit quiet. Everybody will hear you.'

'What do I care who hears me? I understand that you sneaked out of my house tonight, like a kitchen maid, to meet this whelp, to whom you have got yourself clandestinely engaged.'

'We're not engaged,' shouted Solly. He was badly frightened by the Professor, but a shout was the only possible tone in which this conversation could be carried on.

'You're coupled in the public mouth,' roared Vambrace.

'We're not coupled anywhere, and never intend to be!'

'Do you dare to say that to my face?'

'Yes, I do. And stop banging on my car.'

The Professor was now quite beyond reason. 'I'll bang on what I choose,' cried he, and began a loud pummelling on the roof. Whereupon Solly, who was not without resource, leaned on the horn and delivered such a blast that even the Professor was startled. He seized Pearl by the shoulder.

'Get out,' said he. And he pulled at her coat so sharply that she fell sideways out of the car on to the pavement. Solly leaned forward.

'Have you hurt yourself?' said he. 'Can I help you?'

It was involuntary courtesy, but it was like gasoline on the flame of the Professor's wrath. Gallantry before his very eyes! The product of who knew what shameless familiarity! He stooped and jerked Pearl to her feet.

'You dirty little scut!' he cried. 'Roaring drunk in the car of the one man you should be ashamed to see! God!'

And he pushed Pearl toward the gate, and as she fumbled with the latch, he cuffed her shrewdly on the ear.

The quietest, but most terrible sound in this hurly-burly was Pearl's sobbing as she ran up the path. Solly started his car with a roar.

HALF AN HOUR later, the Professor sat in his study, white with anger. In the circumstances he should have been drinking whisky, but there was never any whisky in the house, and he had made himself some wretched cocoa, that being the only drink he could find. His thoughts were incoherent, but very painful. He had played the fool all night; he had been bested. Yet unquestionably he was right—the only person connected with this villainous business who was right. He hated Pearl who, he was now convinced, was no longer pure, perhaps—O torturing thought!—no longer a virgin; certainly no longer his little girl. He had struck her! Struck her, like any bog-trotting peasant beating his slut of a daughter. And it was all for love of her.

The Professor was suddenly, noisily sick, and then, in the silence of his ugly house, he wept.

SOLLY CREPT quietly into his mother's house, removed his shoes, and crept past his mother's bedroom door to the attic where his living-room and bedroom were. Quickly he made himself ready for bed, and then, from inside a folio copy of Bacon's *Works*, where he fondly hoped that his mother would never think of looking, he brought out his photograph of Griselda Webster. It was of her as she had appeared as Ariel in *The Tempest*. Stealthily he mixed himself a drink of rye and tap-water, and sat down in his armchair for his nightly act of worship. But as he gazed at Griselda, the sound of Pearl Vambrace, weeping, persisted in his ears. He thought it the ugliest sound he had ever heard, but none the less disturbing. He should have done something about that.

PEARL WAS still weeping, but silently, when dawn came through her window. She felt herself to be utterly alone and forsaken, for she knew that she had lost her father, more certainly than if he had died that night.

PART FOUR

THERE ARE not many people now who keep up the custom of At Home days, but Mrs Solomon Bridgetower had retained her First Thursdays from that period, just before the First World War, when she had been a bride. Without being wealthy, she had a solid fortune, and it had protected her against changing customs; this made her a captain among those forces in Salterton which sought to resist social change, and every First Thursday a few distinguished members of this brave rearguard were to be found in her drawing-room, taking tea. At half-past three on the First Thursday in November tea had not yet appeared, but Miss Pottinger and Mrs Knapp, the Dean's wife, were seated on a little sofa at one side of the fire, and Mrs Bridgetower, regally gowned in prune silk, with écru lace, sat in her armchair on the other. The atmosphere, though polite, was not easy.

'It seems perfectly clear to me,' Miss Pottinger was saying, 'that the two events are linked. Both happened on Hallowe'en, and both concern the Cathedral. Then why should we not assume that both spring from the same brain?'

'But as we do not know what brain it was, what good can it do us to assume anything of the sort?' said Mrs Bridgetower, who had been highly educated, and would undoubtedly have had a career of some kind if she had not relinquished it to be all in all to the late Professor; the consciousness of this education and this possible career led her, in all but the most intimate circumstances, to talk in a

142

measured, ironical tone, as though her hearers were half-witted.

'If everyone told everything they knew, we wouldn't be in doubt for long,' said Miss Pottinger. This dark comment was directed at Mrs Knapp, a small, rather tremulous lady who tried to follow her husband along the perilous tightrope of urbanity.

'I'm quite sure you're right,' said she, 'and I am sure that the Dean would dearly love to know who put that false engagement notice in the paper. He was dreadfully angry about it. But he has never suggested that Mr Cobbler had anything to do with it.'

This was not pedantically true, for the Dean had said to her many times that he hoped to heaven Cobbler had nothing to do with it, for it would mean firing him, and the Dean wanted to keep his excellent organist as long as Cathedral opinion would permit. But Mrs Knapp was on thin ice, and she knew it.

'I happen to know that Mr Snelgrove has told the Dean that he thinks it was Cobbler,' said Miss Pottinger sharply, for she thought it ill became a Dean's wife to palter with the truth, and she suspected, quite rightly, that the Dean told his wife everything. Loyalty between husbands and wives appeared to Miss Pottinger only as a shabby betrayal of the female sex.

'If Mr Snelgrove has interested himself in the matter,' said Mrs Bridgetower, 'I am sure that we can leave it in his capable hands.'

'You mean that you don't intend to take any action yourself, Louisa,' said Miss Pottinger.

'I have not yet decided what I shall do,' said Mrs Bridgetower, with a reserved smile.

'You don't intend to take this lying down, I suppose?'

'I think you know that it is not my way to pass over a slight, Puss dear.'

'Well, it is now three days since that piece appeared, and your friends are wondering when you are going to declare yourself.'

'My friends need not be concerned; my real friends know,

143

I am sure, that I am not one to take hasty or ill-advised action in any matter. I have not the robust health which would permit me to scamper about the town, making useless mischief. Even if I had a temperament which took pleasure in it.'

In Mrs Bridgetower's circle, this was tough talk, and Miss Pottinger ground her false teeth angrily. But Mrs Knapp, who had known these ladies for a mere ten years or so, and was thus a virtual newcomer to Salterton society, interjected an unfortunate attempt to make peace.

'Oh, I am quite certain dear Auntie Puss has no such desire,' said she. 'We all know that her intentions are of the very best.' Then, catching the lightning from Miss Pottinger's eye, she subsided with an exhalation which was meant to be a social laugh, and sounded like fright.

'I suppose I am old-fashioned,' said Miss Pottinger, 'but I still do not see why sacrilege and assaults on people's good names should be passed over without a thing being done. You have a phlegmatic temperament, Louisa, and are perhaps too ill to care what goes on, but I would have thought that Solly would have had something to say for himself by this time.'

'My son has faith in my judgment,' said Mrs Bridgetower.

'Of course, but a man with any real gimp in him would have done something before he had had time to talk to you.'

This was insufferable! Mrs Bridgetower moved into action, which, in her case meant that she relaxed in her chair, allowed her heavy lids to drop a little farther over her eyes, and smiled.

'And what would he have done, Puss, pray? Would he have rushed to Mr Cobbler, and struck him in the face? To have suspected Mr Cobbler in this matter he would have had to take guidance from you, for you seem to be the one who wants to hang Mr Cobbler's hide on the fence, as the boys used to say when we were young. And I do not think that it has ever occurred to Solomon to consult you in any matter, particularly. And a certain gallantry which you, dear, might not appreciate, forbids a man to deny in the open market-place that he is engaged to a girl after such a report, without knowing precisely what he is doing. There are still gentlemen in the world, Puss, whatever our experience may have been.'

This was dirty fighting indeed, and referred to the sudden disappearance, many years before, of a man who, without being actually engaged to Auntie Puss, had put that lady into a mood to accept him if asked. Pouring salt into wounds was a specialty of Mrs Bridgetower's, and the older the wound was the better she liked it.

Auntie Puss took refuge in hurt feelings. Her chin quivered and she spoke in a tremulous voice. 'If you don't take care, Louisa, that is all there is to be said about it. My concern was for you, and for the good name of the Cathedral. A soldier's daughter probably sees these things differently from most people.'

'I think that even a soldier's daughter should know who the enemy is before she fires,' said Mrs Bridgetower who, as a women herself, set little store by wobbling chins and tearful voices in others. She might have gone on to demolish Auntie Puss completely if, at this moment, reinforcements had not arrived in the person of Mrs Roger Warboys. Because of her connection with *The Bellman* it was impossible to say at once if she were friend or foe, and all the time which was occupied by bringing in the tea, and pouring it out, and passing thin bread and butter, was needed before it became perfectly clear that Mrs Warboys had come expressly to talk about the great scandal, and that she was on the side of those whose privacy and inmost feelings had been so grossly violated.

Mrs Warboys' position was a peculiar one, distinguished by many interesting shades of feeling, and she enjoyed it very much in a solemn, stricken way. She felt a family loyalty to *The Bellman*, of course. She thought a newspaper a powerful influence in a community and a great trust; she yearned to see *The Bellman* conducted according to the highest standards of journalism, as she conceived them. She had repeatedly impressed these views of hers upon her father-in-law, Mr Clerebold Warboys, who—although she was the last one to say a word against the late Roger's father—paid no attention to them. If she could, only for a month, have a free hand at *The Bellman*, it would be a very different paper thereafter. Some heads would roll, and although she named no names, certain powerful editorial influences would be removed. She was humiliated by the incident of the false engagement notice, and had come to Mrs Bridgetower's First Thursday most unsure of her welcome. She appreciated perfectly how she would feel herself, if she were in Mrs Bridgetower's position, but she did not wish to lose friends over a matter which she had been powerless to prevent, but which she might be able to amend.

She permitted all of these admissions to be wormed out of her, as it were unwillingly, with Auntie Puss as chief inquisitor, and gained immense moral prestige by fouling her own nest, which was a situation especially congenial to her temperament. She might have been some noble-minded Russian who had, at immense personal risk, escaped to give aid to the democracies.

As Mrs Warboys was basking in her glory, the doorbell rang, and the elderly maid admitted Mrs Swithin Shillito, who was accompanied by Mr Bevill Higgin.

'Dear Louisa,' said the old lady, 'I hoped that I might introduce Mr Higgin to you, for I know you have so much in common, and as he is still a stranger in Salterton—'

'But of course,' said Mrs Bridgetower. 'It is rarely nowadays that I see gentlemen at my Thursdays, and so Mr Higgins is doubly welcome.'

'I am honoured,' said Mr Higgin, bowing, 'to meet a lady of whom I have heard so much. The name is Higgin, *without* the "s". Yes.' And Mr Higgin was introduced to everyone and was very much at ease, rather like an indifferent but experienced actor in a comedy by Pinero. At last he seated himself on a low pouffe next to his hostess, and looked rather like a pixie on a toadstool.

'And where are you living in Salterton, Mr. Higgin?' said Mrs. Bridgetower, after some general conversation.

'For the time being I have taken rooms, rather in the north of town,' said he.

'With some people called Morphew,' said Mrs. Shillito.

'I don't know anyone called Morphew,' said Mrs Bridgetower.

'I'm sure you don't,' said Mr Higgin. 'They are a very good sort of people in their way, and I am very comfortable there, but it is not the sort of place in which one would wish to stay indefinitely. But until I have acquired some pupils, and have had an opportunity to look round for a bachelor flat, with a studio, it will do very nicely.'

And then, without much prompting, he told the company that he taught singing and elocution, and Mrs Shillito said all the complimentary things about his abilities which he wanted said, but which he could not suitably say himself.

'Connection is everything, of course, for an artist like Mr Higgin,' said that lady, 'but it takes time to meet the right people.'

'Less so, perhaps, in a university town than elsewhere,' said Mr Higgin, with a bow which included all the ladies. 'And in a young country, so avid for culture as Canada I hope that it will not take me too long to make my way.'

'I have been urging Mr Higgin to seek some connection with the Cathedral,' said Mrs Shillito. 'Perhaps, Mrs Knapp, you can tell us if there is any part of the musical service in which Mr Higgin's talents could be of use?'

Mrs Knapp said that Mr Cobbler looked after everything of that kind.

'Oh, my dear, you are too modest,' said Mrs Shillito, who was a rosy, round little old lady, got up in grey and purple and, like her husband, English with the peculiar intensity of English people abroad. 'We all know how musical Mr Dean is, and I am sure that Mr Cobbler does nothing except on his advice.'

'I have been trying to see Mr Cobbler,' said Higgin, 'but he is a very elusive man.'

'He may soon be downright missing, if I am any judge,' said Miss Pottinger, who had been seething for some time. Mrs Bridgetower's opposition to her conviction that Cobbler was at the root of the great scandal had served only to intensify her certainty of his guilt.

This pregnant remark brought the conversation back to

the great theme again, and as Mr Higgin was acquainted with it, having heard much about it from the Shillitos, he was able to enter into it with some spirit, though modestly, as befitted a newcomer. He listened with wide-open blue eyes, and said 'Oh!' and 'Ah!' with the right amount of horror at the right places.

'If I may venture to say so,' said he, smiling at all the ladies in turn, 'I think that it will not be at all easy to get satisfaction from Mr Ridley. I have only met him once, of course, but he seemed to me to be a very saturnine kind of man.' And he told the tale of his visit to Ridley, under the wing of Mr Shillito; and, as he told it, it appeared that Ridley had shown a strongly Philistine attitude toward the cultural advancement of Canada, and the improvement of *The Bellman*. He told his story so well, and imitated Ridley so drolly, that it made the ladies laugh very much, and gave particular satisfaction to Mrs Warboys.

'When I think of him sitting there, without a word to say for himself, and snapping at the air with those scissors,' said Higgin, 'I really can't help smiling, though I assure you it was rather embarrassing at the time.'

This lead to further discussion of Ridley, whose eccentricities, habits of cooking, and single state were all thoroughly rehearsed.

'Perhaps it is as well that he never married, if he is so disagreeable,' said gentle little Mrs Knapp.

'Is it widely believed that he is unmarried?' said Higgin, with a very knowing look.

'Why, whatever do you mean by that, Mr Higgin?" said Mrs Knapp.

'Perhaps I'd better say no more—at present,' said Higgin, leaving Mrs Knapp most unsatisfied, and the other ladies even more incensed against Ridley for daring to have a secret, though they admired Mr. Higgin for his discretion in not explaining it, to the only one of their number who did not know it.

'And that is the man,' said Auntie Puss, 'to whom Waverley thinks of giving an honorary degree! Strange days we live in.'

'Because of Swithin's association with him—his strictly professional association, I should say—it would ill become me to comment on *that* matter,' said Mrs Shillito. 'But I would have thought that the University would have wanted its new course in journalism to be formed by those with a— shall I say?—more literary approach to the matter? Writing —the light touch—the formation of a style—you know the sort of thing I mean.'

They all knew. It meant Mr Shillito, and whimsical little essays about birdseed and toothpicks.

'The degree has not been conferred yet, or even formally approved,' said Mrs Warboys, in a marked manner. And as everyone present knew, or thought they knew, that she had several members of the University Board of Governors in her pocket, this was a great stroke, and brought forth a good deal of murmuring and head-nodding.

The tea, and the thin bread and butter, and the little cakes, and the big cake, having been pretty well disposed of by this time, it was a pleasant diversion when Mrs Shillito begged Mrs Bridgetower, as a personal favour to herself, to permit Mr Higgin to try her piano. This instrument, which was an aged Chickering, was a great ornament of the drawing-room, for its case was beautifully polished, and its top was covered with photographs in silver frames, and the late Professor Bridgetower's military medals, exhibited on a piece of blue velvet. Mrs Bridgetower graciously gave her consent.

'I hope that an artist like yourself will not be too critical, Mr Higgin,' said she. 'I do not play so much now as once I did, and it may not be completely in tune.'

With appropriate demurral, Mr Higgin sat down at the piano and struck a chord. It was not so much out of tune as out of voice. The sound board had split under the rigours of winter heating, and the old wires gave forth that nasal, twangling sound peculiar to senile pianos and Siamese cats. Some of the photographs jingled as well. But Mr Higgin dashed off a few brilliant arpeggio passages, and smiled delight at his hostess.

'May I give myself the pleasure?' said he. 'Oh, do say that I may.' And without waiting for further permission he began to play and sing.

It might be said of Mr Higgin that he brought a great deal to the music he performed—so much, indeed, that some composers would have had trouble in recognizing their works as he performed them. He had a surprisingly large voice for a small man, and he phrased with immense grandeur and feeling, beginning each musical statement loudly, and tailing off at the end of it as though ecstasy had robbed him of consciousness. He enriched the English language with vowels of an Italian fruitiness, so that 'hand' became 'hond', and 'God' 'Goad'. It was plain that he had had a lot of training, for nobody ever sang so by the light of Nature.

His first song, which was *Because* by Guy d'Hardelot, he sang with his eyes opening and closing rapturously in the direction of Mrs Bridgetower, in acknowledgment of her ownership of the piano. But when he was bidden to sing again he directed his beams at Auntie Puss.

'I should like to sing a little thing of Roger Quilter's,' said he, 'some lines of Tennyson.' And he launched into *Now Sleeps the Crimson Petal*. It is doubtful if, at any time in her life, anyone had sung directly at Miss Pottinger, and she was flustered in a region of her being from which she had had no messages for many years.

> *So fold thyself, my dearest one, and slip—*
> *Slip into my bosom, and be lost in me.*

Thus sang Mr Higgin, and in that instant Miss Pottinger knew that here was the man who must succeed Humphrey Cobbler on the organ bench at St Nicholas'.

'Sorry to be late, Mother,' said Solly, coming into the room. He caught sight of Mr Higgin, who was still at the piano, and frowned.

'My son, Mr Higgin, my great, grown-up boy,' said Mrs Bridgetower fondly.

'We have had the pleasure before,' said Mr Higgin, with what Solly thought an impudent grin.

Solly was always late for his mother's First Thursdays, and they kept up the pretence between them that it was pressure of university work which made him so. Very soon after his arrival the guests went home, well pleased with their afternoon's work. For they all thought that Mrs Warboys would see that the insufferable Gloster Ridley lost his job, and received no doctorate from Waverley. Miss Pottinger thought that she had done much to undermine Cobbler with Mrs Knapp and thus with the Dean. Mrs Knapp thought she had made it clear that the Dean exonerated Cobbler, and that this would divert the wrath of Miss Pottinger. Mrs Shillito thought that she had further ingratiated herself with Mrs Warboys, thus securing her husband's position. And they all felt that the matter of the great scandal had been brought somewhat nearer to the boil.

WHEN HER guests had gone a dramatic change came over Mrs Bridgetower. Solly had seen them to the door, and he returned to the drawing-room to find his mother, as he knew she would be, slumped from her splendidly relaxed but commanding position in her armchair, with her eyes closed, and her face sagging with fatigue.

'Do you want to go upstairs at once, Mother?'

'No, dearie, give me a moment. Perhaps I'd better have one of my white tablets.'

As he climbed the stairs her voice reached him again faintly. 'Bring me one of my little yellow pills too, from the table by my bed.'

'Don't you think it would be better to leave that until you are in bed? What about a dose of your medicine instead?'

'If you think so, dearie.'

In time Solly returned, and when the tablet and then the dose of medicine were taken with much histrionic disrelish, he took off his mother's shoes and put on her slippers, and covered her knees with a small tartan rug. She opened her eyes and smiled fondly upon him.

'Bad, bad little boy! Late again!'

'I had a lot of papers to mark Mother, and I simply had to get them done. Anyway, I knew you'd want to talk to your friends alone.'

'Friends, dear? What are friends compared with you? And I so much need someone to help me now, passing things and so forth. I wonder how much longer I shall be able to keep up my First Thursdays. They take so much out of me now.'

'No, no; you mustn't give them up. You must see people, you know. The doctor said you must keep up your interests.'

'You are my only real interest now, dear. If your father had lived—but it is useless to talk of what might have been. But I need you to help me. There was a gentleman here today. You should have been here to help entertain him.'

'It looked to me as though he were doing the entertaining.'

'Yes, dear, but suppose he had wanted to wash his hands? Who would have taken him?'

'If he needs to wash his hands in the course of an hour's visit he ought to stay at home. Or wear one of those things.'

'What things do you mean, dearie?'

'Those things soldiers wear when they're on sentry duty.'

'Don't be coarse, dear. I can't bear it.'

'Sorry, Mother.'

'So nice to have someone sing at one's Afternoon. It's been years since it happened. Such nice songs, too. Your father loved *Because*—

> *Because God made thee mine*
> *I'll cherish thee—*

I was terribly moved. Lovey—'

'Yes, Mother?'

'I think I could take a glass of sherry. Perhaps with a little something in it.'

Solly obediently brought a tray and gave his mother a

glass of dry sherry, in which he had put a generous dollop of gin.

'Thank you, dear. It takes away the taste of that horrid medicine.'

'Mother, how did that fellow Higgins get here?'

'Higgin, dear. No "s". Maude Shillito brought him.'

'Do you think he is the sort of person you ought to have in the house?'

'Whatever do you mean, dearie? Maude Shillito brought him.'

'I know, but the Shillitos know all kinds of terrible people. I've met Higgin before, and I thought he was an awful little squirt.'

'Please, lovey; you know how I dislike rough talk. Where did you meet him?'

'He hunted me up at the University. Wanted me to let him talk to my classes about how to speak English.'

'Well, lovey, from what you tell me about them, I think your classes might well have some instruction in how to speak.'

'That's not what the classes are for. And I can't bring in odd visitors just as I please. Anyway, he was terribly patronizing about it, and obviously thought I'd jump at the chance. I was a bit short with him.'

'Really, dear? Was that wise?'

'He rubbed me the wrong way. Talked as if we were a lot of barbarians out here.'

'We must learn all that we can from Older Civilizations, lovey.'

'Just what Older Civilization does Higgin represent? Second-rateness comes out of his pores like a fog. There's something disgusting about him.'

'Dearie, you are speaking of a gentleman who was introduced into our home by an old and valued friend. I don't know why you are so severe on English people, dear.'

'I'm not severe on English people, Mother, but I hate fourflushers, wherever they come from, and if Higgin isn't a fourflusher, I don't know one.'

'Let us not discuss it, dearie. When you are vehement you weary me, and I can't stand much more today. I think I could take another glass of sherry.'

STRENGTHENED BY two heavily spiked sherries, Mrs Bridgetower was able to go upstairs—'to tackle the stairs' as she gamely put it—moving upward very slowly, with Solly half-boosting, half-pulling, and with a rest at the landing. When at last they reached her room, he helped her to undress, for it was understood that the elderly maid had all she could do to clear up after the At Home.

There was no unseemliness in this assistance. Seated on her bed, Mrs Bridgetower undid various mysterious fastenings through her gown, and Solly was able to pull off her stockings and put on her bedsocks. Then she toiled to a hiding-place behind a screen, and herself struggled out of the remainder of her garments, returning at last in a voluminous bedgown. Solly gently boosted her into bed, in which he had already put a hot-water bottle, and propped her up on her pillows. When he had picked up the discarded clothing from behind the screen and put it away, Mrs Bridgetower was ready for her tray.

It was understood that there could be no proper dinner on First Thursdays, as the servant had burnt herself out in preparing dainties for tea. But from the kitchen Solly fetched two trays, upon which suppers consisting chiefly of tea debris had been arranged, and he sat in a chair with one, while his mother took the other in bed. With the sherry and two kinds of medicine mingling uneasily inside her, her appetite was capricious, and to use her own expression, she picked at her food. But her spirit appeared to be refreshed, for she attacked Solly on the subject which had been uppermost in her mind for three days.

'We must make some decision, dearie, about what we are going to do.'

'I suppose all those women talked about it all afternoon.'

'It is no good being resentful and childish. This is a serious matter, and we cannot dilly-dally any longer.'

'I think the best thing is to ignore it.'

'Your father certainly would not have thought so.'

'How can we tell what Father would have thought?'

'The enmity between us and Professor Vambrace was not of your father's choosing, but he never permitted Vambrace to get the better of him. We owe something to your father's memory.'

'Oh, Mother, let's talk sense. About three years ago I took Pearl Vambrace to the Military Ball. You had her here to dinner beforehand. You were very decent to her.'

'There was a very good reason why you took her. I don't entirely recall what it was, but there was something to do with that play—that one in which the Webster girl showed so much of her legs. I have no quarrel with Pearl Vambrace, poor creature. But her father is a very different matter. I will not have people thinking that we have knuckled under in that affair.'

'Oh, Mother, we can't go on fighting forever.'

'Who said anything about fighting? It has been publicly announced that you are engaged to Pearl Vambrace. You are nothing of the kind. Someone has done this for spite. And I think I know who it was.'

'Who?'

'Professor Vambrace himself. It's just the kind of crazy thing he would do. To make us look ridiculous.'

'You can't be serious. He couldn't do that to his own daughter.'

'Pooh, he could. She's completely under his thumb. And that poor Elizabeth Fitzalan that married him—utterly crushed. The man's insane. He did it. Within six months they'll have to put him away, you mark my words.'

'Mother, do you realize that Vambrace is threatening to sue *The Bellman?* He's telling it all over the campus, as a great secret. Everybody's talking about it. He says it's a plot to bring him into disrepute by associating his name with ours.'

'More madness! A great many people are very peculiar. Puss Pottinger is absolutely insane about that organist at the Cathedral—what's-his-name. She won't rest until she has taken his position from him. She thinks *he* put that piece in the paper.'

'Good God! Cobbler! What makes her think that?'

'Because there was some skylarking in the Cathedral on Hallowe'en and she is sure Cobbler was at the bottom of it. And if he was at the bottom of that, why shouldn't he have made other mischief the same day?'

'And does she call that logic?'

'Puss Pottinger doesn't know what logic is. But that's the kind of thinking that gets big rewards for detectives, whatever the mystery-writers may say about clues and deduction and all that rubbish. But I think she's wrong. Vambrace did it. I have more insight in my little finger than Puss Pottinger has in her whole body.'

Solly chewed wretchedly on a dry sandwich. He was thinking, as he had been thinking all day, of Pearl Vambrace running into her house, pursued by her father.

'Well, what do you think we ought to do?' he said at last.

'The dignified and sensible thing is for you to go to *The Bellman* and see this man Ridley. You must give him an announcement which he will insert, denying the report of the engagement and apologizing for having printed it. You must speak to him very firmly.'

'No good. Vambrace did that on Tuesday and Ridley flatly refused. So there's going to be a court action. That's the talk on the campus.'

'And what are the grounds of this court action to be?'

'Libel.'

'Libel? And where does the libel lie?'

'In suggesting that I am going to marry his daughter. Now, Mother, there's no use looking like that. That's what he says.'

'Libel! Libellous to suggest that you—'

Solly was very much alarmed, for it seemed that his mother might have a seizure. But anger is a powerful stimulant, and Mrs Bridgetower's wrath did her good. She seemed to drop twenty years before his eyes, and for ten minutes she called up the past iniquities of Professor Vambrace and uttered violent judgments on his present conduct. Her peroration was delivered in trumpet tones.

'Let him bring such a suit if he dare! We'll bring a counter-action! Libellous to suggest that you should marry his daughter! Calculated to bring him into shame and disrepute? We'll fight! We'll spend money like water! We'll break him, the old hound! Libellous to suggest that a Bridgetower would so lower himself! If there is any libel it is against us! But we'll fight, my boy, we'll fight!'

'Mother, please be calm. What's the good of saying we'll fight? We'll all look like fools, that's what we'll do.'

'How can you talk so? Puss Pottinger was right. You haven't any gimp!'

'All right, then, I haven't any gimp. But it seems to me that you and Vambrace have no thought for Pearl or me; you'd make us look like a couple of children in leading-strings.'

'You have a lot of consideration for Pearl Vambrace, I must say. More than you have for me, it seems. Nasty, scheming little thing!'

'Very well, then, leave Pearl out of it. What will I look like if you go to court to fight a counter-action against Vambrace's libel suit?'

'No, we will not leave Pearl out of it. It seems to me that you are very ready to fly to Pearl's rescue. Solly, tell me honestly, is there any crumb of truth in this report about you and Pearl?'

'If you aren't going to listen to my advice I don't think you can expect me to answer that question,' said Solly, and was quite as surprised as his mother to hear himself say so.

The dispute went on, without anything new being added to it, for another half-hour. It ended with Solly fetching five volumes of the *Encyclopaedia Britannica* to his mother's bedroom, so that she might read all that pertained to the law of libel. He also gave her her pink medicine, and arranged her reading light. Later details of washing and re-

157

moving her teeth would be attended to by the elderly maid. In spite of these filial acts there was a barrier between them, for Solly had created an uncertainty, and an uncertainty about Solly was something which his mother found frightening and intolerable. But she was so stimulated by hatred and the love of combat that she was able to retain some composure, and contented herself by saying that she hoped that in the morning he would be in a more reasonable frame of mind, and see things as she saw them. Thus he left her, and went upstairs to his attic study.

SOLLY'S FIRST act when he was in his own room was to take down Bacon's *Works* in order that he might refresh himself with a look at his photograph of Griselda Webster. It was not a particularly good photograph, but the eye of adoration could see much in it, and it had been his solace in every dark hour since Griselda herself, several months before, had gone to Europe to travel for an indefinite period. In the picture she appeared as Ariel, in *The Tempest,* an unquestionably beautiful girl, even in the tabby-cat greys of a poor photograph. He had other photographs of the Salterton Little Theatre's grand assault upon Shakespeare, hidden in other chapters of Bacon, but he did not look at them often, for his interest was in Griselda alone. But tonight he hunted them down in the large folio, supposing that in this way he was putting off the moment when he must settle down to his work. They looked like the photographs of almost any Little Theatre production; the cast had been taken in groups, some of the players self-conscious in costume and grinning at the camera, others keeping 'in character' with great ferocity, and acting very hard, though without movement. Griselda was in two or three of these, and the one for which he was looking showed her standing on a grassy mound, obedient to the command of Prospero, who was Professor Vambrace. At Prospero's side, but apparently unconscious of Ariel, stood Pearl Vambrace as Miranda.

She had looked well as Miranda, thought Solly. He had

to give her that. She stood well, and had dignity, and the dark stillness of her face suited the part. She was not to be compared with the wonderful Griselda, of course, for Griselda was a goddess. But as mortal women went, Pearl had good gifts. A pity they didn't show more in the costume of every day. And when he had last seen her, white with anger and nervous irritability, at the Yarrows, and then stumbling toward the Vambrace house, she had looked awful. As he thought about it, the sound of her miserable cries came into his ears again, and to rid himself of that memory he closed Bacon, and went to his desk to work.

A pile of fifty-two essays lay before him, in which First Year Science men had expressed their opinions on 'The Canterbury Pilgrims and their Modern Counterparts' or 'The Allegory of the Faerie Queene in Terms of Today'. Imposing as these titles were, and productive of large and learned books as they might be, First Year Science was expected to say what it had to say in not more than a thousand words, and to base its opinions on a small red book called *Magic Casements, Vol. 1: Beowulf to the Elizabethans;* nobody supposed for a moment that Science students had time or inclination to read and ponder Chaucer and Spenser at first hand: indeed, it went against the grain with Science students to bother with English at all.

Solly picked up the first essay, which was by Igor Kaczabowski, and read the first sentence: 'The poems of Geoffrey Chaucer are among the richest jewels of our British heritage. He was called the Father of English Poetry because everybody who came after him sprang from him. In an age of unbridled licence he was an honest civil servant and wrote many poems in his spare time of which the best known are *The Canterbury Tales, Toilus and Criseyde* and *The Treatise on the Astrolabe.* Couched as they are in what is to the modern reader virtually a foreign tongue we will go a long ways before we improve on his ability to size up our fellow man.'

Sighing, Solly tucked Kaczabowski into the middle of the pile, to come upon him as a surprise later on. Picking up another, from Jean Thorsen, he found another reference in the first paragraph to our British heritage, and a further hunt revealed that two more Scandinavians, a Pole and three Russian Jews had claimed Chaucer as their own. He was annoyed; lifting from *Magic Casements* was legitimate enough, all things considered, but he wished that they would read what they lifted with greater care and introduce a little artistry, some hint of individuality, into it. Nobody seemed to have tackled the problem of allegory in modern life, and he didn't blame them; *The Faerie Queene* had little to say to First Year Science.

He had lost the battle, he knew, the minute that he faltered with Kaczabowski; in marking essays the great thing is to go straight ahead, without deviation or consideration of personal taste. To admit that one paper might be more pleasing than another was to allow his critical powers to work on the wrong level; his job was to correct the grammar of First Year Science, and to untangle the more baffling syntactical messes; to begin thinking about Chaucer, or even common sense, was fatal. He pushed the heap of essays aside; if the worst came to the worst he could always award marks between B minus and C plus arbitrarily, and not give back the papers at all.

Our British heritage; what a lot was said about it in Canada, one way and another, and it always meant people like Chaucer and Spenser; it never seemed to mean people like Bevill Higgin who were, after all, more frequent ambassadors from the Old Country. He wished that he had not mentioned Higgin to his mother. But to find the little pipsqueak in the house, mooing Tennyson to all those old trouts in the drawing-room! He had thought himself rid of Higgin.

It was—how long?—three weeks at least since last he had seen him. Solly had been having a difficult morning; he had talked to First Year Science at eight o'clock, and at ten o'clock he had met another group who were getting a quick run through Our British Heritage; these were students of mature years, who had already taught in primary schools for some time and were getting university degrees in order that they might teach in high schools, and most of them were older than Solly. After his lecture one of these men, who was perhaps thirty-five, and had glasses and a bald spot, had approached him and said: 'Professor Bridgetower, I'm not getting anything out of your course; I don't mean anything personal, you understand, but frankly I don't think you have any pedagogical method; in our work, you know, pedagogical method is everything, and if you'd give me a little extra time on some of this Milton, why I'd be glad to give you some pointers on pedagogical method; as you explained to me, I could point out to you where you weren't doing it right, do you see?' Solly had rejected this kindly offer with abruptness, and had told the well-meaning fellow that a university was not an infant class, and that he was welcome to exercise his pedagogical method upon himself. But the student's words had hurt him; he knew that he was a bad teacher; he hated teaching; he shrank from eager minds, and was repelled by dull ones. It was with a sharp increase in his haunting sense of failure that he mounted the stairs to his office.

And there, in his office, where he had hoped to sit down and mope quietly about his failure, had been Bevill Higgin, who had introduced himself with the most ridiculous affectation of what he considered to be a university manner, and who had proposed that he, Solly, should permit Higgin to give readings from English poetry to his classes, in order, as Higgin put it, to give them the sonorous roll of the verse and to illuminate what had, it was implied, been presented to them in a dull and lifeless manner. To make his meaning perfectly clear he had declaimed a few lines of Satan's Address to the Sun, in an embarrassing, elocutionary manner, like a man trying out his voice in a bathroom.

It was a bad moment to approach Solly with such a scheme. He was conscious that he left much to be desired as a teacher of English; this point had just been rubbed into him by one of his own students who had—a final insult—meant it with sincere kindness. It was obvious that Higgin had approached him because he was the most junior member of the English staff, and thus, presumably, the easiest mark. He had sulked, and said that the thing was impossible.

161

And then, to his astonishment, Higgin had said, very confidentially, that he was on the lookout for pupils, and that if he drew any pupils from Solly's classes, he would be willing to remit to Solly one-half of their first month's payment for lessons.

Of course, Solly knew now, he should not have done what he did. But, in a mysterious way, the man offended his sense of propriety. It was not the offer of the kick-back on lessons—no, no, it was something that he had felt before Higgin got that far. It was, he supposed, a snobbish feeling. The little man was such a second-rater, such a squirt, such a base little creature. And so he had risen, and pushed Higgin toward the door, not hard or roughly, but just a good firm, directing push. He had said, he remembered, 'No soap!' which was a sadly unacademic remark, but the best that he could think of at the moment. And when Higgin was in the corridor he had slammed the door.

Undignified. Silly. But he was too disgusted with himself to think of what he was doing, and since that time he had thought little about the incident. But when he had met Higgin at Mother's At Home, there was no mistaking the look of malicious triumph on Higgin's face.

Solly tried to banish thoughts of Higgin by further work. Not intimate communion with the finer thoughts of First Year Science, but with his Grand Project, his Passport to Academic Preferment. From a shelf above his desk he took down a book bound in dingy brown cloth, upon the front of which, inside a border of ornamental stamping, was printed the title, *Saul*. Inside, on the title page was:

SAUL

A DRAMA

IN THREE PARTS

———————

Montreal

Henry Rose, Great St James Street

MDCCCLVII

This was it, the principal work of Canada's earliest, and

in the opinion of many people, greatest dramatist, Charles Heavysege. Had not Longfellow, moved by we know not what impulse, declared that Heavysege was the greatest dramatist since Shakespeare?

Solly had not been drawn toward Heavysege by any kinship of spirit. Heavysege had been given to him, with overwhelming academic generosity, by the head of the English Faculty, Dr Darcy Sengreen. He remembered the occasion vividly when, a few months before, Dr Sengreen had asked him to lunch. And, when they had eaten, and were sitting at the table from which everything had been removed but a bouquet of paper roses, Dr Sengreen had said: 'Now, Bridgetower, you've got to get down to work. What are you going to do?'

Solly had muttered something about having a lot to learn about lecturing and the preparation of his courses.

'Ah, yes,' Dr Sengreen had said, 'but that isn't enough, you know. You've got to get to work on something that will make your name known in scholastic circles. You've got to publish. Unless you publish, you'll never be heard of. You've nothing in mind?'

Solly had nothing in mind save apprehension as to what Dr Sengreen might say next.

'Well, if I were a young fellow in your position, I wouldn't hesitate for an instant. I'd jump right into Amcan.'

Solly knew that Dr Sengreen meant the scholarly disembowelling of whatever seemed durable in American-Canadian literature.

'Amcan's the coming thing, and particularly the Canadian end of it. But there isn't much to be done, and the field is being filled up very quickly. Now, I'll tell you what I'm going to do. I'm going to give you Heavysege.'

And half an hour later Solly had left Dr Sengreen's house carrying first editions of the two plays, the three long narrative poems, and the single novel of Charles Heavysege, which Dr Sengreen had let him have at the prices which they had cost him. And, within a week, he had written to

several learned papers asking for information about Heavysege, to be used in connection with a critical edition of that
author upon which he was at work. Not, of course, that he
expected any information, but this was a recognized way of
warning other eager delvers in the dustheaps of Amcan
that he had put his brand on Heavysege, had staked out a
claim on him, so to speak, and that anybody trespassing on
his property was committing an offence against the powerful, though unwritten, rules of academic research.

And here he was, landed with Heavysege. Within a year
at most Dr Sengreen would expect a learned and provocative article on Heavysege, from his pen, in some journal or
quarterly of recognized academic standing.

Amcan. A new field in literary study, particularly the
Can half. In twenty years they would be saying, 'Dr Bridgetower? The big man in the Heavysege field; yes, the collected edition is pretty much all his own work, you know,
though he let X and Y do the bibliography, and Z did
a lot of the digging on Heavysege's newspaper writings; yes,
a monument in Canadian scholarship; wonderful tribute to
old Darcy Sengreen in the general introduction, but the
dedication is "To my Mother, who first taught me to love
Amcan, *Si Monumentem requiris, circumspice*"; yes, one
of the very biggest things in Canadian literary studies.'
Holding the brown book in his hand, a sudden nausea
swept over Solly, and he gagged.

Why do countries have to have literatures? Why does a
country like Canada, so late upon the international scene,
feel that it must rapidly acquire the trappings of older
countries—music of its own, pictures of its own, books of
its own—and why does it fuss and stew, and storm the
heavens with its outcries when it does not have them?
Solly pondered bitterly upon these problems, knowing full
well how firmly he was caught in the strong, close mesh of
his country's cultural ambitions. Already he was being
asked for advice by hopeful creators of culture. Who was
that fellow, that reporter on *The Bellman,* who had been at

him only a few days ago? Bumble, was that his name? No; Rumball; that was it. Poor Rumball, toiling every spare minute of his time at what he was certain would be the great Canadian prose epic, *The Plain That Broke the Plough.*

Rumball had approached him with great humility, explaining that he had no education, and wanted to find out a few things about epics. Solly, capriciously, had said that he had more education than he could comfortably hold, and he was damned if *he* could write an epic. He had advised Rumball to model himself on Homer, who had no education either. He had expressed admiration for Rumball's theme. God knows it had sounded dreary enough, but Solly felt humble in the presence of Rumball. Here, at least, was a man who was trying to create something, to spin something out of his own guts and his own experience. He was not a scholarly werewolf, digging up the corpse of poor Charles Heavysege, hoping to make a few meals on the putrefying flesh of the dead poet.

But this was not getting anything done. He looked at his watch. Nine o'clock. He put *Saul* back on the shelf, removed his shoes and crept downstairs with them in his hand. Outside his mother's door he listened; though the light was still on, thin, tremulous snores assured him that she was asleep and would probably remain so for many hours. He stole down to the ground floor, shut himself into the telephone cupboard and dialled a number.

'Yes?'

'Is that you, Molly? It's Solly. Is Humphrey at home?'

'Yes.'

'May I come over? I need you.'

'Righto, ducks.'

IN THE dimness of *The Bellman's* news room a cone of light shone from above Henry Rumball's desk, illuminating his typewriter; Rumball, balancing on the back legs of his chair, gazed fixedly into the works of his machine, as though seeking inspiration. He was alone, having returned early from an entertainment given by a class of backward boys before a Home and School Club. He should have been thinking about the backward boys, but he was thinking about *The Plain That Broke the Plough.*

It was an epic, there could be no doubt about that. It seemed to become more epic every day. It swept on and on, including more and more aspects of life in the great Canadian West, until he was thoroughly astonished by it. He had read about this business of books getting away from their writers, taking their own heads, so to speak, but he was astonished to experience it himself. He was happily amazed at the wilfulness of his own creative mind; this ability to go on and on, without much effort or conscious control, certainly made him feel that he was, well, in the grip of a power greater than himself. It was humbling to feel so.... Now, about those backward boys—

But at this moment the footsteps and the rumblings of which he had been conscious at the back of his mind became fully audible, demanding attention, and Mr Shillito walked into the news room.

'Ah, good evening,' said he. 'Just out for a breather and thought I'd look in to see if anything was doing.'

He went to the city desk, rummaged among the papers on it, and looked at one or two copy-hooks, and then walked over to Rumball's desk and sat down familiarly on one corner of it.

'Knocking out your stint, I see,' he said. 'Good. Good. Always write your story while it's fresh in your mind; never leave it till tomorrow. What is it?'

'Backward boys, gym and handicraft display,' said Rumball.

'Hmph, yes; even that—do it while it's hot. Well, well; I'll push on. Always walk a mile or two every evening. Find some of my best ideas come to me then. I still carry a notebook, you know,' said Mr Shillito, with the arch manner of one confiding a surprising secret. 'A good phrase comes into my head while I'm walking, out comes the notebook, under a street lamp, and I pop it down. Then, in the morning, I look at the book and sometimes I find something already written in my head, ready to pop out when the right phrase calls it up. Strange how the writer's mind works.'

Rumball grunted. He did not like to think that Mr Shillito's mind worked along lines so closely resembling his own.

'Yes, it's all part of the romance of the craft. You're young in the craft, and I'm old in it—the greatest game in the world.' Mr Shillito's voice trembled with emotion. Then his mood became conspiratorial. 'Nothing new about the great mystery, I suppose?'

'Nothing that I've heard.'

'Wish that could be cleared up. It isn't good to have a thing like that hanging over a paper.'

'Oh, I don't know. It'll all come out in the wash.'

'I wouldn't say that, lad. No, I wouldn't say that.'

'Sure. A libel threat isn't anything. The lawyers will probably fix it up between them.'

'You think so?'

'Even suppose they don't, it couldn't cost the paper much. It's not serious libel, if it's libel at all. No court would give much in the way of damages on a thing like that.'

'It isn't the public result I'm thinking of. It's the secondary results. Here in the office, for instance. Some pretty big apples could be shaken from some pretty high branches.'

'You mean Boney?'

'Don't say I said so.'

'No, of course not. But Gee, Mr Shillito, what would bring it to that?'

'Towns like this, my boy, are very close-knit—at the heart, I mean. You may tread on some people's toes, and nothing will happen to you. But if you trouble the waters in the wrong quarter, you wish you hadn't. Divide families, turn father against daughter—that kind of thing—no good comes of it.'

'Father against daughter? You mean Vambrace and his daughter?'

'I shouldn't speak of it. Still—I saw what I saw. I'm an old man, and I've seen a good deal of life, but I'm still shocked, thank God, when I see a woman beaten.'

'Beaten! You mean Vambrace has been lighting into Pearl?'

'Did I say so? Well—off the record, mind—he was dragging, positively dragging her into the house. I was out in the garden calling Blue Mist, our Persian, and I saw most of it. And when I went out into the street, do you know what I found, Rumball?'

'What?'

'A blackthorn stick, broken right across. Right across, mind you. When you bring a white man to that pass, Rumball, you've got to answer for it.'

With his usual dramatic sense Mr Shillito rose from the desk, and went to the door, thoughtfully sweeping aside his ramshorn moustaches. Before leaving he fixed Rumball with a stern glance, and flourished his walking stick at him.

'Off the record, mind you,' he said, and was gone.

Once again Rumball was alone, peering into his typewriter. Was it up to him to do anything? He knew Pearl. Indeed, he admired her. He had first met her when he sought some information for TPTBTP (which was the cabbalistic way in which he thought of his book) in the Waverley Library. She had been very helpful and nice, and he had told her about the book. She had seemed interested. Lonely as he was, he had two or three times asked her if she would like to have a meal with him at the Snak Shak, and talk about TPTBTP, but she had always refused, though nicely. And so he had put her out of his mind. After all, he had to save himself for the book. But—beaten with a blackthorn stick! Should he do anything? And if so, what? Should he go to her in the morning, and offer himself for any service she might command? Pearl, in distress, seemed much more desirable and important than before.

But then, what about his duty to TPTBTP?

Professor Bridgetower ought to be considered, too. He was involved in the mess. And he was the first professor who had ever been human to Rumball. Usually, when Rumball was on the University beat, he called on a few professors who said 'Nothing today' as soon as he approached them.

But when he had wanted to talk to Bridgetower about his novel, Bridgetower had asked him to sit down, and had taken him seriously. A nice fellow. For his sake, as well as for Pearl's, something ought to be done. But what?

Much troubled, Rumball began to type: 'An audience which almost filled the gallery of the gymnasium of Queen Elizabeth School witnessed the annual display by the Opportunity Class on Thursday evening. . . .'

NORM AND Dutchy Yarrow lay happily in bed. Her head was snuggled on his breast, and his left arm held her close to him. A bedside lamp with a pink shade threw a rosy glow over the scene. They were deeply content, and almost asleep, until Dutchy spoke.

'Gee, it's wonderful to be so happy.'

'That's right, honey-bunch.'

'It just makes you sorry for everybody in the world that isn't as happy as we are.'

'That's a sweet thought, sugar.'

'It just breaks my heart, thinking about those two poor kids.'

'Certainly is tough for them.'

'D'you s'pose they'll ever have anything like this? D'you s'pose they'll ever be as happy and as close as we are, right this minute?'

Norm thought about it. He tried to imagine Pearl, lying beside Solly in the connubial bliss which enfolded Dutchy and himself. Somehow the vision did not seem quite right. Happy lovers very often feel the generous wish that others may be as happy as they, but it is only human to think that one has gone a little farther in this sort of happiness than others are likely to follow.

'Well, I don't know, sweetie. Happiness is a kind of a talent. And the physical relationship is a talent, too. Solly and Pearlie are both kind of nervous. I don't think their background is right for it. I mean, they could be happy, but as for being as happy as we are—well, that's expecting a lot.'

'I'll say so. I don't suppose anybody was ever as happy as I am right this minute.'

Far down in the bed, Norm tickled her with his toes. She tickled him with hers. They scuffled and giggled and kissed.

'See?' said Dutchy. 'Can you imagine Solly and Pearlie playing toesies? I just can't.'

'I don't know about that,' said Norm.' There's a touch of the gammon in Pearlie.'

'The what?'

'The gammon; it's a French expression for a delinquent girl. Still, you can't tell. There are people,' said Norm portentously, 'who never get any fun out of sex at all.'

'Oh sure, I know. Case histories. But you don't think they'll end up as a couple of case histories, do you?'

'Could happen. I mean, if it's true about Pearlie and her father.'

'Oh, Norm, don't you think there's been some mistake about that?'

'You ought to know. It was you that Jimmy phoned about it.'

'Yes. I just hate to believe it, but he phoned just as soon as Mrs Shillito was out of his office. She's the Vambrace's next-door neighbour, and she practically saw everything. And Jimmy told it to me just as she told it to him. She was in getting her lower plate tightened up a little bit, so she was able to talk all the time he was working on it. And she swears it's true.'

'She actually saw Vambrace break the stick over Pearlie's head?'

'Not over her head, her back.'

'Ah, well, psychologically that makes all the difference. I mean, even where on her back makes a difference. I mean, if he hit her over the shoulders it might have been just rage, but if he hit her over the fanny it was definitely sex.'

'You mean there's sex between Pearlie and her father?'

'Honey, you're a trained recreationist; you know that there's a lot of sex everywhere.'

'Oh, Norm, how awful. I mean, imagine!'

'Jimmy said Mrs Shillito actually saw it, did he?'

'No, her husband saw it. At least, he heard an awful noise, and went to his front door, and there was Vambrace walloping Pearlie with the stick. And a car was dashing away which must have been Solly's car, because he drove her home from here, remember? And old Mr Shillito ran out and found the stick, and it was one of those blackthorn sticks, smashed in two over Pearl's body. And you know what awful thorns those sticks have, and she was wearing just a thin dress and a short coat, so the lacerations must be something awful.'

'It makes you think, doesn't it? I mean, right here in Salterton, among university people—that kind of thing, that you only associate with case histories.'

'Norm, after a thing like that, do you suppose they could ever be really happy?'

'Well, I couldn't say, honey-bunch. But I'll go this far: it doesn't look too good.'

There was silence for a time, until Norm felt a wetness on his shoulder.

'Lambie-pie! What's the matter?'

'I just can't bear to think of those two having such a tough time, when we're so lucky!' And the good-hearted Dutchy sobbed loudly.

'Oh, honey, that's wonderful of you! Gee, that's just wonderful. Come on, now, cheer up. Give daddy a smile. Come on, just a little, teentsy-weentsy smile.'

'How can I smile when there's so much unhappiness in the world?'

'Well, take that attitude, peachie, and everybody would commit suicide. It's not normal to take other people's troubles so hard.'

'Yes, but Norm, these are people we *know*.'

'Well, now, you cheer up, honey, and we'll see what we can do.'

'Aw, Norm, do you really mean you can *do* something?'

'Well, for heaven's sake, isn't that our whole life? Isn't that what we're trained for?'

'You mean you think we could do some social engineering, and make everything jake for those two poor kids?'

'We can certainly try. Now it's plain that the place to relieve the pressure is with Professor Vambrace himself. His attitude simply isn't normal. I don't like to butt into a man's private life, but this thing is bigger than our personal feelings. I'll just have to go to him and explain to him what's biting him.'

'Oh, Norm! I think you're wonderful!'

'Yes, I'm going to have to explain to the Professor about the Oedipus Complex.'

'What's that?'

'It's rather a complicated concept. And, honey, I don't want to talk about it right now.'

'Gee, Norm, I think you're just the most wonderful person!'

'Don't wriggle around like that.'

'I'm going to get up and get us some coffee and stuff.'

'No, you're not.'

'You mean you don't want to eat?'

'Later.'

'Oh, Norm!'

THE COBBLERS lived in a row of small, impermanent-looking houses, all exactly alike and all—though not more than a few years old—with an air of weariness, like children who have never been strong from birth, and have a poor chance of reaching maturity. Molly Cobbler opened the door to Solly's knock, and in her usual silent fashion nodded to him to follow her upstairs.

When they entered the bedroom Humphrey Cobbler was invisible, but in the old-fashioned bed, shaped rather like an elegant sleigh, a heap of bedclothes showed that he was sitting up and bending forward, and a strong smell, and some very loud sniffings and exhalations, made it clear that he was inhaling the fumes of Friar's Balsam.

'Come along, now; you've had enough of that,' said his

wife, unveiling him. His mop of black curls was more untidy than ever, and the steam had given his face a boiled look.

'Bridgetower, you find me very low,' said he.

Solly said that he was sorry.

'I have a cold. It would be nothing in another man, but in me it is an affliction of the utmost seriousness. I cannot sing. Suppose I lose my voice entirely? I am not one of your fraudulent choirmasters who *tells* people how to sing; I *show* 'em. I'm at a very low ebb. Don't come near me, or you may catch it. You wouldn't like a precautionary sniff of this, I suppose?' He held out the steaming jug of balsam.

'I've brought you the only reliable cold cure,' said Solly, producing a bottle of rye from his pocket.

'Bridgetower, this is an act of positively Roman nobility. This is unquestionably the kind of thing that Brutus used to do for Marc Antony when *he* had a cold. God bless you, my dear fellow. We'll have it hot, for our colds. Molly, let's have hot water and lemon and sugar. Would you believe it, Bridgetower, I have been so improvident as to fall ill without a drop of anything in the house?'

The invalid looked very much better already, and was now sitting up in bed in a ragged dressing-gown, wrapping up his head in a silk square which obviously belonged to his wife.

'Have a chair, my dear fellow. Just throw that stuff on the floor. I can't tell you how much I appreciate this visit.' He fetched a large and unpleasant-looking rag from under his pillow and blew his nose loud and long. 'E flat,' said he, when he had finished. 'Funny, I never seem to blow twice on the same note. You'd think that the nose, under equal pressure, and all that, would behave predictably, but it doesn't. See this?' He held out the rag. 'Piece of an old bedsheet; never blow your nose on paper, Bridgetower. Save old bedsheets for when you have a cold. They're the only comfort in a really bad cold, and the only way of reckoning its virulence. I consider this to be a two-sheet cold.'

By this time his wife had returned, with glasses, lemon and sugar, and an electric kettle which she plugged into an outlet in the floor. Solly chatted to her, and Cobbler plied the bedsheet, until the water was hot and the toddies mixed.

'Aha,' roared the invalid, who seemed to grow more cheerful every minute. 'This calls for a toast! What'll it be?'

'It had better be to Solly's engagement,' said Molly. 'After all, it's his whisky.'

'Engagement? What engagement? Oh, yes, I remember. I heard about it last night, but this pestilent rheum knocked it right out of my head. Who are you supposed to be engaged to, Bridgetower?'

'Pearl Vambrace was the name given in the paper,' said Solly, watching Cobbler very closely.

'That's nonsense,' said Cobbler. 'I simply don't believe it.'

'Nor do I,' said Solly. 'But why don't you?'

'It's psychologically improbable, that's why. You are, as everybody within a fifty-mile radius knows, an ardent but unsuccessful suitor for the hand of Miss Griselda Webster. Very well. Suppose you *do* get some sense? Suppose you *do* get it into your head that she will never marry you if you both live to be a hundred? Very well. You bounce. On the rebound you get engaged to somebody else. But would that somebody else be Pearl Vambrace? Most certainly not! Intuition and reason alike are outraged by such a supposition.' And here Cobbler took a very big drink of his boiling toddy, and for the next few minutes Molly and Solly were busy patting his back, fanning his face and assuring him that he would survive.

'What I mean to say,' he continued in a whisper, mopping his eyes with his piece of sheeting, 'is that Pearl Vambrace is not the kind of girl to catch any man on the rebound. Such girls are either the soft, squeezy kind, who secrete sympathy as a cow secretes milk, or scheming old mantraps who will accept a man when he's not himself.'

'Well, I'm glad to hear you say so,' said Solly, 'for somebody put a notice in the paper that I am engaged to her, and there is a very strong body of opinion which thinks that that person was you.'

Once again Cobbler got himself into trouble with his hot drink, and when he had been put to rights again Solly told him of all the dark suspicions of Auntie Puss, and Cobbler told Solly of the Hallowe'en party in the Cathedral, and of his serenading Professor Vambrace in the park, which he said that he had been unable to resist.

'Well, there you are,' said Solly. 'Everybody knows you can't resist any lunatic notion that comes into your head. And so, when something like this happens, your name is bound to crop up.'

'Only in such a diseased fancy as that of Auntie Puss Pottinger. I am many reprehensible things, in the eyes of the bourgeoisie, because I am unlike them. But therein lies my defence. Can you conceive of any practical joke more tiresomely bourgeois, more quintessentially and ineluctably lower middle class, than shoving a fake engagement notice in the paper? Is Cobbler, the running sore of Salterton society, the man to do such a thing? Never! What's more, this trick required careful planning, deft execution, and prolonged secrecy to assure its success. Is Cobbler, the man of impulse, Cobbler the Blabbermouth, the man to bring it off? Once again I cry—Never! And to conclude, this has been done by someone who knows you, some false friend who is privy to your bosom, yet ready to exhibit you as a Merry Andrew to the jeers of the mob. Could this be Cobbler the True, Cobbler who has eaten your bread and salt, and drunk your rye toddy, Cobbler who is to you as secret and as dear as Anna to the Queen of Carthage was? No! The echoing air repeats it—' And Cobbler was about to shout 'No' again, in a very loud voice, but he was seized with a terrible fit of coughing. 'God,' he said, when he could speak again, 'I'm going to fetch up the callouses off the soles of my feet in one of those spells.'

'Well, that's what I thought myself,' said Solly. 'It just didn't seem like you.'

'Your simple eloquence touches my heart,' said Cobbler. 'Molly, my pet, I need another length of old sheeting.'

Molly took the sodden rag from his hand and left the room.

'What would you do if you were me?' said Solly.

'What would I do in your place?'

'No, no; you'd do something fantastic and get farther into the soup. I want to know what you would do if you were intelligent but prudent. What would you do if you were me?'

Cobbler pondered for a moment. 'Well,' he said, 'I suppose if I were you—that's to say a somewhat inert chap, half content to be the football of fate—I'd go right on doing whatever I was doing at the moment, and hope the whole thing would blow over.'

'Yes, but I can't do that. I'm absolutely fed up with what I'm doing. I'm a bad teacher; I loathe teaching; I'm expected to teach English literature to people who don't want to know about it; I'm expected to make a name for myself in Amcan; damn it, sometimes I think seriously about suicide.'

'Lot's of people do,' said Cobbler, 'but don't delude yourself. You're not the suicidal type.'

'Why not?'

'You're too gabby. People who talk a lot about their troubles never commit suicide; talk's the greatest safety-valve there is. I always laugh at that bit in *Hamlet* where he pretends to despise himself because he unpacks his heart with words, and falls a-scolding like a very drab; that's why the soliloquy about suicide is just Hamlet putting on intellectual airs. A chatterbox like that would never pop himself off with a bare bodkin. No, the suicides are the quiet ones, who can't find the words to fit their misery. We talkers will never take that way out. Anyway, you wouldn't dare commit suicide, because it would upset your mother; she'd need more than six kinds of medicine to get her out of that.'

Molly came back into the room. She had put on her

nightdress in the bathroom, and her black hair hung loose about her shoulders. Solly had never seen her look so striking.

'You look like one of those wonderful Cretan women,' said he, in honest admiration.

'Thanks. I'm going to go to bed, if you don't mind. The furnace is out. But don't think that means you have to go. We'll be very jolly like this.'

And with a flash of legs she was in bed with Cobbler, and settled back against her pillows with a basket of socks to mend.

'Solly is thinking of suicide,' said her husband, making a beginning on his new piece of sheeting.

'Solly needs a wife,' said Molly.

'But not Pearl Vambrace,' said Cobbler, with great decision. 'She's too much like him in temperament. Married couples should complement each other, and not merely double their losses. There's much to be said for the square peg in the round hole, as the Cubist told the Vorticist.'

'I don't want a wife,' said Solly, passionately. 'I've got a mother, and that, God knows, is enough to warn me off the female sex for life. I don't want a wife, and I don't want my job, and I don't want Charles Heavysege.'

'You want to run away to sea,' said Cobbler. 'But you wouldn't like it, you know.'

'I suppose not,' said Solly. 'Don't pay attention to anything I say tonight. I'm utterly fed up.' He looked into his glass, which was empty.

'Perhaps you are beflustered by the blabsome wine,' said Molly Cobbler.

'Impossible. I've only had one. But where did you get that business about being beflustered by the blabsome etcetera?'

'You used it last time you were here.'

'That was weeks ago.'

'Yes. But it stuck in my mind.'

'Molly, do you realize that you have been quoting from the great Charles Heavysege?'

'Oh? Never heard of him. Yes I have, too. You've mentioned him.'

'I've mentioned him! What an understatement! He obsesses me. He is my incubus—my succubus. He is becoming part of the fabric of my being. I expect that within ten years there will be more of Heavysege in me than of the original material. Do you realize what Heavysege is? He is my path to fame, my immortality and the tomb of my youth. I wish I'd never heard of him.'

'Mix us some more toddies, like a dear,' said Molly. 'If he's so important to you, why do you wish you'd never heard of him?'

Solly busied himself with the glasses. 'Do you really want to know why?' said he.

'If it's not too long, and not a bore,' said Molly.

'It is very long, and it is a bore, but I'll tell you anyhow. You can go to sleep if you like. Fortunately you are in a position to do so. It's getting cold in here.' And Solly lifted a red eiderdown from the bed and draped himself in it.

'I am now gowned as Dr Bridgetower, the eminent authority on the works of Heavysege,' said he. 'The great scholar in the Heavysege field will now address you.

'It was on May 2nd, 1816, that Charles Heavysege first saw the light of day in Liverpool. When I write my introduction to his *Collected Works* I shall embellish that statement by pointing out that the shadow of the Corsican Ogre had but lately faded from the chancelleries of Europe, that the Industrial Revolution was in full flower in England, that Byron had been accused of incest by his wife, that Russia's millions still groaned under the knout, and that in Portland, Maine, the nine-year-old Longfellow had not, so far, written a line. I'll make it appear that little Heavysege hopped right into the middle of a very interesting time, which is a lie, but absolutely vital to any scholarly biography.

'What happened between 1816 and 1853, when Heavysege came to Canada, I don't know, but I'll fake up something. He was a wood-carver by trade, which is good for a few hundred words of hokum about craftsmanship, but he soon became a reporter on the Montreal *Witness*.'

'That was the trumpet-call of the Muse,' said Cobbler, and blew his nose triumphantly.

'Exactly. From there on it's plain sailing, as scholarship goes. Heavysege's major work was his great triple-drama, *Saul.* Now *Saul,* ladies and gentleman, presents the scholar with the widest possible variety of those literary problems which scholars seize upon as dogs seize upon bones. The first of these, of course, is: What is *Saul?* It is in three parts, and fills 315 closely-printed pages. Therefore we may fittingly describe it as "epic in scope"—meaning damned long. It is brilliantly unactable, but is it fair to call it a "closet drama"? Is it not, rather, a vast philosophical poem, like *Faust?* We dismiss with contempt any suggestion that it is just a plain mess; once scholarship has its grappling-hooks on a writer's work there is no room for doubt.'

'Nobody has ever written a great play on a Biblical theme,' said Cobbler. 'Milton couldn't pull it off. Even Ibsen steered clear of Holy Writ. There's something about it that defies dramatization.'

'Please do not interrupt the lecturer,' said Solly. 'Heavysege did not write a mere Biblical drama; he wrote a vast, cosmic poem, like a fruit-cake with three layers. Only the middle layer concerns Saul and mankind; the top layer is all about angels, and like everything that has ever been written about angels, it is of·a deadly dreariness; the bottom layer, which is thicker than the others, is about devils, and much the best of the three. Heavysege was awed by angels, sobered by Saul, but right in his element with the devils. He makes them comic, in a jaunty, slangy, nineteenth-century way; he provides love-affairs for them. In fact, he is at his best with his devils. This obviously suggests a parallel with Milton; in scholarly work of this kind, you've got to have plenty of parallels, and Heavysege provides them by the bushel. Heavysege reveals traces of every influence that even the greediest scholar could require.

'But in your eyes I see a question of the greatest import. Was Heavysege, in the truest sense, a Canadian writer? I hear you ask. Set your minds at rest. Who but a Canadian could have written Saul's speech:

179

> *If Prompted, follow me and be the ball*
> *Tiny at first, that shall, like one of snow,*
> *Gather in rolling.*

Does not Jehoiadah behave like a Canadian when he refuses
to cheer when his neighbours are watching him? Is it not
typically Canadian of Heavysege's Hebrews that they take
exception to Saul's "raging in a public place"? Is it not
Canadian self-control that David displays when, instead of
making a noisy fuss he "lets his spittle fall upon his beard,
and scrabbles on the door-post"? Friends, these are the first
evidences of the action of our climate and our temperament
upon the native drama.

'I could go on at some length about the beauties of
Heavysege, as they appear to the scholar. *Saul* is full of misprints. Correcting misprints is the scholar's delight. On
page 17 we find the word "returinag". Did Heavysege mean
"returning"? That's good for a footnote. On page 19 we
find the word "clods" where we might expect "clouds".
But can Heavysege have meant something deeply poetic by
"clods"? That's good for a paragraph of speculation, for we
must be true to the printed text at all costs, and avoid any
mischievous emendations. Does the poet allow anything of
his own life to colour his drama? Well, at one point Saul
speaks of "poignant emerods", and the adjective opens up
an alluring avenue of speculation; we must find out all we
can about Heavysege's state of health in 1857, when *Saul*
was published. Had Heavysege a personal philosophy?
What else can we call the four lines which he gives to an
Israelite Peasant? (Incidentally, this peasant makes his appearance smoking a pipe; Heavysege has not even denied
the editor the luxury of a nice, juicy anachronism.) This
Peasant says:

> *Man is a pipe that life doth smoke*
> *As saunters it the earth about;*
> *And when 'tis wearied of the joke,*
> *Death comes and knocks the ashes out.*

Can we hear that unmoved?'

'I can hear it totally unmoved,' said Cobbler.

'Then you have no soul, and do not deserve the intellectual feast that I am spreading before you,' said Solly. 'But there, in a nutshell, is Heavysege. I spare you his other play, his two long poems and his newspaper writings, which it will be my duty to find and sift. There, my friends, is the ash-heap upon which I must lavish my efforts and thought, in order that I may loom large in the firmament of Amcan. It's devilish cold.'

'Poor Solly, you look miserable,' said Molly Cobbler. 'You'd better get in with us.'

Solly looked at the bed dubiously. 'But how?' said he.

'Give us all nice hot drinks again. Then loosen the covers at the foot, take off your shoes and hop in. You can put your legs up between us. We'll warm you. And I'll spare you one of my pillows.'

Solly did as he was bidden, and a few minutes later was surprised to find himself snugly tucked in, facing the Cobblers, and with his feet in the remarkable warmth which they had created.

'I feel like the sword which Lancelot laid between him and whoever it was,' said he. Molly Cobbler said nothing, but laughed and tickled one of his feet, which made him blush.

'You know, you tell a very pathetic story,' said Cobbler, who had been blowing his nose and pondering, 'but it doesn't hold water. You want us to be sorry for you because you're tied to Heavysege and teaching people who don't want to learn. But you're not tied, you know. Nobody has to teach if they don't want to. I remember my own fiasco as a teacher of music appreciation at Waverley. That repulsive Tessie Forgie came to me one day and said, "Mr Cobbler, do I understand that I am responsible for all the operas of Mozart?" I said, "Miss Forgie, if you were responsible even for one of Mozart's overtures I should clasp you to my bosom, but you aren't; if you mean, do you need to have a knowledge of Mozart's work to appreciate music,

the answer is yes." That finished me as a teacher. I expected
my students to know something, instead of being examina-
tion passers. That's why I only see a few of the university
brats privately now, as on that memorable Hallowe'en. If
you don't like teaching, get out of it.'

'But what else can I do?'

'How do I know? But you won't find out while you are
hugging your miserable job. And why do you bother with
Heavysege? Why don't you write something yourself?'

'Me? What could I write?'

'How should I know? Write a novel.'

'There's no money in novels.'

'Is there any money in Heavysege?'

'No, but there are jobs in Heavysege. Get a solid piece of
scholarship under your belt and some diploma-mill will
always want you. Don't think I haven't considered writing
something original. But what? Everything's been written.
There aren't any plots that haven't been worked to death.'

'You've read too much, that's what ails you. All the
originality has been educated out of you. The world is full
of plots. I'll give you one. In a town like Salterton lives a
wealthy, talented and physically beautiful couple who have
two beautiful and talented children. Arthur is a boy of
twenty-one and Alice is a girl of eighteen. Although they
live in wealthy seclusion the news leaks out that Alice has
had a child, and that Arthur is the father. There is a scandal,
but nobody can do anything because no charge has been
laid. Then Alice and Arthur enter their child in an international baby contest sponsored by UN, and it sweeps off
all the first prizes. They explain that this is because incest
strengthens the predominating strains in stock, and as their
physical and mental predominating strains are all good,
they have produced a model child. Their parents reveal
that they also are brother and sister, and that the family
has six generations of calculated incest, practised on the
highest moral and eugenic grounds, behind it. UN takes
up the scheme and the free world has a race with Russia as
to which can produce the most superior beings in the

182

shortest time. Amusingly written, it would sell like hot-cakes.'

'You don't think it a little lacking in love-interest, do you?' said Molly.

'Oh, that could be taken care of, somehow. What I am saying is that it is an original plot. If every story has to be a love-story, you'll never have any originality, for a less original creature than a human being in love cannot be found. But I get sick of hearing people crying for originality, and rejecting it when it turns up.'

'Your plot is utterly impossible,' said Solly, 'it would offend against the high moral tone of Canadian letters, for it is at once frivolous and indecent.'

'Oh, very well,' said Cobbler. 'Go on ransacking the cup-boards of oblivion for such musty left-overs as Heavysege; that is all you are good for. I have a horrible feeling that in two or three more years I shall despise you. Quite with-out prejudice, mind.'

The hot toddy and the bed were working strongly upon Solly's spirit. 'I have a strong sense of being ill-used,' said he murmurously. 'I am in seven kinds of a mess. I am trapped in a profession I hate, and I am saddled with a pro-fessional task I hate. I am the victim of a practical joke which puts me into a very delicate relationship with a girl I hardly know and whom I don't think I like. I ask advice of the one man I know who seems to be free of petty con-siderations, and all he does is mock me. Very well. Loaded as I am with indignity I can bear this also.'

'Hogwash!' said Cobbler, groping under his pillow for his piece of bedsheet. 'Don't come the noble sufferer over me, Bridgetower. You are in a richly varied mess, true enough. But, much as I like you, I am clear-eyed enough to see that it is the outward and visible reflection of the inward and invisible mess which is your soul. You think life has trapped you, do you? Well, my friend, everybody is trapped, more or less. The best thing you can hope for is to under-stand your trap and make terms with it, tooth by tooth. If this seems hard, reflect that I speak from what may well be

183

my deathbed.' He blew his nose resoundingly. 'B natural,' said he, 'my cold drops more than a full tone every hour. Obviously I am dying. Well, accept these hard words as a parting gift. You are the prisoner of circumstance, Bridge-tower, and it is my considered view that you are not one of the tiny minority of mankind that can grapple with circum-stance and give it a fall.'

Solly pondered. 'We'll see about that,' he said, after a time, but his host and hostess were both asleep.

MUCH LATER Solly woke, and found that Molly Cobbler was kicking him, gently but persistently. 'It's time you went home, ducks,' said she. 'It's long after three.'

'Good God,' cried Solly, sitting up. 'What'll Mother say?'

'Tell her you were in bed with a married woman, and didn't think it polite to hurry away,' said Molly. And then, surprisingly, she kissed him. 'Don't pay any attention to what Humphrey said; he was ill and cross. You'll find a way out.'

Her kindness went right to Solly's heart, and he felt a sudden warmth there.

'Thanks,' he said, and kissed her in return. 'I know I will.'

From force of habit he began to tiptoe down the stairs, then, recollecting where he was, he clumped noisily to the bottom, and thence out into the cool night. At least his mind was made up about one thing: he should have tried to protect Pearl from her father.

PART FIVE

GLOSTER RIDLEY sat at his breakfast. From the kitchen came the voice of Mrs Edith Little, his housekeeper, raised in song. It was a high voice, wiry, small and tremulous, a carefully modulated snarl. When she had finished *Just A-Wearyin' For You* she addressed her son Earl.

'Like that, lover?'

'Goog.'

'Good? Aw, you're a flatterer. Are you going to be a flatterer when you grow up?'

'Blub.'

'You going to be a flatterer like Ugga Bev?'

'Ugga Bev.'

'Aw, you're crazy about Ugga Bev, aren't you? Eh? You're just crazy about him.'

'Gaw.'

'Well, you just grow up half as smooth as Ugga Bev and you'll be all right. Ugga Bev is certainly a smoothie. You going to be a smoothie, lover?'

'Smoo.'

'You are? Say, you're just too smart, that's what you are. Just too smart for your old Mommie. But you'll always be Mommie's fella, won't you?'

'Blub.'

'Yes, sir. Mommie'll always be your best girl, eh? Tell Mommie she'll always be your best girl.'

'Blaw.'

'Aw, you're a flatterer.'

Ridley sighed as he spooned up the last juice from his

185

grapefruit. This was, he knew, a carefully staged scene, intended to impress him with the beauty of mother love, and the delightful cleverness of little Earl. He was not a vain man, and it had never occurred to him that his housekeeper sought to ensnare him with her charms, but he knew that she was, for some mysterious purpose, intent upon calling his attention to her son. She frequently told him stories of the child's brilliance and whimsical humour, and she had once asked him if he had never longed for a child of his own? He was both too weak and too kind to tell her the truth, which was that he feared and mistrusted virtually all children, and he had temporized somehow. But when Christmas came, a few weeks later, he had bought a large and expensive toy panda for Earl, and after that Mrs Little had begun to bring the child to work with her occasionally, and to stage these dialogues within his hearing. And he had, though somewhat ashamed of the emotion, begun to hate Earl intently.

Was it ever permissible, he wondered, to describe a child as a slob? Surely slob was the only accurate word for little Earl. Though the child was not much more than three, he already had a hulking, stooping walk, his round abdomen suggested the prolapsed belly of middle age, and in the corner of his mouth was a damp hole, as though provided by nature for the soggy butt of a cigar. If ever a child were a slob, Earl was a slob. Not that he thought of him as Earl; he had some weeks ago christened the child Blubadub in the secret baptistery of his mind. The name had come out of the deep past, when, as a child, he had seen a picture in a bound volume of some English magazine (was it *Punch?*) of a pretty young mother talking with just such a surly brat: 'And what does Mama call her darling?' 'Blub-a-dub,' the brat replied. 'That's right,' said Mama, 'Beloved Dove!' Blubadub, the son of Constant Reader.

Mrs Little brought him his egg and a rack of toast. 'I hope I don't bother you with my singing,' said she.

'Not at all,' said Ridley. It would have been true, but churlish, to say that he would prefer silence; bachelors pay a high price for any sort of female care.

'I'm a regular lark these days,' said Mrs Little, 'singing all the time. I'm taking voice.'

'Indeed.'

From the gentleman who boards at our place. Mr Bevill Higgin. He's a wonderful teacher; he just seems to get it out of you, kind of. I often tell him he could get music out of anything. We're all taking, me and my sister and her husband and even Earl.'

'The little boy too?'

'Oh yes. Mr Higgin says you can't start a kiddy too young. He could sing himself before he could talk. Would you like to hear Earl?'

'Some day, yes.'

'Oh, but he's right here. I sometimes bring him with me, while I'm working here mornings. He just sits as good as gold, while I'm working. I'll bring him in.'

Ridley felt a wave of despondency sweep over him, as she hurried to the kitchen. I should be a happy man, thought he. The sun is shining on my breakfast table; I have a very nice apartment; my housekeeper is clean and capable. But I feel wretched, and now I shall have to listen to Blubadub sing. Well, I'm not going to let my egg get cold anyhow.

Mrs Little returned, leading Earl by the hand. The child was nicely dressed in a yellow jumper and brown corduroy overalls, but in Ridley's eye he was a slob. He hulked, and in his dimple a ghostly cigar butt seemed to nestle.

'Now, lover,' said Mrs Little, kneeling, 'sing for Mr Ridley. Just like you sing for Ugga Bev. That's what he calls Mr Higgin. He means Uncle Bev, of course. Come on, lover —Jack and Jill went up the hill—'

'Faw down, bo cown,' mumbled Blubadub.

'Ah now, lover, you know that comes later,' said Mrs Little, playing the loving mother with many an arch glance toward her employer and quarry. 'Come on, lover; Jack and Jill,' she prompted in her own tiny, wiry voice.

'He got baw head,' said Earl, fixing Ridley with a surly stare.

'Now, lover, that's bold,' said Mrs Little, blushing very much. 'You sing for nice Mr Ridley.'

'Not nice,' said Earl, and struck at the air in Ridley's direction. 'Stinky. Got baw head.'

Ridley saw no reason why he should help Mrs Little out of her difficulty, and went on eating his egg, after casting a malevolent look at Blubadub. The child well understood its meaning, and stamped and struck at the air again. Mrs Little thought that the time had come to show that she could be firm, as well as sweet, in the motherly role, so she took Earl's fat fist in her hands and shook it mildly.

'Now, lover, Mommy wants you to sing for Mr Ridley just like you sing for Ugga Bev. Now, come on.'

'Ugga Bev bastard!' said Earl, with greater clarity than he had given to any previous speech. 'Baw head bastard!'

With a smothered cry Mrs Little seized her child in her arms and fled to the kitchen.

Ridley was much cheered. He hoped that Earl was in serious trouble. He ate his egg with better appetite, and positively enjoyed his toast and coffee. After all, he thought, the day which lay before him might not be so painful as he feared. He had slept badly. The thought of a difficult day to come always gave him a restless night. But looking out of the window at the autumn sunshine it seemed that things might not be quite so laborious as he supposed. He must see Balmer this morning. He must see Mr Warboys, and in all likelihood his enemy Mrs Warboys, late in the afternoon. Well, it must be lived through, somehow.

Fighting down anxiety he changed from his dressing-gown into his jacket, gave a final brush to what remained of his hair, collected some papers into his briefcase and sought out his hat and coat. As he was about to leave the apartment, Mrs Little appeared again from the kitchen, with swollen eyes, from which tears still welled.

'I just don't know what to say,' she said. 'What you must think of Earl's language I don't know. I don't know where he picks up that kind of talk.'

'Don't give it a thought,' said Ridley, seeking to make his escape.

'Oh, but I do! I never think of anything else. That child's

all I've got, and really, well—I guess I just live for him. You'll never know what it is to try to bring up a boy single-handed. Sometimes it just gets to be too much.' And Mrs Little wept again.

'Please don't distress yourself. He'll probably be much like other boys.'

'That's what I'm afraid of. I just dread that he'll end up just such another as his father was before him. In front of you, of all people! And when you're so worried about the paper and everything.'

'Eh?' said Ridley, who thought, like many another worrier, that he showed no outward sign of his distress.

'Of course you're worried. *I* can tell. I guess I see you the way nobody else sees you. It's that piece about Professor Bridgetower and Professor Vambrace's daughter, isn't it?'

'What makes you think that?'

'There's a lot of talk about it, and I hear a good deal. Of course everybody knows I'm connected with *The Bellman*, sort of. I know how you've been worrying. I can see how your bed is all screwed up these mornings, and how you've been taking soda, and everything. Oh, I wish there was something I could do!'

This was a cry from the heart, and though she stood perfectly still before him, Ridley had a dreadful sense that in a moment Constant Reader might throw herself into his arms. He was alarmed, and without a word he rushed out of his apartment and down the stairs. He had a sense that even his home had become menacing.

Mrs Little, overwhelmed by the thought that she had been bold, sat down in Ridley's armchair and wept.

'THE ROOT of the matter is the malice of X, and the party to the action which can find X first will win it,' said Gordon Balmer.

'I see,' said Ridley.

'The whole business is ridiculous,' Balmer continued, 'but it would make a very pretty case, for all that.'

189

'I don't see that it's ridiculous,' said Ridley. 'You tell me that it could cost *The Bellman* a heavy sum in damages. That wouldn't be ridiculous.'

'It depends what you call a heavy sum. *The Bellman* could stand a few thousands. But what the judge would advise a jury to grant the other side, if you lost, mightn't amount to very much, especially if Vambrace and Snelgrove asked for something very big. A judge often takes a poor view of a big claim. No, it's precedent you have to avoid. If they got a judgment, even for a thousand dollars, on a thing of this kind, people all over the country would be trying to shake down newspapers because of all kinds of trivial errors, and getting settlements out of court. That's where it could cost you a lot of money. Anyhow, I said it *could* cost you money; I didn't say it *would*. It's my job to see that it doesn't. That's why I want to get my hands on X.'

Mr Balmer poured a glass of water out of a vacuum jug on his side-table and drank it with relish. His office was very different in atmosphere from that of Snelgrove, Martin and Fitzalan; indeed, it could hardly be said to have anything so needless as an atmosphere at all. Mr Balmer sat behind a steel desk, in a scientifically-sprung chair; Ridley sat in a chair which matched it exactly. There was nothing on the desk but a blotter, nothing on the floor but expensive linoleum, and nothing on the walls save some framed evidences that Mr Balmer was a lawyer, and a QC. Mr Balmer himself, though a stout, bald man, managed to suggest that his flesh was merely some scientific modern substance, as it might be foam rubber, over a steel frame. The glass of water set some lawyer-like and explanatory machinery at work inside him, and he continued.

'They will charge libel. Snelgrove was in to see me yesterday, and that is what they have in mind. It will be a difficult charge to prove, but it could be done. However, it is one thing to prove libel, and another to get anything substantial in the way of damages for it. The judge might very well take the line that the libel didn't amount to much. Still, you published the libel, and you're guilty. If the judge didn't like newspapers—and judges don't, as a usual thing—he could be ugly about it. Now, our defence should be that you are a victim of malice. Malice is a vague term in law, but though it's hard to define it isn't hard to understand. You are the victim, along with Miss Vambrace and Mr Bridgetower, of the malice of X. Give me X, and I'll put him in the stand and pretty soon the whole issue will be fogged over, because you, and Vambrace, will both be anxious to get at him. The judge probably won't be able to do anything to X, unless a charge is brought against him— a charge of malice. Whether that could amount to anything will depend on who he is. I wouldn't advise such a charge, unless the circumstances are exceptional; malice is even slipperier than libel.'

'And what happens if they get X?' asked Ridley.

'Ah, then they would probably keep him under wraps until they had got what they could out of you, and bring another case against him. Or they might even bring him in late in the case, as a surprise, and question him in such a way as to further discredit you. X is the key to the case. Give me X, and the whole thing will be sewed up.'

'But I can't give you X. I'm trying to find him; Marryat's trying to find him; Weir is looking for him. But we haven't a thing to go on. We'll never find him.'

'Don't say that. Snelgrove is looking for him, and so is Ronny Fitzalan. Vambrace is hunting him, and I hear some very queer rumours about that. When a lot of people are looking for a thing, it usually turns up. Not many people can cover their tracks, and even fewer can keep from telling a secret if they know one. I'm sure X will be found. I just want our side to find him first.'

'I suppose compromise is quite out of the question?' said Ridley.

'No, not by any means. Ronny Fitzalan has been to see me, without Snelgrove knowing. He's a cousin of the Vambrace girl, and he wants to keep the thing quiet for her sake. But to shut Vambrace up you'll have to eat a lot of dirt and do it in public, what's more. I'd advise against it. Technically, you're in the wrong; morally, you're in the clear. Give in on this, and God knows what demands you won't face next. You've got a good case, and I think you should fight it. Next time you might not have such a good case; the time for a show of strength is when you're strong.'

'I see. Well, can you suggest anything? Should we hire detectives, or anything?'

'I've been in the law for twenty-five years, and I've yet to see a detective who could work effectively in anything except a very big city. In a place like this you can smell 'em. Anyway, they do a lot of their work through the underworld, and the underworld of Salterton is just one man, Pimples Buckle. He controls everything crooked in a fifty-mile radius. Leave it to me. I'll establish diplomatic contact with Pimples. Meanwhile keep up the search.'

And with this Ridley had to be content.

IT WAS on Monday morning, at the same hour when Gloster Ridley was in consultation with *The Bellman's* solicitor, that Solly at last found Pearl in the music room of the Waverley Library. Since the previous Friday, following his visit to the Cobblers, he had been in search of her, for he was now convinced that if they could talk over their difficulty they could find a way out of it. At least, that is what he told himself when he sought Pearl at the Library on Friday morning, and that was his certainty when he sought her again on Friday afternoon. At both times she had been busy and he felt a shyness about asking for her at the main desk, so he had mooned about the reading room hoping that she might come into view and, unsuspected by himself, attracting a good deal of attention among the other librarians, who assumed that he had come for a sight of his fiancée, or a word with her. By Friday night his need to talk to Pearl had become a source of discomfort to him, but he dared not call her on the telephone, and he knew of no place where he might find her.

On Saturday morning he had visited the Library again,

but without better success. The Library closed at one o'clock, and he had hung about in the street outside, thinking that he might see her as she left to go home. Had he known it, Pearl was watching him from a window, and did not leave until he had gone. Lunchtime in the Bridgetower house was a fixed appointment; the Vambraces did not care when they ate. Pearl told herself that she could not imagine what he wanted to say to her; by a not uncommon trick of the mind she resented and even hated Solly because he had been a witness to the disgraceful scene between herself and her father. If he chose to hang about on a wet day, hoping to speak to her, he was free to do so. She rather wished he might catch cold.

This was a harsh thought, and harsh thoughts were a new and luxurious experience for Pearl. Since that dreadful Wednesday night, when she had lain awake weeping for the loss of her father, she had thought many harsh things about a wide variety of people. And although uncharitableness is widely believed to be an enemy of beauty, and may be so if continued for many years, a few days of it improved Pearl's appearance remarkably. Feeling herself now to be alone in the world, she stood straighter, her eyes were brighter, and she moved with brisk determination. As she was no longer burdened by a sense of family, and felt free for the first time in her life from the Vambrace tradition of despising all worldly things which cost money, she drew a substantial sum from her savings account and bought herself two new outfits, smarter than she had thought proper before. She went farther. She had grown up under the shadow of her father's belief that short hair for women was a fad, which would quickly pass, and her own black hair was long and indifferently dressed. But on Saturday afternoon she went to a hairdresser and had her hair cut to within three inches of her head, and curled. It was an act of defiance, and at the evening meal that night, as her parents consumed a trifle composed of left-over blancmange and jelly-roll, she was powerfully conscious of their eyes upon her. But they said not a word.

The fact was that Professor Vambrace was cowed, for the first time in his relationship with his daughter. He was bitterly ashamed of the scene that he had made in the street, ashamed because he had behaved in an undignified fashion in front of young Bridgetower, ashamed because he had clouted his daughter over the ear, like some peasant and not like a cousin of Mourne and Derry, ashamed because he had allowed his daughter to see how deeply he was hurt by the failure of his attempts as a detective. His mind refused to admit that he was ashamed to have hurt the feelings of his child, who had worshipped him; but his heart's pain was the worse for this refusal. Yet it was not in the Professor to ask forgiveness, to explain, to make any move toward reconciliation with his daughter; he desperately desired to be forgiven, but in his hard way of thinking it was out of the question for a parent to ask forgivenesss of a child. A child was, through the very fact of being a child, always in the wrong in any dispute. He told himself that he would wait until Pearl was in a proper frame of mind, and then he would allow her to creep back into his good graces. This was his attitude until Saturday morning, and Thursday and Friday were dark days in the Vambrace home.

THE PROFESSOR had no lecture to deliver on Saturday morning, but he went to the University all the same, and he was sitting in his office, reading a quarterly devoted to classical studies, when there was a knock on the door and a tall, heavily good-looking young man entered without waiting for an invitation.

'Professor Vambrace,' said he, 'I'm Norm Yarrow.'

'Indeed?' said the Professor, without expression.

'We haven't met, but I'm a new boy on the student guidance staff. A friend of Pearlie's.'

'Of—?'

'Pearlie. Your daughter.'

'So? I am not accustomed to hear her called that. Hypocorisms are not employed in my household.' The Professor was very much the cousin of Mourne and Derry that morning.

'Professor, let's get down to brass tacks. I'm only here because I want to help. I want you to understand right now that my job is simply to understand, not to accuse. Now, you're an intelligent man, so I don't have to beat about the bush with you. We can take the gloves off right at the start. I take it that you've heard of the Oedipus Complex?'

'I am familiar with all forms of the Oedipus legend.'

'Yes, but have you understood it? I mean, as we moderns understand it? Have you got the psychological slant on it?'

'Mr. Yarrow, I should hardly be head of the department of Classics at this University if I were not thoroughly acquainted with all that concerns Oedipus.'

'But the Complex? You know about the Complex?'

'What Complex are you talking about? All art is complex.'

'No, no; I mean do you recognize what the story of Oedipus really is? I mean about every man's childhood desire to kill his father and marry his mother? You've heard about that?'

'I have naturally heard something of such trash. Now may I ask the purpose of your visit, Mr Yarrow? I am engaged, as you see, in reading.'

'I'll put it in a nutshell. Has it ever struck you that there's a kind of an Oedipus thing between you and Pearlie?'

Professor Vambrace was not a merry man, but he was not without his own sort of humour. After a long look at Norm, he replied.

'An extremely interesting suggestion, my dear sir. Perhaps you would like to expand it?'

Norm beamed. As he always said to Dutchy, they were easier to deal with when they had some brains, and didn't weep, or shout at you.

'I'm glad you're taking it like that, Professor. Now about Pearlie; there's been talk. And particularly about that scene in the street a night or two ago. They say you were walloping her with a pretty big stick—'

'They say? Yes, much has been said about me, Mr. Yarrow. I can guess who your informants were. They have been saying such things for many years. And now they say that I have been chastising my daughter in public, do they?

With a stick? I am not in the least surprised. And how does the legend of Oedipus bear upon this accusation?'

'Professor, you love Pearlie.'

'Do I, Mr Yarrow? An extraordinary idea. That a man should love his daughter is understandable, but surely my detractors deny me any such natural feeling?'

'I mean, you love Pearlie too much.'

'And so I chastise her in public with a stick?'

'Exactly. You're jealous, you see. You're jealous of her normal love-object, young Solly Bridgetower.'

'Oh, you believe her to be in love with Bridgetower, do you?'

'Well, isn't she engaged to him?

'What makes you think so?'

'Well—wasn't it in the paper?'

'Aha, so you believe what you see in the papers? A strange confession for a psychologist. No, Mr Yarrow, she is not engaged to him, nor has the idea of being engaged to him ever entered her head. Now, to return to your opinions about Oedipus, which I find refreshingly novel, what has Oedipus to do with all this?'

Norm had a feeling that he had lost the upper hand in this interview; it was not normal for the interviewee to be so icy calm, so impersonal, as this.

'From the piece in the paper it was natural to assume that she was engaged to him. You'll admit that. Now Oedipus is a kind of symbol of a particular kind of love, you see, and. . . . '

'Oedipus might be taken as a symbol of many things. In accordance with the prophecy, he slew his father Laius, and married Epikaste, the widow of Laius, to discover later that she was his mother. A strange love, certainly. But my dear mother died when I was a child of two, Mr Yarrow, and I have no recollection of her. I fail to see the resemblance between Oedipus and myself.'

'Perhaps you don't know yourself as thoroughly as you should. Not that I mean to blame you, of course. It takes training to know yourself in the way I am talking about.

But if you turn the Oedipus legend around, you get a daughter who kills her mother and is in love with her father. Do you follow me?'

'Inverted legends are no novelty to a classicist, my dear sir. Let me help you out; it is your idea that my daughter loves me to excess, and that in order to correct this undesirable condition I beat her publicly with a stick? Is that it?'

'No, not exactly. You're being too literal. What I'm trying to get at is that your desire to keep Pearlie from her natural love-object, to keep her all to yourself, is—well, let's not say unnatural; let's just say it isn't usual. Go on that way, and you may be headed for a crack-up. Maybe I shouldn't have brought Oedipus into this. All that Freudian stuff is pretty complicated, and anyway I'm sure things haven't got that far yet with you and Pearlie—if I make myself clear.'

'But you do not make yourself clear. And I am anxious that you should do so before you leave this room. After all, it is not every day that a man of my age, and of my quiet and retired mode of life, is confronted with a stranger who suggests that he lives in an unnatural relationship with his daughter. I should like to hear more.'

'Now, Professor, let's not get extreme. When I was talking about Oedipus I was talking symbolically, you understand.'

'I do not profess to understand psychological symbolism, Mr Yarrow, but it does not require much training to realize that Oedipus is a symbol for incest. Isn't that what you imply?'

'Oh, now just a minute. That's pretty rough talk. Not incest, of course. Just a kind of mental incest, maybe. Nothing really serious.'

'Fool!' said the Professor, who had been growing very hot, and was now at the boil. 'Do you imply that the sins of the mind are trivial and the sins of the flesh important? What kind of an idiot are you?'

'Now, Professor, let's keep this objective. You must

understand that I'm talking on the guidance level, not personally at all. I just want to help you to self-understanding. If you understand yourself, you can meet your problem, you see, and I'm here, in all friendliness, to try to help you to understand yourself, and to help Pearlie, and so forth, do you see?'

'But you have not yet told me what all this has to do with Oedipus.'

Norm was by this time sick of the name of Oedipus. A horrible suspicion was rising in his mind that the Oedipus Complex, which he had for some time used as a convenient and limitless bin into which he dumped any problem involving possessive parents and dependent children, was a somewhat more restricted term than he had imagined. The chapter on Freudian psychology in his general textbook had not, after all, equipped him to deal with a tiresomely literal professor of classics who knew Oedipus at first hand, so to speak. Norm had received his training chiefly through general courses and from some interesting work which proved fairly conclusively that rats were unable to distinguish between squares, circles and triangles.

'Let's forget about Oedipus,' he said, and smiled a smile which had never failed him in all his career in social work.

'Not at all,' said the Professor, grinning wolfishly. 'I am increasingly reminded of Oedipus. Do you not recall that in that tragic history, Oedipus met a Sphinx? The Sphinx spoke in riddles—very terrible riddles, for those who could not guess them died. But Oedipus guessed the riddle, and the chagrin of the Sphinx was so great that it destroyed itself. I am but a poor shadow of Oedipus, I fear, and you, Mr Yarrow, but a puny kitten of a Sphinx. But you are, like many another Sphinx of our modern world, an undereducated, brassy young pup, who thinks that gall can take the place of the authority of wisdom, and that a professional lingo can disguise his lack of thought. You aspire to be a Sphinx, without first putting yourself to the labour of acquiring a secret.'

'Aw, now, Professor, let's not be bitter—'

'Bitter? Have I not a right to be bitter? You intrude upon me with your obscene accusation, and your muddle of old wives' tales about me beating my daughter in the streets, and you tell me not to be bitter! No, you listen to me: I shall inform your superior of this, and if you dare to repeat any of this filthy nonsense to anyone else, I shall not only drive you out of this University in disgrace, but I shall take you to court and strip you of everything you possess. Get out of here! Get out! Get out!'

The Professor had worked himself up into a rage by this time; flecks of white bubbled from his lips, and his eyes rolled horribly. He seized his walking stick—not a blackthorn, for that was broken, but a knobbly ashplant—and he might have struck Norm with it if the expert in guidance had not darted into the corridor, to escape down the iron staircase so rapidly that it rumbled like thunder.

But when he was in safety he felt a certain comfort coursing warmly through him. The Professor's rage, though alarming, was the normal response to what Norm had said; when a man was shown to himself he invariably wept or raged. It had been the Professor's period of quiet, controlled watchfulness which had worried Norm. That was definitely abnormal, and hard to figure out. In fact, the more he thought about it, the less he understood it. And all that talk about Sphinxes—that didn't sound too good. Simply made no sense at all. The Professor would bear watching.

The more Norm reflected on the interview, the more he was convinced that he had understood it all thoroughly. Which, as he was the expert on human behaviour, was perfectly normal.

ALTHOUGH NOTHING would have made him admit it, Norm's visit had had some effect on the Professor; it made him yearn toward his daughter more painfully than at any time since that Wednesday night when he had wept alone in his study. But this also he could not admit. If only she would show signs of wishing forgiveness, how quickly, how magnanimously he would forgive her! But there she sat

across the table from him, in clothes which he had not seen
before, and which even his unpractised eye could recognize
as better than her usual garb, and with her hair cut short
and dressed in a strange new fashion. His spirit was nearly
broken, and he decided to make the first move toward
reconciliation.

'I received a visit from a friend of yours today,' he said
to her, 'a young man from the chaplain's department, who
called himself Yarrow.'

'He is not a particular friend of mine.'

'Indeed? He appeared to know a good deal about our
family affairs.'

Pearl said nothing.

'Tell me, Pearl, is it your custom to discuss family matters
with outsiders?'

'No, Father.'

'But you have discussed your home with this man
Yarrow?'

Pearl's first instinct was to lie. Before that dreadful,
emancipating Wednesday night she would certainly have
done so. But three days of bitterness had changed her.

'Yes, Father.'

'I see. And may I ask why you did so?'

'I must talk to someone occasionally.'

The Professor said no more, and his heart was very heavy.
He did not suppose, of course, that Pearl had told Yarrow
that he had beaten her with a stick, or that he had an in-
cestuous passion for her. That was plainly the spiteful talk
of the cabal which had so long been at work against him.
But he knew that Pearl had shut him out of her life because
of that night.

Sunday was a black, silent day in the Vambrace home.

SUNDAY WAS not much better for Solly than it was for Professor Vambrace. He was possessed by the seemingly con-
tradictory convictions that Pearl was a wretched, inconsiderable, bungling creature who had introduced a last

intolerable complication into his already complicated life, and by the feeling that he must talk to her as soon as possible. In his mind's eye he could see her—dark, dowdy and withdrawn. Therefore it was with surprise that he encountered the reality in the music room in the Library on Monday morning; it was as though a picture, previously much out of focus, had been made clear to him.

'Ah—can I have a minute? I mean, I've simply got to talk to you. It's desperately important.'

'I'm very busy.'

'I can't help that. You must listen; it's as much your business as mine.'

'Please go away.'

'I won't go away. I've been chasing you for days. We've got to have a talk. How can we get out of this bloody mess if we don't discuss it?'

'I don't know. And I don't think you are likely to find a way.'

'Oh, I know; you're angry with me because I didn't do anything the other night. Well, what could I do? How would it have been if I'd knocked your father down when he was cuffing you? Or called a policeman? Damn it, I'm sorry. I'd have done something if it could have made any difference or settled anything. But I couldn't think of anything, so I got out of the way. Look: I'm terribly sorry. And don't think I came here for fun. I'm not enjoying this a bit more than you.'

'That's a very charming remark.'

'Well, how charming have you been, since I came? Can't we behave like sensible creatures and talk this thing out? I hear your father is suing *The Bellman*.'

'Yes. What's that to you? All you have to do is get up in the witness box and swear that you never had any intention of marrying me, and you will be as white as driven snow. The judge will probably offer you the pity of the court in your wronged condition.'

'Well if that isn't the most nauseating feminine attitude

I've ever heard! Do you suppose I want anything of the kind? I don't want anything to do with a court action. Do you?'

'Oh don't talk like a fool! Of course I don't. How do you suppose it will make me look?'

'Well, then, why don't you repudiate the action?'

'How?'

'Simple. You hire a lawyer. When the case comes up he gets on his feet and says, "Your Honour, my client, Miss Pearl Vambrace, wishes me to say that she does not consider herself libelled, and wants it understood that she has nothing to do with bringing this action, and that it's all a pipedream of her father's, who has got into a fantod about nothing very much." Or however lawyers phrase these things. It'd blow the case sky-high.'

Pearl gazed at Solly with reluctant admiration. She had been agonizing about her situation for several days, and had seen no ray of light. But here was a man who cut through the complications with easy brilliance.

'If it was known you were going to do that, I doubt if the case would ever come to court,' Solly went on. 'It'd just be a waste of money. Do you know a lawyer?'

'My cousin Ronnie is a lawyer.'

'Fitzalan? No good. He's old Snelgrove's partner, and Snelgrove has been telling half the town, in strict confidence, that he is going to take the hide off *The Bellman*.'

'Well, and so he should. It's libelled me. And you too.'

'Don't be silly. If it's libel to say I'm engaged to you, and if it's libel to say you're engaged to me, surely we are both such lepers that the two libels cancel out. It's a mistake, a damn silly mistake, but still a mistake.'

Once again Pearl was dazzled by Solly's grasp of the fundamentals of her problem. His law might be shaky, but his reasoning was sound.

'You mean you don't care about that engagement notice appearing?'

'Of course I care. It can make a hell of a mess of things for me. But it isn't the end of the world, you know.'

'You mean it would be awful for you if Griselda Webster came to hear of it?'

'Well, it certainly wouldn't make things any simpler.'

'I'm sorry I was so nasty about Griselda and you the other night.'

'Forget about all that. You were upset, understandably. So was I. All that crawling about on the floor, and hitting me on the nose, and playing those blood-soaked games. Very unnerving.' Solly caught her eye, and Pearl smiled. And she was so surprised to find herself smiling after four bitter days that she laughed and he laughed with her. They were so delighted and relieved to be laughing that they did not notice that the door had opened, and that the Librarian, Dr Forgie, stood beside them. A chronic sufferer from asthma, he spoke bubblingly, like a man under water.

'Well,' said he, looking up at them from his five foot three of scholarly obesity, 'I have surprised you, I see. Now I really must protest, Bridgetower, against these, ah—tender assignations during Library hours. Miss Vambrace has her work to do, and I must beg you to confine your meetings to leisure time, which is ample—ample. We shall not quarrel about this single transgression of rules. Cupid plays strange tricks upon us all. Permit me to congratulate you both!' And here Dr Forgie seized Solly's hand and wrung it powerfully. He then reached up to Pearl's shoulders and dragged her down to a level with his own face, and kissed her with a smack. 'I must beg that there will be no repetition of this incident,' said he, and strutted out of the room.

'Unless you want to be kissed again by Dr Forgie, we'd better part,' said Solly.

'How do you suppose he knew we were here?'

'His daughter Tessie told me where to find you. With many tender and insinuating sighs and glances, I may say. Cupid has a firm friend in Tessie. Then I suppose she regretted her kind action, and blatted to Pa.'

'How like Tessie. You must go.'

'When do I see you again?'

'Eh? What for?'

'We haven't half settled things. I keep telling you that we must talk. Unless we have a united plan of action, this is going to be bad for both of us. Can I see you tonight?'

'I suppose so.'

'Where shall I call for you?'

'At home.'

'What? Won't your father mind?'

'I haven't any notion. Come about half-past eight. I'll be watching for you. No—just blow your horn, will you?'

It was Solly's turn to admire. Casually blown motor horns, he was sure, would not soothe the breast of Pearl's father. And yet she did not seem to care. Clearly Pearl was a girl of greater spirit than he had supposed.

PUNCTUALLY AT half-past four Ridley arrived at the home of his employer, and as concisely as possible he reported to him the conversation which had passed between him and Gordon Balmer, *The Bellman's* solicitor, earlier in the day.

'So he's going to Pimples Buckle?' said Mr. Clerebold Warboys.

'Yes. I didn't tell him that Weir went to Buckle last week; we know just as much about Buckle's influence as he does. But it's no good. Buckle knows nothing about the affair, and isn't interested. He has his pride, you know. He says this isn't crime—merely kid stuff—and he's only interested in crime. He wouldn't budge unless we would promise him a good deal of newspaper protection next time he comes into court, and of course we can't do that.'

'So we're still up in the air about X.'

'Yes. Worse than up in the air, I'm afraid. Snelgrove has nabbed X.'

'What!'

'I had a call from Balmer just as I was leaving the office. Snelgrove had called him not long before; they say they've got X, but of course they won't tell us who it is. Balmer's guess is that it is a woman. Anyhow, Snelgrove wanted us to meet him tomorrow, for a show-down, in his office. Balmer fought that, because he wanted the meeting to be in his office. But after a lot of wrangling I've arranged that the lawyers, and Vambrace, and X, should all meet in my office. We have to keep some sort of face.'

'Quite right. If we have to climb down and make terms, we'd better do it on our own ground.'

'You think we should climb down?'

'I don't know. And I'm not going to be there. You must handle this. Let them think they have winkled me out of my house and down to the office, and they'll imagine we are worried. Which, of course, we are. But we mustn't show it. That's why you must deal with it yourself.'

'Very well; if you think that best.'

'I do. Fight to the last ditch. We mustn't climb down if we can possibly avoid it.'

'I'm glad you feel that way.'

'I certainly do feel that way. There is nothing lawyers like better than to score off a newspaper. In fact, you might say there is nothing most people like better than to score off a newspaper. And it's understandable that they should feel that way. There have been times in my political life when I would have been glad to silence every newspaper in the country. Newspapers, as you very well know, can be damned nuisances.'

Ridley smiled. 'There have been two or three times in my life when I would have done anything to keep something out of a paper,' said he; 'anything, that is, except give the order for a story to be killed.'

'I know what you're talking about,' said Clerebold Warboys. 'But in spite of all the hogwash that is talked about the freedom of the Press, and in spite of the nauseating slop which the newspapers sometimes write about it, the freedom of the Press is a damned important thing. Not that this pin-prick has much to do with it. At worst it will cost us some money. But what I don't like is being pushed around by people who hate the paper and want to make it look foolish. God knows we can make overselves look silly enough, without any outside help. We've got a case of some sort. We are as much abused as Vambrace. So we'll fight, just to show that a newspaper doesn't have to look like a fool to please a few cranks. We'll get Pettypiece to fight the case for us, if it goes to court. He's forgotten more about news-papers and libel than old Snelgrove will ever know. We won't climb down unless they can show that we have really been careless and haven't a leg to stand on.'

'I'm afraid we have been careless,' said Ridley.

'It could happen to anybody. Anyway, they don't know we've been careless yet. And they won't, unless this comes to court. Don't let this thing worry you, Ridley. A pin-prick.'

'I'm afraid it is a little more than a pin-prick for me, sir,' said Ridley. 'This is not easy to explain, because it makes me look vain and probably a little foolish. You know I've done a great deal to arrange the new journalism course at Waver-ley. In fact, I might say that I've done all the real work. It's meant a great deal of time for several months. There has never been any talk of reward, and I don't want money. I can say quite honestly that I haven't done it for money. But it has crossed my mind, once or twice, that I might be named for an honorary degree.'

Thus modestly he brought out the ambition which had been his constant, lively companion for many weeks.

'Well, what about it? Vambrace has no say in such things. He isn't a Governor.'

'He is very close to several Governors.'

'Which ones?'

'This is rather embarassing, but I think he carries a great deal of influence with your daughter-in-law.'

'With Nesta? Oh, I don't think she sees much of him.'

'Mrs Roger Warboys has been interesting herself in this matter to a greater degree than you apparently know. And you are aware that she has a poor opinion of me as an editor. She is a friend of Mrs Bridgetower's as well.'

'Well, God bless my soul! You think she's out to sink you, for this honorary degree, or whatever it is?'

'I'm afraid so.'

'Well, what do you expect me to do about it?'

'I have not mentioned it to you before because I do not expect you to do anything about it. I have too much pride to appeal to you in a thing of this kind.'

'I'm glad of that,' said Mr Warboys who, like many people, had a keen sense of the triviality of ambition in others. 'I couldn't interfere, you know. Most of the Governors are friends of mine, but I couldn't go hat in hand to them and ask them to do something for somebody who was working for me. They might take it amiss. But you can leave it to me to put Nesta straight. It would be a fine thing for you to have a doctorate. A very nice crown to your career. A good thing for *The Bellman*. But if it doesn't work out, don't worry. These things are pretty chancy. Anyhow, you don't care much about it, do you?'

Ridley longed to say that he cared passionately about it. But life had not encouraged that sort of boldness in him, and he muttered something which suggested that he cared little for worldly gauds. Mr Warboys was plainly relieved, and after a few further remarks, Ridley rose to go. As he was about to leave the room Mrs Roger Warboys entered.

'There's a taxi at the door,' said she to Ridley. 'I thought, it must be yours. You always come and go in taxis; why don't you get yourself a car?'

'I prefer taxis,' said he. 'I find them much more convenient.'

'Not a bit convenient, really,' said Mrs Warboys, contradicting absent-mindedly and without interest. Then something seemed to strike her, and she looked at Ridley keenly. 'What news of Mrs Ridley?' said she.

Ridley turned very white, and the bony structure of his brow stood out in stronger relief. But when he spoke it was quietly and with self-possession. 'The news does not change very much, and never for the better, Mrs Warboys,' said he, and hurried out of the room.

'You shouldn't have asked him that, Nesta,' said Clerebold Warboys. 'Anyhow, you're not supposed to know.'

'Nobody's supposed to know,' said his daughter-in-law, 'but somehow everybody does.'

DRAWING UP outside the Vambrace house at about half-past eight o'clock, Solly sounded his horn in a discreet, rather than a challenging blast. He did not wish to see Pearl come through the door pursued by an angry father.

A light in an upper window went out at once, and immediately afterward Pearl came down the walk, perfectly self-possessed, and stepped into his car as though this were the most ordinary thing in the world. Solly could not refrain from admiring comment.

'You made it all right?'

'Of course. What did you expect?'

When he had hunted down Pearl that morning in the music room she had been too surprised to assume her new role of woman of the world, which she had not yet been able to make fully her own. Thinking about their conversation afterward, Pearl had decided that she had been too friendly; the truth was that she had been so amazed by the common sense which Solly had brought to their common predicament that she had been pleasanter than she intended; he had even made her laugh. But he had referred tactlessly to her father's treatment of her; he had let her know, quite needlessly, that he had seen that cuff on the ear, had heard those sobs. Therefore she was determined to give him a double dose of the woman of the world tonight.

Solly was properly intimidated. He had thought, that morning, that Pearl would be easy to deal with; she had laughed with him, and he set great store by laughter. So he drove in silence along a country road until he came to a point where it ran directly beside the bay upon which Salterton faces, and there he brought the car to a stop.

There was a silence, which Solly and Pearl both found embarrassing, but after a very long time—perhaps two or three minutes—he broke it.

'Well?' said he.

'Well?' countered Pearl. She did not mean to be difficult, but she could not think of anything better to say.

'Well, here we are. The meeting is now open. Ladies first; what do you want to say?'

A woman of the world should always be able to say something, and Pearl felt herself to be at least as much a woman of the world as the Old Woman in *Candide,* so she plunged into speech.

'We must look at this reasonably,' said she. 'There's no use getting excited; there's been quite enough of that. We've been reported engaged. We're not engaged and aren't going to be. We want the report contradicted. It isn't really so dreadful. Of course Father thinks it is. He hates your family.'

'He doesn't,' said Solly. 'Only a couple of years ago when we were all working on *The Tempest* he was easy enough to get on with. And not so many years ago he and my Mother appeared together on some sort of public committee about some current affairs thing, and they got on like a house afire. What's all this about hating my family? It's a good fifteen years since my father nosed him out as Dean.'

'Father's hates ebb and flow,' said Pearl. 'He hates you now and that's all there is to it.'

'He's as mad as a hornet at the thought of your marrying anybody. That's what it is.'

'Please. We aren't here to discuss my father.'

'Very well, Madam Chairman. But I'll bet we can't keep off him for long. Go ahead.'

'As I was saying, this report is a nuisance, and it will take some living down, but there is no very great harm done, provided there is no legal action.'

'No very great harm done?'

'Father thinks so. I don't. After all, you're a human being. It is within the range of possibility that I might have been engaged to you. There are people who aspire to that condition, in case you don't know it; and in the case you do know it and are conceited about it, I may tell you that Tessie Forgie is the most avid of them all. But the fact is that I'm not engaged to you, and while I am annoyed at the report that I am, I do not consider it to be libellous or insulting.'

'You overwhelm me.'

'Please don't be sarcastic. I'm simply trying to be objective.'

'You are succeeding magnificently. I hardly feel as if I were present in the flesh at all.'

'Unfortunately, my father takes a very serious view of

this whole affair. He thinks it is part of a plot to make him appear ridiculous.'

'Please! You're turning my head with all this subtle flattery.'

'He wants to bring an action against the newspaper. The editor is behaving abominably. Do you know this man Ridley?'

'I've met him once or twice—

A poor, unfruitful, prying, windy scribe,
Who scratches down hell's witsome sprits, that he
May show them to her vulgar, gaping crowds,
Extended on his tablets.'

'What?'

'I am amazed that you, a librarian cannot place the quotation instantly. From the great Charles Heavysege, Canada's earliest and foremost dramatist. I presume that when your father formed his opinion of me he did not know that I was the coming big man in the Heavysege field.'

'The what field?'

'It's a rich new vein of Amcan. We scholars are pegging out our claims in this new Yukon.'

'Please be serious. Ridley has behaved with dreadful discourtesy to Father. So far as I can see there's only one way to appease Father, and that's to find whoever put that notice in the paper.'

'And how are we going to do that?'

'Well, surely you have some ideas? Am I expected to do everything? All I can think of is that it must be somebody who knows us both.'

'Quite a wide field.'

'Not too wide when you think it must be somebody who knows us both and hates us both.'

'Oh, come, surely whoever it is only hates you. I'm just an insulting accessory to this business. Still, you're right. Who can it be? What goblin of ignoble mind?'

'Heavysege again?'

'Quite right.'

'I think Father knows already.'

'Really?'

'He was being extremely mysterious and hinting a lot this evening.'

'Well, why didn't you ask him?'

Pearl hesitated for a moment. 'At present it isn't very easy to ask him questions,' said she.

Solly thought he knew why, but this time he had tact enough not to refer to the happening of Wednesday night.

'If we could find out who it was,' said Pearl, 'without asking Father, naturally, we might be able to do something. Perhaps even go to see the person.'

'Have you thought of calling your cousin Ronnie?'

'I did. I went out to a public phone, and called him. All he would say was that Mr Snelgrove knew, but wouldn't tell him. He thinks there's to be some kind of big pow-wow tomorrow at Snelgrove's office at three.'

'If we're to catch whoever it is first, we'll have to be quick. Frankly, I don't think we have much of a chance.'

'Oh, don't be so defeatist! Don't you want to get this settled?'

'Pearl, have you said your say?'

'Why yes, I suppose so. For the present, anyhow.'

'Well, then, it's my turn. So far as I'm concerned this affair is settled, in its most important aspect, already.'

'How?'

'You mentioned Griselda this morning. I got this cable this afternoon.'

Solly brought a yellow cable form from his breast inside pocket, and gave it to Pearl, turning on the light on the dashboard of the car. She read:

DARLING DELIGHTED NEWS PEARL DEAR GIRL JUST RIGHT FOR YOU HAPPY FOR YOU BOTH GIVE PEARL KISS FOR ME MUCH LOVE WRITING GRISELDA

'Oh, Solly,' said Pearl, in a stricken voice.

'Yes,' said Solly. 'That's the end of an old song.' And he switched off the light.

In the half-darkness Pearl stared at him. She had ceased to be a woman of the world. Her eyes filled with tears, and very slowly they brimmed over and ran down her cheeks.

Solly was wretched, for he thought his heart was broken. Very probably it was so, in the meaning which is usually attached to the phrase. Most hearts of any quality are broken on two or three occasions in a lifetime. They mend, of course, and are often stronger than before, but something of the essence of life is lost at every break. Still, hurt as he was, he could not see Pearl weep unmoved. He took her in his arms, and comforted her as well as he could, and for a time they were miserable together.

'I wouldn't blame you if you threw me into that bay,' said Pearl, when she felt a little better, and had been accommodated with a clean handkerchief out of Solly's breast pocket. 'I've been a self-centred fool. I talked endlessly about myself and what this meant to me, and now you've lost Griselda. Everybody knows how much you loved her.'

'Yes,' said Solly, 'I'm afraid I have been rather obvious for a couple of years. Well, I don't care. I suppose it's better to feel something and look a fool than to take damned good care to feel nothing, and *be* a fool.'

'Would it help if I wrote to her? I could explain everything.'

'No you couldn't. This doesn't really concern you. I knew some good friend would be quick to tell Griselda. They even went to the expense of a cable. I'm sure it was a relief to her. She never cared much about me, really. I'm certain that cable means every word it says, quite literally. She'd be happy to think I had stopped crying for the moon, and had taken up with somebody else. Sorry, I didn't mean that the way it sounded.'

'Please don't feel guilty,' said Pearl. 'I said dreadful things to you. You must loathe me.'

212

'I don't loathe anybody,' said Solly, 'except myself.'

But Pearl was not to be denied self-abasement. 'I'm not very good about other people's feelings,' said she. And then, much more fully than she had ever been able to confide in Norman Yarrow, she told Solly about her life at home. About the division which her mother's religiosity and her father's agnosticism had made there. About the hard egotism, rising sometimes almost to the point of madness, which possessed him. About the life she led between them, torn this way and that, and cut off from young people, from ordinary pleasures, and with little before her save a continuance of this weary course, ending undoubtedly in the bitter role of the unmarried daughter who nurses both parents into the grave. She spoke without self-pity, but she spoke with point.

Solly was horrified. 'My God,' said he. 'It's monstrous. Of course everybody knows you have a grim time in that house, but everybody's always thought of it as a kind of joke. They're horrible.'

Pearl shook her head. 'No,' said she, 'that isn't it at all. They have done everything they have done out of love. They loved each other very much, and I think they still do, if they could hear one another, in their private worlds. And they loved me as much as they were able. They did the best for me that they could—the best they knew. Don't try to persuade me to think differently now. It's all I can bear at home now—more than I can bear for long, I know. But in spite of it all I love them very much.'

Solly's heart, which had contracted and grown hard that afternoon, when he received Griselda's cable, seemed to melt and beat freely now for the first time.

'I know what you mean,' said he. 'It's much the same with my mother. I'm tied to her apron strings. I'm a joke, I know. Griselda was very bitter about it once. But filial piety isn't simply a foolish phrase. It's a hard reality. Some people never seem to feel it. In happy families it is never put to any real test. But duty to parents is an obligation that some of us must recognize. However hellish parents

213

may be, the duty is as real as the duty that exists in marriage. God, what a lot we hear about unhappy marriages, and how little we hear about unhappy sons and daughters. There's no divorce for them. You've told me about your parents. Well—you know my mother. And that reminds me that it's half-past ten, and she won't go to sleep till I come home, and she needs sleep.'

Saying no more, he started the car and drove Pearl back to her door.

'Good night,' said she, and held out her hand to him.

Solly turned toward her. His face was set and white. But as their eyes met his expression softened, until he smiled.

' "Ah, lovely hellsnake, wilt thou stare at me?" ' he whispered.

'Heavysege?' said Pearl.

He nodded, and for the second time that day they laughed together. Solly suddenly seized Pearl, and kissed her again and again. Then, once more he seemed to be angry.

'Damn it all,' said he, 'haven't you any name but Pearl?'

'I've got a saint's name,' she said. 'Veronica.'

'That's a little better,' said Solly, and kissed her again.

'I must go in,' she said, struggling free.

'Yes,' said he, and this time the shadow of Wednesday night did not divide but united them.

SOLLY TIPTOED up the stairs, but the light under his mother's door was shining, as he knew it would be. He tapped and went in.

'You're late, lovey,' said Mrs Bridgetower. Without her teeth, and with her thin long hair in a braid, she was both pitiable and terrible.

'Not really, Mother. It's a little after eleven.'

'It always seems late when you're out, dear.'

'Sorry. Now you must go to sleep.'

'Where were you, dear?'

'Just out, Mother.'

'Dearie, it hurts me so to be shut out of your confidence.'

214

'Oh, you know I haven't been up to anything very terrible.'

'Dearie, I'm worried.'

'What about, Mother?'

'I'm worried that I'm going to lose my little boy.'

Oh God, thought Solly, here we go. She's coming the pitiable over me. There ought to be rules for these encounters—an inter-generation agreement about hitting below the belt.

'Well, and how do you expect to lose him this time?'

Mrs Bridgetower had had a sedative pill, and was groggy, but Solly knew her well enough to know that she could be most dangerous when at her groggiest. She spoke lispingly from her toothless mouth.

'Dearie, there's nothing in it about this girl, is there?'

'What girl?'

'This horrid Vambrace girl.'

'She's not horrid, Mother. You know her.'

'The whole family is horrid. Dearie, say there's nothing in it.'

'But, Mother, you know the whole thing began as a practical joke.'

The old eyes filled with tears; the old chin quivered a little.

'Then say it, lovey. Mother wants to hear you say it. There's nothing in it, is there?'

'Now, Mother dearest, you must get off to sleep, or you won't be able to get up tomorrow.'

Solly kissed his mother and turned off her bedside lamp. A nightlight glowed from the floor. As he reached the door his mother's voice came to him, lisping still, but sharp and without assumed infantile charm.

'I wouldn't like it to be said that *my* marriage had begun as the result of a practical joke.'

He closed the door and hastened to his attic. What a demon she was! It was impossible to conceal anything from her. She could smell a change of emotion in him!

Yet what Pearl had confided to him about her family life

had strengthened him, and as he lay in his bed he pitied his mother. And the more he pitied his mother, the more he thought of Pearl, until he could think of nothing else.

Veronica; as Veronica she seemed to be someone quite new.

Mrs Bridgetower also lay awake, and her heart yearned toward her son. He was all that she had in life. All—save a large house and nearly half a million dollars very shrewdly invested. Her heart longed toward him.

How easy, how utterly simple, for Solly to turn back to Mother—to drive away the powerful but still strange vision of Veronica, and to give himself to Mother forever! Should he run down the stairs and into her room *now*, to kiss her, and tell her that he would be her little boy forever? Thus life and death warred in Solly's bosom in the night, and in her bedroom his mother lay, yearning for him, willing him to come to her.

Of course, sensible modern people, though they believe a variety of strange things, do not believe in any such communion in emotion as this which seemed to be at work between Solly and his mother in the darkness of their house. That is why such things are never mentioned by those who have experienced them.

GLOSTER RIDLEY had fled for comfort to Mrs Fielding as soon as he felt that he could decently do so, and he arrived in her house precisely at half-past eight, but it was ten o'clock before he had a chance to speak to her intimately. No man should ever assume that he will be able to get the immediate and undivided attention of a woman who has children. Miss Cora Fielding was going to a dance, and needed her mother's help in certain fine details of dressing. Even Ridley was called into service, Mr Fielding being out, to help with a stuck zipper; the women had a pitiful faith in the ability of a man to meet such a problem, and Ridley broke two fingernails, and pinched Cora severely, in order to sustain the credit of his sex. Young George Fielding, who was seventeen, was encountering the Crimean War for

216

the first time in his history lessons and, although he did not
say so, he clearly had a feeling that Ridley remembered this
encounter as a personal experience, and repeatedly came
into the living-room to ask him questions about it. Ridley
finally found it quicker to dictate an essay on Balaclava than
to help George to find the facts himself. But at last the essay
was done, and at last Cora's escort called for her, and at last
Ridley was alone with Mrs Fielding.

'Now, Gloss, tell me all about it,' said she, leaning back
in her chair and turning her level gaze upon him.

This was exactly what Ridley was aching to do, but he
could never get used to the way in which Elspeth Fielding
cut corners. He had expected at least a quarter of an hour
of preliminaries before he got to his theme, and without
them he was not completely sure that he knew what that
theme was.

'All about what?' he said, to gain time.

'All about what's worrying you half to death. Dear old
Gloss, you come here white as a sheet, you smoke without
a stop, your hands shake, you pinch poor Cora, you lecture
Georgie as if he were a public meeting, and then you try
to pretend that everything is all right. Richard will be home
in about an hour, and unless you tell me quickly, you may
not tell me at all. Is it about this lawsuit with Professor
Vambrace?'

'How did you guess?'

'It comes out of you in strong rays. Now let me get you a
drink, and then you can tell me all about it.'

Ridley told her all that he thought was relevant. And
because he was a good journalist, and was used to getting a
story straight, he told it briefly and with all the points in the
proper order. But Mrs Fielding was not to be fooled.

'But you don't really care about an honorary degree.
Don't tell me that. Of course it would be very nice, but you
don't need it and you don't want it—not as much as you're
pretending.'

'How do you know, Elspeth? I'm not a university man.
An honorary degree to me means the degree I might have

earned years ago. I've earned it a different way. I've always missed a university training. I didn't have an easy time when I was young. I thought you understood all that.'

'Of course I understand it. But you're not a vain man. An honour of that sort wouldn't mean all this to you. You wouldn't shake and look sick at the thought of missing it.'

'I'm not a very self-assured man. I need things to bolster me up. Comfort, for instance. People think me a fussy old bachelor to take so much thought for my own comfort, though I really don't think I live any more comfortably than most married men I know. And the position I've made for myself. I'm really very well thought of as an editor, you know. And money. Of course I haven't a lot of money; my expenses have been heavy. But what I've got is rather carefully placed. All these things are necessary to me in a way that I don't suppose they are to most people. I've got to be secure.'

'Yes, that's an obsession of yours. But what has this particular trouble got to do with your security? How can it shake you, even if you do have a lawsuit, and lose it? Even if you lose your piddling degree. You'll still be you, won't you?'

'Don't hector me, Elspeth. I don't feel up to it.'

'Gloss dear, I'm not trying to hector, only to find out. Tell me truly—I'll never breath it to a soul—do you terribly want that red gown? I'd understand, if you said you did. Nearly everybody has some hankering like that. Please tell me? Does it mean something very special?'

'It would be one more thing between me and—'

'Between you and what?'

'And—it sounds strange, but it's the only phrase that fits —between me and being found out.'

'Found out in what?'

'You know very well. Of course you do.'

'You mean about your wife?'

'Yes.'

'But, Gloss, everybody knows about that!'

Ridley's face was more white and drawn than ever. He looked at Mrs Fielding coldly, almost with dislike.

'Precisely what do you mean, "Everybody knows about that"?' said he.

'Not everybody, of course, but dozens of people. I suppose that several hundred people in Salterton know that your wife has been in an asylum for nearly twenty years. Really, Gloss, for a newspaperman you are very stupid about secrets. How many Salterton secrets do you know? It must be hundreds. Scandals about money; adulteries; suicides; even murders. And you know how all those secrets came to your ears, and how many people know them beside yourself. Did you really, truly suppose, that your little secret could be kept when so many others were known? I have never mentioned it, because I knew you wouldn't want me to do so. But Dick knows, and somebody told him. And I've heard it mentioned several times. Gloster Ridley's wife is in an asylum near Halifax. Nobody thinks about it, but all kinds of people know it. Gloss, is all this passion for security an attempt to rise above that? You poor darling, what a lot of unnecessary agony! Why didn't you tell me about that years ago? When you told me about your wife?'

'I have never really told you about my wife.'

'No? Is there more to it? But it can't really be very dreadful.'

'Can't it? Elspeth, I visit my wife twice a year. I make myself do it. She hasn't recognized me once in the past fifteen years, and now I don't even see her. They let me look into her room. She lies there all day, curled up on a mattress in a corner, with a blanket pulled over her head, She has to be fed artificially.'

'Poor Gloss! How dreadful! But really, my dear, wouldn't it be better not to go? If you can't do anything, I mean?'

'No. I must go. It is absolutely necessary for me to go.'

'But why?'

'Because she is there through my fault. And—this is what shakes me, Elspeth—there is still a chance, remote, but a chance, that she might recover. Might be well enough to return to me, the doctors say. Can you imagine that? The murderer's victim to rise from the dead, to live with him

219

and share his daily life! Do you think murder a strong word to use? Do you? I use it, in my thoughts; often I can't escape it. Murder! She is in a living death, and I cannot stifle the feeling that I murdered her.'

'Oh, Gloss! I'm sure you didn't.'

'I wish I were sure, one way or the other. But I'll never know. However, as Salterton knows so much about my affairs, I suppose this is all stale news to you?'

'Oh, darling, don't be bitter. Of course I want to know everything about it, if you'll tell me. But I won't pry.'

'It isn't as though there were much to tell. You'll find this hard to believe, Elspeth, but when I was young I was very romantic. I was always falling in love—not lightly, but deeply and painfully. When I was twenty-one I met a girl who seemed to me to be the most beautiful and desirable creature that I could conceive of. I wanted to devote my life to her. She had no very strong feeling for me; she had no strong feeling about anything; but I talked her into marrying me. That happens oftener than people suppose. Love is a great force, and because I was a stronger character than she, I was able to persuade her. I was sure that she would grow to love me after we were married. She didn't. Perhaps she couldn't have loved anyone. I suppose I was an impossible fool. I know that I reproached her. She was stupid, and she was a wretched housekeeper. I know that sounds petty, in a love story, but we lived a pig's life, for I had a job with a very poor salary, and it was all intolerable. I thought I couldn't bear it. I considered running away from her, and do you know why I didn't? Because of my mother; I didn't want her to think ill of me. I didn't know what to do. But one day my wife and I were driving in a borrowed car; I was going, I remember clearly, to report a small country fair for my paper. We quarrelled for several miles. Suddenly the car went out of control, and we turned over in the ditch. That is the phrase the papers always use—"the car went out of control"—you see, it accuses nobody. It is for the court to make accusations. But in this case there was no court. I wasn't very much hurt, but my wife was

220

badly shaken. It was shock, the doctors said, and after shock came pneumonia. And within a year, a serious breakdown. Schizophrenia, Hallucinations, thinking she was somebody else, all that kind of thing. No need to go into detail about it. That meant the hospital, and that's where she has been ever since. Now she is as near to being dead, to being nothing at all, as a living human creature can be. And what I have never been able to decide is whether that accident was really an accident, or whether I created it.'

'But of course you didn't create it! You mustn't think such a thing! I'm sorry, Gloss; I know that was a silly and useless thing to say.'

'It's very sweet of you to have such belief in me. Of course I, as I exist at this moment, didn't create it. But I was a very different person then. I wished her dead, or myself dead, time and time again. And you see, so much of my life has been devoted to making myself into a person who couldn't possibly have created that accident, who couldn't possibly have done that murder. And if you think the red gown of a Doctor of Laws wouldn't be a help in that, you haven't understood what a very inferior creature I am, and how much apparently small things can mean to me.'

'But, my dear, a red gown can't change your own opinion of yourself. The man you live with, and feed and wash and dress and go to bed with doesn't wear a red gown. He's the man that counts. Oh, Gloss darling, you must stop torturing yourself. What's the good of winning honours and the good opinion of the world if you can't live on good terms with yourself?'

'Do you know anybody who isn't a fool who really lives on good terms with himself?'

'Yes, of course I do.'

'I shouldn't have married her, but I did. Very well. Having married her, I should have borne it better, shown more restraint, and more kindness. But I didn't. Can I forget that, or forgive myself?'

'But it's done and past repair. Now, Gloss, you must listen to me.'

221

It would be of little avail to set down in detail what Mrs Fielding said to Ridley. None of it was extraordinarily wise, or uncommonly deep, but it was all rooted fast in love and womanly tenderness. Nor would it be truthful to say that Ridley was set free from his bugbear forever. But his burden was so much lightened, and confession had so cleansed him, that he was very much changed, very much cheered, and when at last Mr Fielding came home Ridley greeted him with a warmth of affection that surprised that gentleman, old friends as they were.

When at last Ridley set out for home, his step was light, and he felt free and vigorous. If only, he thought, I had had the good luck to marry somebody like Elspeth. But that was fruitless speculation, and he had learned that night how profitless, how diminishing, fruitless speculation can be. At fifty he was perhaps rather old to be coming to such conclusions, but we all subscribe thoughtlessly to many beliefs, the truth of which does not strike home to us until experience gives them reality. Wisdom may be rented, so to speak, on the experience of other people, but we buy it at an inordinate price before we make it our own forever.

'If I could hold fast to this state of mind I am in now, I might at last be free,' thought Ridley exultantly.

When he went into the vestibule of the old mansion in which his apartment was, he found a figure huddled on the floor, partly asleep. It started up, and revealed itself as Henry Rumball.

'I've been waiting for you sir,' said he. 'I've found X.'

He held out his hand. In it was a pink slip for a *Bellman* classified advertisement.

MRS EDITH LITTLE had completed her self-imposed nightly task of marking the typographical errors in *The Bellman* and was knitting on a sweater for little Earl. It was a complicated pattern, designed to make the finished garment look as though it had been made from heavy cable, and she was often compelled to consult her pattern book, from the

page of which smiled the photograph of an offensively neat
and handsome little boy, wearing the sweater in question.
The Morphew's living-room presented a peaceful domestic
scene. Mrs Morphew was painting her toenails coral pink,
having spent an agreeable hour rubbing the hair from her
legs with a pad of fine emery paper. The radio had been
discoursing music, comic repartee, news and advertising all
evening but neither Ede nor Kitten had paid any attention
to it. They were lost in their thoughts. But when an an-
nouncer said that it was, at that very instant, eleven o'clock,
Ede spoke to her sister censoriously.

'You'd better stop that. The boys'll be home soon.'

'What of it? I got a whole 'nother foot still to do.'

'D'you want them to catch you at it?'

'Why not? Georgie knows I do it. Georgie likes it.'

'What about Bev?'

'Bev's an old sport. He'd like it.'

'It isn't right for men to know what women do.'

'If you'd let Bob Little know a little more what you did,
maybe he wouldn't've run out on you.'

'That is one hell of a thing to say.'

'Yeah, ain't it though!'

'Yes, it is! If I wanted to throw my legs around I could
get men to look at me too. The way George looks at you
sometimes, it makes me creep!'

'I'll bet it does.'

'All right, if you're proud of that kind of thing.'

'George is still living right here with me, and glad to, in
case you hadn't noticed.'

'And so he ought. You're a wonderful housekeeper. I give
you that.'

'That's only part of what I am.'

'Oh, you both of you make so much of that! Still, it
hasn't brought you any children.'

'Ede, that's a dirty, lousy thing to say, even between sis-
ters!'

'Well, who threw Bob Little up to me a minute ago? I

223

may not have a husband, but I've got my child, and I'd a lot sooner it was that way than the other way.' And Ede knitted ostentatiously.

'You're a liar but I forgive you,' said Kitten good-naturedly. 'Listen, why don't you start looking around?'

'I'm not interested, thank you very much.'

'Well then, get interested. Earl's going to need a daddy. If you don't think much of George, get a man of your own to bring up the boy.'

'I can manage Earl without any man.'

'All right. Go on wishing old Baldy Ridley would take a tumble to you. And I'll bet you wouldn't wait for any ring if he did either.'

'That's a fine thing to say about your own flesh and blood.'

'Ede, you got more refinement than sense; that's what's wrong with you.'

'I've got a child to think of; I can't just let myself go.'

'Oh, so I've let myself go, have I? I can get into clothes you can't even touch.'

'I meant mentally. Living with George you've just sunk to his level. You've just become George's Thing, if you want to know what I really think! Just his Thing!'

Kitten was unable to reply to this, for she had thrown herself backward in her chair and was kicking her feet vigorously in the air in order to dry her nail-varnish. It was at this moment that the front door opened and George and Mr Higgin walked in, followed by a stranger.

'Looka there!' shouted George, and seizing one of his wife's feet he nipped her playfully on the big toe with his front teeth. 'What I always say, kid, you're good enough to eat!'

'Georgie, lemme down! Georgie!' squealed Kitten, and after a great deal of bare leg and frilly panties had been displayed, and after George had pretended to strum on her leg as upon a guitar, he did let her down, and she made a great show of modesty, tucking her feet up under her.

'What a pleasant homecoming,' said Mr Higgin, laughing delightedly, his bright eyes missing nothing of Kitten's display. 'You would have been proud of George, Kitten, indeed you would. He was quite the hit of the smoker, wasn't he, Mr Rumball?'

'Uh-huh,' said Rumball, without much enthusiasm.

'Meet m'friend Henry Rumball,' said George; 'Hank, meet the wife. Meet Ede. Siddown. Getcha drink.'

'Don't bother, Mr Morphew,' said Rumball. 'I'll have to go in just a minute, anyway.'

'Hank's a reporter,' said George. 'Gonna write us all up in *The Bellman*, aintcha, Henry?'

'I can't promise anything,' said Rumball. 'I only dropped in to see Mr Higgin; Mr Shillito insisted that I should. It wasn't a regular assignment, you know. I only came to see if there was anything about Mr Higgin I might work up into a feature story. There won't be any report of the smoker.'

'No report of the smoker?' said George, greatly indignant. 'And why not? Ain't we boys at the club subscribers? Ain't we got any rights? Listen, son, just tell me one thing; you've heard about the freedom of the Press?'

'Sure, sure,' said Rumball uneasily.

'OK then, why don't the smoker get a write-up?'

'Well, it was a private performance, Mr Morphew.'

'You're damn right it was private. So what were you doing there, sticking your nose into it?'

'Well, as I said, Mr Shillito asked me to go to see what Mr Higgin was doing, and to see if I could write something about it.'

'Now lookit,' said George pugnaciously, 'about this freedom of the Press. That means the club has as much right to a plug in the paper as anybody, don't it? And if not, just kindly tell me why not, will ya? Just explain.'

'Don't get excited, George,' said Higgin. 'It was a private show. And a very good thing too. Oh, if you could have seen George!' He giggled rapturously.

225

'I was good, wasn't I?' said George, restored to good humour. He was not entirely drunk, but he was in a variable mood, and there were traces of greasepaint on his face.

'You were sensational,' said Mr Higgin, giggling again.

'What'd you sing, Georgie?' asked Kitten, who had surveyed all of this with complacency.

'The ones I practised,' said George, then winked at Higgin and went off into a fit of laughter so great that he fell into his wife's chair. When they had sorted themselves out, he was sitting in the chair and Kitten was in his lap, her coral toes hanging over the arm.

'Oh, but it was the encores,' said Mr Higgin, bubbling with mirth. 'That was where he really had them, eh, Mr Rumball?'

'Yes, I guess it was,' said Rumball.

' "I'll be up 'er flue next week," ' sang George, loudly, and collapsed in laughter.

'What?' cried Kitten, who had caught the infection and was laughing herself, without knowing why.

'It's his song,' said Higgin, wiping his eyes. 'He sings it in the character of a chimney-sweep. It's all about his work, you see, and that's the refrain—"I'll be up 'er flue next week"—and the meanings people seem to see in it, you'd never think! What we in the profession call the *double entendre*,' he said to Edith, feeling that she should be included in the gaiety, if possible on a higher level of culture than the others. But Ede merely snorted.

'I'd like to get along now, if that's all right?' said Rumball.

'Yes, of course. You wanted to see my press-cutting book. I'll get it at once,' said Higgin, and trotted up the stairs.

'I'll expect to see something in the paper about the show tonight,' said George, in a loud, bantering tone. 'We got some influence, you know. Ede here's got influence on *The Bellman*, ain't that right, Ede?'

'George, that'll do,' said Edith, with dignity.

' "I'll be up 'er flue next week," ' sang George, *sotto voce*, and pinched Kitten from below. She slapped him playfully and they scuffled under the embarrassed eyes of Mr Rumball until Bevill Higgin came downstairs, carrying a large press-cutting book.

'Here it is,' said he. 'A complete record of my career, with photographs, clippings, programmes—all dated and arranged in proper order. You will be very careful with it, won't you? All my life I have been methodical. I cannot bear to part with any of my little clippings from the past. A few may be loose in the book. When you have done with it, if you will give me a call, I'll pick it up at *The Bellman* offices myself. Please, please be careful. This is my life,' he said, patting the volume with a wistful charm which no one but Edith fully appreciated.

'Yes, I'll be careful,' said Rumball, and then, nervously to the others, 'well, good night, everybody.'

'Remember, we got influence!' shouted George, as the door closed behind the reporter.

'Do you really think you'll get a write-up?' asked Edith very seriously when, a little later, they had all been accommodated with glasses of rye from the bottle which Georgie produced from his bundle of costumes. 'It would be wonderful publicity, Bev—bring you all kinds of pupils.'

'I have hopes,' said Mr Higgin demurely. 'My friend Mr Shillito is, so to speak, editor *emeritus* of the newspaper; I have been given to understand that he carries very great influence—very great. He thinks something should be done. Of course, that young man will write his *critique* on what he finds in my cuttings-book. Tonight's work was not my best line, of course.'

'Oh yes it was,' said George, 'that's the stuff the public wants. You got to give the public what it wants. And it wants the heart stuff and the funny stuff. This arty stuff is all baloney.'

'Listen to who's talking,' said Edith.

'Yeah? Well, if you'd heard how I went over tonight you'd change your tune, Ede. Bev says I got talent and I guess tonight I proved it, eh, Bev?'

'Oh, no doubt about it,' said Mr Higgin, and giggled again. 'You ladies should have heard him. Or no—perhaps

227

you shouldn't have heard him. But for a male audience it was a treat, really it was.'

'Well, I kind of half hope you don't get a write-up in the old *Bellman*,' said Kitten. 'Because if you do you'll get so many pupils and be so famous we'll lose you from here, and I'd certainly hate that.'

'Oh, you dear creature,' said Mr Higgin, tittering.

'Yes, and what would Earl do without his Ugga Bev?' said Edith, throwing him a glance heavy with solicitous motherhood.

'Oh, my dears, you must never believe that I would leave you,' said Mr Higgin, and though he looked tenderly toward Kitten, it was Edith's hand that he patted. 'I've come to look upon this as my own family. I have indeed. And you can never know what that means to a weary, wayworn wanderer such as myself.' There was a tear in his eye.

'Well, Bev, I guess we all understand that, and I know I speak for the girls as well as me when I say that we feel the same in regards to you,' said George, whose tipsiness had suddenly taken a formal turn.

'Sure, Bev, we know how tough it is to make your way in a new country and all that,' said Kitten.

'Yes, we have to remember that everybody was new in Canada once,' said Edith, and then, suddenly, the gathering rose from this solemn and somewhat literary note to a higher plane of enjoyment. The rye went round again, and for a third time, and then Mr Higgin sang *Believe Me, If All Those Endearing Young Charms,* and the Morphews and Edith, as befitted his pupils, provided harmonies of uncertain character but of rich intent. By the time they went to bed all their hearts were high and full.

EDITH HUMMED the lovely Irish air as she undressed, and returning from the bathroom she heard its strains from the door of the Morphews' bedroom. She hummed it still as she stood before her mirror, and arranged her hair in metal curlers, which stood out like a *chevaux-de-frise* around her face. It was a caressing air, and its gentle melancholy aroused agreeably painful feelings in her breast. The way Kitten was always at her about men! But she wasn't the sort to throw herself at anybody that came along, or settle for a big loudmouth like George. Love, if she were ever to feel it (for she had long since decided that her feeling for Robert Little had not been the Real Thing) would be something fine, gentle and wistful. She couldn't bear a man to whom she was nothing but a Body as, quite unjustly, she supposed that her sister was to George. Her love, if and when it came, would be a thing of Mind, of Soul.

There was a very gentle tap at her door. Supposing it to be Kitten she opened it, and Mr Higgin slipped quickly into the room. He was in his pyjamas and a dressing-gown, and with his pink face and small stature he looked like a small boy.

'Shh!' said he, with his finger on his lips. 'After such an evening of true friendship I simply couldn't go to sleep without saying good night to my little pupil.'

He tiptoed to the cot in which Earl lay asleep, and looked tenderly down at him. His thoughts seemed to be too fine for utterance, but he smiled and sighed. Edith, who was somewhat alarmed at being caught in her nightdress, felt reassured, but reached for a kimono.

'Don't trouble,' said Higgin, 'I'm just going.' He looked back at the child. 'Your treasure,' said he. 'What would I not give to have the right to call him mine as well. Still, it is no small thing to be his "Ugga Bev". I want you to know, Edith, how much I cherish that.'

Ede felt that this demanded something equally fine from her, but she was not ready with phrases. 'Well, I want you to understand, Bev, how much it means to Earl, and to me too,' she said at last. 'I mean, your influence, and everything.'

Mr Higgin looked at her and his face filled with tender admiration.

'Thank you,' he said, with a more than ordinary simplicity. 'You can never know what that means to me. Oh, Edith, to see you standing there, in simple loveliness! It's

229

a picture; that's the only expression I can use; a picture!'

Edith was suddenly conscious that she was standing in front of the only light in the room and that her nightdress was thin. She hastily moved toward her kimono again, where it lay on the bed.

'No, no, dear child,' said Mr Higgin, very tenderly, but laughing a little in a disembodied manner. 'Don't misunderstand me. And please don't put on your gown. Your loveliness, Edith, has not been revealed to any profane gaze. Just slip into your bed, and let me tuck you up.'

Obediently Edith got into bed, and Mr Higgin drew the covers up to her chin, and smoothed them.

'The little mother tucks up her babe, but who is to tuck up the little mother, eh?' said he, tenderly. And then, absent-mindedly, he sat down on the bed. 'You know,' he continued, 'my life has been a wandering one, and not easy, but I have always cherished the domestic virtues.' He seemed to turn the expression over in his mouth, savouring its fine flavour. 'Yes, the domestic virtues. An artist seeks his inspiration where he finds it, but I have always felt that, for me, the richest soil of inspiration was a family and a home. But that was denied me.'

Mr Higgin was speaking now in a rich, actorly manner, and the sigh with which he followed his words would have carried to the topmost gallery of a good-sized theatre.

'I have known love,' he continued. 'Love as the artist knows it, fleeting, turbulent, sweet. Love of the sort which for it as few women are. But that is past. I find myself now at the age when all that is a lovely memory. I don't suppose life has denied to you, sweet child, though you are framed that you have any notion of my age. I am forty-eight.'

Edith said nothing. She would have taken him for considerably over fifty, and she was ashamed to have misjudged a man whose suffering had plainly been so deep.

'Forty-eight,' said Bevill Higgin. 'Yet the heart is young. The heart, I may say, feels as young as that of that blessed child yonder. It is, truly, a child's heart. "In the heart of age, a child lies weeping." Do you know that lovely poem? Ah, so true, so true of me. In my heart is a child, a child who seeks the mother.'

Edith was awed by the beauty of Mr Higgin's talk. There was a grandeur and a sweep about it for which she had longed all her life, and now that she actually heard it, addressed solely to herself, she was entranced. Softly but quickly Mr Higgin turned out the lamp, and slipped under the covers beside her. He lay at some distance, and she was not strongly aware of his presence, but only of his voice.

'And where is the mother to be found,' asked Mr Higgin, 'but in every loving, understanding heart? Edith, life has not been kind to me. When Fortune frowns on a man, every hand is against him. Misfortune in the Old Country drove me abroad. I could have fought it out there, with small-minded detractors. But there is such a thing as pride. And so I came here, and though I found a haven in this house, my path was not smooth abroad. No, no; not smooth. I found friends' (here his hand stole under the sheet and clasped hers) 'and I must say I found enemies as well. Shall I name those enemies? I fear that if I do so I shall wound a heart which has become very dear to me.'

Here Mr Higgin moved himself nearer to Edith, and in a deft and practised manner slipped one arm under her head, so that she lay partly on his bosom. He smelled strongly of rye, and his manner suddenly became jocular.

'What a trusting little heart it is,' he murmured. 'Working loyally every day to bring comfort to a man who is unworthy of such gifts. What a dear, trusting, silly little heart.' He giggled.

'Who are you talking about?' said Edith. Her voice came tremulously.

'Can't you guess? About your Mr Ridley, of course.'

'What's wrong with him, Bev?'

'He has been very harsh to me, dear one. Very harsh and scornful. So have some others. But I think they regret it now.'

'Who do you mean, Bev?'

'The young man at the University. I wasn't worth his

231

consideration, though I could have helped him. Snotty young pup! And the girl in the Library. I couldn't use the Library without an introduction. Oh no, I wasn't good enough. And your Mr Ridley, snapping his scissors at me. I'm not spiteful. I don't bear a grudge. But I've had my little game with them, just the same.'

'Bev, did you!—'

'Aha, what a sharp little thing it is! And you are the only one that knows! Because I think I'm on the upward path now. I think I've broken the ice. And when I'm established here, they'll all feel the weight of my hand, and not in little jokes either.'

He was giggling a great deal now. Edith was much puzzled. Here she was, in possession of the secret which had so much troubled her idol, Mr Ridley, and yet now that she was able to be of use to him, he was no longer her idol. This pink, sweet-talking little man seemed suddenly to have filled her whole being with warmth and comfort and wonder.

'You'd never tell, would you?' said he teasingly.

'Oh, Bev, no—never, never,' she whispered.

Bevill Higgin leaned forward and kissed her, very softly, but for a long, long time. A delicious warmth suffused her. She seemed to melt, to move toward him without any will of her own. Gently, very gently, his hand stole in the front of her nightdress and caressed her breast. She shuddered with pleasure as he slipped the straps from her shoulders, and, pushing the nightdress downward, stroked first her stomach and then her thighs with a touch as light as a feather. She heaved gently on a warm, smooth sea.

'Mommie.' It was Earl's voice, sleepy but loud. 'Mommie, I wanna go to the bathroom.'

Edith came to herself with a start. She pushed Higgin roughly from her. 'Get away!' she whispered roughly, 'get away from me, you nasty old thing.'

'Edith,' said he, in a very low voice, 'don't be frightened. It's me! It's Bev! Be calm!'

Hampered as she was by her downthrust nightdress she

nevertheless managed to scramble quickly over him to the floor. Seizing a hairbrush in one hand, and screening her naked breasts with the other, she struck at him, and as he guarded his head from the blows she beat furiously at his hands.

'Get out of here,' she whispered. Earl, concerned only with his own mounting need, wailed from the cot. 'Get out,' she whispered, over and over, until Higgin, scrambling from the bed, rushed from the room. She threw his slippers after him.

LATER, SHE sat up in her bed, marvelling at herself. She had as near as a toucher been seduced! She had always thought of seduction as something that happened in fine hotels, or in the backs of very expensive cars. And right here, in her house and the Morphews', in this little room, with her hair in curlers, and little Earlie asleep not three feet away! It was staggering. It was shattering.

Yet she could not weep. The experience had been immeasurably stimulating. She felt no shame, only triumphant virtue. She wasn't anybody that could be had by any slick old fellow with a line of smooth talk! It had been a narrow escape, but the more she thought about it, the more she knew that she would never have let him go the limit.

And she had the secret! How Ridley would thank her! How he'd be grateful to her! For he wasn't one of the kind that always looked at a woman with one thing in mind. He was above all that. She'd be there extra early in the morning. She'd wake him up with her news.

Her ideal was triumphantly restored to his throne.

PART SIX

AT HALF-PAST two on Tuesday, November 7th, Gloster Ridley was arranging his office for the meeting with the lawyers. Miss Green had done all the necessary work well beforehand, but still he fussed nervously with the chairs, rearranged heaps of paper on his side-table, laid pencils conveniently on his blotter, tinkered with anything and with everything. How different was the demeanour of Mr A. J. Marryat, who stood calmly by the window, smiling out at the beauty of the late autumn. But the difference between the two men was superficial; though the one fussed and the other was at ease, both had an air of confidence.

Mr Marryat turned to Ridley. 'Gordon Balmer has just come in the front door,' said he. 'Now, remember, the important thing is never to lose face. They'll talk a lot about court, but *this* is the trial. We've got to maintain face.'

Ridley smiled, and concealing his nervousness for the first time, he stood behind his desk in an attitude which was almost debonair. It was not long until Miss Green opened the door to admit *The Bellman's* lawyer.

'I'm a little late,' said Mr Balmer. 'I wanted to get over earlier in order to do some arranging; there's a lot in the way these situations are handled.' He made his way directly behind Ridley's desk, and put his briefcase upon it. 'I'll sit here, if you don't mind,' said he. 'I have a good many papers and I'll need somewhere to put them.'

'I've thought of that already,' said Ridley, 'and I've arranged a place for you here.' He indicated a chair on the

234

other side of the desk, 'You see, I've cleared a place for all your papers.'

'Of course I had no intention of taking your chair,' said Mr Balmer, though that was what he had just been prevented from doing. 'But as I suppose I shall be in charge of the meeting I more or less unconsciously made for this place. You see,' he said, lowering his voice confidentially, 'there's a certain psychological advantage about dominating the room, on these occasions. And the man who sits behind the desk always dominates the men whose legs can be seen. It's a funny thing; not one in thousand thinks of it.'

'Extraordinary!' said Ridley, but he did not budge from his position, which made it impossible for Mr Balmer to get the dominating chair without forcibly pushing him aside. 'As a matter of fact, I've tried to give you a psychological advantage of another sort; I've put you with your back to the window, and Mr Snelgrove will sit facing full into the light. I think that's rather good, don't you?'

Mr Balmer muttered something which might have been assent. Certainly he did not seem to think that any advantage of lighting could make up for the loss of the dominating chair, the chair which, by his attitude, he had put in the position of the Bench. With an ill grace he moved to the less desirable chair indicated by Ridley, and began to take some things out of his brief-case.

Ridley looked toward Mr Marryat, who was behind Balmer. Though his expression did not change, his eyes signalled 'Face?', and equally without expression Mr Marryat signalled back 'Face, indeed!'

Again there came a tap at the door, and Miss Green ushered in Mr Snelgrove and Professor Vambrace.

'Good afternoon, gentlemen,' said Ridley. 'I had expected three in your party. I hope that X has not disappointed you?'

'You may be sure that X will appear at the proper time,' said Mr Snelgrove. 'As we are to have this meeting under circumstances which I must say I consider to be very irregular, I must ask for certain necessary accommodations. I have many papers, and I shall want a desk. I presume that there will be no objection if I sit here?' And he also made for Ridley's chair, but the editor stood his ground.

'I am sure that you will find everything you want here, opposite Mr Balmer,' said he. 'Blotting paper, pens, ink, pencils—we have tried to anticipate your wants, but if anything is lacking my secretary will get it for you at once.'

'I would greatly have preferred to hold this encounter in my own chambers,' said Mr. Snelgrove, in a voice which temper was already causing to tremble. 'I consider it most unusual and undesirable to meet a colleague who may become an opponent in his client's office.' And he glared at Gordon Balmer in a manner which was intended to make Ridley, as a non-legal person, feel superfluous and intrusive.

'I am not on my home ground, either, Mr Snelgrove,' said Balmer, and went on ostentatiously arranging some papers. It was to be a source of astonishment to Ridley and Marryat, during the ensuing hour, that both the lawyers had brief-cases containing a great many papers which could not possibly have had any bearing on the matter in hand, but which peeped importantly from their satchels as though they might, at any moment, leap forth to prove or disprove something of the utmost importance.

Professor Vambrace said nothing, but took a chair somewhat to the rear of Mr Snelgrove. He had, for the occasion, put on a suit of dark, heavy tweed, and a black tie, and looked more than ever like a tragedian of the old school.

Once again the door opened, and Miss Green showed in Dean Jevon Knapp.

'Sorry to be late, if indeed I am late,' said he, smiling urbanely at everyone. He fixed upon Mr Marryat, as the most amiable looking person present, and shook him by the hand with great cordiality, to his astonishment.

'I find it difficult to ask the question,' said Ridley, 'but I cannot hold it back. Are we to understand that Dean Knapp is X, Mr Snelgrove?'

'I am not in a mood for facetious questions, sir,' said the lawyer.

'I assure you that I have no wish to seem facetious. But

you have promised to produce X, and the only unknown quantity here is the Dean. I think my question a very natural one.'

'Quite natural,' said Mr Balmer, who felt that, as a lawyer, he ought to say something as soon as possible, and who was himself puzzled.

'I asked Mr Dean to join me here,' said Mr Snelgrove, 'in order that he may be a witness to what I intend to disclose. I have a particular reason for doing so and it is of direct concern to him. I repeat, X will be forthcoming in due season.'

'Very well,' said Mr Balmer. 'Now, I think we have wasted quite enough time, and if you have no objection, I should like to clarify one or two points which are still in doubt.'

As he spoke, Ridley sat down behind his desk, and Mr Marryat, moving a chair from a corner, sat down almost beside him. It was a well-timed move, for both the representatives of *The Bellman* were behind the desk, with their legs concealed; they were on the Bench and the two lawyers were, so to speak, in court. The Dean seated himself in an armchair as some distance, and immediately detracted from the dignity of the proceedings by producing a small and evil-smelling pipe, which he lit with a great deal of noise and sucking. He was the only person present who seemed to have no sense of the importance of face.

'May I ask at once,' said Mr Balmer, 'whether you intend to proceed against *The Bellman* for libel?'

'I shall advise my client on that point when this meeting is over,' said Mr Snelgrove. 'I need not explain to you that the law of libel exists as a safeguard of private reputation. I do not think that there is any doubt whatever that the publication of this false notice of engagement places Miss Pearl Vambrace in an exceedingly uncomfortable position, and will tend to make her avoided and shunned by young men of her acquaintance. A young woman's good name is her most precious possession; not in a legal, but in a moral sense, it is a major portion of her dower. This affair will unquestionably expose her to a certain amount of ridicule, perhaps to a great deal of ridicule and distress of mind. The refusal of *The Bellman* to do anything whatever to mitigate the wrong it has done her can only increase the unpleasantness of the situation in which she has been put. If this is not a civil libel, I should very much like to know what you would call it?'

'I should hesitate to call it libel,' said Mr Balmer, very blandly. 'After all, it is an everyday occurrence for a young woman to be reported engaged to a young man. Many young women take it as a compliment to be so reported, and laugh it off if the report has no truth.'

'A formal notice of engagement, printed in a newspaper, is something very different from social gossip,' said Mr Snelgrove, raising his eyebrows very high, and tapping his front teeth with his eyeglasses. 'It is a deliberate and premeditated untruth, designed to wound and surround the victim with an atmosphere of ridicule.'

'The common description of libel is that which exposes the victim not only to ridicule, but also to hatred and contempt,' said Mr Balmer. 'You will not pretend that anything remotely resembling hatred or contempt could spring from this prank?'

Professor Vambrace, whose face had grown dark during the foregoing, now spoke in his deepest tones. 'I consider that hatred and contempt have been engendered against me,' he said. 'Rumours of the most foul and obscene order are being spread against me. They have been thrown in my face by complete strangers. I can call witnesses to prove it.'

'Will you be good enough to leave this to me?' said Mr Snelgrove to his client. 'I shall bring up these matters at the proper time.'

'Frankly, I am happy that Professor Vambrace has spoken,' said Mr Balmer. 'I should like to know who has been libelled, the Professor, or Miss Vambrace? The lady is not here; that suggests to me that she does not choose to associate herself with this dispute.'

'My daughter is not here because I would not bring her

into a discussion of this kind,' said the Professor. 'I do not consider this a proper place for a young girl.'

'Ah, I had not understood that Miss Vambrace was a minor,' said Mr Balmer. 'That, of course, puts quite a different complexion on the case.'

'She is not a minor,' said the Professor. 'She is a lady, and entitled to be guarded against disagreeable experiences and associations.' He scowled deeply at Marryat and Ridley, who looked as though they did not understand what he meant.

'Not a minor?' said Balmer, with a show of surprise. 'In that case then, Professor, may I ask a pointed question: if she is not a minor, is she still subject to corporal punishment in her home?'

'Do you see?' roared Vambrace at Snelgrove, starting up from his chair. 'These damnable rumours pursue me everywhere! How dare you ask me such a question?' he shouted at Balmer.

'Only because it is a question I should be obliged to ask you in court if this matter were to come to trial,' said the lawyer, blandly. 'Very disagreeable questions may be asked in court, and they cannot be avoided there as easily as here.'

'Sit down, sir, at once,' said Mr Snelgrove. 'Sit down and be silent, or, I warn you, I shall throw up your case here and now. I only took up this matter to help you; I shall not put up with an interference.'

'If Miss Vambrace is the injured party, I really think she should he here, however repugnant the proceedings might be to her,' said Balmer. 'If it is Professor Vambrace who fancies himself injured, we must change our ground. I don't quite see the damage to him in this affair.'

'In libel it is not necessary to prove damage,' said Mr Snelgrove, playing the wily lawyer to the hilt. 'Damage is presumed, as you well know.'

'Damage would be presumed when the jury had decided whether the engagement notice was capable of a defamatory meaning,' said Balmer. 'You can't tell what a jury might make of a thing like this. They might think it was a huge joke. One outburst from your client in court and they would be very likely to do so.'

'Don't tell me what a jury is likely to do, sir,' said Mr Snelgrove. 'I know just as much about juries as you do. The standard in such matters is what the Reasonable Man might think.'

'Are you putting forward your client as the Reasonable Man?' asked Mr Balmer. The Professor growled, but was hushed by Mr Snelgrove. Mr Balmer pressed his advantage.

'My own opinion is that the Reasonable Man would say that my clients have been ill-used, and are, in fact, innocent victims of a hoax. No jury of business men would find against them for an honest mistake. Everybody makes mistakes and nearly everybody at some time is victim of a hoax. They are, I assure you, just as anxious to find the real perpetrator of this hoax as you are.'

'I think the jury's sympathy for your clients would be a good deal cooled when it was explained how negligent they had been,' said Mr Snelgrove. 'They claim to have a system of records which tells them who inserts all such advertisements as this. Why have those records not been brought forward? I think the answer must be because they cannot produce any such record. The matter of a completely impossible date in the advertising copy would take a good deal of explaining to the Reasonable Man.'

'A small matter,' said Mr Balmer.

'Perhaps, but taken in conjunction with the fact that they have no record of who inserted the advertisement it is not a small matter. If they have any records, and are not, in fact, irresponsible, why do they not themselves know who X is?'

'That is something which we shall make known at the proper time—in court, if need be,' said Mr Balmer. 'But I have another question I wish to ask your client.'

'I forbid you to answer, Professor Vambrace,' said Mr Snelgrove.

'Oh, very well,' said Balmer. 'If you have it all cooked up between you, so that he speaks only when you give him leave, I don't mind. But it suggests even more strongly what

I have suspected for some time, that Professor Vambrace is in this thing simply in the hope of getting a big money settlement. You and he are in this together; it's a shakedown.'

'My honour has never been called in question,' shouted the Professor, starting up. 'That is a lie, a damned, malicious lie, and I demand that you apologize immediately.'

'I'll apologize,' said Balmer, 'if you will give me your word of honour that anything you get out of your libel suit —after you have paid your lawyers their very considerable fees—will be given to a charity.'

'Say nothing!' commanded Mr Snelgrove. 'Don't imagine that I don't see what you are up to! You are trying dirty, underhanded tricks to make my client discredit himself or frighten him off suit. Your conduct, sir, is a disgrace to the Bar, and don't suppose that I won't bring it up at the next meeting of the Bar Association!'

The atmosphere of the room had become very hot. The Dean's pipe had gone out, and he tittered occasionally, from nervous tension. Marryat and Ridley were, to tell the truth, a little ashamed of their lawyer, whom they had never seen in action in quite this spirit before.

'Please yourself about that,' said Balmer. 'I'm tired of this discussion, which is not leading us anywhere. You say that there is libel, and that my clients were negligent. All right. Prove it. Let's have X. Where have you got him hidden?'

With great dignity Mr Snelgrove rose and walked to the window. Having trained his eyeglasses upon something in the street below, he took out his pocket-handkerchief, and solemnly waved it three times. He then returned to his chair, and glared at Mr Balmer in silence, which was broken only by a furious nasal whistling from Professor Vambrace.

Some time passed, uncomfortably for the six men in Ridley's office, until Miss Green's knock was heard, and she opened the door to admit Humphrey Cobbler, followed by Ronnie Fitzalan. No one seemed to have anything to say, and no word was spoken until Mr Snelgrove had waved Cobbler into a chair which Ronnie, rather apologetically, placed very much in the centre of the room.

241

'Well, Mr Cobbler,' said Mr Snelgrove, now the stage lawyer to the life, 'I daresay you are wondering why you have been asked to come here?'

Cobbler produced a very large wad of torn sheeting from his jacket pocket and blew his nose resoundingly. 'I'm sure it's something pleasant,' said he, 'and I love the suspense. Whenever lawyers want me for anything, I always assume that it is because somebody has left me a fortune. Just let me have the details slowly, saving up the actual glorious figures for the last.' He spoke in a thickened voice, and his face was pale. Closing his eyes, he relaxed as much as he could in the straight, armless chair which he had been given.

'I'd advise you not to take that tone,' said Mr Snelgrove. 'This may be an extremely serious affair for you.'

'You needn't worry about what tone I take; I have perfect pitch,' said Cobbler. 'As for seriousness, I have risen virtually from my death-bed to be here, chiefly because Mr Fitzalan is a very persuasive fellow. My one thought now is to get back to bed.'

'My dear fellow,' said the Dean, solicitously. 'Are you worse since Sunday?'

Cobbler made no reply, but blew his nose as though painfully expelling his soul from his nostrils.

'Gentlemen,' said Mr Snelgrove. 'Behold X.'

The moment fell short of great drama. Ridley and Marryat seemed unmoved, and Balmer glanced momentarily at Cobbler, only to return to a paper which he held in his hand. The Dean, who did not know what X meant, except that it was something vaguely discreditable, merely looked confused. Only Professor Vambrace scowled upon Cobbler, and as the organist had his eyes shut, this was not particularly effective.

'I shall be brief,' continued Mr Snelgrove. 'Cobbler, I put it to you that on October 31st, on Tuesday last to be precise, you and a gang of hoodlums invaded the premises of St Nicholas' Cathedral, taking liquor with you. There you created a disturbance, the details of which I shall not specify; it was, however, sufficient to arouse the attention of some

of the Cathedral neighbours, and even of the Dean, who
arrived after some lapse of time and drove you forth. Is this
true?'

'Guilty, m'lord,' said Cobbler, without opening his eyes.

'It was on the following night,' said Mr Snelgrove, 'that
you sought out Professor Vambrace in a public place, and
there sang a ribald song, directed at him personally, while
indulging in drunken and derisive antics. What do you say?'

'Guilty as hell,' said Cobbler, indifferently.

'Oh come,' said Ridley, 'Mr Cobbler was not drunk on
that occasion. I was with him shortly beforehand, and I
know.'

'Oh, you do, do you?' said Mr Snelgrove, rounding on
him. 'I was not aware that there was an association between
you two. Where were you and what part did you play in
this disgraceful and libellous action toward my client, may
I ask?'

'You may not ask,' said Mr Balmer. 'Please do not interfere, Mr Ridley. You interrupt my friend's train of reason.'

'If you do not answer me now, I do not greatly care,' said
Mr Snelgrove. 'There will come a time, and a place, where
I shall question you under circumstances where you will be
compelled to answer, and then we shall uncover whatever
link there is between you and this shameless rowdy. You're
thick enough, I dare say.'

'I object to the suggestion that I am *thick* with anyone,'
said Cobbler, as though half asleep. 'It's an expression I
particularly dislike.'

'Go on, sir, go on!' said Mr Snelgrove, who had worked
himself up into a fine forensic fit. 'Be as impertinent as you
please! Now, I put it to you that before you insulted Professor Vambrace in the park, and on the same day that you
so grossly abused your position as cathedral organist, you
caused this to be inserted in the paper edited by your friend,
here.' And with a flourish Mr Snelgrove produced from
among his papers a very large sheet in the exact middle of
which the tiny clipping of the engagement notice had been

pasted, and upon which a secretary had made a notation in a very small hand, in red ink.

Cobbler opened his eyes, and took the paper. 'Aha,' said he, showing little interest, 'so that's what it looked like. I missed it when it came out.' And, handing it back to the lawyer, he closed his eyes again.

'Well, sir,' said Mr Snelgrove. 'What have you to say for yourself?'

'Nothing,' said Cobbler.

'You will now understand, Mr Dean,' said Mr Snelgrove, 'why I asked you to come here. You have, for several years, obstinately defended this man against those of us who understood his nature and his pernicious influence in the Cathedral. You hear him now confess that he has nothing whatever to say in extenuation of this exceedingly mischievous and, I fully believe, libellous action. It has caused great inconvenience to you, to Professor Vambrace and his daughter and, I fully expect, to Mrs Bridgetower and her son, though I am not empowered to speak for them. I hope, sir, that your eyes are open at last. I must say, also, that I hope that in future you will look upon your Cathedral Chancellor as something more than a man of straw. I am sorry to have involved you in a disagreeable scene, but there seemed to be no other equally powerful way of carrying conviction to you. Now, Mr Ridley, will you be good enough to inform me if *The Bellman* intends to take action against this man?'

'No,' said Ridley.

'Then I shall advise my client to take action for libel against *The Bellman* and against Cobbler, and because of his conduct toward my client in the park, I shall prove that libel in the full meaning of the term was intended. Further, I shall bring forward your refusal to prosecute, after what you said earlier, as an indication that you knew of his guilt and tried to shield him.'

'But I don't know of his guilt,' said Ridley. 'Indeed, I know that he is not guilty. I have proof of it here.' And, reaching into a drawer of his desk he drew out a pink receipt for a classified advertisement.

'But he has admitted guilt,' said Mr Snelgrove.

'No I didn't,' said Cobbler. 'I simply didn't deny it. Never deny; never explain. That's my guiding rule of life.'

'Oh, come, that will never do,' said Mr Snelgrove, with elaborate contempt. 'You permitted me to put the question to you, backed by extremely strong circumstantial evidence, and you did not utter a word of denial. That will require a great deal of explanation.'

'Not really,' said Cobbler, still with his eyes closed. 'I was curious to hear what you would say. And a pretty poor show you made of it, I must say, for a lawyer. Circumstantial evidence! Guess-work and spite; nothing more.'

Mr Snelgrove was very angry now. His face was extremely red, and as he had not blushed for many years the unaccustomed feeling bereft him momentarily of the power to speak. The Dean seized his opportunity.

'Mr Cobbler,' said he, 'will you give me your word of honour that you had nothing to do with this engagement notice?'

The accused man sat up smartly in his chair and turned toward his questioner. 'Honour bright, Mr Dean,' said he. 'It's a simple matter of psychology; I do a lot of damn silly things on the spur of the moment, but I'm not a calculating practical joker. Unless you call letting Mr Snelgrove make a jackass of himself a calculated practical joke. Anyhow, Bridgetower's a friend of mine. And I'm sorry I made Professor Vambrace feel cheap; I didn't mean it very seriously. But he looked so funny hiding behind trees, playing I-spy. And I've paid dearly for that; look at the cold I caught, dancing and getting heated. I'll gladly admit that I'm a fool, if it will make anybody happy, but I really don't think I'm malicious or underhand.'

The Dean smiled and nodded several times, and applied himself again to his smelly little pipe. As for Mr Snelgrove, it appeared that he might have a stroke. His face was contorted, and he made gasping noises so alarming that Ronnie Fitzalan hastened to pour a glass of water from Ridley's thermos jug, which he offered to his senior partner.

Ridley's eyes moved to meet those of Mr Marryat. Face? they seemed to ask, and the reply beamed back, Indubitably Face. The editor spoke.

'I feel sure that everyone present would be glad to meet the real X,' said he. 'And as I think he is in the building at this moment, it can easily be managed.' He pressed a bell. 'Miss Green, will you ask Mr Shillito to bring his visitor in here?'

There was another short wait. Cobbler, who seemed much recovered, sang very softly, under his breath,

> *The charge is prepared,*
> *The lawyers are met,*
> *The judges all ranged—*
> *A terrible show!*

—but he caught the cold eye of Mr Balmer upon him, and desisted. Mr Snelgrove appeared to recapture something of his self-possession, and was giving a powerful impersonation of a man who had something very telling up his sleeve. Professor Vambrace was sunk even deeper than before in his melancholy; his face was as grey and forbidding as a rock. Ridley, though he wore a bland and hopeful look upon his face, was kicking one leg furiously under his desk. Would his scheme come off? It was 3.30, and everything should be in readiness, but so often people were unpunctual and—But before his nerves got the better of him Miss Green opened the door again, and this time it was Mr Swithin Shillito who entered, ushering before him Mr Bevill Higgin.

Mr Shillito was about to embark on an elaborate round of greetings, but something in the atmosphere of the room stopped him just as he made a move toward the Dean. Mr Balmer spoke.

'I don't intend to make a stage-play of this,' said he, with

246

a look at Mr Snelgrove, 'and I shall content myself with asking a very few questions. Your name is Bevill Higgin, is it not?'

'That's right,' said Mr Higgin, smirking nervously. The sight of the assembly had put him palpably upon his guard, and his voice shook a little.

'Mr Higgin, did you, or did you not, on the thirty-first of October, at some time in the morning, insert and pay for an engagement notice in this newspaper? This notice, to be precise?' and Mr Balmer produced a sheet of paper, very much like Mr Snelgrove's on which the tiny piece of newsprint was pasted, with a notation in blue.

Bevill Higgin did not reply at once, and the nervous smirk did not leave his face. But his eyes flickered quickly from Balmer to Ridley, and from him to Snelgrove. 'What makes you think I did?' said he.

'Because the receipt for payment was found in that scrapbook, which is your property, and which you are now carrying under your arm,' said Mr Balmer.

'And how do you connect that with me?' said Higgin. 'Is my name on it?'

'The whole text of the notice is written on it in what is demonstrably your handwriting.'

'I deny any knowledge of it. I write like a great many other people. I should like to know why I have been asked here to be questioned in this way?'

'Because you did it.'

'Prove that. I suppose you're a lawyer. You know that what you're saying is libellous. You haven't one scrap of real evidence to connect me with what you're talking about. If it's the text of an advertisement somebody must have signed it. What is the name on the receipt?'

'You signed it with a false name.'

'Oh yes! Very likely! Anything to get a scapegoat! You don't catch me like that! I bet you haven't got any receipt.'

Ridley lifted the pink slip from his blotter, where it had been concealed and waved it gently in the air. 'We have it, and we have you, Mr Higgin,' said he. 'Also, I have a witness—I need hardly tell you her name—who will testify, if necessary, that you confessed to her that this advertisement was your doing. There's no point in keeping up a pretence. We've got you. Mr Snelgrove, Professor Vambrace, allow me to present X.'

This, too, should have been a satisfactorily dramatic moment, but it failed. For, as every eye turned upon him, Bevill Higgin's face changed from its usual bright pink to a deep red, crinkled into a mask of misery, and with embarrassing noise and openness, the little man cried. Cried so that tears ran down his cheeks and dropped upon his threadbare blue serge jacket. Cried so that Mr Marryat and Ronnie Fitzalan looked away from him in deep embarrassment. Cried for what seemed an age, but what was perhaps ninety seconds. Cried until a clear ball of mucous formed at the end of his nose, then swung by a thin string in mid-air. He did not raise his hands to his face, nor did he close his eyes. He wept with the abandon of a guilty child, but his whole figure spoke of failure, of genteel poverty, of hopeless middle age. The sound worked horribly upon Ridley's nerves, and just as he was about to shout at the man, to shout that all would be forgiven him if only he would stop that dreadful weeping, Mr Swithin Shillito drew a very large, very clean white handkerchief from his breast pocket, and handed it to Higgin, deftly fielding the pendulous nosedrop as he did so. At the same moment Fitzalan, taking the water glass from Mr Snelgrove, who still nursed it, offered it to the stricken man. By less than two minutes of weeping Higgin had washed all the starch out of his judges.

Mr Snelgrove was the first to act; his quick legal mind saw in this a chance to recover the prestige which he had lost in the matter of Cobbler. He pounced.

'You admit your guilt?'

Higgin, mopping his eyes, nodded, but said nothing.

'Well, then we have X at last,' said Mr Snelgrove, looking round the room with the air of a man who has at last triumphed over the stupidity and obscurantism of others. He continued, with heavy irony: 'Now, Mr Higgin, perhaps you will have no objection to explaining your motive for inserting that advertisement?'

Higgin mumbled something, in a voice still thick with tears.

'Hey?' said Mr Snelgrove, cupping his hand to his ear. 'I can't hear you. Speak up. Let us all hear what you have to say.'

Again Higgin spoke, somewhat more loudly, but again Mr Snelgrove shook his head.

'He says it was only a joke, sir,' said Ronnie Fitzalan.

'A joke!' said Mr Snelgrove in what was almost a whisper of horror. 'Have you any conception, man, of the mischief you have made? Of the trouble you have brought into the life of my client, Professor Vambrace? Have you any notion of this?'

'Never meant any harm to Professor Vambrace,' said Higgin, his voice tripping over a sob as he spoke. 'Haven't the pleasure of his acquaintance.'

'God bless my soul!' said the Professor. It was a strange comment from a professed agnostic, and it rose to his lips unbidden.

'And if your joke, as you choose to call it, was not directed at my client, just what did you expect to gain by it?' asked Mr Snelgrove.

'Permit me to point out that I also represent injured parties in this matter,' said Mr Balmer. 'On behalf of *The Bellman*, Mr Higgin, I put this question to you: Did you realize when you inserted that advertisement, that you were involving this newspaper in a fraud, and a possible action for libel? Did you think of that?'

Higgin shook his head.

'Do you realize that at this moment you stand on the brink of suit both by my client and this newspaper?' asked Mr Snelgrove. 'Well, man? Say something! And don't attempt to impose upon us by any more tears. They will have no effect upon me. None whatever. I can assure you of that.'

Higgin raised his head, and spoke with more self-

249

possession than before. 'It was only my little joke,' said he.
'I never thought it would cause any real trouble. I just
wanted to play a little joke on Professor Bridgetower. No
real harm meant.'

'And what moved you to involve my daughter in your
joke?' said Professor Vambrace, menacingly.

Higgin giggled weakly, and blushed. 'I really do assure
you, sir, I meant no harm,' said he.

'Do you know my daughter?'

'I only had the pleasure of meeting Miss Vambrace once.
In the Waverley Library. A charming young lady.'

'You meant this to be a joke on Mr Bridgetower and Miss
Vambrace?' said Balmer.

'Yes, sir.'

'No one else involved? No reference to Professor Vambrace at all?'

'Oh, none, I assure you.'

'I think you also meant it to be a joke on me,' said
Gloster Ridley. 'And I think I know why. It was because I
refused to publish and pay you for articles about yourself,
which you wanted to write for this newspaper. Wasn't that
it?'

'Oh, no, Mr Ridley.'

'Oh, *yes*, Mr. Higgin. I recall your visit here very clearly.
You got Mr Shillito to introduce you. This advertisement
was to make trouble for me because I ignored you. Isn't that
right?'

'Oh, no, Mr. Ridley'.

'Oh *yes*, Mr Higgin. You did it to spite me, didn't you?'

Higgin was silent, but a nervous grin flitted across his
face, and disappeared.

'If it was spite against me, was it spite against Mr Bridgetower and Miss Vambrace? Was it spite against Professor
Vambrace?'

'No indeed. I have never met Professor Vambrace until
now.'

'Then it was spite against my daughter,' said the Professor. 'And what reason had you to play this vile trick upon
her, you scoundrel?'

Again Higgin was silent, but again he smiled, the imploring, sick smile of one who strives to avert another stroke of the lash.

'Had she ignored you at some time?' said Ridley. 'Had Mr Bridgetower ignored you?'

Still Higgin said nothing, but looked from face to face, still with his imploring smile, a figure of cringing abjection.

'Are we to understand that this whole matter was prompted by malice?' asked the editor.

There was a longer pause, and at last the sickly smile faded from Higgin's face, and he nodded.

No one spoke for a time, and it was Mr Marryat who first broke the silence. 'Well, what are we going to do about that?' said he.

'Malice is a very ugly charge,' said Mr Snelgrove. 'A rare charge in law, but a horrible one. The law brings us face to face with some detestable things—things from which the minds of decent men withdraw in loathing—but few more detestable than the charge of malice.'

'But is it a possible charge at all?' The question came, to the surprise of everyone, from Dean Jevon Knapp, who had been forgotten in his corner.

'Rather an obscure offence,' said Mr Balmer. 'You recall what I told you about malice, Mr Ridley. I've never met with it, as an isolated charge, before.'

'And may that not be because it is an offence more in my realm than in yours?' said the Dean. 'I don't find malice so horrible as you, Mr Snelgrove; perhaps because I see more of it; or perhaps I should say because I recognize it more readily than you do. But it is horrible enough, certainly. In the Prayer Book you will find a special plea to be preserved from it, appointed for the first Sunday after Easter: "Grant us so to put away the leaven of malice and wickedness that we may always serve Thee in pureness of living and truth". The writer of that prayer understood malice. It works like a leaven; it stirs, and swells, and changes all that surrounds it. If you seek to pin it down in law, it may well elude you. Who can separate the leaven from the lump when once it has been mixed? But if you learn to know it by its smell, you find it very easily. You find it, for instance, in unfounded charges brought against people that we dislike. It may cause the greatest misery and distress in many unexpected quarters. I have even known it to have quite unforeseen good results. But those things which it invades will never be quite the same again. I assure you that you will always have the greatest difficulty in isolating the leaven, once it has set to work. I do not wish to preach out of my pulpit, but I doubt if any of us here can truthfully say that he has not been touched by the leaven of malice, either in the remoter past, or during the past week.'

What might have been said in reply to the Dean must always remain a matter of conjecture, for as he finished speaking, there was another tap at the door, and this time Miss Green admitted Solly and Pearl. Professor Vambrace started to his feet at once.

'Pearl,' said he, pointing at Higgin, 'do you know this man?'

Pearl was taken aback, but after a moment she spoke. 'No, Father,' said she, 'I have never seen him before.'

'And what have you to say to that?' demanded the Professor of Higgin.

'Some mistake,' said he. 'I thought Miss Vambrace was a short, stout lady with reddish hair.'

'My God,' said Solly, 'he's got you mixed up with Tessie Forgie!' And to the astonishment of the others, he and Pearl began to laugh.

'Though I would ordinarily be pleased to see you,' said Ridley, 'I must ask if you can wait for a few minutes. As you see, I have rather an important conference here at the moment, and if you have not come to join it, I hope that you will not be offended if I ask you to retire.'

'We have come to join the conference,' said Solly. 'We know what it's all about, of course. We've come to ask you not to do anything about a law case, or a retraction of that engagement notice, for at least a week. We want time to discuss several important matters.'

'And what, precisely, do you mean by that?' said the Professor.

'Surely it's plain enough,' said Mr Marryat. 'They mean that they may become engaged after all. I can tell by looking at them.'

Pearl went to her father. 'Please don't say anything now,' she said; 'let us talk to you tonight.'

It was a critical moment. The Professor looked black, but for the first time in a week his daughter was talking to him with earnest affection. Her hands were on the lapels of his coat. Suddenly, moved by some deep wisdom, she stood on tiptoe and kissed him on the mouth, a thing she had not done in several years.

The Professor's face did not seem to relax greatly, but a look of nobility and almost of peace came over it. His eye was bright, and he said; 'Of course I shall do nothing further until my daughter and I have talked the matter over thoroughly.'

'Well, that blows the whole case sky-high,' said Mr Balmer, rising and putting papers back into his brief-case.

'How so?' asked Mr Snelgrove, whose emotional apprehensions had never been keen, and who was still chewing over the Dean's lecture on malice, and wondering if any of it could possibly have been directed at him.

'Because if these two young people are engaged, or become engaged, there is no libel in that advertisement. Justification is a perfect defence. Not that I think that there would be much sense in suing this man,' said Mr Balmer, looking at Higgin.

'I have exactly nine dollars and twenty-five cents in the world,' said Bevill Higgin, and for the first time that afternoon he had a touch of dignity.

'Let me warn you, my friend, that poverty is a poor protection, if you choose to make a hobby of public mischief. You've had a very narrow escape, and you'll never be so lucky again.' With these minatory words, Mr Balmer nodded to Ridley and Marryat, and left the room.

'May I go now?' asked Higgin.

Ridley nodded. The little man, some of his usual jauntiness restored, looked about him, as though to take his leave. No one would meet his eye. At last he turned to Swithin Shillito, and put out his hand. 'Shall I give you a call in a few days?' said he.

'No, Mr Higgin,' said the old gentleman; 'in future neither I nor Mrs Shillito will be at home to you.'

Bevill Higgin drew on his thin, mended cloth gloves, and went.

PROFESSOR VAMBRACE and Mr Snelgrove walked down the stairs a few steps behind the Dean.

'May I offer you a lift, Professor?' said the lawyer. 'Fitzalan will be happy to drop you anywhere you want to go.'

'I prefer to walk, thank you.'

'An extraordinary business, that. I could have sworn Cobbler was the guilty party. It was on the tip of my tongue to accuse him directly. But of course, one learns to be cautious in our profession; I merely put it to him as a possibility. As for that other fellow—Beneath contempt. However, I am deeply indignant, Professor, on your behalf. Deeply indignant.'

They were on the pavement by this time. The Professor faced Mr Snelgrove, very much the cousin of Mourne and Derry.

'Your indignation, sir, is a purchasable commodity; it will be healed by tomorrow. Mine, I assure you, is made of more lasting stuff. Be good enough to send me your statement at your earliest convenience.'

The Professor walked away, leaving Mr Snelgrove gaping. But though the Professor had spoken of indignation, his head was high, and there was even a proud smile on his face. His daughter had been restored to him. He would talk to Pearl that evening. Yes—perhaps he would even talk to young Bridgetower. He had never really had anything personal against the boy.

As he overtook and passed the Dean, he raised his hat

with a sweeping gesture. 'An uncommonly fine day, Mr Dean,' said he; 'we are having a wonderful autumn.'

OUTSIDE THE offices of *The Bellman* Solly and Pearl were tucking themselves into the little English car when Cobbler hurried up to them.

'Let me come with you,' said he.

'We're going for a drive in the country. We'll be glad to drop you at your house.'

'No, no; I don't want to be dropped. I'll go with you on your drive.'

'But we have several things to talk about.'

'I know you have. I'll help you.'

'They're private.'

'Not from me, surely? Not from your old friend? I'll be a great help. Let me come along.'

'You won't be a great help at all. Anyhow, you've got a cold. You want to go right back to bed.'

'Not a bit of it. I found that meeting most refreshing. You missed the cream of it, when old Snelgrove tried to put the finger on me; he thought I put that piece in the paper. The desire to think ill of me completely submerged his judgment. I led him on, I'm afraid. Very wrong of me, but utterly irresistible. I'll have no trouble with him, for a while.'

'Cobbler, Miss Vambrace and I want to be alone. Can you understand that?'

'Worst thing in the world for you. You'll brood, and upset each other. I'll just hop in the back seat.'

He did so.

'I'm taking you straight home,' said Solly, pulling away from the curb.

'If you do, I'll lean right out of the window and shout "Solly Bridgetower loves Pearl Vambrace" over and over again, and the whole place will know. I warn you.'

'By God, I believe you would.'

'Of course I would. I want to go for a drive. My cold has

reached that stage where it absolutely demands a drive.
Let's go out across the bridge.'

Solly turned a corner. They were passing the Deanery,
and at that instant Miss Puss Pottinger was hastening up the
steps. Thrusting all of the upper half of his body out of the
window, Cobbler waved to her.

'Yoo-hoo, Miss Pottinger, looking for news? I'm free!
Free! Not a stain on my character! Bye-bye!' He pulled
himself back into the car. 'I'd like to be a fly on the wall
when the Dean talks to her,' said he. 'The old boy is very
hot on malice this afternoon; she won't enjoy her sandwich
and bit of seed-cake, I'll bet.'

Until they were out of the city, Cobbler sat quietly in his
place, and no one spoke. But as soon as they had crossed
the river he hitched himself forward on the back seat, and
thrust his smiling face between Solly and Pearl.

'Now,' he said, 'let's get down to business. When are you
going to announce your engagement? Perhaps I should say,
when are you going to confirm Higgin's premature announcement? Listen, Bridgetower, what has he got his
knife into you for?'

Briefly, Solly told him of his first encounter with Bevill
Higgin.

'Well, well,' said the organist. 'And he thought Miss
Vambrace was Tessie Forgie. Now why, I wonder?'

'I think that she must have been sitting at my desk on my
day off, and refused him library privileges, or something
like that,' said Pearl. 'She has a very short way with people
she thinks don't matter.'

'Remarkable! Obviously a very impetuous fellow. And
full of conceit, I suppose. Thought he'd show you all that
you couldn't slight him. Poor bleeder! I'm sorry for him.'

'I could cheerfully kill him,' said Solly.

'Oh no! You'll be grateful to him in a little while. And
years from now, as you sit at the door of your rose-entwined
cottage, with your grandchildren tumbling on the grass
before you, you'll be saying, "I wonder whatever became

of Bevill Higgin, that fragrant old soul who brought us together." '

'Listen, Cobbler,' said Solly; 'get this through your head. We're not even engaged. It seems remotely possible that we may be, but we're not yet. We have a great deal to discuss, before we can contemplate any such step. So will you please stop your nonsense? It's embarrassing.'

'My dear children, I'm only trying to be helpful. Most couples who are going to get engaged think that they have a lot to talk over before they really do it. Utter waste of time. Forget all I said to you the other night about Miss Vambrace not being suitable, Solly. I was wrong. Now the scales have fallen from my eyes. Not only is the hand of Fate discernible in this affair; Fate has been leaving finger-prints all around the place ever since Higgin got his bright idea. Miss Vambrace—or may I call you Pearl?——'

'I'd rather you called me Veronica,' said she.

'How very wise. Much, much better. Well, Veronica, help me to bring this fellow to his senses. I'm sure that you, with your infinitely superior emotional grasp, see that this marriage is fated. Believe me, I've seen a lot of couples get engaged, and they could cut down their time by three-quarters if they would just stop talking and creating abso-lutely artificial difficulties once the thing was in the bag. You'll enjoy being married, you know. You can help Solly with Heavysege.'

'Ah, but that's one of the difficulties,' said Solly. 'I've given Heavysege the heave-ho. I met Dr Sengreen this morning, quite by chance, and entirely on the spur of the moment I told him that I was putting Heavysege aside because I had something of my own, something original, that I wanted to write. I told him I wanted to be a creator of Amcan, not one of its embalmers. I should have been more careful, I suppose, but Oh hell——. But I can't get married—not in fairness to Veronica—until I've written it, and it has proved either a success or a failure.'

'Nitwit!' said Cobbler. 'Your first book won't be a success. Don't make marriage conditional on the success of a book, or your mother dying, or anything unlikely of that sort. Put first things first. Get married, and plunge into all the uproar of baby-raising, and loading yourself up with insurance and furniture and all the frowsy appurtenances of domestic life, as soon as you can. You'll survive. Millions do. And deep down under all the trash-heap of duty and respectability and routine you may, if you're among the lucky ones, find a jewel of happiness. I know all about it, and I assure you on my sacred honour that it's worth a try. Come on! You know how all this will end up. You'll act on instinct any-how; everybody does in the really important decisions of life. Why not get some fun out of it, and forget all the twaddle you'll have to talk in order to make it seem reason-able, and prudent, and dull.'

They drove in silence for a time, and then Pearl turned her head toward Cobbler.

'I think you're right,' said she. 'And I hope you'll always be our friend.'

For once, Cobbler said nothing, but for the rest of the drive he leaned back in his seat and sang very pleasantly, in an undertone.

WHEN THE conference broke up, Gloster Ridley was left alone with Mr Marryat.

'Well,' said the general manager, 'I hope we've heard the last of that. The trouble you can get into in this business! And mostly because so many people take themselves so seriously. Still, we kept up face, eh?'

'Yes, we did that,' said Ridley. 'In fact, I think we've even gained a little, in some quarters. Vambrace was posi-tively human when he said good-bye. He had the decency to say that a misunderstanding might happen to anyone.'

'So he might,' said Marryat. 'When I think how he car-ried on in here just a week ago——!'

'Yes, but it was more than old Snelgrove saw fit to do.'

'A fine monkey *he* made of himself! Well, I've got some things to do.' And Mr Marryat went.

But as he left the room another figure, who had been

lurking outside the door, slipped into the editor's office. It was Mr Swithin Shillito.

'Chief,' said he, 'what can I say?'

'I really don't know, Mr Shillito. Perhaps it would be best to say nothing.'

'No, no; I feel that much of what has happened is my fault. After all, I introduced Higgin to you. Had it not been for that, all this trouble might have been spared. I've many faults; I don't have to be told that. Perhaps when I am gone it will be said that a foolish generosity was one of them. I wanted to do the poor chap a bit of good. Loyalty to a fellow Britisher, you know. But I realize that in the Craft there can only be one loyalty—to one's paper, and of course to its Chief. I'm in the wrong. I admit it, freely and even gladly. At my age I can still admit that I am often foolish. But not small, I think. No, not small.'

'Please do not feel it necessary to accuse yourself,' said Ridley. 'Anybody can make a mistake, and yours was undoubtedly a generous one. But as we are together, Mr Shillito, I shall take this chance of telling you that the publisher has raised the matter of your retirement. No, please do not protest; Mr Warboys will not hear of you being tied to the daily routine any longer, and I am in complete agreement with him. Confidentially he is organizing a banquet in your honour, and you are too old a hand at these things not to realize that such a tribute will involve a presentation, as well. I understand that it is to be a full-dress affair, with the Mayor present, and some representative journalists from other cities. It will take place between Christmas and the New Year. You will want to prepare a speech, I am sure, and I suggest that a valedictory article, in your own characteristic style, would be welcome.'

It was the sack. But it was a silken sack, lined with ermine, and the Old Mess knew it, and responded accordingly. He spoke of generosity, of long ties, of his hope that *The Bellman* would call upon him whenever he could be of use, of his high regard for Mr Warboys, and his admiration for the Chief.

'I had hoped,' said he, in conclusion, 'that I might remain in harness until next Convocation. It would have been a keen pleasure to me to write an editorial on the occasion of your honorary degree.'

'To be quite frank,' said Ridley, 'I'd rather not have a degree. For a working editor it might prove an embarrassment. When the time comes for me to retire—well, the University might like to do something for me then. But I've thought this matter over very carefully, and if I'm offered one now, I shall decline, with thanks. I'd be grateful if you would pass that information on to people who might be interested—to Mrs Roger Warboys, for instance.'

'You may depend on me,' said Mr Shillito, and turned to go.

'And Swithin,' said Ridley, recalling him. It was the first time in their years of association that he had used the old man's first name, and he was somewhat surprised to find how gently it came off his tongue. 'I didn't want to show that receipt slip to the lawyers, for a reason that will interest you. It was signed, you know, with a false name.' He handed the slip to the old man. The name written, very clearly across the bottom, was Swithin Shillito. There was a pause while the old man took it in, and then, 'I should have known that fellow wasn't a sahib,' said Mr Shillito, with dignity, and walked out of the office.

Ridley sat down at his desk. The afternoon was almost gone, and he did not feel in the mood for work, but it was too early for him to go home. What would he do at home? He would call Mrs Fielding later and angle for an invitation to dinner. Meanwhile, he savoured the poignant sweetness of renunciation. How painfully, how exhaustingly, he had desired a doctorate. Now, for the past eighteen hours, he had known that he did not need this honour to silence the voice of his inner guilt. He was a man released from bondage.

Silently Miss Green entered, and laid a copy of the afternoon's edition of *The Bellman* on his desk. The editor picked it up and idly leafed through it. Truly, *It is a barber's chair, that fits all buttocks.* . . . Now that this hubbub was over he might find a few hours in which to prepare his Wadsworth Lecture; he was more determined than ever to make it a distinguished piece of work . . . *The pin buttock.* . . . Poor Mrs Little, poor Constant Reader, who had come to him that morning even before he was out of bed, trembling with her great news about Bevill Higgin, destroying her idol, and Blubadub's Ugga Bev, in order that *The Bellman* might be vindicated. Indeed, for a moment he had almost suspected that she had some personal feeling toward himself . . . *The quatch buttock.* . . . That boy Rumball must be given a rise. He had shown a lot of gumption by discovering that receipt. Loyalty was a great quality in a reporter—but no, he was thinking like the Old Mess . . . *The brawn buttock.* . . . Professor Vambrace was not a man that he could ever like but, as an editor cannot allow himself the luxury of many friends, so he must also be careful not to use his power unjustly, and pursue enmities beyond the grave. Quickly, Ridley opened a locked drawer of his desk and took out the emended obituary of Walter Vambrace which he had prepared in anger the week before. To restore it to its original form was confidential work, too confidential even for the close-mouthed Miss Green; he would do it himself before he left his office. As he slipped a piece of paper into his typewriter to do so, his telephone rang. Was Miss Green not there, to take the call? After three rings, he lifted the receiver himself.

'Yes? . . . Yes, I see . . . Yes, of course I shall be very happy to do so . . . But may I ask if you are quite certain that there will be no objection from either family? . . . You can guarantee that? By tomorrow morning? . . . And you will speak to the Dean at once? . . . Well, in that case, would you both be able to come to my office some time tomorrow in order to sign the order? You will understand my caution, I am sure. . . . And may I offer my congratulations? . . . Oh, very kind of you to say so . . . Goodbye.'

Turning back to his machine he typed, slowly and precisely:

> Professor and Mrs Walter Vambrace are pleased to announce the engagement of their daughter, Pearl Veronica, to Solomon Bridgetower, Esq., son of Mrs Bridgetower and the late Professor Solomon Bridgetower of this city. Marriage to take place in St Nicholas' Cathedral at a date to be announced later.

In red pencil he wrote beneath this: *To be set, but not inserted until I OK the copy.*

He looked at it for some time, and then he wrote again: *Debit the cost of this advertisement to me personally.*

Face? No, no; he felt that it was the least that he could do.

FOR THE BEST IN PAPERBACKS, LOOK FOR THE

In every corner of the world, on every subject under the sun, Penguin represents quality and variety—the very best in publishing today.

For complete information about books available from Penguin—including Pelicans, Puffins, Peregrines, and Penguin Classics—and how to order them, write to us at the appropriate address below. Please note that for copyright reasons the selection of books varies from country to country.

In the United Kingdom: For a complete list of books available from Penguin in the U.K., please write to *Dept E.P., Penguin Books Ltd, Harmondsworth, Middlesex, UB7 0DA.*

In the United States: For a complete list of books available from Penguin in the U.S., please write to *Consumer Sales, Penguin USA, P.O. Box 999— Dept. 17109, Bergenfield, New Jersey 07621-0120.* VISA and MasterCard holders call 1-800-253-6476 to order all Penguin titles.

In Canada: For a complete list of books available from Penguin in Canada, please write to *Penguin Books Canada Ltd, 10 Alcorn Avenue, Suite 300, Toronto, Ontario, Canada M4V 3B2.*

In Australia: For a complete list of books available from Penguin in Australia, please write to the *Marketing Department, Penguin Books Ltd, P.O. Box 257, Ringwood, Victoria 3134.*

In New Zealand: For a complete list of books available from Penguin in New Zealand, please write to the *Marketing Department, Penguin Books (NZ) Ltd, Private Bag, Takapuna, Auckland 9.*

In India: For a complete list of books available from Penguin, please write to *Penguin Overseas Ltd, 706 Eros Apartments, 56 Nehru Place, New Delhi, 110019.*

In Holland: For a complete list of books available from Penguin in Holland, please write to *Penguin Books Nederland B.V., Postbus 195, NL-1380AD Weesp, Netherlands.*

In Germany: For a complete list of books available from Penguin, please write to *Penguin Books Ltd, Friedrichstrasse 10-12, D-6000 Frankfurt Main I, Federal Republic of Germany.*

In Spain: For a complete list of books available from Penguin in Spain, please write to *Longman, Penguin España, Calle San Nicolas 15, E-28013 Madrid, Spain.*

In Japan: For a complete list of books available from Penguin in Japan, please write to *Longman Penguin Japan Co Ltd, Yamaguchi Building, 2-12-9 Kanda Jimbocho, Chiyoda-Ku, Tokyo 101, Japan.*

FOR THE BEST IN PAPERBACKS, LOOK FOR THE

Other titles by Robertson Davies, available from Penguin Books:

☐ **THE MANTICORE**

A monster with the head of a man, the body of a lion, and the tail of a scorpion, the manticore appears in the dreams of Boy Staunton's son David, as he learns surprising things about his father and about himself.

"Rarely has psychoanalysis of any ideological stripe been so successfully depicted in fiction." —*Newsweek*　　　*310 pages　　ISBN: 0-14-004388-8*

☐ **WORLD OF WONDERS**

The finale of the Deptford Trilogy is the story of Magnus Eisengrim—formerly Paul Dempster, whose premature birth was spurred by an errant snowball—now a master illusionist and the most illustrious magician of his age.

"A novel of stunning verbal energy and intelligence." —*The New York Times Book Review*　　　　　　　*316 pages　　ISBN: 0-14-004389-6*

☐ **TEMPEST-TOST**

Salterton's amateur production of *The Tempest* seems more like *A Midsummer Night's Dream* when the members of the company pursue one anther madly in a satirical look at unrequited love.

"An exercise in puckish persiflage." —*The Toronto Star*
　　　　　　　　　　　　284 pages　　ISBN: 0-14-016792-7

☐ **LEAVEN OF MALICE**

Initiated by the insertion of a false engagement notice in the Salterton *Evening Bellman*, the leaven of malice continued to work until it had changed permanently, for good or evil, the lives of many of the citizens of Salterton.

"A comic novel that shows Canada's finest novelist near the top of his form."
—*The Washington Post*　　　　　*262 pages　　ISBN: 0-14-005433-2*

☐ **A MIXTURE OF FRAILTIES**

More than a story of Monica Gall's life in London and her education as a singer, the finale of the Salterton Trilogy is an absorbing, comic, and moving account of Monica's education as a human being.

"First rate . . . abundantly funny." —*The New York Times*
　　　　　　　　　　　　380 pages　　ISBN: 0-14-016791-9

☐ **THE REBEL ANGELS**

A remarkable cast of gypsies, defrocked monks, mad professors, and wealthy eccentrics stars in a brilliant spectacle of theft, perjury, murder, scholarship, and love at a modern university.

"Full of the splendid ironies and fateful turns, as well as the fascinating characters, one expects from Davies." —*Chicago Tribune*
　　　　　　　　　　　　326 pages　　ISBN: 0-14-006271-8

FOR THE BEST IN PAPERBACKS, LOOK FOR THE

☐ WHAT'S BRED IN THE BONE

This wonderfully ingenious portrait of Francis Cornish—art expert and collector of international renown—is a spellbinding tale of artistic triumph and heroic deceit.

"A deliciously readable story . . . An altogether remarkable creation." —*The New York Times*   *436 pages*   ISBN: 0-14-009711-2

☐ THE LYRE OF ORPHEUS

"A biting satire on the artistic muse . . . Just what one would expect from Canada's leading man of letters and literary virtuoso." —*Chicago Tribune Books*   *480 pages*   ISBN: 0-14-011433-5

☐ THE DEPTFORD TRILOGY

A glittering, fantastical, cunningly contrived trilogy of novels that centers around the central mystery "Who killed Boy Staunton?" *Fifth Business*, *The Manticore*, and *World of Wonders* lure the reader through a labyrinth of myth, history, and magic.

"[Davies] conveys a sense of real life lived in a fully imagined . . . world." —*The New York Times Book Review*   *864 pages*   ISBN: 0-14-014755-1

☐ THE SALTERTON TRILOGY

Three hilarious and wonderfully shrewd novels—*Tempest-Tost*, *Leaven of Malice*, *A Mixture of Frailties*—reveal the schemes and dreams of the denizens of Salterton, a place described by some as "the place where Anglican clergymen go when they die."

"[Davies's] writing is full of zest, wit and urbanity." —*The New York Times Book Review*   *776 pages*   ISBN: 0-14-015910-X

☐ THE CORNISH TRILOGY

Woven around the pursuits of the erudite scholars of the University of St. John and the Holy Ghost, this dazzling trilogy—*The Rebel Angels*, *What's Bred in the Bone*, and *The Lyre of Orpheus*—lures you into a world of mysticism, historical allusion, and gothic fantasy.

"A trilogy that stands as a major fictional achievement." —*The New York Times Book Review*   *1142 pages*   ISBN: 0-14-015850-2

☐ ONE HALF OF ROBERTSON DAVIES

These stories, essays, and jeux d'esprit reveal the heart of Robertson Davies: novelist, scholar, teacher, and master storyteller.

"The voice is soft and gentle, but it is full of the strength of wisdom." —*Chicago Tribune*   *286 pages*   ISBN: 0-14-004967-3

FOR THE BEST IN PAPERBACKS, LOOK FOR THE

☐ **HIGH SPIRITS**

This collection of wildly inventive ghost stories presents eighteen original appari-
tions, rendered with Davies's special touch—a bit of parody mixed in with true
scariness—and all emanating from high spirits.

"The reader's own spirits will be happily elevated by these wonderful and grace-
ful tales." —*The Washington Post*   *198 pages*   *ISBN: 0-14-006505-9*

☐ **THE PAPERS OF SAMUEL MARCHBANKS**

Originally written as editorials and signed "Samuel Marchbanks," these humor-
ous essays comprise writings of anecdote and opinion, liberally spiced with
scorn, spleen, irony, and wit in the grand tradition of the cantankerous old devil
himself.

"Davies is prickling sensibilities, puncturing pretensions, and obviously enjoying it all immensely." —*Time*   *560 pages*   *ISBN: 0-14-009771-6*

☐ **THE ENTHUSIASMS OF ROBERTSON DAVIES**

An urbane and wonderfully opinionated collection of articles in which Robertson
Davies addresses topics ranging from love affairs to bean-snipping.

"What a fiction writer's collected nonfiction should be . . . absorbing, polished,
elegant, occasionally disquieting, and usually funny." —*The Washington Post
Book World*   *384 pages*   *ISBN: 0-14-012659-7*

Questions:

1. What did I do to make him want to treat me so poorly?
2. How do I meet the right people for me?
3. Why does the thought of that scary me?
4. What now?

I still suffer from lack of confidence · social, academic
I still envy Lindsey's confidence   creative
Thanks, tot. Bye Bye Lindsey. Bye Bye.

meet new people
stand on my own two feet.

work today 12-4
            5:15-8
home to sleep tonight & tomorrow.